The Destructive Element

Duff Brenna

The Destructive Element

Duff Brenna

SERVING HOUSE BOOKS

Published by Serving House Books

South Orange, NJ

www.servinghousebooks.com

ISBN: 978-1-947175-55-6

Library of Congress Control Number: 2021939598

Member of The Independent Book Publishers Association

First Serving House Books Edition 2021

Cover Art: Wlliam Blake, The Ancient of Days

Serving House Books Logo: Barry Lereng Wilmont

Acknowledgment: My thanks to Sam Hamod for his 2006 poem entitled "The Zoo." I altered a few lines that support the theme of destruction guiding much of this novel.

To the destructive element submit yourself

—J. Conrad

Books by Duff Brenna

The Destructive Element
Murdering the Mom
Minnesota Memoirs
Winter Tales: Men Write About Aging, with Thomas E. Kennedy
The Law of Falling Bodies
The Willow Man
The Altar of the Body
Too Cool
The Holy Book of the Beard
The Book of Mamie
Waking in Wisconsin (poems)

For Christine & Dean

1 – Remembrance of Things Past

The last time he saw her, she had said: "You look like death warmed over. How'd you get so old? Gray temples. Bags under your eyes. You're getting old. An old lug. How old you be?" He was two months short of fifty-four. Fifty-three had seemed old eight months ago, but now he was used to it. But what about six years on? *Sixty*—definitely the cusp of old age.

•

He had driven north to Rancho Bernardo that day, turning east at Gateway Avenue. Ahead of him: the Gateway Retirement Home. Gateway to what? The American Dream? Gateway to Heaven? Gateway to Hell?

He had punched in his mother's password. The gate sliding open. The winding driveway beckoning, the parking lot, the conifers, the shrubbery. A sparkling sky clear as God's conscience.

•

Commodities inside the building: expendable homos-not-so-sapient. The old bones rattling. Crafty sundowners lurking naked in their rooms waiting like werewolves for the moon to rise. That's when they wandered. A hundred ancients marking time. The final adventure. Any last words, old sot? The hoarse voice dog-paddling through a stream of mucus.

"I . . . want . . . to . . . say." (Eyes moistless. Cough infantile.) "Ba ba da da ack. I . . . was . . . once . . . the . . . king . . . of . . ."

"Yes, yes, the king of? The king of?"

"Wall Street. Made millions. Look at me now. It's a rip off."

"Yes, look at you now, old sot. Happy trails to yooou."

"Thur-nunk."

"Is he gone? What did he say? Did you write it down?"

"He said he wants the most expensive coffin ever made. Titanium exterior. Silk pillow, satin sheets inside, *Playmate*'s Miss July glued to the ceiling."

•

Death: "A cock-up maladaptation making us incapable of thriving," was what Harley's mother told him. How bright she *was*. Vivacious. A femme fatale. Irresistible *joie de vivre*. Upon a time years ago.

•

Park your car in front of the three-story complex filled with souls circling the halls in holding patterns. Surrounding them are thick walls, fences, manicured lawns fringed with stiff poinsettias, tiger lilies, juniper bushes, tangles of honeysuckle leeching friable stucco. The building: desert pink, a red tile roof. Fireproof.

You climb the stairs to the entrance. Follow the hall with its industrial strength rug, its wooden rails running the length of the walls, giving wobblers something to hang onto. Music bubbling from the ceiling. Lawrence Welk. Dead for more than two decades, but there he was: musician-immortality.

An old man takes your arm and says, "I had to fly to my mum in Florida twice this year. She's ninety-five. Hospitalized. Lung cancer. Now she's back in her apartment. Oxygen tank. That's the stuff we're made of. Last week my forty-year-old niece in New Jersey died of cancer. Cancer's the King. My father died of cancer a decade ago. My younger sister died of cancer. She left behind two boys and a husband. *Shameful*. She barely begun life, you know what I mean? I mean what's happening? So much cancer. Cancer's the King." He shakes his head as he wanders off repeating, "Cancer's the King." You watch him approach a woman inching along the rail. He snags her arm and repeats the same story word for word.

Then he continues collaring others.

Long ago, you dubbed him The Ancient Mariner.

•

You can replay every minute in the old folks' home, the same way you can replay the exact moment when you first heard JFK had been shot: you were thirteen years old, playing baseball. Coach yelling for the team to stop and "Listen up! President Kennedy was shot and killed today in Dallas, Texas. The game's cancelled. Go home!" The most startling thing was Coach himself. A brawny man with an iron jaw, his knees trembling, the note in his hand trembling too.

•

Your mother had tried to write like Proust, had tried to distill memories of her youth, her moods, her feelings where real life occurred. It wasn't what you did that counted; it was what you felt.

She claimed to have a thousand stories that would, in effect, create a symphony of sensations that would rival Beethoven. All she needed was the time to write them down. She tried. You saw her trying. You even read a portion of the manuscript but couldn't follow the storyline. What she was writing had seemed bloated. Fuzzy. Over-written. One line caught your imagination: *He was omphalos: a phallic stone of dizzying proportions.*

All flash and spark and dazzling liveliness, her students adored her. One of them told you, "It's like being taught by a great actress. How lucky you are to have her for your mother."

"Have you ever seen Three Faces of Eve?" you asked.

She said, "Who's Eve?"

"That's my mom's name."

"Mrs. Olsen?"

You ended the conversation with, "You're right, I'm lucky."

•

Round the corner and there she is, your mother standing in line outside the din-ing room. Her hair is swept into a black bun fastened by knitting needles (muggers beware). She is easy to spot among the gray and white mops sprinkled here and there. As she turns her head, you can see her surgically tightened forehead broad and pale, her lavish eyelids aping Cleopatra. A gash of deep red screams across her mouth. She is lending an ear to whatever over-the-hill Ella is saying.

"Speak up, dear."

A line of old ladies and old men are waiting for the cafeteria to open. They al-ready have their trays. You know your mother has made the rounds that morning and gotten her gang out of bed and into their jogging togs, the little club of disciples she coaxes through the halls and water aerobics and dance classes, followed by four times around the building (one-mile) whisking them along—a hen with her chicks. Gotta keep moving. You can rest forever in your grave, girls. But for now, move it or lose it. Keep dancing.

•

Spotting you, she and Ella wave.

"Gimme hug, Harley man," your mother says. "What you doing here? Come to eat with us?"

"Stopped to say goodbye, Mom." You hug her, and shake hands with Ella, her soft, palm always mildly surprising. Girlish for her age.

"Where you going, Harley man?" says your mother.

"Minnesota. On tour."

"No one tells me nothing." Her eyes examine you closely. "Harley man, you look like death warmed over. How'd you get so old? Gray temples. Bags under your eyes. You're getting old. An old lug. How old you be?"

"Fifty-three."

"Wish I was fifty-three," she says. "I was a tiger at fifty-three. Stand up straight. You're getting stooped. The back has only so many bends in it, you know; the heart has just so many beats."

"I didn't get much sleep, Mom."

"You look like death warmed over. How you feel?"

"Tired. I didn't get much sleep."

"You're always tired. Quit repeating yourself. That's what old people do." She turns to Ella. "You know, when this son of mine was a boy he drove me crazy. I wanted to kill him. A buzz saw. He made me prematurely gray, yes he did. He's why I had to start dyeing my hair."

"Because he had so much energy and wouldn't sit still," says in-the-know Ella.

"That's right. We know him, you and me."

They both scrutinize you. Ella, however, is smiling. "Difficult boy," she says, putting her hand over her mouth and tittering. "But we love him so."

"I love him to death," says your mother. "You know what I did last night, Harley man? I danced. We did ballroom dancing."

"Did you? Well, good for you."

"This old boy what took me, he's cocked up today. I tried to wake him, but he called me crazy and told me to go away." She throws her head back and hoots. She still has that owlish laugh. A laugh announcing her love of life. She takes your hand and does a twirl under your arm, a pirouette, while she says, "These gams can still cut a rug. I could've been professional."

"Professional what?" Ella asks, sniggering.

"Don't get smart," your mother replies.

•

Turning to you and jerking her thumb at Ella, she says, "I got her off her ass. She's lucky I found her. She was a stale cracker till I come along and give her the up and at em. Right, Ella?"

"I won't deny it. When they put me in here, I thought I was done for. I never been so depressed in my life. Your children get sick of you and they stuff you into one of these joints and tell you it's for your own good. You'll be with your own kind, they tell you. You'll have activities and such. You'll play games." Ella scrunches her face into a pout, wrinkles imploding. Her eyes look as if they sting. She dabs them with a hanky.

"Now, now Ella, now Ella," soothes your mother.

"Who the hell cares about games at my age, Eve? I'd like to know. Put me in here so they wouldn't feel guilty. 'Look how nice we took care of Mother. Aren't we grand?' Bah! I got their number. They ain't fooling me. Out of sight out of mind. Don't worry, their turn's coming. They'll see what it's like. What goes round comes round. Ain't leaving them a dime, not a penny."

Eve pats Ella's shoulder. "Next thing we do is get your hair dyed, put some color in you. Send you to Dr. What's-His-Face for a facelift. How old do I look? My boyfriend said no more than fifty."

"Fifty-five max," says Ella.

"You betcha, baby. Barely a senior citizen."

•

The red rope falls, the line shuffling to the serving counter, bony fingers pointing to what they want. The smell of scrambled eggs and toast. The aroma of coffee.

"You gonna eat, Harley?"

"I ate already, Mom."

"Eat again. You're too skinny. Your whole life you been too skinny."

They sit at a round table with two other ladies shoveling O'Brien potatoes and eggs, grape jam on buttered toast.

You sip coffee, your cold hands glad for the warmth of the cup.

There is tea in a Brown Betty in the middle of the table, along with packets of blue and pink sweeteners. A din of voices. Clattering dinnerware. Champagne music. A tidy little world living meal to meal. On the other side of the fence: a portal to the past, people scrambling to get somewhere, live in a mini-mansion, have 1.5 kids, a pedigreed dog to match the American statistics, drive a Hummer like it's a weapon, wear clothes in the latest style—for boys to cover their flaws, for girls to look like the latest shame-on-you shaking her bootie on MTV—own every high tech gadget available: TVs that cover entire walls, computers and iPhones and iPods and DVDs and navigational devices and—

•

"How long you gonna be gone? You better write me," your mother says. "None of those damn email things, neither. I want a letter. Give me all the low down. What'll you be doing?"

"Readings."

"Readings?"

"From my book."

"You wrote a book?"

"I gave it to you last week. *So Much Heroism.*"

She waves her hand in dismissal. "They pay you for that?"

"Sometimes."

"Sometimes. How'd you ever get mixed up in such a racket?"

"You used to write, Mom. Remember?"

"Me? What the hell I wanna write for?"

"You said you wanted to freeze time. Leave some of you behind."

A tiny light goes on in her eyes. "Yes, coffee cake. My mother's kisses always smelled whisky. She died of stroke. She died fast, a hunched up old blowsy. And now I'm in this cock-up loaded with afflictions. Get it down. Write about it."

"I do."

"Why don't you come and read for us?" says Ella.

"Read to these characters?" says your mother. "Look at em. They'd fall asleep. Got attention span of kittens."

"I think it would be fun," says Ella.

"When I get back, we'll see," you tell her. "I'll look into it."

"Goodie!" says Ella.

"Haven't read a thing of his and don't intend to," says your mother frowning. "Christ a' mighty, I changed his diapers. What can he tell me? Tell me nothin. Nobody tells me nothin."

You see she is on the cusp of a mood. They always come sudden, sliding towards "black depression" as she calls it. Shadows clouding her newly carved face, washing out her Scandinavian pinkness, replacing it with an oxygen-starved haze, the smell of acetone. Beneath the surface you see fine lines lurking, waiting to show themselves, the whole face soon hanging like it was before she had her operation, paying twenty thousand the surgeon charged her.

"Did you take your blood pressure today?" you ask.

She ignores the question. "Harley man, you ain't getting no inheritance. I'm gonna spend it on fun. Goddamn, I earned it."

Which is what Ella echoes, adding: "Not a nickel for those betrayers."

Your mother's head roams side-to-side, eyelids drooping, eyes gazing wall to wall, searching for an exit? For seconds her attention rests on you. She seems mystified. How could you have done this to me? Lousy son. Selfish bastard. You and that cowardly bitch.

•

Two or three weeks after her facelift she started getting goofy. You thought it had something to do with the anesthetic and she'd snap out of it. But she didn't. She had always been rather outré anyway, so for a while you were able to overlook what was happening. But one day you dropped by her apartment and found her wearing a checkered blouse (orange and white stripes), purple polka dot hot-pants and galoshes, the old-fashioned black buckle-ups. A delicate gold chain around her neck, along with an Indian bead choker, black beads saying in Navajo *TSEGI* (sacred ground), and the key to her apartment hanging from a safety pin pushed through a hole in her earlobe. Thick red lipstick zigzagging. Rouge brightening her cheeks. Her teeth on the kitchen counter grinning. The smell of old skin, damp rug, something exhumed, something not quite dead, but beginning to rot. The bed hadn't been made and the sheets were gritty. All her bookshelves were empty. Hundreds of books had vanished. Dirty clothes lay strewn over the furniture. Dirty dishes and half-eaten TV dinners piled in the sink. Your mother saying "Yum, yum" as she stood in front of a full-length mirror admiring herself.

"What are you doing, Mom? Where'd all your books go? You sell em?"

"I met this *man*. I got a date. How do I look? Eye candy?"

"I think I should take you to the doctor."

She loved going to doctors, so she gave you no trouble. She was out the door and into the car before you could lock up her place.

•

The doctor examined her and told you she was early stage Alzheimer's. He gave you a prescription to fill, some brain stimulator called Aricept, and told you to get her on vitamins and make sure she ate well and exercised and drank coffee every morning or at least something with caffeine in it. Gatorade during the day to keep her electrolytes in balance would be helpful.

"Give her plenty of liquids, she's mildly dehydrated. She'll need lots of care now," he said. "Someone to watch over her." He looked at you out of the sides of his eyes, a look that said he didn't believe you were up to the task.

Is anyone?

"I like this man," your mother said. "Make him my doctor for everything."

"He is your doctor for everything, Mom."

"Whoopee."

"Except he doesn't do facelifts. That's Dr. Cox."

"Dr. Cox? Who's Dr. Cox?"

•

Later, you told Franny about the diagnosis. "And the prognosis ain't so good neither. Slowly but steadily, she's going to get worse. We're losing her. She's heading south."

Franny freaked when you told her you wanted to convert the patio into a granny-flat and get a part-time caregiver to come watch your mother while you were at work.

"We can't do that! We can't do that! Oh, my God!" cried Franny, her hands framing her head, reminding you of Munch's screamer.

"But she's my mom," you said. "We got to take care of her. I'm the son, Franny. The son has to take care of the mom."

"I won't be able to stand it. I'm half-crazy with my own aliments. Don't ask me to take on hers."

Was that the moment you stopped loving her?

•

Looking back now, you can see Franny was right. One sick woman was barely bearable. Two would be impossible. So with Franny's arthritis, indigestion, sciatic nerve, gall bladder and other health troubles as your excuse, you took your mother around to a number of assisted care homes and found GATEWAY.

WE'RE ALL FAMILY HERE said the brochure, a picture of an elderly couple sitting in a courtyard under an umbrella. Elysium in the background. Your mother was given her own apartment, a kitchenette, a bedroom, living room, bathroom, and a caregiver who came in everyday to bathe and dress her and make sure she got her meds and that she ate well. All for only four thousand a month, of which you paid a thousand, while your sister Shanna paid five hundred. Your mother's social security and teacher's retirement handled the rest. The money you got for her house was put in an annuity with you and Shanna as joint beneficiaries.

•

Within a month or so of living at GATEWAY she was almost a different person. She was still having her "spells," but sometimes it seemed as if the doctor might have made a misdiagnosis. Maybe it was just dehydration that had caused her dysfunction. Or maybe the medication was actually doing its job.

You came to visit her one day and found her bouncy and chatty and giving orders. She had a notion she had been hired as an employee to work with the elderly. She took her job seriously. She was a joy to have around, the staff told you. Except those times when she sank into black depressions, a lifelong affliction that had been part of your childhood, when your mother would lie in a dark room and not talk to anyone.

"I'm gonna take the gun and shoot myself," she would yell. And then Shanna and you would look at each other, because both of you knew that for a few days she would be off her rocker. Her second and third husbands divorced her because of her broody moods. The third one swore she was what drove him to drink. Which gave him cirrhosis. Which eventually killed him.

•

"What would you like me to bring you from Minnesota, Mom?" you ask, hoping to pre-empt the doldrums entering her head. "I've got lots of readings and signings in Minnesota, a thing called UMBA, it's a booksellers association. They're the ones who invited me for *So Much Heroism*."

"What do I care?"

"How about a new ball gown?"

"What for?"

"For your ballroom dancing."

"Ballroom dancing! Listen to the man. Square dancing is about the best my crew can do. If the caller uses a bullhorn. Half deaf. The other half so arthritic they sound like they're stomping on Rice Crispies. Ballroom dancing, where'd you get that one?"

"I'll look for a nice square dance dress, then. Would you like that?"

She gives you a look. "Quit trying to buy me off, Harley man. You lock me away in here and then you try to buy me off. Some son you turned out to be."

"Got to go, Mom. Got to hit the road."

"Abandon me. Go ahead deceive me. All you want is for me to die."

"That's not true, Mom." *(Sort of true.)*

"It's true. You and that Franny. That bitch. If you had left her back when she was having her affair and deserved the boot, I could have lived with you. Now it's too late. I got this job to do. But some daughter-in-law. Some son. Tell me the truth, do you love her?"

Do you love her? Do you love Franny?

"I don't know," you answer.

She glares as if you have told her something contemptible. "Just remember this from your mother who knows everything there is to know about this subject." Wagging her chipped nail in your face she says, "You can't control what you love. Don't even try. It ain't possible. I tried four times. Or was it five?" She starts counting husbands on her fingers. "Jim, your father. George one. George two. Emmett the bastard who broke my arm. Henry Flower, I loved his name, but he was another no-goodnik. Emmett, hmm." She pauses. "What happened to him?"

"He died of liver failure."

"Too much booze killed that bastard. He bled to death internally. Dumb bastard. So how many is that?" She counts them on her fingers again. "I haven't been married that many times, have I?"

To change the subject you say, "Eat your breakfast, Mom. You're wasting away to nothing."

"You should talk. Nothing but skin and bones. You look like death warmed over. What kind of man you turned into?" She leans confidentially toward Ella, "It's his fat fool wife, she feeded her own fat face, but not my son."

"She feeds me," you say.

"How come she never come see me? Twenty years I'd knowed her and she never come see me. I should have stayed where whats-her-name is, your sister—"

"Shanna."

"Shanna is my real friend. You talked me into coming to this godforsaken ..." Eyes confused, she looks around. "Where am I?" she asks.

"California," you tell her.

"California?" she says, her tone baffled.

●

Twenty years ago moving from Colorado to be with the baby that never made it alive into this world. (And the next neither.) Franny and Eve had desperately wanted them. Eve never forgave those miscarriages. God getting her. God punishing fool-around Franny. Lots of miscarriages. Very common if you're a tart and a tippler and you get pregnant before you're married.

●

"You mark my words: she'll end up in here before long in a wheelchair."

"That's what she says, Mom. Franny suffers terribly."

"So does me. You ever think about *that*?"

Standing up, you pat her shoulder. "Got a plane to catch. Got to get moving." You kiss your mother's nest of hair and leave the dining hall.

Seconds later, she is beside you, catching your elbow and saying she will walk you to the door. "This job is wearing me out," she says. "I'm so exhausted I can't think straight. I fall in bed and sleep like a dead toad."

"This place would fall apart without you, Mom."

"That's what everyone tells me. It's always 'Eve, Eve.' Everywhere I turn they want something from me."

"It's good to be useful."

"I want to drop dead with one foot in front of the other. I want to drop dead in harness, like the old gray mare." The hallway light shining on her profile reveals silver roots running through her once ebony hair. The bun pinned to the back of her head is coming loose. The knitting needles sagging.

At the top of the stairs you hug her and say, "I hope you get your wish, Mom. You better get back now. Your girls need you."

"See you next week," she says.

"I'll be gone a month," you remind her.

"Where you going so long?"

"I'm going to . . . nothing, nowhere. Never mind. I'll see you next week."

"Take me for a hamburger and Pepsi. Pepsi is my favorite."

"I'll do that. You be good now."

"Be good? That's all I ever am. Whatever the hand finds to do, do it for there is no work . . . um . . . what's the rest of it?"

"Nor device nor knowledge nor wisdom in the grave whither thou goest."

"Are you sure? That doesn't sound right, Harley. Are you sure? Do you know? What do you know, Harley man?"

.

When you get to Minneapolis and have checked at the hotel desk, there is a message telling you to call Franny. An emergency.

Franny answers her phone on the first ring. Before she can say anything, you say, "It's Mom."

"I'm sorry."

"What happened?"

"Stroke. A massive stroke. She went fast."

Your throat tightens. You fight back tears. "Do you know what she was doing? Was she out marching her troops around the building?"

"I don't know. Are you coming back to take charge?"

.

You catch a shuttle back to the airport. While you wait on standby for a flight, you call your sponsor at Upper Midwest Booksellers Association and tell her what has happened and that you are cancelling your appearance and the tour.

"I'm so sorry," says the woman. "You'll probably never get a chance like this again, but I understand. If it were my mother, I'd be on the next plane, too. Mothers, they're special. If you can't love your mother who can you love? Mothers teach you how to love. Love and mother are synonyms."

.

Harley remembered the woman's words as he rose from his easy chair and stood gazing at the portrait of his mother hanging on the wall. She was eighteen then. Young forever. Her smile expressing her joy of life, her capacity to love.

Mother's love. Is there such a thing? Beyond the word itself is there anything real? Love. A word used to describe something incoherent, illogical, something that comes in a rush of overwhelming feeling. Something that can be lost as fast as it's found.

Or is it just me? Do other people know love? They don't need logic. They don't need to be rational. People say: God is love. And they say: I know God exists because I know God exists. I feel God in my soul. I feel God in my heart. I feel God in every organ of my being. I know because I *know*. Why hasn't that way of knowing ever worked for me? Who am I to say none of it makes sense, none of it is reasonable? Who am I to say show me the *data*?

But then again if there is God, there may also be Heaven, a place of many mansions where Eve knows Eternal Bliss now. Not ashes in the rose garden. Dusty discards. She shuffled off her mortal coil. The essence is elsewhere. It knows nothing of pain or fear. It knows nothing of senility and loss of dignity. It knows nothing of no longer being. Nothing of children turning away with tears in their eyes and saying, "That's not my mother. That's just a shell we called Eve."

•

The whereabouts of Eve's many books remained a whodunit, a strange puzzle as puzzling as how such a vital woman, an intellectual, a writer, a teacher could sink into senility. Would she have kept her wits longer if he had built her that room and taken care of her? Would he have stayed true to his wife? Would he not have fallen into an affair with a woman who takes his breath away every time he sees her?

2 - Bodies in Motion

Harley was fifty-four when he did the Border's reading and met Didi for the second time. This was a year after he had met her at Norman's poetry gig in San Diego. Driving home from Border's that night, Harley saw himself standing behind the lectern, spotting her in the audience. All eyes on him. Some eyes saying: you're-probably-no-good-and-can't-entertain-me. (Always his first impression.) He had done his best to amuse her (them), quoting passages from his third book— *Bodies in Motion*. Harley had started with the scene in the topless/bottomless bar called The Body Shop—the bodybuilder chanting:

I'm the man for sat-tis-fac-tion,
The one who owns the main at-trac-tion.
Oh, it always gets re-ac-tion
From the girls with giddy hair.

Whenever Harley read the scene of Naked-Girl-Dancer watched by Bodybuilder in grip of Ravishing-Intentions, his eyes licking every millimeter of her squirming skin, it always got attention, the listeners waiting to hear what would happen next. Maybe the bodybuilder was going to ambush her when she left after her shift was over. Or maybe he would lose control, leap on stage, carry her off to … wherever. There were always looks of surprise when she ended up turning the tables. Coming to the booth. Taking his hand. Leading him out to her van. Beginning the process of destroying his life.

For writers like Harley, readings were crucial. He gave them for the purist of reasons: he wanted to sell books. Enough so his publisher would want to publish him again. Critics said his work was odd, edgy, quirky, character-driven, plotless, highly literary (terrible term: "highly literary"—code for miserable sales). In interviews Harley had argued with critical assessments of his books, explaining that he was trying to write a small slice of life as seen through a glass darkly. He insisted that his work wasn't plotless. Wasn't quirky. Wasn't (gasp!) "highly literary."

•

He wrote mainly to entertain readers and to keep himself sane and off a psychiatrist's couch. No brain pickers for Harley. No "experts" telling him he had this or that unpronounceable disorder. All he wanted to do was tell stories. Good stories, of course, though he knew some of them were stinkers. The trouble was: how did the writer know which stories were good, which bad? It was judgment. Sometimes Harley's judgment was on par with an 80 I.Q. Other times it soared (in his humble opinion) beyond calculation. Years ago his mother told him that when he was growing up a cyclone of energy making her "climb walls," she couldn't figure out what she had given birth to, a genius or a nincompoop. The genius was the one who taught himself to read before he went to kindergarten and could memorize whole books and quote them verbatim without looking at a single page. Children's stories to be sure, but …

•

The nincompoop stabbed all his mother's plants and gave them wounds that wouldn't heal. Then lied about it. "Not me, Mama, them plants got a disease." The nincompoop hid dirty underwear beneath clean underwear in the underwear drawer and was found out and whacked with a switch. Because cleanliness is next to godliness. And why had Harley done that, anyway? He didn't know. The clothes hamper was ten steps away in the bathroom. The nincompoop was the one who jumped off the roof with a sheet as a parachute and sprained both ankles. But the genius got to kick back in bed and read while his ankles healed. Harley remembered his father shouting: "You stupid! Look what asinine shit you've done now!"

Both the genius and nincompoop were apparently contributing factors in the father's suicide: The family on vacation in San Francisco; Harley (fiercely five) bouncing on the backseat having a bout of attention deficit; Father saying, "Can't stand this kid's incessant prattle. Why can't he sit still? The back seat is not a goddamn trampoline."

Harley refused to take the entire rap for what happened next. Surely, there must have been something more going on in his father's head that day. His mother and father always at each other. Sometimes over little Harley, but mostly over her being such a flirt. Although she was a high school English teacher, she was also Swedish with a touch of Italian and had a mouth on her that would have had Eric Partridge taking notes: cock-up, balls-up, drive your cobs up your throat, you cow cocker. Tale of Two Titties. The father would plug his ears and hum when she got going. So, maybe Harley's ventilating vocals was the last straw that day, but the groundwork had been laid long before.

Harley watched as his father stopped the car in the middle of Golden Gate Bridge, leaping out, rushing the rail, diving over. Non-stop, no hesitation. Start to finish, perhaps six seconds. How long had he been suicidal? Had he planned it? Doing it so dramatically? Like something from a horror movie. His mother was screaming, screaming, while little Shanna on her lap screamed too. When his sister got old enough to make sense, he asked her about it—Dad's suicide? "Don't know what you talkin bout, Harley. Don't member any of it, not a bit":

Swept up in pieces by a trawler, head here, arms there, torso surfing the foam of a two-footer, bowels, buttocks and legs never recovered.

•

Years later, after he put his mother in the assisted care retirement home, he was going through her personal things, trying to decide what should be kept and what to set out for GOODWILL. He had a pile of clothes she would never wear again. There were dozens of new shoes of all types still in their shoeboxes (never worn as far as he could tell). There was a drawer stuffed with silky underwear. Another drawer stuffed with nylon stockings and pantyhose. Drawers full of low-cut halters and naughty nightgowns and garters. She had a heavy terrycloth robe and another made of black satin hanging on the back of her bedroom door. Harley set aside every utilitarian item she could use.

Searching further, he found a cedar box she kept on the shelf in her closet. Inside were trinkets—a tiny statue of Shakespeare holding a minuscule book, a half-heart necklace inscribed with Harley's father's name, JIM, a diamond wedding ring, several silver bracelets, and a metal chain memory bracelet with a childhood picture of himself and a picture of his father and another of his parents kissing. He found a Bronze Star Medal with a V for Valor and a Purple Heart. He found a Mont Blanc pen with his mother's name printed on it and **TEACHER OF THE YEAR** in tiny gold letters. There were birthday cards. And letters and notes and poems written in longhand.

He opened one of the notes and saw it was written by his father:

Once upon a time I was heroic. Yes, that is the word. The word is Heroic. During the war I was scared to death but did my duty and was decorated by General Patton. Heroic Lieutenant James Olsen. No more. What happened? What happened to him? Life. Life happened. Takes the stuffing out of you. Out of everyone, eventually. It happened when I realized that I had lived beyond my ability to seize my own life and wring something lofty and lasting from it, something that would bring forgiveness for the pain I've caused, the lives I've broken, the lives I've taken. But that dream or hope, or whatever it is, is based on illusion. People who say they've fulfilled their dreams, their great ambitions, achieved their goals -- still have to get up tomorrow and construct a reason to keep living. There has to be more to it than being too afraid to die. My reason for being is as elusive as my under-standing of why I've lived my life the way I've lived it. Why did I survive the war when so many tens of thousands died? Why did I come back to the States and marry Eve? Why did I work all these years as a loan officer for Central Savings saying yes or no, fulfilling wishes or denying them? Why was Harley born? I'm not father material. The kid can't stand me

*and I can't stand him. It's the truth. Who needs to know the truth if the truth destroys you?
I'd rather live a lie, if the lie is kind, if the lie is merciful, if the lie makes me believe there
is really such a thing as love and it's not just a condition of being self-absorbed and simply
wanting what you want and to hell with everyone else. Today I've got THIS. Tomorrow I'll
be tired of it and want something more. Desire: It's an eternally recurring and destructive
curse given to us by warped ancestors. I'm sick of it. Fundamentally, nothing will ever
change. Never. Tomorrow IS another day of Jim Olsen wanting out.*

•

Harley kept the note and said nothing to his mother, who seemed not to notice
it was missing whenever she would go through her box, her fingers tinkering trying
on jewelry while staring into a mirror. Lifting out her husband's medals and staring at
them with a puzzled look in her eyes. Once, she even pointed to his picture hanging
from the memory chain and said, "What's his name?"

Harley wrote about it in *So Much Heroism*, the story of a war-haunted man, a despairing father trying to cope with being bombarded in Europe and then bombarded
even more by his passionate wife and logorrheic son and his dull, unhappy life forcing
him through the motions, a man dreaming of his lost, heroic past. And dreaming also
of following the one thousand three hundred others who had jumped from Frisco's
life-gobbling bridge. People told Harley they liked the novel up to the part where the
father took the long dive. The description of him smiling. The description of him
waving bye-bye and shouting Unk!

Can you imagine how it felt? The air whistling in your ears. The seagulls thinking
you are one of them. Has he spotted some fish? The sparkling water so bright it was
like diving into the sun. A lucid moment: *maybe I shouldn't have done this.*

•

Harley had spent a lot of time outdoors in his youth—a construction worker,
motorcycle rider, ocean surfer burned year after year by UV—and to him he looked
at least sixty (on bad days sixty-five.), a senior citizen toddling towards the boneyard.
It depended on how tired he was. Lack of sleep (all his life—terrible insomnia) had
etched those lines in his face. At certain angles they looked like scars. Blame it on
Scandinavian skin and an inherited depression that turned manic on occasion, which
kept him dependent on drinking too much. Drinking only making it worse, of course,
but for two or three hours awash he usually felt a tide of good will lifting him, telling
him he was fine, just fine. That he wasn't a has-been with a hole in his head where his
common sense used to live.

•

Redux Borders: Harley facing a big crowd—big for him—fourteen people on folding chairs, including the four salespersons running the store. Bless Harley's soul, there was a nice little stack of *Bodies in Motion*—the Thinker on the cover wearing a cowboy hat. His chin resting on his fist. To Harley's eyes the Thinker looked as if he were sitting on the pot relieving himself. Harley had tried to tell his editor that the picture was scatological. The editor had told Harley to mind his own business. And when Harley kept complaining the editor said, "Who do you think you are John Grisham?" Harley apologized and hung up. He once had an agent tell him that she had to get off the phone because she had a two hundred thousand dollar author on the other line: "Whom would you talk to? A five-thousand dollar author, or a two-hundred thousand dollar author?"

No contest.

But that was then. This night at Border's had been open-ended, a night that might be a triumph or a retreat into chaos. Like the chaos that happens to Harley's anti-hero in *Bodies in Motion* who falls for Naked-Girl-Dancer and lemming-like follows her up to and over the edge that threatens all of us now and again. Whatever the future held, there in front of the audience was Mr. Harley J. Olsen floating apart watching himself answering questions.

•

No nuance. No mention of past-their-glory icons. Not one idea in Harley's head. Smile and they usually smile with you. He learned that was the way the formula worked. For some of them. Not that dour old lady with brittle hair that would turn to powder if you squeezed it. Or the scowling marine in camouflage fatigues with the James Ellroy book in his hand. He (the marine) was wandering by as Harley was reading the line: *Look at that pussy pooch begging someone to nibble.* Harley watched him take a chair. Head forward, elbows on knees, he listened intensely to the rest of the passage. Harley also remembered the fidgeting teenager, whose mother kept whispering, telling him to sit still (a kid after Harley's own heart). Make Mommy climb the walls. At least the salesclerks and Didi grinned in the right places. Laughed at the jokes (the silly bodybuilder salivating over silly Naked-Girl-Dancer gyrating on stage), leading others to laugh as well.

During the question and answer period a toothy woman up front had said, "What do you do about writer's block? I've been stuck on a page of my novel for ages."

"If you're a writer stuck on a page," Harley answered, "bring a woman and a man together in the same room. Don't ask me how, just get them together. Man. Woman.

Same room. A lock on the door. They don't really have to do anything much. Let them jabber. Let him check out the curve of her hip. Let her check out those shoulders. The reader's anticipation keeps the pages turning. See what I mean? You've got your heart into it again. What can your man and woman do? Figure it out and let them do it or not. Be a tease. One word follows another and you're off and running."

•

Smile, Olsen. Smile like you mean it. You were giving them tricks. You hate tricks.

Glancing at the speedometer, you realized you were doing eighty. Three martinis in you. Breathalyzer waiting. You moved two lanes over. Slowed down.

•

He didn't used to smile at reading events at all. But one night at a bookstore in La Jolla someone asked him why he looked so grumpy. The question came as a shock. "I look grumpy?" he said. He didn't want to look grumpy. "No, it's simply concentration. Focus. Intensity." Plus deepening age lines. Maybe attitude, the prostitution of my work, the idiocy of trying to be charming. A personality. Why am I here? Why am playing the whore? What do you people want? Why don't you go home and read?" The compassionate ones.

Now when he gave readings he smiled more. He tried to project kindness and caring. But behind his mask was a man who hated being a member of an obtuse, greedy species. As the poet phrased it: "Homo Satanicus".

Thinking of the seven billion-plus cluttering this groaning planet made Harley claustrophobic, anxious, irrational. All that food slithering into seven billion mouths and out seven billion asses. Landfills overflowing, the lungs of the ocean collapsing, viruses mutating, biding its time, all things waiting for other things to bite them, eat them. Ad infinitum. "Xanax," his mother would say if she were still alive. "Take your Xanax, Harley. Life is full of sorrow an' sufferin. And then you cock-up die, so relax, relax."

•

Didi, petite, hair gone blond, dark-eyes wide with what? Wonder? Wearing denins and black leather jacket, raised her hand and asked for the secret to becoming a published writer. She said she had sent out "dozens of stories and poems, all of them rejected. I'm at my wit's end. Tell me what to do. Tell me what to do."

Tell her what to do.

Give her the blueprint.

Harley frowned, knitted his brows, bit his lips. Felt totally inadequate.

He would tell anyone how to get published if he could. But he didn't know how. "According to Petrarch," he said, "remorseless labor conquers all."

The look on her face was dissatisfied. Harley knew what she wanted. She wanted him to read her work and advise her—edit it, revise it, add the professional touch.

He smiled sympathetically. Pretended to care and that he wished to be helpful.

Despite her exaggerated frown, she was even more attractive than he remembered. The cascading blond hair was striking. Her flawless skin stretching over starlet cheekbones, come-hither mouth. The acne-scarred man sitting next to her looked like he wanted to kick Harley's ass. It sometimes happened that there would be a person at a reading whose face projected menace. Which caused Harley to think—Sees right through me. Sees what a phony I am. Knows I lucked out somehow and shouldn't be up here. You're a stupid bastard, the face says. You're a wise ass. How did you ever get that piece of shit published?

"Working on anything new?" Didi had asked.

"Yes. Well, fiddling with the words."

•

Afterwards, he had drinks with her, kissed her, and now he was driving home believing he had handled things reasonably well. Except for the kiss. Maybe he shouldn't have allowed that to happen. Just an impulse on her part, stopping his mouth with her mouth. A nice kiss. Glutinous lips. Wet with wine. Smelled of wine. Write that down, how her mouth smelled like wine.

Quickly the night passed, but Harley would remember it with gratitude. And he might use it to create a sex scene. One of those harmless flings. Or perhaps adultery? The sneaking around. Sex at every opportunity. Then the demands. She wanted to get married. Children. A house. A long life together. All he had to do was leave his wife. "If you really love me, you will."

•

When Harley got home, Franny was sleeping. He tiptoed into the bathroom, brushed his teeth. Washed his face. Put on pajamas. Went into his bedroom/office. Sat at the desk. In his journal he wrote a synopsis of the reading.

Later, he lay in the dark staring at the ceiling, thinking of Didi and the kiss. Two kisses, actually. It hadn't been the same as when he was younger. There hadn't been that instant fire, damn the torpedoes, full speed ahead, throw caution to the winds. Age slowing him down. Testosterone on the low side of normal according to his blood test. The doctor once offered him a testosterone gel, but Harley said no. He didn't need to get stirred up. There had been many women in his life. Thirty, perhaps, maybe more. Doubtless, he could have had Didi. Her nervous smile, her uneasy finger rubbing her lip, her exotic eyes telling him: you want me I'm yours.

In his youth he might have taken her to the car and found some secluded spot and added a notch to his memories of orifices. But that was not his way on the cusp of fifty-four and senior citizenship. Far more meaningful things to do than get laid. Those bewitchments of the body were ultimately lies, anyway. Years ago he had thought with each one that maybe she was it. Maybe her body would make him believe in love. But in the end each body became a void. Wanting them became an ailment. No deathless light ever entered his head. Seen with a cool eye, the act itself was ridiculous. Nothing but revulsion and disappointment after. When at thirty-two, he met twenty-five-year-old Franny and got along with her so well, he made up his mind to marry her and love her as best he could. Keep things under control.

Calm life.
Order.
Stability.

•

It was fine at first, but then as the years flew she started wanting more passion than Harley could supply. His neglect sent her into the arms of another, an office romance. Harley never met him. But he could smell him on her and knew when he made love to her that her lover had been there that day. She had already had three miscarriages but was still in a breeding time of life. It was only sex, he told himself. But it bothered him just the same. He didn't want to care. But he cared. Not that Harley owned her. The odor clinging to her was often a perverted turn on.

They almost broke up when he told her he knew what she was doing and offered her a divorce. She offered him one too. No fault. No blame game here. They cried in each other's arms.

He looked for an apartment.

Days later she told him the affair was over. Her lover's wife had found out and was threatening him. Franny had wrung her hands. She had bawled as only the bereaved can bawl. The next morning she woke with a rash on her forearms. Her cheeks and her belly flaring with more rashes. She took Benadryl.

Later, when she asked Harley if he was going to leave, he said if she wanted him to stay he'd stay.

She hoped he could forgive her.

"We all make mistakes," he told her, feeling everything shriveling below his waist and around his heart.

When he moved into the guest bedroom, Franny had a fever. The doctor ordered numerous tests, but nothing was conclusive. Some kind of virus, the doctor decided. Stay in bed, drink lots of fluids.

For two weeks she was sick. She claimed God was getting her for what she had done. She slept with the Bible in her bed. Harley took care of her. Kept her clean. Kept her fed. She couldn't eat much, just bouillon and crackers. Sometimes chicken soup. She cried in her sleep. She stared at the cross hanging on the wall. She murmured prayers. When she was awake she asked Harley for forgiveness. He would say there was nothing to forgive. Nothing at all.

"I'm such a fool," she would say.

One night the fever broke and she recovered. It took months to regain the weight she had lost. But then she just kept gaining, ballooning to a hundred and sixty-five pounds. One-seventy. One-eighty.

•

Years. And more years. Franny and Harley settled into a mock sister and brother relationship. Perhaps others had grand passions for which they would die, but not Harley. He took whatever passion he had and put it into his work. "No iron can stab the heart with such force as a period put in the right place," he constantly reminded his students, echoing what a favorite professor had told him. (Years later he discovered he was quoting Isaac Babel).

The novels were written and published. Harley won some small awards. The reviews were mostly positive, respectful. At the university he was promoted. His life was peaceful, predictable, and sane. Until Franny got breast cancer. Which scared both of them witless. Cancer! Jesus!

Harley became a cheerleader cheering her on. He told her she wasn't going to die. Said it so many times and so firmly that she believed him. Harley kept thinking how simple life would be if she did die, how her life insurance would free him to live for his art. Not responsible for anyone. Except selfish Harley Olsen.

Again, she slept with the Bible. Again, she claimed God was after her. Again, she wept copiously. Again, she prayed doggedly.

After the surgeon took the lump out, he told Harley the cancer was encapsulated and there was no trace in the lymph nodes. Prognosis: good. Franny would be on Taxol for five years as a preventive.

But then she was diagnosed with rheumatoid arthritis and went on weekly doses of methotrexate, plus painkillers like Ultram and Vicodin. Prilosec for her stomach. Natural healers glucosamine and chondroitin with MSM. She had to have an operation on her feet to remove inflamed nerves between her toes. She started catching lots of colds. The methotrexate wreaking havoc on her immune system. Her gall bladder filled with stones and had to be removed. She always had backaches and diarrhea. She got deeply depressed and went on Zoloft.

Which eventually helped her cope well enough to get a part-time job editing for Harvest Home, the job evolving, years later, into her position as senior editor. Between the Zoloft and the other medicines and her job, Franny's outlook on life improved. She insisted she owed it all to God, to Jesus Christ her Savior. She became a cheerful, optimistic person, trustworthy and kind. Proud to call herself a cancer survivor. When friends asked her about her arthritis, she told them she had her good days and her bad days. And she always added that things could have been so much worse. What if the cancer had spread? God forbid.

•

Had Harley been the one to get cancer and all Franny's other aliments on top of that, he doubted he could have coped so well. Would he have turned to God? Maybe Harley would have mimicked his father, taken a dive, hung himself, put the gun in his mouth. Maybe he would have become an alcoholic nincompoop. Which was what had happened to his grandmother and mother as they aged. Both alcoholics. Both brave when they were drunk, but otherwise anxious , worried, fearful covering it up with bluster. Harley hoped he would never get that way.

But as his mother always told him when she was alive, "You never know what you'll do until faced with a moment of truth." What her moment had been, she never said. But Harley suspected it was the death of his father, watching the long leap, watching him waving. The rest of the scoop was fish food, the missing bowels, legs, buttocks. Harley's tranquilized mother still managed to function as a teacher and out-live four desperate husbands, all of them younger, all of them exhausted, ready to go like characters in her "Tale of Two Titties."

3 - In the Palm of Your Hand

Norman Ten Boom's eighth book of poetry, a collection called *Ecstasy: Love Poems for Lovers*, was a thin thing containing seventy short poems exploring themes of love and violence, May/December romance, morality and sin, war and peace, health and illness, time and death. Its cover depicted a cloudy border surrounding a blue, impressionistic flower opening its mouth. The dedication inside was to his new love: *"For Didi my muse."*

"She completes me," Norman told Harley.

They were sitting in the university cafeteria, Norman quoting his own poetry when he said: "We are the same blood, breath and heart." With his chest swelling, ample chins quivering, he repeated, "Breath and heart, breath and heart. You've read the collection."

"Of course," said Harley.

"Every word a gem, a nugget of simplicity, yes?"

"Yes," said Harley.

Norman played with his coffee cup, turning it in circles, staring into its opaque interior as he continued, "Well, who knows if it will be appreciated? But I don't care because it brought me her. You see what I'm saying? I'm saying that without Didi, *Ecstasy* would never have been written. Nothing else matters." He laid a hand on Harley's forearm. "I'm saying that at nearly sixty-two I have finally found my soul-mate."

Soul-mate.

Mate for the soul. One of those.

•

When *Ecstasy* debuted Harley had blurbed:

Norman Ten Boom confirms his place as one of the most distinctive poetic voices of his generation, a man musing on love as a value system that makes its own laws, its own occasionally mystical world of morality, where we would (if we could) embroider the one we love into the very valves of our heart.

[Not very inspired, but it was the best he could do given his limited opinion of the book.]

Not that it mattered anyway. To Harley's relief, Norman declined to use it. More prestigious names marked the back cover, all of them more or less putting Norman's name in the company of Pablo Neruda and Garcia Lorca.

"You're coming to my reading," said Norman, tapping Harley's forearm.

"Wouldn't miss it."

"You're in for a treat, my friend. You're in for a ride. I always put on a good show."

"Do you?"

"Let me tell you something. This is the voice of experience, so you should listen. At least ninety-eight percent of the audience will be women. Every one of them will believe herself a poet. They'll coo and swoon over what I read them. You watch, you'll see. I know these things." He was nodding his head. "I'll have them creaming their pants. Watch how they cross their legs and jiggle their foot. You know what that means when a woman crosses her legs and jiggles her foot?"

"She's nervous."

"She's masturbating, Harley. She's masturbating. She's squeezing her vulva. She's milking it. It happens all the time. I've seen it for years, my man, for years. This is what my poems do to women, the love poems and the violent poems. Love and violence gets them off, believe me."

"Whatever you say, Norman."

"Got to go teach my class, but let me leave you with this proverb: Sour, sweet, bitter, pungent—all must be tasted." Rising, he pulled a stack of flyers from his briefcase. "Here," he said, "pass these out to your classes."

The flyers announced:

ACCLAIMED POET NORMAN TEN BOOM WILL BE LAUNCHING HIS 8TH BOOK OF POETRY TUESDAY, MARCH 10 AT 7:00 P.M. THE POET'S GROOVE, BLUE NILE RESTAURANT
2027 E. FRANKLIN, SAN DIEGO, CA

•

Even though Franny was having one of her bad days, she and Harley went to Norman's reading arranged by a local writers' group, consisting of a number of poets who got together monthly to critique each other's work and give advice.

The audience sat at dining tables. Inspirational Norman stood behind a lectern, his shaggy silver hair haloed, the key light shimmering around him like white, transparent fire.

Accompanying his recital was a clatter of dinnerware, the soft prattling of the staff, double doors shuffling as waiters came and went. At the table closest to the stage sat Didi Godunov. She kept stealing glances at Harley. He made sure he didn't meet her gaze, even though he wanted to gawk at her, trim as she was, her hair cascading, her crescent eyes magnetically bright—everything about her the opposite of Harley's overweight and unwell wife. The image of her kissing him after his reading at Border's kept fluttering in front of his eyes.

In spite of the setting and disturbances, Norman read beautifully—arms waving, lion's head jerking side-to-side, mane flourishing, his silky baritone rising and falling in full command of his language.

The lines he read were mostly romantic, but romance injected with something clinging like syrup to the syntax, words seeking to pierce the heart, devastate the soul, disconnect the rational powers and flow with the emotional tide; yet, like the rabbit racing the tortoise, never quite getting where they wanted to go—the elevation of love as something spiritual, a higher calling. Harley's impression was that a talented teenager might have written many of Norman's poems.

Norman had been right about women being ninety-eight percent of the audience, many of them cooing over each rendition, their oohs and aahs exhaling rapture, audibly longing for a love as sweet and true as the love expressed in his seductive voice. The applause at the end of each poem seemed on the verge of ovation, passionately urging him to give more vis-à-vis—*Love vast as the sky*. Harley watched them crossing and uncrossing their legs. Feet jiggledee-jiggling.

A number of his poems may have been as brilliant as Norman claimed they were. The ones exploring jazz, political chicanery, the treachery of warmongers, the lamented death of innocence at the hands of evil men, the blamelessness of children caught in the midst of unjustifiable wars—Harley thought those poems were insightful and a pleasure to hear (though doubtfully linked with the theme of Love Poems for Lovers). He believed that Norman would have been more impressive if he had stuck to currently crucial topics, rather than mingle the reading with the soul inflamed. Romantic revelations arriving in the form of a muse named Didi Godunov:

I need these ethereal transports that set the nymph of
uncontrollable cravings throbbing towards the beacon of
beauty's passionate promise.

Ladies all around Harley and Franny nodded their heads knowingly. So did some of the men. Didi sat starry-eyed and trembling over "*a love like this seemed out of reach/ lost as I was in the slough of despond that aging brings.*" Falling in love had restored Norman's youth and made him believe that soul-mates truly exist, for he had found such a mate—

in the form of an angel
who treads so lightly upon the earth
she never leaves a footprint except in the softest sands of a summer beach
where waves wash in greedily caressing the slender signs
of immortal beauty passing by.

•

After the reading, Norman and Didi drove to the Olsen house for a late supper. It was a cozy celebration to honor the new book, and also to make Norman feel that Harley and Franny believed he was as important as he said he was—"Contemporary poets rank me as one of America's finest. Many say I am simply the best of my time."

(At the university library Harley had looked for critical opinions and studies that might verify Norman's statements, but couldn't find any. All eight books of his poetry had been published by small, independent presses, most of which had come and gone, except for Purity Press based in Berkeley, California, which still advertised that they published "where no publisher has gone before.")

•

The evening started with champagne toasts to Norman's new book and to the new love of his life, lovely Didi Godunov.

"Slainte."

Harley lifted his glass and quoted Omar Khayyam. *"Drink! for you know not whence you came nor why. Drink! For you know not why you go, nor where."*

"In vino veritas! boomed Norman.

Franny touched the wine to her lips. She didn't dare drink any. Under a daily bombardment of prescription drugs her liver had become a liability. Medical problems hadn't weakened her cooking skills, however. She served deep-fried shrimp and calamari hors d'oeuvres, followed by sole with lemon and caper sauce, tossed salad, saffron rice sprinkled with ground walnuts and fresh parsley, toasted sourdough dipped in olive oil. Wine and more wine. Three bottles by midnight. Harley knew he was drinking faster than usual, but he didn't care. He loved the wine. Loved the background music, Telemann's Viola Concerto in G Major filling his ears, mixing with and muting the monologue flowing from Norman, whether his mouth was empty or full.

•

After the four of them retired to the living room, the guest of honor sat cross-legged like a pasha on one of the great cushions near the fireplace, Didi by his side. He told them he was going to get her first collection of poetry published. He was going to write the forward and arrange some readings. The book would be out in seven months, at which time Harley and Franny could give a dinner in Didi's honor.

"Yes, of course," they both agreed.

Didi's smiling eyes sparkled with gratitude. She stared at Harley and childlike stated, "You would do that for me?" He noticed a slight cast in her left eye and found it curiously alluring.

"I'd love to read your collection, Didi."

"Oh no, not yet, Mr. Olsen," she demurred. "I'm still working on it."

"Call me Harley."

"What I mean, Harley, is that I'm still revising. Cant' help myself."

"She doesn't need to revise. The collection is perfect," said Norman, Didi looking down modestly, Norman stroking her cheek. "She writes like an angel I tell you. Don't you think she's beautiful? Have you ever seen such delicate cheekbones? Look at her eyes. How they always seem to be smiling. She could have been a model. No, no, I'm serious. Let me tell you something—I know these things. She and I met in another life and she was the model for Iphigenia in my *Cymon and Iphigenia,* 1848. No, I'm serious. Take a look at it sometime. It's her. Didi to the core. Just hers is a darker complexion. She's part Moroccan, you know. Aren't you, Didi?"

"A drop of Moroccan, but mostly blond Russian," she replied.

"Your Iphigenia?" quizzed Franny, one eyebrow rising.

His arm pointed godward as he declared, "I was the Pre-Raphaelite John Millias in one of my other lives. Do you know how I know this?"

No one could say. Harley heard Didi whispering, "Cyclic return of body and soul."

"Transmigration of the heart the instant I saw a Millias' painting," insisted Norman. "It was *Christ in the House of His Parents*. I recognized every detail. The carpenter's shop, the open door looking out on the sheep in the field, the figures of Mary and Christ that I had drawn. The very wood shavings on the floor were intimately familiar. That was just a year after I met the 1848 Didi and had her pose as Iphigenia. Later I used her in my *Ophelia*. Different color hair, but the same face. Didn't I tell you that you and I were old souls, my darling?"

"That's what he said." Eyes closing on a breath of laughter.

"And I took her straight to the painting in *Nineteenth Century Paintings*. Didn't I, my darling? Didn't I just stick my finger in and flip the book to the exact page?"

"It was uncanny."

"Preordained," said Norman. "And there you were. Wasn't it you?"

"If you say so."

"But the point is we are eternal lovers. Remember when we turned over the Tarot cards and we both got the Sun as the last card? We did. It's true. These are phenomenon we can't ignore. A higher power. It's spiritual! What else could it be?"

Franny's stare shrieked at Harley: *This man is woo-woo!*

Harley, a mite tipsy, was thinking: But how do we know? Maybe there are special beings that can see into the occult, into the Beyond where our many lives litter the scene like beads of dew waiting for sunrise. Hmm, maybe I should write that down.

He looked above Franny's head at the print hanging on the wall: *The White Calico*

Flower. Beneath the snowy flowers was an epigraph: *If winter comes can spring be far behind?* Harley had written the epigraph to remind himself of Percy Shelley's indomitable spirit. Whatever life threw at him, he handled and went on with his work. That's how Harley wanted to be, a doer, a survivor, and a believer in the mission of art and artists.

"Shelley believed that artists were the higher power," Harley offered.

"The unacknowledged legislators of the world," said Norman, his finger a rigid wand. "The artist mirrors the future. He's often not conscious of what he's doing, he's a medium. I'm a medium, a clairvoyant who expresses the beauty of the earth by what I create. My words on paper outlast pyramids. Even if you bury my words they will rise again and conquer. You see what I'm saying? My words are immortal. Oh, my friends listen to me; listen to Norman Ten Boom saying yes to the universe, yes to life, yes to his desires, yes to the adrenalin rush of being in love. Yes to withering and rebirth."

"Yes to the risen Jesus," said Franny beatifically. "We die to be born in the bosom of God."

There was an awkward pause.

•

Then:

Norman continued, "The desire to live or die moves in cycles. If, over time, the cycle to go on living doesn't return and possess you, then you are done for. You'll die and that will be that. Snuffed out completely. Your soul floating nowhere. Which is why you must never commit suicide. It's an irrevocable denial of life. It sweeps you out of the cycle forever. Didi and I, in our many lives, have always said yes to life. Yes, yes, even as we were dying. Isn't that right, Didi? We say yes we will, yes!"

Didi agreed.

When she glanced at Harley he fancied the cast in her eye was signaling an apology. Were his own eyes rolling? Be serious, he counseled himself. Nothing is pure humbug. Truth as evanescent as snowflakes. Truth variable. Truth dependent on the true cause, *vera causa.* Today's fiction: tomorrow's truth. And who was it that said there is no science so hard as to know how to live this life well? Maybe Norman knows best. Say yes to withering and rebirth. He almost laughed, but turned it into a cough.

"We read each other's thoughts all the time," continued Norman. "We finish each other's sentences. We are so in tune that if I have a panic attack from missing her so badly, she will always call me and say, 'What's wrong?' And one way or another she'll get out of the house and come over. Isn't that right, Didi?"

"Sometimes it's hard. My kids and my husband don't approve, of course. My kids call me bad ..." She grimaced. Looked away. "Well, never mind about that."

"They're both adults," said Norman. "But right now they're behaving like selfish brats. They want their mother to stay with their father, but the man is a brute. Isn't he, Didi? He has no respect for you as a persona, my darling."

"He has no respect for me as a persona," she echoed.

"He cheats on her. He's a doctor and he cheats on her with his patients. He uses her like his personal slave. She's everyone's personal slave. Those two kids will be in college in the fall and still clinging to her apron strings. Isn't that right, Didi? They want to own her. They don't want her to have an identity of her own. Isn't that right, Didi?"

"To them I'm only a wife and mother," she said, voice hollow, the thin line of her smile, the inward curve of her brow expressing *martyrdom*.

"I want to give her freedom," cried Norman. "I want her to live with me and let me make her into a great poet. I'm her truest lover, friend, and mentor. Isn't that right, Didi?"

"He's helping me realize my potential," she said.

•

After a clumsy moment Norman added, "You know, I wake in the night and feel like I'm having a stroke. And I have to call her. But one night she didn't answer the phone." He looked at her with accusation in his eyes.

"I turned my phone off by accident. It's an old habit," she explained.

"Tell them about your heart monitor."

"I had to wear a heart monitor," she said. "I was having pains in my left arm. My blood pressure is dangerously high. So is my cholesterol."

"See what I'm saying?" said Norman. "It's stress. She needs to get out of there before they kill her. They're killing you, my darling. That husband. You should hear some of the things he says to her. I won't repeat it, but if he ever said those things in my presence I'd break him in half." His eyes narrowed dangerously, "I can be dangerous," he said.

Harley believed him. Corpulent, bearish Norman could probably do it, snap that husband like a piece of kindling. But another part of Harley was saying beware of a bragger, beware of braggadocio. As Norman stared at Didi, his eyes glistening with hunger hope uncertainty, something else was revealed—anger? fear? a mixture? And what for? Because she wouldn't leave her family and move in with him? He was terribly lonely he had told Harley. He hated the silence in his apartment. Lying in bed, the silence. Waking at three. Staring at the ceiling .

"All I want is what is best for her," he told them, stroking her hand, gripping it, kissing it. "It's not for myself that I do what I do. I do it all for her. I wrote *Ecstasy* for her. I didn't know it at the time, not until she became my real estate agent. The instant

I saw her, I fell in love and the poetry poured out of me. Didn't it, Didi? Don't tell me about Romeo and Juliet or Ferdinand and Miranda. Did we not exchange eyes that first day, Didi? We looked at each other and I knew I had found her once more in the halls of time. But I didn't say anything. Not right away. I'll tell you this from my heart: a voice inside me kept saying, 'Your eternal lover has returned.' But I didn't act on it because I was married. Right, Didi?"

"He changed the title and completely rewrote the book. All these love poems were pouring out, and as I'm reading them I'm thinking how lucky his wife is."

"It wasn't until weeks later I pulled out the book and showed her Millias' *Ophelia*," said Norman, "and beautiful bare breasted Iphigenia." He laughed hugely, his chins quivering. "The hairs on Didi's arms rioted as if those paintings were electric. Or maybe it was my standing over her. I saw my breath playing with her hair. I'll never forget it. She looked at me like I had popped out of a bottle. Poof, I was her genie." Norman threw his head back and roared. Then he pointed his finger and said, "Ah, but I knew. I knew."

"What about you, Didi?" asked Franny. "Did you feel like he had popped out of a bottle?"

Didi massaged her lips with her index finger. Her eyes searching Franny's eyes. "I can't say exactly how I felt. Except I was confused. I remember thinking: did he really say that? Had he told me he painted the Ophelia when he was John Millias? We were sitting there flipping through the book, and Norman is pointing out painting after painting he had done. I think one was a Titian?"

"*Venus of Urbino*," bellowed Norman. "I defy anyone to look at it and my Ophelia & Iphigenia and tell me they are not the same woman.

"You were Titian?" said Franny.

Norman's eyes protruded. "Of course you don't believe me. But there is more in heaven and earth than found in your Christos, Franny."

"No, no, I don't mean to doubt you," Franny protested.

"Eternal lovers know nothing of time. Didi and I have had countless lives together, and that's all that counts. Right, Didi?"

Didi flexed her fist. "My hand keeps going asleep." She shook the hand. Norman grabbed it, rubbed it between his palms.

"So cold," he said, "for someone so beautiful and young. Hold it in front of the fire. It's those BP pills she takes. They make her hands and feet cold all the time. She's only forty. This shouldn't be happening to her. It's the stress of her home environment this past three years, no doubt about that. She's been married twenty years to that monster. This is what it's done to her. Broken her heart. It's criminal. A philandering husband who accuses her of having a fling with the neighbor next door. He even said he wasn't sure their son is his. That's how twisted the bastard is. She's so cold, Harley. Fuel the fire, will you?"

The room was already overheated, but Harley put another log on and stirred the flames with the poker.

•

"It's really hard," said Didi. "My children have turned against me. They don't understand I fell out of love with their father when I was thirty-two and caught him having an affair. I stay in the marriage because I don't want them to be products of a broken home. I don't care what feminists say, children need both parents. Fathers are as important in their own way as mothers. I stay for my babies. I want so much to create a—"

"All he does is take advantage of her," blurted Norman.

"—secure home."

"He never helps around the house. She cooks and cleans and buys the groceries. She does everything. All he does is sit on his fat ass giving orders."

"Actually, his ass is slender. He's slender all over."

"He's a parasite and the kids are the same way. A pair of parasites still sucking Mommy's titties."

"Norman."

"Well, it's true, isn't it? Metaphorically speaking."

"They're not even twenty yet, they don't know anything."

Norman's eyes shifted as if looking for enemies. His round face was flushed, his jaws grinding. His heavy lips petulant and wet. His white hair falling forward like a bushy curtain.

•

Then:

In sympathetic tones, he told Didi she was absolutely right. "And I will do everything in my power to help those two make their way in life. I can snap my fingers and get them into any number of first-rate universities. I know famous political and literary figures all over the world, and they will know you and your children because you'll be connected to me. A letter or phone call will open any number of doors, my darling. I'll take care of them just as lovingly as I'll take care of you. But the thing you've got to do is make your decision to live, not just exist. Pack your bags and come to me. Everything else will fall in place. I know these things. You've got to believe me. Do you believe me, Didi?"

"This is one of the hardest decisions I've ever had to make in a life full of hard decisions. Sometimes stupid decisions."

"It will kill you to stay there. It will kill both of us. I'll die."

"Oh, Norman."

"No, I mean it! I don't want to live without you. I can't." Norman grabbed his left arm, rubbed it. "You see?" he said. "Sympathetic pains. You see?" He dug in his shirt pocket. Pulled out a bottle of pills. "Some water," he ordered.

Franny rose painfully. Waddled to the kitchen.

"Bring me an aspirin, too," he said.

"What are you taking?" said Harley.

Norman was taking a blood pressure pill and Prozac. Franny brought him the aspirin. Didi was hovering, her lips pinched with worry.

"I had a mild stroke," he said, almost blissfully. "When my marriage was breaking up I was going cuckoo. I was dizzy all the time. I couldn't walk straight. I was walking into walls. I didn't know what was wrong with me. I'm telling my wife that maybe I'm having a stroke and she's telling me to get out of her house. The look on her face said she wanted me dead. You never know, you understand what I'm saying? You never know who you can count on. I mean I hadn't done anything wrong. Sure, I might have been attracted to Didi, but we hadn't done anything, had we, Didi?"

"I was showing him houses," she said. "We were together a lot."

"Well, we had to be. But the wife got jealous and started accusing me of having an affair. She said she wanted me out of her life. She said I had driven her crazy for years. And here I am having a stroke and she won't lift a finger. I had to get the guy next door to drive me to the hospital. Have you ever heard of such a thing? A hard woman. A cold-hearted woman. Cold as ice cubes let me tell you."

"She's throwing you out and you're having a stroke?" said Harley.

"Lucky for me it was very mild. They fixed me right up. I've been exercising like mad ever since. Don't you think I've lost weight?"

"I can see that."

"Except for these poetic chins," he said, laughing. "I'll need surgery to get rid of them."

"He has such a sense of humor," said Didi. "My husband is just the opposite. No humor at all. He was raised on a farm. Farms are dour."

"I love this unspeakably marvelous life!" Norman quoted. "God, I love living. I want to live forever. Every day I wake up wondering what wonderful thing is going to happen to me. Yes, yes, and one wonderful day it was *wunderbar*!" He pointed at Didi.

"I had no idea what would happen when he came to me, wanting me to show him houses," she said. "I looked him up on the internet and boom, there he was in all his glory, an acclaimed poet, a professor of literature. I don't mind telling you, I was hugely impressed. I returned his call and started showing him around."

"It was love at first sight," said Norman. "Isn't it so, my darling?"

"I guess so. I don't know. All I knew was how sick to death I was of Danny Walker. I was going crazy. I wanted out."

"Walker?" said Harley. "Not Godunov?"

"I kept my maiden name. I'm Deidre Annaba Godunov. Which probably says something Freudian about my marrying a Walker." She sighed. Shook her head. "I've had enough to drink, so I'm brave enough to tell you. He was my doctor. One day after a physical, he asked me to have lunch with him. He's a good looking guy, so even though I knew I shouldn't, I did. Long story short, I got pregnant, knocked up. He talked me out of an abortion. I married him, had the kid. Got pregnant again. I already knew I'd made a mistake, but it took me twenty years to get to this point. I had to stay for the kids. Well, that's what I told myself, but who knows the truth? Maybe they would be better adjusted if I had left when they were little. For one thing, I didn't know how I could afford it. Danny had the money, the wherewithal and could have given them a better life. I felt stuck, but as soon as they were in school, I went to community college and studied real estate. By the time they were teens, I had a job selling houses, condos and stuff. Then what happens? Norman comes along and overwhelms me. And look how he's changed my life. Everything used to be so ... so predictable. Now it's like I'm riding a whirlwind."

"Their life a storm whereon they ride," said Norman. "But what I was saying is ... when are you moving out, Didi? We're getting old. We don't have time to waste."

•

Didi pulled back. Her finger stroking her mouth as if zipping it. "It's so hard," she murmured. "So hard it seems impossible. I wish you wouldn't pressure me, Norman."

"But what can you expect, my darling? I'm a poet. Every fiber of my being throbs with love of you. I'm like an over-wound violin, an E string ready to break. I feel it right this moment getting tighter and tighter. Can't you hear my soul shrieking?"

"No."

"I can. It's driving me crazy. Listen, my darling, all I want is to protect you and nurture your talent. If it were possible I would take you to some island and keep you there writing poetry, while I waited on you hand and foot."

"Norman, now—"

"No, I mean it. I wouldn't hesitate a moment, not a second." He turned to Harley, his eyes imploring. "Do you see now how I love her? Do you see?"

"No ordinary love," Harley admitted.

"Shattering," Norman answered.

Didi closed her eyes. The fingers of her left hand kept flexing.

"Don't worry, I'll get you out of that house," said Norman. "If it's the last thing I do."

"What can I say to this wild man?"

"Between us there is no need for you to speak," he said. "It's always been obvious that you understand everything I say. I see things. And I know far more than what I see. All that matters is that we love each other. The rest can go to hell."

"I can't wish that for my kids. Don't ever ask me."

"Didi, listen to me. This will never come again in this life. There is only now and the two of us. He who hesitates is lost."

"Oh, can't we talk of something else? We're monopolizing." She looked at Harley, her eyes apologetic. "Poor you and Franny having to listen to this."

"No problem. What are friends for?"

"We make good sounding boards," said Franny.

Norman's finger was in front of Didi's face, admonishing. "Life breeds excuses," he told her. "Rationalizations. And we miss our chances and they never come again. A hundred years from now no one will remember anything about us except the art we've left behind. With me you'll become an artist. Without me, your family will pull you back into servitude. You'll be dying an inch at a time and as you're dying you will know that you've never really lived." He paused. Words hanging. Fire crackling.

•

Didi stared at Harley and said, "I suppose he's right." She glanced at the books lining the shelf behind the couch. "I've read your books," she told him, "all of them. They're amazing. *So Much Heroism.* I think that's my favorite. The one about your father. The war and all that."

Norman said, "He had to be selfish to write them. He didn't let anyone get in his way. Isn't that right, Harley?"

"I guess so."

"A writer who doesn't live for his art is no artist."

"Is that how you feel, Harley?" said Didi.

Harley looked at his novels and wondered if they were products of selfishness. He decided they were.

"He's selfish," said Franny. Quickly adding, "But he has to be. Art comes first. Then his teaching. I'm somewhere down the line, God knows." She chuckled, her chubby cheeks wiggling, her mildly warped fingers covering her mouth, her eyes sad slits nesting within circles of what was obviously aching flesh.

•

"That's all I have to say," said Norman. "Let's talk about something else. The reading went well, don't you think? I had them in the palm of my hand." He gazed at his palm.

Didi was leaning forward, rubbing her belly round and round. Her other hand covering her mouth as she brought forth a burp. "Oh, excuse me!"

"As good an opinion as any," said Harley.

"Take a Tums," said Norman. "You got any Tums, Franny?"

"Do I have Tums!" Franny reached in her pocket and pulled out a roll. "Keep it, honey, I've got plenty." Smiling wistfully, Franny looked at Harley.

He knew what she was thinking. She was wishing he would say to her what Norman said to Didi. All that matters is that we love each other. The rest can go to hell. Harley loved dear Franny. But not the way Norman apparently loved Didi. Norman's way of expressing his feelings was far beyond Harley's unreliable heart.

At times he wished he were different, wished he could let himself go the way Norman and Didi were letting themselves go, letting themselves have this passionate affair that didn't take their ages or marital status into account. But it wasn't possible for Harley. He was who he was. They were who they were: Norman and his poetry—his ego its own universe; Didi and her abusive husband, her ambitions bleeding outside the boundaries of a house that had become a prison; Franny and the numerous ailments that her cruel god refused to cure; and himself trying to find a *raison d'être* in the life of the mind, in the life of art.

•

Make the most of it. Everyone plagued by isolation, everyone groping blindly, never making anything other than dreamy connections. Stay warm. Bless your reveries. Be humorous. Be cynical. Be decent. Be kind while you can. Keep babbling. Babbling gets us through. Harley, inclining towards Norman, waited for him to pick up where he had left off. His volubility faltering, making him instantly old now, chins hanging, lips hanging, cheeks hanging, hair hanging. Vulnerable in the moment.

Harley nudged him, coaxing him gently while saying, "You had them in the palm of your hand."

4 – Eternal Lovers

The car door chunks shut. She listens for the engine. Is Harley buckling his seatbelt? Adjusting the mirror, the radio? Thinking deep thoughts? Is he looking at the house? Maybe wondering if he should go back inside? Stay where he belongs? Is Harley hesitating?

The engine starts.

She hears it idling.

"Harley, don't go," she whispers. "Don't leave your Franny."

Why does he have to move out now?

Twenty-three years for what?

What's it all about, Harley? You're depressed. You need time alone, time to find yourself? Sounds phony to Franny. She knows whom to blame, though. She knows it's God again. God getting her. God making her pay for the sins of her youth.

And if your right hand causes you to sin, cut it off and throw it away.

"I'm willing but the flesh is weak."

She squeezes a roll of fat (the fat flesh of her fat belly), grimaces and says, "Who could love such a slob, anyway? Not Harley for sure, he's always had an eye for thin. But geez, it's not my fault I'm sick. I didn't ask to get old and fat and sick."

Heavy, mushy, repulsive, that's how she sees her body. She blames it on rheumatoid arthritis, aplastic anemia, fibromyalgia, chronic sciatica, plus tendonitis in her knees and feet, which make exercise painful. That and all the medications making her retain water, while slowing her metabolism. She drinks mostly green tea with her meals, drinks it so the antioxidants can savage those ravaging free radicals shattering her cells. Sometimes she drinks red wine for her heart. She drinks a martini or two (occasionally three) to help her sleep better at night. She doesn't like meat, but she eats it (mostly chicken and fish) for the protein. She eats scrambled eggs and hash browns on days when she can't stand another carnivore morsel.

"I'm such a mess, it's a wonder I can even get out of bed. I try to be good. I try to eat right and control my booze. Booze is beneficial, though. Booze makes me gutsy. It makes me not care so damn much about Harley or myself or … or anything. But you know with liquor you gotta be careful. You gotta control your intake, Franny, that's the thing."

Careful as she is, her stomach still gives her trouble. Food gets in there and creates a mushball, an impaction, which will send her to the cupboard for milk of magnesia, which will give her days of diarrhea. The acid churning. Digestive tract a raucous cavern of spasms. She has had numerous colonoscopies. They never find anything wrong.

Maybe it's some untraceable poison. Something hidden. Something sinister. Maybe Harley has been poisoning her? There are times his eyes say he'd like to. Times he's looked at her with contempt, even disgust, his whole face saying I wish you were dead.

Did he have it in him? Would he ever murder his Franny?

She read a story about a man who poisoned his wife over the course of a year. Sprinkling her salads with cadmium. The doctors didn't know what was destroying her organs. They tested her for every disease imaginable, even for heavy metals like lead, arsenic and mercury. But not cadmium. She nearly died several times, but somehow rallied and against all odds continued living. The cadmium was ruining her kidneys, her colon, everything. But still she wouldn't die. Until finally her husband got sick of waiting and injected her with raw nicotine, which smothered her lungs. It was her insurance money he wanted, a million dollar policy.

"I only have a little insurance," Franny says aloud. "Like ten thousand is all. Would Harley kill me for ten thousand? Of course not. Don't be silly. Harley cares. He's a sensitive man. Heart of gold mostly. Given my impulsive nature, I'm more likely to murder him than him me. In his heart of hearts he loves me. I'll get well and slim down and he'll come back, you'll see."

Bad nerves that's the thing. That's what causes all her digestive woes. Nerves and stress strangling her body, not letting it work the way it should, the way healthy bodies work. She envies healthy people. They don't know how good they have it. Twenty years ago she ate anything she wanted. Took it all for granted and didn't understand her mother's outraged complaining. All those antacids the old lady takes by the handful. Zantac and God knows what. She bitches about everything ever since Franny's father died of prostate cancer. His wife went sour watching the process, a sourness that rarely leaves her these days. Fiercely, she keeps saying she's dying: "I'm dying, Franny, I'm dying." Been saying it for four or five years. Every phone call, every visit: "I'm dying, Franny, damn it, I'm dying." And Franny has become more and more like her. Feeling diseased inside. Breast cancer lurking. It's true, you never get rid of it, not really. It hides within, biding its time, until it is ready to eat you alive.

"Baby, you used to be a trim chickee-poo," Franny says, smiling at the memory. "When you first met Harley you weighed a hundred and four pounds. Could have been a model, everyone said so. Harley said you looked like that movie star, the one who got drunk and drowned herself. Natalie Wood—*Splendor in the Grass*. You were so cute, so adorable, Franny."

A new image ignites her: She and Harley on his motorcycle. Through the Laguna Mountains roaring, leaning on the curves. Scary. Exhilarating. She felt her breasts pressing against him and she knew he felt it too, her hands clinging to his abdomen, her fingers dipping down giving him a hard-on. His leather jacket rubbing her mouth, making her wet, making her oral. The machine vibrating between her legs filling her with anticipation. The fear, the thrill, the thrust. Harley was Franny's man back then.

Those were groovy times just after college. Times when she believed their love had been predetermined eons before they were ever born. Eternal lovers. Part of God's ongoing plan. The cosmic formula. She had believed in Harley totally. She knew that no one better mess with her when he was around. She had seen him in action. The anger, the quick reflexes, the power in his fist when that guy at the Christmas party caught her under the mistletoe and kissed her hard. And she, high on vodka and pot, gave tongue for tongue. And Jesus, Harley almost tore the fellow's face off. Broke his jaw with one punch. And hated himself after. And blamed Franny. Your fault, Franny. Your fault for flirting. But lordy-lordy Harley had looked so ... so heroic. A warrior, a Viking. It had been worth the world to see him fighting for her.

So far away now it seems like another life when she was someone else and it happened to her, not Franny. The years flew and a morning came when she knew that her ten trillion cells had morphed and she no longer had the strength to rise up singing. When she looked in the mirror, nothing about her was what it was.

Except her eyes.

Eyes her father once compared to the dewy eyes of a doe—"A sweet one." Her hair had gone from lush chestnut to stale brown. She no longer permed it. She let it hang straight down covering the furrows on her forehead, the strands ringing her neck half-hiding sags and wrinkles. Why is the neck the first to go? A necklift is what she needs. A facelift. An Everything lift.

Bah, who cares what she looks like?

No one.

Nobody.

Franny hates her bloated carcass. She wants to be a curvy redhead bouncing like a model down a runway. Instead of what she is, a repellent, pear-shaped drudge with flat feet and swollen ankles. Varicose veins mapping her waterlogged calves. It happens to every woman, eventually. The body goes. The skin no longer elastic. Health is never forever. Hers went a little earlier than usual is all. No one is immune. Look at Harley. He turned fifty four and has indigestion problems and irritable bowel. His hair thinning. Dry lines around his eyes. He looks so old sometimes it's shocking.

But for years Franny has felt older than Harley looks. Feeling those pains that never leave her body. Just like her mother in the retirement home. Her mother, the angry harridan who complains about her health and everything else, but refuses to let any of it inhibit her. Her tank is full; it runs on rage. "I'm dying, Franny, I'm dying."

"Oh dear oh dear," whines Franny, "why can't I storm the way Mama does? Be mean. Kick ass. Tell Harley to go to hell."

Life isn't fair. Life picking on every body, not just Franny's body. It comes with maturity; with parental genes fusing weirdly. All the generations preyed upon by that spiral thing invented by God. An outcome of your mother and father making love.

The acts of love that doomed Franny and her sisters. All three of them harboring their parents' problems. Diabetes for Judy. Diabetes and emphysema for Ruthie who smoked for thirty years. Numerous other illnesses as well. These crazy kids today, they have no idea what's coming to get them. Damn fools, they live as if there's no tomorrow.

But tomorrow comes. Tomorrow gets you for having the wrong physique and the wrong urges. Booze booze, sex sex. Impulse-driven Franny has done it all. She didn't know it when she was young—something evil was coming. No clue what nasty things were looming. Attitudes changing, getting worse year by year. Imbeciles piercing their stupid faces. Even their tongues! Covering themselves in tattoos as if they loathe the sight of their own skin. Filling their heads with that pounding noise they call music. Ugh. A noise proven to cause deafness and shriveled brains. What do they live for, anyway? Living for the next deviant concert. The fad drug of choice. Is it Ecstasy? What does Ecstasy do for you? Is it for better sex? Or maybe a substitute for sex?

"Don't ever do that to me again," Harley had told her after her mistletoe mishap. "Don't push that jealousy button. I can't control it and I don't want to act that way. I'm grownup, Franny. I'm a college graduate, for Christ's sake. I might be only an adjunct professor, but dammit I've earned my M. A. and I'm trying to make something more of myself without the help of my goddamn family, especially my mother."

How many years ago, Franny? Too many.

She listens to the engine rumbling. The transmission slipping into gear as she whispers, "Don't go, Harley." Holding her breath a moment, she hears the tires rolling over asphalt. The noise fading. Her husband of twenty three years leaving.

She grumbles, "Self-centered bastard. Shithead"

Franny, will you look at what you're doing? You're teary-eyed again. Over what? Quit being such a baby. Learn to cope. Quit blubbering. Oh, Franny, you make me sick!

She reaches for a tissue. Dabs her eyes, blows her nose. Looks at the clock. Five-thirty. She can snooze a half hour if she wants to.

Snuggling deep in the pillow, Franny tries to concentrate on sleeping. But sleep eludes her. She keeps sliding back to her sinful years. The shameless slut she used to be. Sluttish ways that had continued even after she married Harley. She pictures herself at twenty-six—how she and Judy's husband had been desperate for each other. Sexy Cecil. Bald as a cue ball now and has a bad heart. Had a triple bypass when he was only forty. But once upon a time he had been a hunk, a knockout. Blue eyed. Sexy. Very attentive to Franny. Always making her laugh. Always touchy-feely when no one was looking. He gave her the hots and she nearly did it with him that day in the car. Did everything but.

She sees them tonguing each other. How did she ever stop herself from letting him in? What stopped you, Franny? You stopped you. You said no to Cecil. No, we can't. Not all the way, Cecil. Because I'm married to Harley, and God will punish me. You put your hand over your heart, remember? Feeling like God lived there and was ready to bust out like that alien in *Alien* wreaking havoc. Cecil said you were killing him. Here, Cecil, here. I'll fix it. And you did, Franny. How many times did you do that to him?

Stop. None of it matters now.

She vacillates. She whispers, "A long time ago. Years and years and I was awfully young. Young and dumb and always hot for someone. So what? That's normal. I was just being a normal girl ready for childbearing. Lordy, lordy how I loved it. Simply the best feeling in the world. He could never give me enough, my once-a-week Harley. He called me horn dog Franny. Told me I was a nympho."

She giggles and her heart skips a beat as if God just flicked it with his finger. Warning her. *Watch yourself, Franny. Watch it.*

"Yeah, but Cecil backed off when I mentioned God and how if either of us died during intercourse, it would be straight to Hell. Then that other time we were making out, he told me to divorce Harley. Divorce him and I'll divorce Judy. We'll get married. I want you, Franny. So delicious. Oh, how I want you! Slow down, Cecil, let me make it all better."

That was the first time she actually considered leaving her husband. What kept her from doing it? Love for her sister and love for Harley. In the moment of decision, she realized she and Cecil could never work. Not in the long run. Yes, Cecil was sexy and Franny liked him a lot, but Harley was her one and only true love. Eternal lovers, remember? And besides that—Judy would never have forgiven her. Franny would have lost her big sister. No man is worth that. Christ, the mess it would have caused. The heartache.

Harley had been suspicious during that time, but he didn't confront her. He had closed off that side of himself by then. It was an act of will. No more jealousy. No more threats. The fight at the party had changed him. As far as Franny knew, it was the last fight he ever had. How serious he became afterwards. I'm a college grad, he kept saying. Saying it like a mantra, like he couldn't believe it and had to convince himself by repeating the words over and over.

He worked at SDSU for fifteen years as a part-timer. Then he got an award for his first novel. Got an agent. She sold two more of his books, all reviewed in *The New York Times* and other major newspapers. Now he's a full-time professor and writer at Cal-State, San Marcos. He ignores Franny. Concentrates on sending his work out and getting published, getting grants and awards. She knows he's still searching for validation, the self-esteem his father had shattered when Harley was little and unloved.

Damn books, anyway—Franny is a copyeditor who hates books. Well, not all books, but a lot of them. When she asked him why he was pushing himself so hard, he said it was because he wanted to prove he was special.

"I want to prove it to those who gave me up for lost. I want to prove it to myself and everyone who wrote me off all these years. In her cups my mother told me I was a loser, and I believed her. But I don't believe her anymore. What did that bitch know? Teenagers have holes in their heads. Teenagers can't think straight, especially if their home life is fucked up. Christ, I was in my mid-twenties before I had a clue, Franny. When I met you I was over thirty and just starting to think straight, starting to see life's long haul and that only the dumb and the unlucky die young and lost. When I finally found the way forward, I promised myself that nothing was going to stop me. Just stand back, Franny. Stand back and watch me."

And then Harley took up yoga, of all things! Learning it, of course, from a stupid book. Learning how to meditate. Be spiritual. He became an "atheist Buddhist," a term he uses that continues to baffle Franny. He walled himself off, and ultimately didn't care what she did. Not her or anyone. He became so cold it wasn't him, not the exciting man she had married. Is it any wonder she cheated?

"Face it, Franny," she says, "you wanted him jealous. Jealousy showed he cared. You wanted him to fight for you again. Years later when you had that affair with Chata Johnson, he of the thick whip, Harley's reaction broke your heart. He shrugged you off and offered a divorce.

After that, everything fell apart and Harley withdrew to the point of being so emotionally detached it was as if he had no heart at all. Totally dead-faced. And so unconcerned it crushed you. He was above adultery, the tawdry way that tawdry people behaved. What a prig. You knew then he didn't love you, at least not in any romantic sense of the word. Loved you more like a sister than a wife. How long has it been since you've been laid? Fourteen years? Fifteen?" Franny looks at the drawer where she keeps her vibrator.

Not now.

But the thought makes her picture Chata Johnson's penis in her hands. She never saw another one like it except in the porns they watched together. Nothing like that full feeling he gave her. The orgasms, oh my!

So maybe Chata should have been her eternal lover, not Harley?

If he had left his wife, Franny might have left her husband. Loved him but left him. Because what could you do with a don't-touch-me man like that? She had dreamed about making a new start with Chata. Buying a house and having children. Normal stuff. How bizarre it all seems that Franny could be divorced from Harley and living with another man. Would it be twenty years since then? Twenty years quick as a wink. Twenty years and so much has happened to her body. The honeymoon period wouldn't have lasted very long and Chata would be feeling gypped, married to a woman who was always ill. But then again, maybe Franny wouldn't be ill if she were married to a loving, caring man who touched her. Who desired her desperately the way Chata had. Well, no matter what, it wouldn't have worked. Her family would have disowned her. Called her a whore. Miscegenation was a mortal sin back then.

Pale light glimmering, outlining the lamp, the chest of drawers, the wall of books from floor to ceiling, vertical-tight—like soldiers guarding what is Harlan J. Olsen's tight-ass world. Books. Novels mostly. Brain-warping words, that's what happened to him. It's a known fact that too many novels can cripple your mind, confuse you, make you unable to focus on the important things in life.

Like wives.

True love.

Romance.

Each other.

Fractures in the mirror of life, that's what novels are.

Fractures.

Her husband fractured. Fractured their relationship.

Inconsiderate, inexplicable—synonyms for him.

Because he hated Catholicism, she dropped her Catholic faith to marry him, but missed God so much she became Born Again. Another religion he refused. And then what does he do instead? Becomes a damned to hell atheist Buddhist.

"Freeeak me out."

She wants the old Harley back, the motorcycle rider making his tough way in a tough world. She had trusted him to take care of her and he did, but college with its bias eventually changed him. Made him … cerebral.

She has boxes full of junk in the garage. She could empty those boxes and fill them with his books and sell them at the used bookstore on 8th street. She could empty the shelves and lie about it, tell him, "I don't know what happened, Harley. A burglar stole them, maybe?" Or maybe she would fess up and say, "They changed your personality, ruined you, so I sold them, Harley. What you gonna do about it?"

Franny doesn't want to get out of bed. But if she doesn't, the aching will get worse. The flu feeling in her joints will be there all day if she doesn't get moving. She needs to put something in her stomach and take a pain pill. And something to soak up the acid that gives her heartburn. She prays it won't be one of those Vicodin days. Sometimes those things make her feel like a zombie. "Like whose head is this on my shoulders?"

Franny wonders why Harley always mumbles and thrashes and groans in his sleep and gets up and down and never stays in bed past five. Maybe because he has a guilty conscience about neglecting his wife? When the two of them used to sleep together, did she ever get a full night's rest? She had been glad to have him in his own room. Except some nights she gets lonely and wishes he were beside her holding her hand. His warm presence. The sense of security whenever he's near.

Not near now. Maybe never again. Maybe he'll have an accident and die. Or find another woman.

"I'd kill him. Swear to God I would."

Franny, he hasn't been gone fifteen minutes and you already miss him. Your heart breaks for the umpteenth time.

You're hungry now. Hungry for what? Not that. Forget it. Yeah, but it would be nice. Something to make her feel good for a while. Is that asking too much?

"Jesus, I'm lonely."

Franny gives loneliness a smack upside the head. "Nuts to that," she says. "There's my sisters. And there's Mama in the retirement home to visit. There's my job. There's TV. There's emails. Yeah, and the phone I can hang on and get all the gossip. Movies on weekends. Church on Sunday. QVC on TV. I'm going to order whatever I damn well want. What are credit cards for, anyway? And I'm going to dye my hair flaming red. Get a facial. And slutty new clothes. And go on the veggie/ fruit smoothie diet. I'll start exercising. Do water aerobics like Judy. Cecil is jealous of her looks. He watches her like a hawk these days. Would she ever do anything? Has Ruthie? Or Mama? Is it in the genes? Was my behavior an aberration? It wasn't the real me. Or was it? Blame it on neglect. I'm the black sheep, just like Harley is the black sheep. Just like his mother was the black sheep, even as she aged. What was she, seventy when she got that facelift and boob job? Dead and gone now. She needed to stop bar hopping and boozing and sleeping around. She needed to find God. That's what would have helped her best. That and if she had stopped smoking. God knows if her soul went up or down."

●

Franny had smoked for ten years. It was the thing to do back when she was young and with it. When she met Harley he had smoked Marlborough's. But when Franny got sick, she quit smoking and so did he. Cigarettes had gotten her just like the Surgeon General had said they would. But God Most Merciful came through. He gave Franny the strength to bear what was happening. He taught her the power of faith. With God and the Bible (and the fact that the tumor in her breast was encapsulated) she found ways of coping.

Franny turns on the lamp. Opens the drawer. Takes out the Bible she slept with when she was fighting cancer. At random she stabs a page with her finger.

And on the eighth day the flesh of his foreskin shall be circumcised.

"Maybe if we had had children," she murmurs. "A son."

Closing her eyes, she flips through the pages. Stabs again:

Enjoy life with the wife whom you love, all the days of your vain life, which he has given you under the sun, because that is your portion and your toil at which you toil under the sun.

"Bingo. I'll send this to Harley. I'll email it to his office."

Then she thinks not. He would say she was nagging him.

"Harley, what more do you want? Why don't you stop running all over creation and come home to me? Let's grow old together. Take care of each other like we should."

That's your egocentric Harley, Franny. That's how he works.

"Oh, Harley honey, my dear, I pray God you don't end up a lonely old man without a woman who loves you. But it will serve you right if you do." Franny snorts with instant anger, murder filling her heart. She would like to throttle her husband. Hit him over the head with the fry pan.

She looks at the clock and says, "Time to get your lazy butt out of bed. Take your shower, wash your hair and set it. Boil green tea. Get some celery and stuff it with Cheez Whiz. Read PEOPLE under the hair dryer. Get dressed. Drive to work in that stupid traffic. Spend the day with your mind focused on manuscripts that will bore you to death."

And count your blessings, Franny. Things could always be worse.

•

She kisses the Bible. Puts it back in the drawer. Forces her legs over the side of the bed, sits up. Coughs. Farts. Winces at the sciatic pain running down her leg and into her foot. Her stomach is full of gas. Her lower tract loose. Tomorrow she'll probably be constipated. That's how it works: loose one day, hard and dry the next. Maybe she has colon cancer. It sneaks up on you. Her fingers are so swollen this morning she can barely bend them. When has she ever been this tired? Poor, anemic Franny. She needs another blood transfusion. After the last one she actually had some energy. But now she's back where she started. Back to running on willpower. Eat more leafy vegetables, the doctor has told her, eat more spinach. She is maxed out on folic acid. Five pills a day and he is saying eat more spinach. Who does he think she is—Popeye?

"Get up and go to work," she commands herself. "Edit those stupid texts and chat with your co-workers, all of them afflicted, their lives a mess same as mine, yeah. When I talk to them about God, it comforts them. At work I'm doing God's work. I may be miserable now, but all misery will turn to bliss when I become the dear departed." And she thinks: *Now there's a comforting thought.*

Rising from bed, hobbling to the bathroom, she counsels herself: "These torments are part of the cosmic plan. Endure them with patience, Franny. Cling firmly to the Lord and permit nothing to keep you from your duties or your worship. For Jesus' sake suffer, Franny. If you suffer enough, God will keep you safe. God will reward you. God loves you. Especially if you suffer bravely.

Do it bravely, that's the thing.

5 - Danny & Didi

Because of her mother's continuous nagging, Didi went to see him. They talked about the kids, both in college and doing well. They talked about the past, Danny using her as his Confessor. She didn't want to hear what she heard. How when they were married, he didn't trust her and he didn't trust Jerry Fields. Thought they were lovers. He said Didi had been right about him when she said he didn't trust her because he didn't trust himself. He married her and was almost immediately unfaithful. Over the course of their years together he had deceived Didi so many times he had lost count. For two or three years prior to her leaving, most of his infidelities were with April Fields. Now and then it would be with some sex-starved patient. Some easy lay. Round heels, he called them. Very daring to make love to a woman in an exam room. It had been his experience that doing it there heightened the erotic effect. He said he did it twice with April that way. Had to muffle her moans with his hand over her mouth. Patients being escorted past the door. What's Doc doing to that poor girl?

•

In those times, April was a high-hipped restless woman of thirty. Always complaining about the brevity of a woman's looks. How a woman was called a matron a frump a crone in old age. But good-looking older men were said to be distinguished.

Didi also hated the idea of growing old and did her best with creams, facials, diets to look young. But she didn't complain. Did not chase youth the way April chased it. Saying to her, "Well, since we have to grow old, we might as well do it gracefully. There's something repulsive about women who overcompensate. Going under the knife and all."

April agreed. But her heart seethed whenever she detected a new wrinkle or gray hair. Found one in her pubis and freaked.

"Get over it," Didi had told her. One hair does not a crone make. April had a theory that semen contained hormones that would keep her youthful. Sex to her was like taking an injection. She said she always pushed Jerry to make love to her at least twice a week. And of course now Didi knew April had sex with Danny whenever she could. Usually when he took his two-hour lunches and they met at a hotel near his practice.

April and Jerry had two kids before they finally divorced. Maybe the kids were Danny's. Who knows? April went to cosmetology school after she left. As far as Didi knows, she is still working for some salon in San Diego.

Didi waited until her kids were grown (eighteen and twenty) before she found enough backbone to leave Danny. Her mother came over often to help Danny. She cleaned his house once a week, made dinner, listened to his problems. He has a bad back now. Also, his feet swell because he's on them all day seeing patients. Didi's mother was always saying, "That man needs you, Deidre. He still loves you. He told me you're the only woman he's ever loved."

Didi didn't buy it. She didn't care much, anyway. Well, just a little, maybe. She knew in her heart of hearts that he was still getting laid. Doctors have that power, especially if they still look virile, which Danny does. Didi bet he and April were an ongoing item.

Also thinking: what you are is what you're forced to deal with. Your acts tell on you. People don't change their spots. Or maybe some do? She doesn't know. Does anyone?

•

Didi's spots: For months her secret life revolved around Harley. But there were things she kept from him, too. Sounds odd, but there was something to be said for having him elsewhere two nights a week ministering to ill Franny in San Diego. Two nights when she could do anything she wanted. Not have to explain herself. The sort of freedom she felt in college. She took advantage of those Friday and Saturday evenings when Harley was gone. What was she supposed to do, sit around watching television?

Nothing serious. Some flirtations. A few dinners with this or that man. Or woman. Some groping. Some kissing. Usually stopping if things got heavy. The only exception was Carlson. With all others, it was only sex-light, a blithe version that had nothing but surface to it, mouths, tongues, hands. Never deep. Not in her head. Not anywhere. Certainly not fuckbuddy stuff like she had for a while with him. First time it happened was when she showed him the property he bought for GO QUANTUM, his popular fitness gym. He looked into her eyes and said, "Didi, you're simply stunning. You make me weak-kneed." A caress, an abrupt, overwhelming desire. Sometimes you just can't help yourself.

Didi was over him now. Hadn't seen Carlson in a year.

Also thinking: SEX—no big deal unless you make it a big deal. There were safe ways to handle it. Ways that didn't include penetration. Have fun. No one hurt. A little disloyal, of course, but she didn't want to stop. Although, she was worried about STDs. Also worried about someone becoming obsessed with her. Wanting to see her more than she wanted to see him or her. She had often considered such possibilities when it came to Carlson. Such a mind-blowing sex machine. Yeah, it was good with him, but not as good as Harley. No one better ever, though he was aging, slowing down and in need of more stimulation. They had mused about threesomes lately. Didi always got a tingling in her groin whenever she pictured herself with men at both ends.

•

Also thinking: Moral letdowns, but these were fantasies she would be dealing with until her inner-sanctum withered, taking her urges with it.

Sometimes she argued with her mirror:

No big deal.

Very big deal, Didi. The morals of a monkey.

What Harley doesn't know can't hurt him.

That's not the point, Didi. It's you that's hurt, not him.

Harley's fault for leaving me alone on weekends to play nursemaid to her, that stupid Franny.

No one can be corrupted if corruption isn't already in her. You're born with it. You inherit it, a heritage of self-destruction, just like Danny and Harley have. And you, Didi. You too. Your wild days, your wild-eyed youth when you dyed your hair platinum and wore short skirts with no undies, your blouse open, flaunting your cleavage.

It was Danny's example. His example corrupted her. Ripped her out of her fabricated self. Manufactured innocence manufactured by her busybody mother.

Nice to have an excuse for everything you do. Stealing another woman's husband. Doing it casually.

She wanted to *LIVE*. That was all. Was it a sin to want to live? Here and now was all we have, and then everything's over and this world knows us no more—forever.

This attitude, this sort of egocentric thinking can get you killed. No one gets away with anything, Didi. One day, sooner or later, you'll pay.

Then she'll pay. Life on her terms. Or no life at all.

•

Also thinking: Danny spilling his guts, damn him. He told her a story about April lying naked on a bed beside him. The two of them discussing the possibility that Jerry and Didi had created sweet little towhead Keats. April offering that Jerry was probably unfaithful when he went on those business trips to Chicago and Denver, but that Didi was not the unfaithful type. "Certain women just won't do it," April told him. She wanted to believe there were women who had unbreakable codes. Wanted to believe there was an immovable spot in the world. Which such women represented. A place where you could touch bottom and knew there was no further to go. Her mother had been like that. Or so April believed. Her mother had had moral absolutes. Didi was another who had moral absolutes.

Danny had scoffed. No one knows anyone. We're infinitely mutable all of us. He had thrown the blanket off, exposing her body. His fingers cupping a breast, squeezing it until she whimpered. You see that door, he had told her. As long as you can lock it, as long as a woman feels safe behind it, as long as she's sure she won't get caught. What I mean is—I've never met a woman who wouldn't come across. Not ever. Of the women I've had since my marriage, at least twenty of them had husbands. So don't give me moral absolutes. There is no immovable spot. You're all corruptible, thank God! What a boring world it would be if you weren't.

Listening to Danny reminiscing, Didi remembered Harley's words at the Escondido reading of *Bodies in Motion*. Telling the wannabe writer who was suffering a mental block: "Man. Woman. Same room. A lock on the door." His novel was so sexy it made her think he might be a libertine. But that's the last thing he turned out to be. What he was—was a contradiction. Also thinking: yeah, so what are you, Didi?

Danny schizoid: The last thing he told her that day was that her unfaithfulness hadn't bothered him, as much as her carelessness in getting pregnant with Keats. And perhaps Emily as well? It wasn't fair that Danny had to raise another man's kids. It was the worst thing about women, how sneaky they could be in crediting their children to gullible men.

"Both those kids are yours, Danny. You know you're crazy, don't you?" she said.

"Yep."

"You're losing it."

"I'm sick."

"You sound sick."

"I wanted to dump you, Didi. Every time I looked at you I wanted to …"

"To what?"

"Wave a wand."

Didi was, perhaps, paraphrasing a bit, but mostly she believed she remembered their conversation fairly well. She had repeated it to herself over and over, trying to figure out why she didn't know him, even after she had been married to him for nearly two decades. How could he not believe that Keats and Emily were his kids? Didi was a good girl then. Mostly. Until Norman Ten Boom swept her off her feet.

Madness. Madness.

•

Until Danny told her of his doubts about Keats and Emily, he was generally decent enough. Not a clue that he was making love to his patients and probably coming home and making love to her too. Being a doctor he would have known the ones he had sex with were clean.

Her not knowing anything was a blessing. Thought she was lucky having such a fine man. In many ways that mattered, it might be true. But then what do you do with all the deception going on behind your back? Your husband screwing, screwing.

Coming home and being this great guy. Which one was he?

Every visit with Danny turned her into a priest to whom he unburdened his conscience. Listing sleazy details. Sad eyes apologizing. Eyes begging forgiveness. Never dreamed he had it in him: almost groveling. In fact, she felt so sorry for what he was enduring she found herself wanting the old, hardnosed bastard back. Still, she was all ears when it came to his behavior. It was as if he thought examining his past would keep him out of hell after he died. Would Danny go to heaven? Didi wasn't sure he believed in heaven. Or hell. Or God. And she still didn't understanding why he told her his many sins.

•

Also thinking about when they married: how she was Silly Putty. Play Dough. He could have shaped her any way he liked. Also thinking he did, in fact. And then hated her for it.

She recalled the day she said to him: "I am the way I am because of you. You and Mommy. There is no me here."

"Who doesn't want to be a victim?" he told her.

"I don't."

Wiggled his finger at her. Raw whisper: "Yes you do. It gives you every excuse, Didi. I am a victim of my mother and father and that brutal farm. You are the victim of your mother and me. On and on. Pick a point and it will lead to finger pointing. We both could have been so much better, you know. I let my libido rule and it ruined you. Ruined me too, but ruined you more. You were sweet, a flower child, not totally innocent, but basically good inside. But I broke the good in you. Given the right handling you might have become ideal."

•

His eyes were dewy. Tears ran down his cheeks. I turned away. This crying shit driving me crazy. Especially when a man does it. Also thinking: maybe I am broken, but I don't want to waste one second trying to be ideal. Fuck that. An ideal wife, mother, daughter: fuck that. The way I see it: every life—a Pandora's Box. Chaos clamoring. Danny's infidelity turning the key, opening the lid. Don't try to explain anything, not the self, not Danny, not Norman, not Harley, not Carlson, not Mommy. The why: what does it matter?

Also thinking: It matters.

Also thinking: Where's my conscience?

Also thinking: the last thing I need is a fully functioning conscience.

Feeling nutso. Does it show?

Save As Documents: The World According to Deidre Annaba Godunov.

6 – Playing the Man Well

Two years into his affair with Didi, Harley Olsen made his escape. Before him lay the Sonora Desert, freeway 8, El Centro, Yuma. He hoped to make Flagstaff before nightfall and find Lloyd Bean.

Lloyd and Harley had been friends in Denver during their teen years. They lost track of each other for decades, until Lloyd came across one of Harley's books dusty on a shelf in the Flagstaff Library. Lloyd read it and wrote the publisher, who forwarded the letter to Harley. Lloyd's letter saying he was shocked to find the book wasn't half-bad, given that a turnip wrote it. He ended with directions to his house and an invitation to: "Come see me sometime, big boy." So that was what Harley was doing. Getting out of town. Getting away from his part-time wife. Getting away from his mistress. Harley was jittery and tired. He had been drinking too much lately and at Lloyd's he knew he'd be drinking more. Harley promised himself to stop boozing after his visit with Lloyd. He was sure he would write better without alcohol pickling his brain. Maybe his hand wouldn't shake so much when he picked up a pen.

•

"What are you doing?" he questioned the pounding traffic—everyone in a furious hurry. "How did the world get so goddamn crowded? Where are we going? What in the world are we after? We're after movement. Keep moving. The thing to do is just keep moving." Harley's mother had always told him, "Put one foot in front of the other. And don't be thinking too much about it. Take it from me, Harley man, life is a cock-up from cradle to grave, you'll never be happy. The best thing you can do is distract yourself." Harley knew she was right. Distraction was the key. Work and booze and sex and work and booze and sex. Good to be amused by your musings. Good to be sidetracked. Good to be absorbed in the belief that what you were doing was not marginal. In the long run pointless.

•

"Art deco!" enthused Harley passing the outskirts of El Centro: slants of light lighting desiccated lands, tufts of shrubbery, shacks, geometric junkers in yards dysfunctional. An antique tractor framed by fractal sagebrush and cacti, flashes of glittering eclecticism. Pyramidal sand dunes narrowing through Yuma, the Colorado River becoming a trickle gasping all the way to *Mar de Cortés*.

Harley was not the fearless traveler he used to be. He was fifty-seven now. His re-flexes slowing. The traffic on the freeway unnerved him so much he missed his turnoff, staying on the 8, until a sign announced:

AJO 85 SOUTH

BUCKEYE 85 NORTH

He understood he needed to go north. North was Prescott. Beyond Prescott was Flagstaff. Head for the mountains he told himself. Why weren't there more signs to guide him? He needed signs telling him what to do. Signs pointing the way, saying do this and you'll be safe: life will be fine if you follow the signs. It was Arizona's fault. Arizona didn't believe in spending money on signs.

•

In Buckeye he pulled into a gas station and asked directions. The attendant told him to take the 10 to Phoenix, then 17 north. Harley had wanted to avoid Phoenix. All around him he saw monster pickups, behemoth semis trying to bully his Honda Civic. To distract himself he put on a taped lecture—some professor telling him that Philip Roth wrote absurdist comedy influenced by Freud and Beckett, all three men writing essentially an extended joke. Woody Allen. Mel Brooks. Richard Pryor. Absurdisms. All of them. They reminded Harley not to take life seriously. Take life seriously and the first thing you know—you are fucked, man. And, ultimately (finally, in conclusion, toe-in-the-grave) what is the last thing you know? You were fucked, man. Harley chuckles. The whole caboodle so goddamn goony.

•

Settling into rhythm, the car swallowing miles of black pavement, Harley listened to the lecture. He was driving sixty-five. Cars flaming by him like missiles. All of them rushing to destruction. Mayhem in the making. Days like this, Harley hated everyone.

It was just a theory: "Comedy," said the professor, "is a mixing of otherwise separate kinds of people, words, events, or situations and submitting them to criticism and/or ridicule, mainly satire. Illicit love is full of comic possibilities." The phrase echoed in Harley's mind—illicit love, illicit love. The professor talking about Sheridan's *The Rivals*, whose center was built on linguistic pretense—especially Mrs. Malaprop, who used words mal a propos, out of place: "As headstrong as an allegory on the banks of the Nile." "Illiterate him, I say, quite from your memory." The professor's tone was reassuring. Also comforting.

•

Harley, no longer anxious, found himself not listening, but rather wondering what those trees were, their flowers spreading out like butterflies, tiny yellow clouds that appeared to be levitating. Yellow beds of blossoms for Vishnu to lie upon. Palo Verde in bloom. Palo Verde. Poetic Palo Verde.

He drove by a sign claiming:

+ A LIBRARY IS A TREE OF DIABOLICAL KNOWLEDGE +
+ TRUST IN THE WORD OF THE LORD ONLY +

Burn the libraries, burn the books, especially Harley Olsen's books.

•

A few miles past Prescott he watched the sun sliding below the horizon. Sunsets always reminding him that he was only a guest on earth. Before long he'll lose it all. All of it taken away. Given to other guests who will watch sunsets and remember their mortality. Like a manipulated machine designed to break down, the body dribbling molecules, a particle here, microbe there and one night you can't see where you're going: no night-vision cones. He stopped at a motel called TIRED EYES, its neon sign saying V CANC. And: BROADBAND. TIRED EYES was a rundown relic, with an empty swimming pool and a weed-infested playground for restless progeny—rusty jungle-gym, an A-frame for swings but no swings, a slide (more geometric deco, he mused).

•

Spending a restless night in a room smelling of stale walls and musty bedding, he listened to roaring diesels, the whirr of cars, monster pickups with tires baying. Sleepless and filled with agitation, he whispered to the dark, "I am an absurd man, an absurd comedy. An illicit lover. A vow-breaker. Contemptible cheater." Climbing out of bed, he turned on his laptop and wrote his soul-mate an email:

Dear Didi,

No way can I continue to do this, not to you, not to her, not to myself. This is killing all of us, Didi. I've never been so wretched, have you? Our affair is a great cliché filled with insane joy and endless pain. A blessing. A curse. Take a look at Franny and you'll see a woman terrified of losing it all, willing to put up with whatever I do, just so I don't totally leave her. How can I live with that? How can I live with the evidence of my behavior written on her face every weekend when I go to San Diego and take her to dinner and talk to her as if what we're doing is normal? You don't turn your back on someone you've been married to for more than twenty years, someone you've experienced the ups and downs of life with. So what if she betrayed me once or maybe twice? It's so long ago I can barely remember how I felt. I was hurt. I was angry, but not very much, because I blamed a lot of it on myself for cultivating what a psychiatrist might call the emotional sterility that fed Franny's hunger for intimacy. You somehow broke though that barrier and brought me back to life, Didi. And I thank you for that, I think. The thing is: you may have also, ironically, instilled in me the emotional means of my death. For I feel something dying in me daily, certainly not the least of which is my self-respect. I don't feel like much of a man anymore. I'm ashamed of the way I'm living. Sick to death of the pain I'm causing poor, ill Franny. Her little affairs are puffs of nothing compared to mine, but it caused her just as much anguish and she turned her anguish inside and she's never been the same since. She's a physical wreck to this day, and I truly believe if she hadn't given into temptation she would be okay now. But it's too late. Her aliments are real. She's not a hypochondriac like you say, Didi. Or maybe she is. How does one judge these things? The point I'm making is that she's suffered enough. I've got to break it off with you and go home and take care of her. If I don't do this I won't be able to live with myself.

I feel like I'm coming apart. I am not the fortress I thought I was. I've learned that my nature is like a weathervane, it shifts with the wind. It tells me I am ugly. I like me NOT. I'm sorry to be hurting you this way. I love you, but love isn't enough. You'll get over it in time. You're not a woman to lie down and die over losing your lover. You're a dynamo. You're full of life. You'll find someone new. Franny hasn't the strength you have. In the terrible shape she's in she'd never find a companion, she's too old, she's too ill, she's too fat, she's too depressed, she's a walking advertisement for despair. Leaving her is the same as handing her a death sentence. Maybe someday you'll see how impossible this was and how stupid we were to even try balancing our screwed up lives. Maybe twenty years ago we could have done it, but not at my age. You're still attractive and can easily find a man who will love you and the two of you can grow old together. I'll be a distant memory long gone out of this life when your journey is over. I hope you will have forgiven me by then. We knew this was going to happen. We've known for three-plus years that this was just an interlude that couldn't last forever. Grieve if you must. Then pick yourself up and move on, Didi.

•

Harley re-read the letter. It said enough, but not everything. He might have mentioned she was why he drank so much, the accumulation of what they had done the past three years haunting him whenever he stayed sober. The depression, the sense of hopelessness, the longing for oblivion. In between the lines it was all there. How many times had he sat with the gun in his hand? Telling himself that suicide was the only way out. Some of us don't die soon enough. Living too long can be a mistake. Everyone glad to be rid of you by the time you finally go. No tears, heartbreak, grief. Thank God that bastard's gone. They forget you as fast as they can. But what do you care? You're reduced to ashes and life moves on easily without you. No chance to mend anything. No chance to erase the page and start over.

•

His hand moved the cursor to SEND. Finger hesitating. One click and this mess would be over. He would get back to being his boring old self, fussing with the words. One click was all it took. The message onscreen telling him: YOUR MESSAGE HAS BEEN SENT.

One click.

One.

Harley held his breath. Felt his heart protesting.

Did he really want it over? Did he really want to go back to what was? Did he really want never to see Didi again, make love to her, mentor her, argue with her, discuss politics and poetry and movies, philosophy and literature with her? Did he never want to see her cherished face again? Never? Yes and no. If he could only split himself in two, be Franny's loyal husband, her ultimate support (in her and his declining years) and Didi's lover until he (or somebody) dies. Might this be the best he can do?

His hand moved the cursor to DELETE and the letter to Didi vanished. Not yet, he told himself. Inevitably it will have to be, but not yet. Tomorrow—

We all have one more tomorrow, don't we?

•

Closing the computer, he stood up. Got a glass of water. Washed down a milligram of Xanax. Then stared out the window, listening to traffic and looking at silhouetted hills in the distance, a crescent moon rising, its horns tilting as if wanting to gore something. There were stars, but he could barely see them. In the scheme of things, what did any of it matter? For the umpteenth time his murderous heart fantasized killing Franny. Beyond the Franny barrier lay freedom. Sort of. Didi would own him if Franny were dead. Did he want that? Did he want to be owned by another woman? Be accountable?

Kill both of them, Harley.

In fact one night not long ago he went into Franny's room with the gun in his hand. Watched her sleeping. She looked sad. Helpless. Her compressed mouth deeply frowning. He pointed the gun at her, his finger on the trigger, the safety off. He could have shot her in the head, shot her close, so she would have powder burns on her skin. Put the gun in her hand. And say to the investigators: She couldn't handle the pain anymore. He would shoot her and leave her there. Go back to his apartment in Riverside. Wait a day. Then call Judy and Ruth and Franny's boss. Can't get in touch with her, he would say. Do you know where she is? No, they haven't heard from her. She didn't show up for work. Maybe something is wrong. The sisters would rush over and find her. Call the cops. Everyone would accuse Harley. They would say what a horrible man he is, no loyalty, no sense of duty, no self-restraint. You killed her, Judy would say. Killed her, Ruth would echo. They'd never be able to prove it. It seemed a perfect plan, but when it came to the moment of truth he couldn't do it. He thought about consequences. How her death would prey on him. Haunt him.

How do you wipe out all the years of caring, of seeing one another through illness?

How do you delete indelible memories?

How do you wipe out years of love that somehow got muddled in middle age?

•

In Chino Valley he stopped at a liquor store. Bought a twelve-pack of Miller's and a bottle of vodka. Back in the car he took a pull on the vodka. Then another. And opened a beer. A few sips from each container and he was fine. A little too little was just enough.

He needed to find Lloyd Bean's house. "I'm lost," he said aloud.

After thirty minutes of snooping along one street after another in Flagstaff, he crossed the highway to the other side and dumb-luck stumbled onto Mustang Way and the right address over the entrance to Lloyd's trailer park. Harley counted the numbers (the trailers lined up like boxcars side-by-side) and stopped at number nine. In front of him: a trailer that was perhaps forty feet long, twelve feet wide, listing starboard. Dead honeysuckle vines draping the rail of a porch hosting white plastic chairs, white plastic table. Brittle bushes leaning against the skirt in front. The trailer was white with cinnamon trim fading. It needed a bath, one of those high-pressure wash jobs. Why was everything so dirty? On all sides and across the street were similar moody monuments to indigence advertising gimme a paint job.

•

When the door opened, Harley didn't recognize him. Lloyd Bean's eyes saying he didn't recognize Harley either. Lloyd had a scraggly white moustache *(white!)* and a paunch and his hair was thin on top, wispy strands like anemic strings combed left to right across a balding dome. But he was still handsome. Ruggedly so: bullish neck full of wrinkles, square jaw that looked like it could still take a punch.

"Is you is, or is you ain't?" his raspy voice asked. "Jesus Christ, Harley Olsen losing his hair. Salt and pepper moustache. Skinny as a rail. Fuck, whaddaya know? Shit, I hate it. I wanted you to look like that pimply punk who couldn't get a date in middle school and jacked off looking at *Playboy's* playmate."

"Weren't me, man, that was some other pervert. That snotnose with the Vaseline jar in his pocket. Wasn't his name Lloyd Bean?"

Lloyd laughed. His teeth were yellowish, but he had the same gap-toothed grin. "Now I recognize you," Harley told him.

Lloyd said, "You're taller than I remembered, but still a twig. Come in here and have a beer. That is beer tucked under your wing, I take it."

"Does a swim duck? Does a fuck mink?"

"Are the woods a dung deal?"

•

They sat at the abused table on Lloyd's porch drinking beer. Lloyd served flavored potato chips in three large bowls, vinegar and salt in one, barbecue in another, plain can't-eat-just-one in the third bowl. Harley was starving, coffee and toast long ago tunneling through his duodenum. Lloyd kept opening beer, kept filling bowls with potato chips that disappeared, kept lighting Camel cancer sticks, eyes full of sarcastic comments, blue chips of cynicism. Interlaced wrinkles crawling over his forehead and cheekbones. Harley noted that those same age lines squirmed around his own eyes whenever he smiled in the mirror. He remembered the lineless face of Lloyd the boy, his wavy blond pompadour attracting hopeful stares from Denver schoolgirls. Where did all that go? We're not that old, are we?

As if reading Harley's thoughts Lloyd said, "I can't get over it. You sonbitch, Harley, you've ripened."

"You should talk."

"Prematurely gray, Harley." Sweeping his fingers through his hair, he added, "This happened twenty years ago. I've had a hard life, Harley. But I'm still youthful in my mind." He tapped his forehead. Then touched his chest gently. "Got a dicky heart."

"Yeah? So do I."

"Bet you don't have one of these."

He opened his shirt and Harley saw something that looked like a tiny pack of cigarettes buried beneath the epidermis above Lloyd's left breast. "Pacemaker," Lloyd said. "I'm living on currents courtesy of Edison." His laugh sounded as if he was gasping. "Every five years I take this box in and get a new battery. I got a year to go and I'm thinking I might skip it, you know. I'm fifty-eight now. Fifty-eight is long enough for anyone to live. What you think?"

"Lloyd Bean with a pacemaker," marveled Harley. "Jesus Christ." But Harley was glad to learn that Lloyd was fifty-eight, while himself only fifty-seven. His heart skipped a beat now and then and had a flabby valve. High cholesterol and high blood pressure taking a toll. How long could a body stand such ruthlessness?

He and Lloyd reminisced about Denver. They caught up on who was dead and who was a loser and who lucked out and made a million dollars inventing some kind of fastener for Target Stores to hold up shelves—Gordon Bourgeois. Harley remembered Bourgeois being voted Most Likely to Succeed, while Lloyd was voted Best Looking, and Harley got votes for nothing.

Lloyd grinned, the gap in his teeth revealing the tip of his tongue. Harley asked him what was so funny. And Lloyd said, "Just remembering how we used to play with words, make them up and fool kids into thinking they were in the dictionary. Do you remember sentence-sillyism?"

"Huh?"

Lloyd leaned forward. "I'll go first." He cleared his throat, the phlegm bubbling as he orated: "As I approach some vestige of parallelism in my search for literary wholeness I am trying to absorb poetic vibrations exhuberating and regurgitating from the phkatorial depths of my ass-oral being."

"Oh, fuck yeah," Harley said. "I remember that."

"Come on," Lloyd coaxed. "It's like Hot Potato, you got to keep it in the air. Don't drop it, Harley. Babble!"

And Harley was thinking—what did that professor say? Comedy is a mixing of . . . words built on linguistic pretense. Absurdities.

"Hold forth," Lloyd commanded. "Speak to me of the shortcomings you showed Mary Lou in the park that day. Mary Lou, I am so into you!"

"Oh, shit, you still remember that?"

Lloyd referring to a time at the park when Harley's cock fell out of a hole in the crotch of his jeans. Popping out like a curious grub when he joined some friends sitting in a circle talking. Half hard and looking earnest, his cock was eying Mary Lou Fuller. She was staring at it. Riveted.

"God yes. How embarrassing. I didn't even know it was out until you got hysterical and pointed."

"Like a squinty-eyed mole wanting her hairy hole to hide in. I want you, baby! That's what it was saying. Shit, she couldn't tear her eyes away. You could have had her that day, Harley. You could have flogged the bog."

"I don't know."

"I'm serious."

"After that I couldn't look at her. I avoided her from then on."

Lloyd said, "Let's stop being so intellectual and so wonderfully poetic in our efforts to cast you in a heroic light of rectitude, phallically speaking, of course. Give me the straight poop, Harley. I'm listening."

"Okay," he said, pausing to gather a mouthful. "The park pecker gave us a feast of poetic phkatude fantasies. Next in our rhyming let's be very down to earth, down to grassroots. Fear must not studify the minds of any who, including you and I, pissiffying or radically underthinking the monumental task now at hand. Dammit, I hate to be such a conundrum, but the park pecker facing us may be challenging beyond our capissities. But we must rise to the challenge, or die trying."

"Where is the Harley I used to know-and-love who never shirked his duty when literature called? I think resting on his laurels when his conscience reminds him of Mary Lou and the hideous blame he put upon her for the farts he himself let that day. Our park pecker needs to be honest, it must be simple and it needs to be as portential as we can make it. Twas brillig, you know, and the slithy toves did gyre and gimble in the wabe. Let us rhyme on for the sake of Lloyd Wadsworth Shortfellow."

"And Harlan Edgar Alien."

•

Several beers later, the chips were gone and also a dinner of fried sausage sandwiches, because both Harley and Lloyd were definitely too drunk to drive to the Mexican restaurant, where Lloyd had made reservations. Harley had learned that Lloyd was married three times. He has six kids, five girls, one boy. He worked as a cement finisher, until his heart forgot how to keep time. He received disability now. And a bit from the union. He said it was hard work and fooling around that broke him down. The long hours under the sun, the sweep of the trowel getting heavier and heavier, wrecking his shoulder and elbow. Forcing him to drink for the pain. Beer didn't help his health. Nor did the women he kept on the side. Nor did the four to five hours sleep before he had to get up and play cement again. Thirty-plus years of that kind of thing gives a man a rebellious heart. Lub-a-doo-doo; instead of lub-a-dub. Gives you chronic pains in your lower back as well. Puts calluses on your knees that match anything a surfer squatting on his board could brag about.

"Hope you've been able to avoid beating up your body like that."

"Not quite," said Harley. "My heart has gotten weak the past two years. Might need a bypass."

"No shit?"

"I try not to think about it."

"Me too. Fuck hearts. So, you're, like, all professor-author shit now."

"I guess."

"You were always the smart one," Lloyd told him. "But I never figured any of us for college. And I sure as hell never figured you for a fuckin novelist."

"I'm faking it," Harley said. "Olsen the imposter. One of these days they'll find me out."

"Well, it just shows to go you how wrong you can be about youngsters. Especially how you don't know shit about nobody's future. I mean a smart asshole like me might have got a degree and wrote books, you know. Shit, I've read so many damn books I shit pulp paper and ink. I should own the Flagstaff Library. But here you are with three novels published, and I don't mind telling you the one I read was okay. Except you got a way of pulling back when it comes to describing sex. You kept getting that girl on her knees and then wouldn't put her mouth where it wanted to go. You'd just go off to some storm or something and I'd lose my erection. You and your metaphors."

"Metaphor rates a writer."

"Ah, what do you know? I'll tell you what rates a writer. Are his characters realer than television?" Lloyd leaned forward and burped. His face had a florescent tinge. Eyes shiny with mockery, youthfully bright, belying the wrinkles surrounding them. "Harley," he said, "what'cha tryin to do with all the words pouring out? Impress people?"

"Hell, Lloyd, I'm trying to tell a story that entertains someone for a while. Make a few dollars."

Lloyd shook his head. "Don't try to bullshit a bullshitter, old boy. Every real writer is a murderer. Destructive bastard, he wants to murder all the drivel that rules our lickspittle lives. He wants to drive his words into us like Mack the Knife. Scarlet billows, man. He wants to tear up our insides. Make us bleed the garbage out of our quaking bodies. He's the carney barker crying out, 'Here she is, folks. Come see life as the fucked up mess it is. Don't be afraid. What you see will make you free.' Because look, Harley, if you can't take it straight-no-chaser, you'll be a lying sack of shit all your pointless life and you'll never have the guts to see delusions popping up everywhere you turn. You'll never be able to see things down the middle. There is no eternal truth, Harley, but what little whiff of truth there is nests in the middle. The writer, the artist goes sniffing out that middle ground and whatever he finds he puts it in his art. That's if he's real and not just a bullshitter like me, Lloyd Bean, mister know-nothing major asshole."

"Straight-no-chaser," said Harley. "I like it. Yeah, I'll steal it."

Lloyd's smile was cunning. "I stole it from the title of some book in the library."

Moths dive-bombing the porch light, battering their bodies. Leafless bushes scratching the trailer, emitting a scrawny, pain-bitten sound. "Look at them crazy fuckers," said Lloyd, pointing to the moths. "Falling like cinders." And then he said, "We're all like that, don't you think? Killing ourselves to get to the light."

Harley kept silent. He wanted to change the subject.

Lloyd, chuckling, said, "I'm such a dumb asshole."

"No way, Lloyd. I think you still got it"

"Fuck, who cares what you think?"

"You don't care what I think? Then you are a dumb asshole."

Lloyd and Harley gave into coughing guffs of laughter.

Wiping happy tears from his eyes, Lloyd said, "Got no more love nor life in me than a lug nut. Life without love—who needs it, son? I bet you got women smothering you, don't you? All them coeds and lady fans, I'd be banging em."

•

The mountain air got cold. They went inside. Lloyd inventoried the beer and announced two more apiece.

"I've got a bottle of vodka," Harley told him.

"You holding out?" said Lloyd. "You sonbitch. Get that vodka and let's have some real drinks."

So out to the car and back with the Stoli. Two stiff ones over ice. Lloyd and Harley saluted their fucked up childhoods in Denver, where everything seemed simple when they were young and had perpetual hard-ons.

"Careless I was about it," said Lloyd. "You remember when I wiped out Timmy Benton? You remember when I swung that car antenna so hard I made it sing and the tip flew off and hit Timmy in the temple? You remember that, Harley?"

"Whatever happened to Tim?"

Lloyd bolted his drink. "He never come around, Harley. Sonbitch lived years curled like a pretzel before he died."

"That's fucked."

"Tell me about it."

"See, I lost touch with all that."

Lloyd said, "Yeah, I went off and harvested wheat in the Dakotas before heading west. I made myself a workhorse by day, a drunk by night. I used to go in the bars and quote poetry for free drinks." He smiled wistfully. "I liked Robert Service best," he said. And then quoted:

The Northern Lights have seen queer sights,
But the queerest they ever did see
Was that night on the marge of Lake Lebarge
I cremated Sam McGee.

"That one would get me a boilermaker ever damn time. Shows how comical life is."

"You used to quote Twain, too. That was cool."

"Twain's cool," Lloyd agreed. And he added, "Ain't God a nightmare from which you'd like to awake?"

"Should you talk like that, Lloyd? Given that little problem requiring pace-making?"

"You pedaled me around my newspaper route when I broke my ankle. I never forgot that, man. I sat on the handlebars and threw the papers and you pedaled your ass off. You were a good pal."

"My little legs just a churning."

"Don't shit me, Harley. This is Lloyd Bean you're talking to. You were the one all the girls creamed their pants for in high school. Us guys always jealous of you."

"No need to be. I tell you what, Lloyd, I was never no good at it. I always disappointed them. I always felt how stupid the act is. I always felt nasty after. All I wanted was to get away."

"Listen to him. What about Judy Sherman? What about Laura O'Neal?"

"Not me, man. Well, once with Laura. That was after I broke up with Judy. But I wasn't proud of that. It was peer pressure. Her pressure. Sometimes you can't help yourself."

"You know we were bastards, Harley. Always in the back of my mind is Tim. I murdered him. No woman could live with my guilty conscience for long. Three wives, Harley. Three fucking wives. How many you had?"

"One?"

"One! Jesus Christ, now I'm really starting to hate you. One fucking wife? One? Jesus, where's your sense of proportion, man? What the hell can you know about life if you've only lived with one woman? And you're a goddamn writer?" He stroked his chin. "So where you get your information?"

"It's all made up."

"Here's the thing, old boy, it's not the bad woman makes a man suffer, it's the good woman. Give me the bad woman anytime. I don't care if she's had a hundred fucking lovers. Give me the ones that when they go, you're better off without them. The last thing I want now is a good woman to make me feel guilty about every god-damn thing I do."

"I know that feeling," said Harley. "My wife is sick. Got all kinds of problems. I feel bad leaving her. I'm rotten, Lloyd, but I had to."

"What do you mean? You mean you left her?"

"Sort of." Harley hesitated, wondering if he shouldn't keep quiet about it. He sighed and said, "I go see her on weekends. See how she's getting along. I left a sick woman. Tell me how rotten I am."

"Yeah, well, I'm rotten, too. But you know what? Fuck it. No regrets, man. You bang her on weekends?"

"Naw, can't get it up for her no more. She's slimmed down some. Looks pretty good, actually. I think she has a lover. I'm fine with that. I hope he makes her happy."

"Are we drunk?"

"Hell, who can stand life if he ain't drunk?"

"That's my philosophy as well. Booze is killing me, but I don't give a fuck."

Neither man spoke for a moment. Harley heard the ticking of a clock. Finally, he leaned forward and said, "The thing is, Lloyd, I've had a pseudo second wife for the last three years."

"What do you mean a second wife? You mean a mistress, or are you a bigamist?"

"Mistress."

"Lucky sonbitch."

"Two years I've been going back and forth between the two of them."

"At your age that's got to be hard on your equipment."

"Honest, I can't get it up for her. I haven't had sex with my wife for over twenty years. Even before she got sick I lost all desire for her. She put on a ton of weight, which didn't help. And then Didi chased me down—"

"You don't have to tell me. I know this story," said Lloyd. "Let me say something, Harley. You know this can't end well. You know it will have a bad ending."

"Yeah, I know."

Lloyd touched his pacemaker again. "This is what that sort of shit did to me. Love affairs, my boy, fuck em."

"I don't know how I keep it up. I'm exhausted all the time, Lloyd. The stress, the anxiety is literally killing me. I lie to my wife constantly and I lie to Didi as well. She loves me. At least I think she loves me. Truth is I don't know what she sees in me. It's a mystery. Maybe she thinks I'll be famous and rich someday. Rich and famous and it'll rub off on her. She's a good poet, kinda. She wants to marry me. But I can't divorce my wife. I can't totally leave her to cope on her own, you know what I mean? How am I supposed to live with myself if I walk totally away from an ill woman?"

"What's she got?"

"Ulcers, liver problems, kidney problems, arthritis, anemia. Other things. I don't know, can't remember em all. She had breast cancer, too. It's cured, I think. She's seven years younger than me, but for years she had the body of an octogenarian."

"Sounds pitiful."

"She is. She breaks my heart every time I see her. She's a good woman. Sweet as they come."

Lloyd nodded knowingly. "What did I just say? A good woman makes a man feel guilty. Stay away from good women."

The bottle went back and forth, never mind the ice. Warm vodka, like the Russians and Poles.

"So, you old sonbitch on the run, ey? Why don't you keep going? Go back to Denver."

"I think about it," said Harley. "Running away from my problems."

"Shit yeah. I'd go with you if I could. Run like hell, Harley. Don't let them catch you from behind and bring you down."

"Jesus, how did I get so stupid?" said Harley.

"It's called playing the man. I tell you it won't end well. It will take a big toll on you, Harley. Women almost killed me." Lloyd kept caressing his pacemaker.

•

They stayed up all night and Lloyd talked nonstop. It was as if he had been starving for an ear. Five in the morning and the bottle drained and Lloyd saying, "It don't matter what the life is you live, it will ultimately break you."

"Shet yab," mumbled Harley.

"Shit yeah," echoed Lloyd. "Finally, somewhere at some unknown moment it will break you for good. No, that's certain. But let it go. Fuck it. No regrets, I say. Because what matters is not the breaking. What matters is how much fight you showed before the end of your sorry ass struggle. You understand me, son? If you can tell me how else you measure things except by failing and rising up and failing again, I'd sure like to hear it."

Harley was doing his best to concentrate, but his mind was foggy. "I'm four or five shots of vodka too far to know, Lloyd. But I'll tell you when I'm sober. If I ever am, that is."

●

At six o'clock, they drove to a café, where Lloyd went for coffee every morning. They ate breakfast. There wasn't any more conversation about words or women or life breaking you. They talked sports: those damn Dodgers. One of the highest payrolls in baseball and can't win the pennant. Money doesn't buy everything. Can't buy pennants. Can't buy love. Can't buy your youthful heart back.

"Where did all the options go, man?"

"Gone with the wind," Harley replied.

"Don't gimme no fuckin Margaret Mitchell."

"To live tomorrow is too late."

"Who said that? Is that Frost?"

"Damned if I know. I think I just made it up. 'You must change your life!' That's Raining Rilke."

"I'll be glad to get rid of you so I can get some sleep. Coming up here getting me drunk. Keeping me up all night. Shame on you, Harley."

"I definitely feel bad about that."

●

An hour later, Harley left him at the door. In the mirror Harley watching him watching back. The sun lighting him from the side. The farther away Harley drove the more Lloyd seemed to burn like a torch in front of the trailer. Brittle bushes burning behind him. Lloyd Bean: a little flame of life using up the last of its fuel. It hit Harley that he would never see him again. They had seen what they are and there was no need for either to see what they would become. No more sentence-sillyism; no more park pecker phkatude fantasies.

Long road ahead and Harley was drained. He needed some sleep. He needed to get away from fixed ideas, absolute conclusions about women or anything.

•

When he got to Phoenix, he turned west onto the 10. Surrounded by brush, cacti, desert sands and speeding cars again. Six more hours, two women and a life filled with lies. Heat flirting with the asphalt in front of him, creating illusions of life-giving water. He knew Lloyd Bean was undeniably right: it was all going to end badly.

7 - Faithfully Yours

She drives to work weekday mornings. Back home at six. Glad she has a routine. So much better than lying in bed feeling abandoned, sorry for herself, her aches and pains, her sciatic nerve killing her, age an ever present threat—Death, it whispers, death, death, death.

Dark strips of exhaust from Lindbergh Field spoil the sky. She grimaces. Feels venomous. Hates what humans are doing to God's creation. Polar icecaps melting, glaciers retreating. Carbon footprints polluting the entire earth. No wonder there's an epidemic of cancer and lung ailments. The jets roar as they pass over the freeway, climbing higher, rattling heaven—as Satan would if God let him.

Airplanes: lethal bombs.

Stigmata.

World's end.

Endgame.

Prophesying the Rapture.

Traffic seething. Drivers giving her looks. Giving her the finger as she waves and sticks to the speed limit. Let them pile up. Let them gnash their teeth and snarl. Defiantly, she slows down even more, forcing the devil's minions to ride her tail. If they rear-end her, it's automatically their fault. They'll get the ticket. They'll pay the fine. The insurance company will raise their rates. She sees it as an object lesson. Don't be in such a rush. Take your time. Be glad you're alive. No guarantees you'll be here tomorrow. Or even one second from now.

She sniggers at their machinations maneuvering their guzzlers around her. Dry brush clutters the hills on both sides of the freeway. The least spark would ignite all of it. Instant Armageddon. In the distance: eucalyptus shading mini-mansions herded together symbolizing Sanctuary. Safety in numbers. It's nearly one hundred degrees already. Global warming. Seas rising. Maniac weather. Tornadoes and hurricanes plaguing the east and Midwest. Drought withering everything west of the Colorado River.

The radio plays her favorite song (*Our God is an awesome God*) as she coaxes her car to the far right lane, angry horns vilifying her, a man bellowing: "Jesus fucking Christ, lady USE YOUR SIGNAL." For sure that man's inevitable end is Satan's lake. The off-ramp takes her to Sixth Street in Hillcrest, where she sees two men strolling along with their hands in each other's back pocket. She says a quick prayer, asking the Dear Lord to smite them. At the entrance to the brick-sided building on the corner of Park Boulevard and Robinson is the building housing *HARVEST HOME PUBLISHING*. In the parking lot, she pulls into her reserved space. A sign on the wall saying:

FRANCIS OLSEN
HARVEST HOME

Going inside she unlocks her office, flicks on the lamp. And sits at her desk perusing the latest proofs from some professor putting together an anthology of essays to use in his classes, a promising way to make back his advance and more. The title is pretentious: *Great Essays about Men and Women and the World Around Them.*

For four hours she line-edits, recognizing the usual suspects: Joyce Carol Oates, John Updike, Gay Talese, Frank Conroy, Susan Sontag, Joan Didion, Joy Williams, Thomas E. Kennedy, Walter Cummins and on and on, all of them showoffs hoping to awe her. In the twenty-five years of doing her job she's read so much crap she's immune to it. Her eyes follow the lines: (You were picturing yourself unattractive and very old and alone and at the mercy of your loneliness), but her mind goes elsewhere till noon, till lunchtime.

She has a book her pastor gave her. A thick thing called *Calvary Witness News.* She's been dipping into it for weeks. It's a compilation of letters sent to a woman in Minnesota named Bobbi Poe, an Upper Midwest's evangelist version of Dear Abby.

●

Franny shuffles to Balboa Park, where she sits on a bench under an elm, while eating an apple and reading Bobbi Poe's advice to timorous sinners.

Dear Bobbi Poe,

Every day I read the letters in Calvary Witness News. All the pain and suffering make me shudder. The people who write you have such difficult lives, and I wonder what is wrong with me because my life is almost perfect, and yet I'm miserable. I have a fine wife, two fine children, a fine dog and cat. I have a yellow canary that sings joyfully when the sun comes up. Everything is fine except my job is a dead end and I hate it. But yeah, I'm lucky to have a job these days. Everything going to hell in this hellish country. And yet God has blessed me, Bobbi. My house is in a gated community and reflects my well-paid, upper-class status. I drive a BMW M6 128i convertible. Get the picture? I have it all but it doesn't make me happy. I feel despair from the time I wake in the morning until I go to bed at night. I'm sick of living, but I don't know why. Maybe it's the awful wars or the deadly weather or our crappy, spineless politicians. Probably a combination of every damn thing. For a while I thought about either killing myself or finding a mistress. A woman at work offered herself to me. We tried to have sex, but I was impotent. Now I find myself avoiding her. Sex has no appeal, not with her and especially not with my wife, a vegan fitness fanatic whose knees and elbows are hard as hammers. But my question is, Dear Bobbi, how can a man have all the blessings I have and still be this depressed? What is missing?

                                                        Suicidal in the City

Dear Suicidal in the City,

I'm looking out my window and God's sky is a pale shade of orange from all the particulates in the air. There are red cardinals darting around like cheerful spirits. A moment ago I saw a monarch butterfly sitting on the sill, its wings breathing like the soul of an innocent child. I'm blessed to see all this and I enjoy it while I can, because I know it won't last. Butterflies, they say, are heading for extinction, along with songbirds, bees, bats, frogs and thousands of other species. The world itself is ravaged. Everything is changing for the worse. One day you will walk in the sun and won't be able to find any branches or leaves to shade you. The roads will be cluttered with cars that have empty gas tanks. A wheelbarrow full of money won't buy you a loaf of bread. People will be dying in the streets of starvation. I hunger, I thirst will be the universal cry of need. The Apocalypse is rushing towards us and you are worried about a life filled with the blessings that all needy humans are praying for? You say you're depressed? What you need is a dose of gratitude to our Lord who, for His own inexplicable reasons, has given you far more than any human being requires. Your good fortune is not going to last. Real misery is coming our way. Real misery that we've brought on ourselves, we dolts who vote for senators and congresspersons who think ME, my way and to hell with everyone else.

Listen, Suicidal, I want you to go to your Bible and read The Book of Job. Read how Satan took away Job's wealth and killed his children and afflicted him with loathsome sores from head to toe and how he sat among the ashes that used to be his home. All this after being the happiest man in town. And you think you're depressed? Do you mimic Job? Do you open your mouth and curse the day you were born? At least Job had reasons for hating his life, but what do you have? A big house, fancy car, a Jenny Craig wife and Toys-R-Us children. Shame on you, Suicidal in the City. Be comforted in the favor shown you by Providence and say the following prayer morning, noon and night:

Make my body and soul rejoice in Thee, most loving God. May I remember that temporal pains and sufferings will be exchanged for eternal joy when I die. Bless me that I may faithfully serve Thee and carry Thy name on my forehead, and reign with Thee after death for all eternity. Amen.

If you pray as I've told you, your suicidal tendencies will pass away and your heart will feel as bright as the brightest cloud in a bright blue sky. So bend your will to the eternal plan of our most loving and generous Lord. And quit wishing for the end that comes soon enough for everyone.

Faithfully yours, Bobbi Poe

Now Franny feels better. Bobbi sure showed him. She gave it to him good, the whiny whimperer. Oh boohoo I have everything, but I'm so depressed. Franny hopes that some nasty disease like COPD gets him. Then he'll know what blessings he once had.

She reads more letters and thinks: So much suffering. I may be a cow and have arthritis and anemia and disgusting bowels, but I've got it good compared to some of these people. Here's a woman who lost her leg in a car accident and has phantom pains. What's so bad about losing one leg? Big deal. Lucky she didn't lose two. Some boys come home from the war with no legs, no arms, blind, mentally ill, impotent.

Bobbi sent One-Leg a verse from the Bible to read daily—*Whatever thy hand finds to do, do it with thy might*—and told her to get on Zoloft and into therapy. She gave One-Leg the name of a Born Again psychiatrist in St. Paul.

Franny believes Bobbi Poe is probably a saint. Franny thinks she will write Bobbi and tell her about Harley walking out on a twenty-three year marriage. What would she say about that abomination?

The next letter describes an emotionally abused woman who wonders if she should leave her husband. He calls her names. He calls her whore, slut, tramp, bitch. Says her ass is wide as a barn door. And he keeps threatening to kill her. Again, Bobbi Poe lists some appropriate verses of comfort. Everything you need is in the Bible, she explains:

As soon as you sit down to read the Bible, an angel alights on your shoulder to protect you from harm. And as for that devil's minion you call your husband, tell him sticks and stones may break your bones, but names will never hurt you. Then pack your clothes and go live with your parents or friends or relatives. Visit your pastor and open your heart to him. He'll pray with you and give guidance. We are not put on earth to be abused by husbands who turn into vicious brutes wanting to murder us.

Franny thinking: Harley doesn't want to murder me, does he? I've been such a ball and chain. I should never have married a man so selfish, so ambitious. Trapped him. Trapped you, didn't I, Harley. That's part of why you left me. But you're a pain in the ass, too, Harley. Don't you know who's sick around here? Don't you know who has become a bog of diseases? And you think you've got troubles. Try handling a painful sciatic nerve, you self-centered prick. Try handling aplastic anemia and fibromyalgia and-and … ah, forget it.

The letters from people who have some chronic illness are the ones Franny likes best. Bobbi Poe tells them the world is full of woe, but when we die all woe is over forever. Nothing but bliss if you've been good, she tells them. Hang in there, you suffering children of a Jesus who loves you. Cling with all your might to the Lord's promises. He will hear your prayers and give you the strength to go on suffering, until he calls you home to perfection.

Turn the page and:

Dear Bobbi Poe, my best friend says PINK is the color of cancer. What do you think of that? You have to be brave to wear pink, I'm thinking. Bad mojo. You have to be brave to walk out the door. Is there a cure for agoraphobia? Do you know if anyone ever takes your advice? Have you ever been sick a day in your life? I'm thinking you're probably healthy as a horse and you're writing pointless letters. Thanks for writing them anyway. They're very entertaining for a shut in like myself. Beware pink, Bobbi.

Yours truly, Rita Recluse

Dear Rita Recluse,

Pink? Pink is the color of GIRL. As in YOU GO, GIRL. Don't waste my time with your "bad mojo." Quit being a coward and get out in the world and do something worthwhile with your life.

Faithfully yours, Bobbi Poe

Franny muses: Why can't I get books like this to edit? I could do this every day and never get bored. I like Bobbi Poe. She takes no shit. She gives comfort, but she also gives a piece of her mind and a wag of her finger. That's what I want to do. Wag my finger and tell the whole world to straighten up and fly right.

•

Lunch hour over, Franny tucks the book under her arm and heads back to the office. Behind her is the San Diego Zoo, where she can hear the birds scolding each other, squabbling like spoiled children.

8 - Appearance vs Reality

Age sixty , three years after finally leaving his wife to cope on her own, Harley bought a condo in San Diego, and Didi moved in with him. Another year crawled by of mornings waking in bed next to her, she breathing the breath of innocence. He has never known anyone who could sleep so deeply. Why wasn't guilt and sorrow troubling her the way it was troubling him? How could Didi be so at ease with what they had done? When he had asked her about it, she had said she loved him too much to care about what their love cost them or anyone else. Given his mood that day, her words had sounded pitiless.

Truth be told, her love scared him. Its vehemence swamped him. At times it was otherworldly. "It's good we love each other so much," she told him, "otherwise what we've done would be unforgiveable. A great love redeems us, Harley."

•

Some days he didn't know if he loved or hated her. Can one do both and not be bipolar? Repeatedly, he believed he wanted to be rid of her. But he lacked willpower. He lacked courage. No matter how weary he was, how much he wished to create a calm, unfettered life, Harley knew he was stuck. *The mind is always the heart's tool*, he continually told himself. Well, things could be worse. He could be living alone and his dithering heart could be so bad it would make him an invalid. And there would be no one to care for him. No one to care if he lived or died. Franny would probably applaud. Who could blame her?

Praise folly: Harley believed it was genetic, a defect handed down by warped ancestors. His destructive mother, his suicidal father.

•

He had a disturbing dream about his mother. She came to his side of the bed, hovering, not touching anything, a wisp of a woman. Gossamer. Her eyes, her mouth were the only things conspicuous. "Harley, who are you?" she had asked him.

Then listed some possibilities as if they were written on his body:

"Hamlet," she said, "ever unready, always making absurd decisions, going through life with your eyes wide shut, unable to see what your actions will do to you and your wife and that immoral Didi lying beside you.

"Oscar Wilde," she said next, "hiding behind a phony façade, lying your way through your days, ever an appearance, never a reality.

"Byron," she added, "ever the hedonist getting his way no matter who it hurts. If you only had Byron's courage you'd be worth something. How did you become such a coward?"

While she continued emoting, Harley felt paralyzed. He felt smothery, as if a great weight lay on his chest pressing the air out of him. He wanted to shout. He wanted to curse and tell her it was all her fault. *I'm smothering, I'm smothering,* his mind panted. He couldn't move. He couldn't breathe. Her words were daggers.

"Don Quixote," she said lastly, "tilting at windmills and breaking your lance, while rationalizing your behavior, ever blaming others for your bad luck, ever chasing fantasies you find in books. You're a symbol of their corruptive power. You're the deviant behind your professor's mask, oh knight of sorrowful countenance. Just remember this, Harley, whatever happens next will not be good and you'll have no one to blame but your ruined self."

A cry broke from him, air rushing from his lungs, his limbs thrashing under the covers. He woke with Didi shaking his shoulder and asking, "What's wrong, honey, what's wrong? Are you having a bad dream?" "A nightmare, a nightmare," he told her. "My mother. She was telling me how horrible I am." Didi put her arm over his heaving chest. She stroked his hair and said, "Shh, shh, you're not horrible at all. You're the best man I've ever known." Didi insisted his mother would never talk like that. "You can't help your dreams," she said. "My subconscious hates me," he told her. He got up. Went to the bathroom. Took a milligram of Xanax. Then sat at his computer and wrote the dream down. An hour later he had calmed enough to lie still and think.

Was this *it* then? Except for making the motions was his life essentially over—self-hatred and guilt shadowing him? Nowhere to go, no curative, no correction? There were obviously no more books in him. No more stories. Not the hint of a poem. He looked at his hands, at the age spots, a trinity of age spots and veins. How did he get so old? So tired? So moldy? Age spots. *Jesus!*

•

Harley slid out of bed at six. Went to the bathroom again. Felt the familiar pain as he sat on the toilet trying to relieve himself. Swollen prostate blocking what needed to get out. All the filth inside. Everything bound up. Tied in a knot. He gave up trying and took a shower. By the time he was done and dressing, he could smell coffee brewing.

Without makeup, Didi's skin had a yellowish tinge, a color more obvious against the backdrop of her platinum hair. The two of them were drinking way too heavily and he wondered if her liver was breaking down. He remembered the last time he saw Franny, how good she had looked. A little overweight still, but nothing like she was the year he left her. Maybe it had all been him. Maybe his neglect made her ill. Could one person give another person a chronic susceptibility to illness?

"Who is it today?" asked Didi.

"Today? Today is Oscar Wilde."

"Wish I could be there."

"Can you take the morning off?"

"I can't. I have four houses to show. They have appointments. I don't dare miss any possibles these days the way things are going. I have a feeling that despite how well the banks are doing we're headed for a double-dip, don't you?"

"In more ways than one," he told her.

Harley finished his breakfast in silence. Carried his plate and cup to the sink. He kissed Didi's cheek. Grabbed his briefcase.

"I love you," she said. "Be careful out there, honey. It's a jungle."

"You be careful, too. I wouldn't want anything to happen to you." As he closed the door he was thinking how they were like an old married couple already. No surprises. No mysteries left. All passion spent.

•

Driving to campus he worried his forehead with the heel of his hand trying to rub away the sense of pointlessness and loss he felt. And a growing headache. He was also thinking: I want what? I want to stay with her. Yes. I want to leave her. Yes. No. What do I want? I mean really. He told himself that the need to call a halt had come too late. The battle for the heart was already over. The cancer of the soul had grown and spread to the brain. The brain's protests were more and more feeble. Reason and will had already handed the reins to emotion. Feelings rule. Feeling was what punished him. Find the switch to turn off feeling and you, Harley, will be cured.

Cured of what?

Are you going to spend the rest of your life half dead half mad? Hating to get up in the morning. Hating to give lectures to students who don't care to hear them. Hating all this traffic, the heat, the noise, the deadening repetition, the bitterness of old age. If this goes on what do you have? You have nothing. Because everything you've done means nothing. Nothing worth living for. The sex that had seemed so crucial had become another occasional diversion. As soon as the act was over sorrow returned. The sense of foreboding. Bring on the booze, the warm, fuzzy glow, the illusion that you don't care what happens to you or to her. All love affairs run their course, Harley. Yours ran its course at least a year ago, but you didn't want to admit it. No more novelty. The familiar is boring. Fervor turning into pretense. Doubtless for her as well. The wild nights of the first three years are slurred memories now. When did it change? Was there an actual moment?

He stared at the concrete bridge pillar in the median of the freeway. At seventy

miles an hour hitting it head on would kill him. An instant of terror and then ...
Socrates said death might be better than the best night's sleep you ever had. Or you
might wake up and find your old friends beside you ready to pick up the conversation.
Either way it seemed like something to be wished for. Turn the wheel, Harley. Turn it
a fraction. Down the center divider. Boom!

•

"Oscar Wilde was born in 1854. He died in 1900. He is one of the great figures
of English comedy in the late nineteenth century. He had the Romantic's belief that
art is simply art and doesn't have to justify itself. He was flamboyant. He wore his hair
long and he dressed eccentrically, always carrying flowers, even while lecturing. It is in
honor of Wilde that I brought this bouquet."

Harley gestured to the spring bouquet on the table. He had stopped at Anita's
Flowers and bought the bouquet from her. Ah, if only he were younger. And unat-
tached. And braver. And full of sap. Harley usually bought flowers from sweet Anita
once a week, keeping them in a vase in his office, filling the air with fragrance. A fragrance that quieted his mind. A fragrance diminishing his doomsday attitude. Often
he quoted poetry to the flowers, reminding them that —"everything that grows holds
in perfection but a little moment." "The meanest flower that blows does give thoughts
that lie too deep for tears." Shakespeare. Wordsworth. Would they trade their fame
for one more day on earth in the arms of a beautiful woman? Will there come a future
when no one will quote either of them? A hundred years from now? A thousand years?

The class was staring at him, eyes puzzled, and Harley realized his thoughts had
wandered again. It had been happening a lot lately, a sense that he barely existed. A
sense he was fading. Already a specter reaching for his dead mother.

He cleared his throat and continued, "Wilde wrote the most engaging comedic
plays of his time. He also wrote a novel called *The Picture of Dorian Grey*. It's a story
about how moral dissipation leads a man to destruction. Dorian has his portrait painted. The painting has supernatural powers, which keep Dorian young on the outside.
The theme is that of appearance versus reality. Who are you? What are you"

He raised his head and looked at the dreary fluorescence reflecting the dull sheen
of his mind's calculations. "What would William Blake have said about that?" he asked,
his eyes scanning for a raised hand. There was an older, heavyset woman in the back row
that he hadn't seen before. Dark complexion. Crescent eyes. Glasses. Brassy hair gleam-
ing like a trumpet. Perhaps she was auditing? Perhaps she was a new evaluator?

A young man with dangling rings in his ears answered Harley's question, "Blake
would say we are what we do. We are not what we think, nor what we say. It's what we
actually do that counts. Nothing else."

"Yes," agreed Harley. "You are what you do. The actions you take are everything we need to know in order to define you. In Dorian Grey's case, what he did was drink. Gamble. Fornicate. And generally live his life for whatever pleasure was obtainable. The painting alters with the passing years and shows us what Dorian really looks like as he ages. As he dissipates, the painting shows a face full of vice and wickedness. One day in a fit of madness, Dorian stabs the portrait, and in stabbing it he is, in effect, stabbing himself. He is found with a knife through his heart. A bit too melodramatic, you might say, but it was popular in its day."

The brassy-haired woman in back said, "You said Wilde was a comedian."

So she was not here to evaluate him. Evaluators were not allowed to talk. "He was," said Harley. "But he wrote some serious stuff as well. In truth he was a deep thinker. Some of his anecdotes rival the depth of Immanuel Kant in my estimation. For instance, Wilde once told a story about a bird that, if seen by you unawares, flies to hide itself. But if it has seen you first, it imagines that it remains invisible and it won't move. Bird trappers catch it easily. And Wilde said that this bird showed true philosophy because having made you the object of its contemplation it has every right to think you have no independent existence. You're just a thing in its mind. You are what you are, says the bird, merely because I have made you the subject of my thoughts. If I did not see you, you wouldn't exist. All of us create the world through eyes continually interpreting what we're seeing. What you see may not be what I see." Harley's hands swept the air as if erasing his students. "There are thirty of us here. That means there are thirty ways of interpreting the world. Every eye sees differently. Such as the eye is, such is the object."

A voice challenged him: "I don't get it. What's Wilde saying about that bird? That you exist because I look at you? Otherwise you don't exist?"

Harley shrugged and said, "I'm getting off course. I meant to say that Wilde's life was built around the theme of appearance versus reality. He was hiding the reality that he was homosexual. He got married, had children, flirted with women, but he was a closeted gay. He was eventually found out and taken to court and charged with engaging in homosexual practices. He was sent to prison for two years at hard labor. It bankrupted him, ruined his health and nearly killed him. It wasn't so long ago that the same thing could happen to gays in this country. Some states still have laws on their books that punish gays if they're caught in flagrante delicto. You probably won't hear of those laws being enforced, but they're there. For the soft palms of the artist, hard labor in prison would be, and was, an excruciating experience. While in prison, however, Wilde managed to write an essay about what had happened to him. Hands down it is one of the greatest essays ever written in English. It's called 'De Profundis,' translated as 'Out of the Deep.' It's an extremely bitter cry of wretchedness and suffering. He also wrote a long poem about prison. 'The Ballad of Reading Gaol.' It's a self-pitying piece about a prisoner sentenced to hang for murdering his beloved. The poem says that each man kills the thing he loves. The coward does it with a kiss/The brave man with a sword.'"

Harley hesitated a moment, the pitiful face of his wife materializing before him. *We kill the things we love.*

Again his mind wandered. Again his students were looking concerned.

"Sir?"

"Yes, well when Wilde got out of prison, he moved to Paris, where he died three years later in despair. And yet he could still be funny on occasion. One of the last things he said as he was dying was: 'Either that wallpaper has to go or I do.'"

The class burst into laughter.

"When they asked him where he wanted to be buried he said: 'It doesn't matter. Posterity will find me.'"

More laughter. Discerning minds: a reason for optimism.

Harley spent the rest of the hour talking about Wilde's trial, telling the class about how he fell in love with Alfred Douglas, whose father was the Marquis of Queensbury, the same Queensbury who wrote the rules for prizefighting, and also wrote nasty letters to newspapers denouncing Wilde.

"Alfred Douglas insisted that Wilde sue Queensbury. Wilde didn't want to sue, but Douglas goaded him into it. Big mistake. Wilde lost in court and was countersued for being homosexual. Oscar lost that battle too and his lover abandoned him."

"What a jerk," a student said. Others nodding in agreement.

"All right then," said Harley, "on that note we'll end this. Next time we'll dive into Wilde's masterpiece, *The Importance of Being Earnest.* Be sure you read it before you come to class."

•

The woman whom Harley spotted earlier approached him as he was closing his briefcase. Up close she looked to be in her sixties, maybe seventy. She was stout, her chest, waist, legs a formidable column.

"I hope it's all right I sat in today," she said.

"No problem. I assume you're an Oscar Wilde fan."

"Heaven forbid. In my opinion that filthy man got what he deserved. I have no sympathy for him."

Harley winced and turned towards the windows, the light.

"A man like that with his mind in the gutter," she added.

"'We are all in the gutter, but some of us are looking at the stars.'"

"That doesn't excuse anything," she said.

"Very true, ma'am. So, how may I help you?"

"I'm Helen Godunov," she said. "Didi's mother."

Harley felt dizzy. He leaned against the table to steady himself. "Didi's mother," he managed to say, his voice breathless, "how good to meet you at last. Yes, I can see her in you now. The eyes."

"Not a bit." Mrs. Godunov's tone was brusque; it was saying: don't try to kiss up. Her nose was long and thin, like Didi's nose. "Is there somewhere we can talk?"

He noticed her fingers slightly trembling and she kept blinking rapidly, like someone lying. Or overly nervous. Yes, nervous as hell and trying to hide it. The thought gave him comfort. "My office," he said.

They walked down the hall. He held the door for her and gestured to a chair. As she walked by him he smelled something sweet.

Cinnamon. A baked cinnamon roll.

He sat behind his desk. The barrier of the desk between them was reassuring. He had no idea what to say. Her eyes behind black-rimmed glasses drilled him.

Her bottom teeth thrusting forward aggressively, she said, "Didi generally has a mind of her own, but sometimes she's easily led, especially by men like you."

"Like me?"

"Intellectuals. Professionals. Men who have succeeded in life. Smart men. Her husband was a doctor when she met him. You happen to be a professor-writer. Reflected glory, that's what she sees in you. No doubt she thinks you know it all."

"Reflected glory?" mused Harley. He wanted to laugh but didn't dare.

"Men like you can lead her astray. I've seen it before."

"I didn't lead Didi astray, Mrs. Godunov. She came to me and—"

"Of course you would say that. It doesn't matter. What matters is what you're up to. I take it you're not going to divorce your wife and marry my daughter."

He murmured, "That's our business."

"No, she's my daughter, so it's my business, too."

"Your forty-seven-years daughter. At forty-seven you're allowed to live as you like."

Her eyes squinted. She had a cynic's mouth. It was hard to imagine those lips being kissed passionately. Impossible to see her tongue probing a man's mouth. Everything about her said: *life has done me wrong, but I'm tough as nails. I can take it.*

"Mr. Olsen, you're no good for her. You're, in fact, very bad for her. The children need her. Her husband needs her. He's a good man, the best. He's been our doctor for over twenty-five years and has treated us like gold. Never a discouraging word. My daughter was wild in her youth, incredibly stupid. Fluff for brains. Promiscuous, did she tell you?"

Harley nodded. Waiting for her to continue.

"She was lucky to land him. He's a kind, forgiving person. He knows what's she's done and he forgives and forgets. How many men do you know who would do that? Most would hold her past against her. He doesn't."

What Helen Godunov was saying was far from what Didi had told Harley. He thought about telling Mrs. Godunov another side of the story. He bit his lip instead.

Meanwhile, Mrs. Godunov kept blathering: "If you would go away, she would go back to him and her children. Think of them. Think of what's best for Didi. I bet you're always selfish. You look selfish. I can see it in your face. Everything about you says selfish."

"Ex."

"What?"

"He's her ex-husband. They're divorced now. And the 'children' as you call them are grown and about to graduate college."

"You think you know it all."

"I'm not young enough to know it all." Again he stifled a laugh.

"That's another point, Mr. Olsen, you're too old for her. Have you ever thought about how she'll cope when time has its way with you and you start looking the way you feel?"

"I'm only thirteen years older than Didi, and I feel fine, Mrs. Godunov."

"No you don't. Go look in the mirror."

"Okay, actually I have thought about that. I think about it quite a lot."

"You look like a heart attack waiting to happen. A stroke in progress. Maybe cancer. Cancer is rampant. Millions of people have it. My husband died of it. Chances are you'll get it and you'll be leaning on her when she's still young enough to find someone else, a permanent partner to grow old with. But she'll be stuck with you, an old, married cheater, and an invalid."

"Are there such things these days? Permanent partners?"

Helen Godunov rolled her eyes, her thick lenses magnifying the gesture. He could see the same fire in her that he saw in her daughter when she got angry or excited. "What do you think she'll do when you start stumbling? You want the real story? I know her and I'll tell you what she'll do. She'll drop you like a hot rock and find someone who can keep up with her."

"You could be right."

"I am right. She'll put up a good front for a while, but then look out."

Of course Harley thought about it often, the gap in their ages that might become a huge liability later. Days come, days go. Nothing to do about it. And at some unknown point your body gives in. Increments of time eating you bit by bit. Yeah, he had thought about it a lot.

"Time," he whispered.

"So, you understand what I'm saying."

"Of course. But, Mrs. Godunov, it's really up to Didi if she wants to return to her ex and her children. I would never stop her. She knows that."

"You're being alive stops her, Mr. Olsen."

The smell of the cinnamon roll made Harley feel sick to his stomach, but he endeavored to look amused, hoping to get a smile out of Mrs. Godunov. "You want me to kill myself?"

She scowled. "I'm not saying that, but who other than Didi would care if you did?"

He knew it was a fair question. Who would cry for him? His sister, maybe. "And you think Didi would go back to him then?"

"What else could she do? He's there with open arms. He's waiting. I've talked to him. He forgives her. You're standing in the way of her future. Believe me I know what it's like to get older and to be looking at a world where no one but your spouse and your children give a damn about you. Everyone else has written you off. You'll get there, Mr. Olsen, if you're not there already."

"I have no one but Didi. All bridges burned, Mrs. Godunov." His hands gestured feebly.

Helen Godunov closed her eyes a moment. When she opened them her face had softened, the mouth no longer looking bitter, the penetrating gaze replaced by what … what … shades of sorrow? The memory of her dead husband, possibly. Harley knew she had suffered, too. Who gets through life without suffering? Without loss? Without huge, life-altering blunders?

"I can see you're not a bad man," she said leaning back in the chair. Her breasts sheathed in black satin rested like dark moles on her belly. Harley envisioned Didi's breasts sagging sadly like her mother's. The wide hips, thick waist, the oval face with its warrior's crown of brittle hair. "I'm going to level with you, Professor Olsen I need help. I need Didi to go home and take care of him.

"Otherwise, you won't be able to walk away. Have I got that right?"

"A mind reader, too. Listen, I endured plenty caring for my husband, easing him out of this world. Yeah, I don't want this. I don't mind pitching in here and there, but I'm doing a full-time job of mothering him. It's not fair. I'm old and I'm tired."

"Didi told me you're the strongest woman she's ever known."

"The strength she's talking about is pouring out of me by the bucket. Taking care of him is killing me."

"Does he really need mothering? What's wrong with him?"

"He's helpless at home. Before his mother died this year, she did everything for him. She cleaned. She cooked. She washed his clothes. She even filled his refrigerator. When Didi married him, she stayed out of the way and let the old woman continue babying him. He can't boil an egg. He eats TV dinners. When the old lady passed, he turned to me. I felt sorry for him, so I took up where she left off. But I got my own life to run. I'm tired. I'm exhausted, can't you see that?"

"You still look formidable."

"Looks can be deceiving. You're sitting there on the outside. What do you know about me? Only I know about me. And I know I'm exhausted." Trembling fingers brushed across her cheek.

"I'm sorry." Harley hesitated. Then asked, "When the kids finish with college won't they come home and help?"

"They might, but I doubt it."

"So sorry," says Harley.

"No you're not. You don't know what it's like to take this on at my age."

"Actually, maybe I do. I spent two decades married to a woman who had everything from arthritis to cancer. There were many times I expected her to die, but she didn't. It was a gloomy, wearing experience. So I may know something of what you're feeling."

"This woman, your wife, you have compassion for her, but if you had really loved her, you wouldn't have walked out, you wouldn't have abandoned her for Didi."

"Maybe so. But I did love her. I still do. Why not? It takes a simple mind to believe we cannot love more than one person at a time. No, I still love my wife, just not in the same way or degree that I love your daughter."

"Perversion."

"No."

"A way to soothe your conscience."

Harley averted his gaze. And thought: *this old bitch might be right.*

She stood abruptly. Turned to the shelves of books lining the walls. "I expected a man who would be easy to hate. But you're more to be pitied. You're so weak. I can see it in your eyes how weak you are. You have kind eyes, nice to look at, but your kindness is the kindness of ill health."

"I used to be strong, Helen. I used to be … invincible."

She stared hard at him, as if trying to see the shadows of his strength beneath the frailty. He thought of how often lately he had seen what she was talking about, the same defects, the same lack of character at his core. Oh, to be noble, wise, full of integrity, full of courage. Oh, to be *good.*

Her continuously trembling hand (common tremor? Parkinson's? exhaustion?) ran over a row of books as she inquired, "Have you read all of these?"

"I'm a liar if I say I have."

"How many?"

"Maybe half. I don't know."

"What's this one about?" She slid out *Anna Karenina.*

The mother of bookworm poet Didi didn't know *Anna Karenina*? Or maybe she did know and wanted him to say what he was about to say: "That's about a married woman who has an affair that ends badly, so she kills herself."

"Yes, it can come to that. The mistakes we make eventually destroy us. Which is what will happen to both of you if you don't reverse course. You think your love is strong enough to handle it, but you're wrong. When the world comes crashing down on your heads, you'll have no one but each other. And believe me each other won't be enough. Under pressure you broke and ran and you'll break and run again. Didi will too. I know her. Neither of you is built to last."

"Are you?" Harley asked her. "Is anyone?"

She gave him a scathing look. "I've done exactly that, mister. There were times I wanted to leave, but I stuck it out. I stayed to the bitter end. There were temptations, believe me, but I refused to give in to them. I had a responsibility. I knew my duty." Her chin jutted stubbornly. She continued blinking. Blinking and blinking. Hand trembling. "When my husband was dying I didn't budge, I didn't run, I didn't whine, I didn't grumble. That's what I'm made of. What are you made of, Olsen? I think we've answered that."

Harley recalled Didi telling him her suspicions about her mother having an affair years ago with a younger man next door named … was it Peter? Did Peter matter now? What would Wilde say? *Most people are other people.*

"Have you ever been frozen by love, Helen?"

"What do you mean by frozen? What does frozen by love mean?"

"Made helpless. Made powerless. Unable to do anything but follow your heart."

She regarded him a long while as if she was anatomizing him. Finally she said, "How old is Harley Olsen?"

"Sixty."

"Sixty," she repeated softly. "Nearly the same age now as a man I used to know when he was hardly more than a boy. The only boy who had ever made me feel powerless."

"You loved him."

"I guess it was love. Do we ever get over a love like that? It wasn't pure, but it was very intense. Young, full of fire." She paused smiling, ran her shaky hand over the spines of the books in front of her. "Those who can, they go their own way. It takes guts. You have to be willing to pay the price. Nobody gets it for free. You understand that, don't you."

Harley nodded. He could tell her what his love for Didi was doing to him and maybe win her sympathy. But he won't. His mind felt infinitely weary.

"What's this book about?" She held up *The Executioner's Song.*

"I don't know," he said. He knew, but he didn't want to talk anymore. He wanted her to leave.

"So you don't know everything after all."

"I told you I'm not young enough to know everything." He offered her a tentative smile.

Her tone became contemptuous again: "So polite. You sit there with your sad face wanting me to feel sorry for you, but I feel sorry for Danny without his wife to lean on. If you really loved her, you would find a way to make her go home again. I'm amazed he would take her back after all this time, but he's a man with a big heart, and he's willing to give her another chance. Do you know why? Because children, no matter how old they are, need their mother. Look how screwed up this country is because mothers run off with the likes of *you*. Women's liberation is for damn fools."

"Actually, I agree," said Harley. "But there's nothing much you or I can do about it. As for Didi's kids, I truly wish she hadn't left them and that nothing had happened between us. But wish in one hand and spit in the other. See which one gets full faster. Look, I had nothing to do with Didi leaving her family. She had done that at least a year before I dated her."

"But she did it for you. Whether you know it or not, you're the ultimate reason. After she moved out of her house, I went to the apartment she rented and you know what I saw? I saw you. She had your picture on her nightstand. And all your books lined up. Let me tell you something about my daughter. Once she sets her mind to something, there's no stopping her. She's patient and she's cunning and she knows how to manipulate people. I know in my heart of hearts that when she left her husband, you were already in her sights. I bet you didn't know what hit you when she came along."

"If she's the way you say she is, then what's the use of telling me to let her go? Even if I broke it off, that doesn't mean she would go back to her ex. She's strong. What she would do is move on. I don't know why you don't understand she would never go back."

"You're wrong. She would go back. You know why? Because a broken heart changes a person. Broken-hearted people need others. She would go back, believe me. With you out of the way, Didi would need the support and love of her family. Of all of us. There would be a vacuum in her life and we would fill it. But first, you have to vanish. As I said before, if you loved her you would do what I say. Staying with her is being selfish and there will come a time when both of you will regret it. Be big, Mr. Olsen, for once in your life."

Be big, Mr. Olsen?

•

After she left his office, he kept repeating her words, trying to see himself as being big. But he was not big. In no way big. Not big-brained, big-hearted, big-souled, big-cocked. Only in bigness of blunder did he measure up to her words. A bigness that thrived on remorse. The need for atonement. He should have been born a Jew, perhaps.

"I've taken on more than I can handle," he realized. "Lost my ... my focus. My concentration. Betrayed my ... yes, because living is a roll of the dice."

A long illness.

Punishment.

Delusion.

What did that professor on the CD say: "Illicit love is full of comic possibilities."

Out the window Harley saw a convoy of army trucks moving west. Heading for the coast? To embark on a ship? Or do they fly the equipment there to that sad, endless war?

The question that trumped all others was: could he live without her? He leaned his head against the windowpane and tried to imagine life without Didi: no more dinners at sunset, a bottle of wine and conversation that stimulated while it soothed. To live alone in his condo without her, without Didi, without her chatter, her laughter. No more cuddling in bed, no more love-making, no more mouth covering his own as if siphoning water from a life-giving well. Was there anyone who could take her place? Would nature and luck ever send another Didi? Not at his age. Could he survive the loss, the shredding of his heart in such a way? His thoughts went back to the morning in bed lying next to her: how he had wanted to get up, get away. Put distance between them. But now it seemed he had changed his mind. For all they had done, for all the pain they've caused others there will be no forgiveness. Harley knew he would keep paying.

But he was willing. Let it all go to hell as long as he and Didi were together. He glanced at his watch. Two minutes until class. Next up: Shakespeare's tale told by an idiot.

9 - A Man's Touch

Friday. She leaves work at four and drives to the clinic. Waits in the waiting room. Leafing through a magazine called *Allure*, she studies pictures of models looking too flawless to be real. She wishes she could look like them. Have this one's wavy hair. This one's flat tummy with the ring piercing her navel. This one's ass is to die for and so are her legs. Scrumptious. Another one has the best breasts—medium-sized, perky, not needing a bra to get uplift. But whose face is best? I'll have her tilted nose. Her fine cheekbones. Her come-kiss me mouth. Her pearly teeth. Her Oriental eyes, ain't they sexy? Her impish chin. Her alabaster skin. Her swan's neck. Put me together and what do you have? A woman that men would fight for. A woman that other women would try to replicate by going to plastic surgeons and showing Franny's picture and saying, This is what I want.

"Francis Olsen?" the nurse calls.

Franny struggles to her feet. Gimps across the floor. Follows the nurse down the hall. The nurse weighs her and congratulates her for losing eleven more pounds. Next Franny is taken to the exam room. She undresses. Keeps her socks on. Slips into a gown. Tying the strings behind her neck. Letting the rest hang open. Who cares if her chubby butt shows? She's been going to Dr. Gold for twenty years. He's seen every inch of her, so what's the big deal.

The doctor enters. His sad Jewish eyes fixing on her. Overhead lights give luster to his bald pate. The file in his hands is six-inches thick.

"Golly, I just noticed how thick it is," she says.

"What's that, Franny?"

"My file, Dr. Gold. Look at all those pages."

"So how are you doing, Franny? Staying on the diet?"

"I've lost eleven more pounds. I bought a stationary bike. It doesn't hurt that much to pedal. Yeah, so I'm riding religiously thirty minutes every day."

Holding his chin between his thumb and forefinger, Dr. Gold studies her face. "How many years were you together, Franny?"

"Twenty-three. It's been three years since he left permanently. I didn't want anyone to know. I mean, I thought it was a phase, a mid-life crisis. I thought he'd come back." Franny looks away. There's a constriction in her throat and she can't trust herself to talk.

"That's quite a number of years. So sorry to hear it. Most couples if they get past the twenty-five year mark, they stay together. But people are changing. That sense of commitment is not what it used to be. I see it a lot these days."

Franny nods. Clears her throat. "I felt it coming, you know. Harley was unhappy, so melancholy all the time. He never laughed anymore. I don't think I've heard him laugh for probably a decade. I think my chronic illnesses wore him down. In sickness and in health, huh? Don't believe it." She smiles sadly. Sad for Harley. Sad for herself.

"You seem to be handling things."

Franny clears her throat again and shrugs. "You know how it is. I got my good days and I got my bad days. Losing weight and exercising helps my attitude. Harley was always after me to exercise and I was always using my bad health as an excuse not to. I should have made the effort while he was still around." Franny chuckles weakly. She feels heat in her ears, heat in her cheeks spreading through her neck.

"You certainly look better," the doctor says. "How are the pains in your feet and knees?"

"Still there, but not quite as bad as they were. Losing weight has definitely helped, but I've still got lots of problems."

"Such as?"

She warms to the subject, meticulously detailing this symptom and that pain, pointing each one out, starting with her headaches, right down to the pains in the joints of her toes. She ends with a deep sigh over how overwhelmingly exhausted she is.

She doesn't want to forget anything. Maybe the combination will make something click in his mind and he'll have an inspiration about how to cure her for good. Lay your hands on, doctor, make me well, make me whole, make me young. Make me cute. Like I was when I was a child and stuck a bean up my nose and couldn't get it out. Until my father tickled my nostrils with a feather and made me sneeze. Ping! He laughed. Laughed harder than he ever did before. Or after. He was like Harley, hardly ever laughing, so moody, so grumpy. When Pa laughed it was memorable. Skin and bones crumpling now. An ocean of earth pressing him down. I wish I missed you, Pa. But nope. You were always on my ass about something. You didn't like me. Your nickname for me was *Fluff for brains.*

"No energy, hmm, yes, that happens," Dr. Gold was saying. "Your chronic anemia. Giving you iron supplements wouldn't do any good. I'm not sure about another transfusion. There's always a risk. Didn't we talk about this already?" As he talks he's scanning a page in her file.

"You told me to eat more spinach and not increase the folic acid because too much of it could harm me, but the amount I'm taking will help my liver, you said. Yes, but the thing is I'm still exhausted, doctor. I wake up exhausted. I can hardly get through my day." She shakes her head mournfully.

"Hmm, yes, depression. I gave you something for that, didn't I?" He keeps flipping pages, his eyes scanning.

"Zoloft. You know what Harley said? Harley said that if you have to choose,

choose quality of life over quantity. I'll risk another transfusion."

"Is that how you feel, Franny?"

"Yes. Well, maybe. I'm closing in on fifty-three, you know, and … well, I just wish I could have one day full of energy without pain, the way I was when I was twenty. Believe it or not I used to be cute. Real cute. Too cute, my pa always said."

She looks for a reaction from Dr. Gold, a smile a wink, but he won't oblige her. He continues to study her file. "We could put you on prednisone for a while. See how that works. How are Ruth and Judy by the way? How's Colleen?"

"You should see Judy. She's been doing water aerobics and looks deeevine. I'm going to start doing them with her. I just have to find time. She's got her diabetes under control. Ruthie had another flare up, but I guess you know about that. You changed her medication."

"Did I? So it's working?"

"It's working. And Mama is good. She says she's used to the retirement home now. She's cheerful. She loves to play bingo and do exercises and sing and dance with the other old people. She gets around. We have lunch or dinner at least once a month. We take turns, me and Judy and Ruthie."

What Franny says about the health of her sisters are basically fibs. Judy's diabetes is still up and down and she can't keep the weight off, though God knows she tries. Ruthie's breath is labored and always rattles. Her ulcers burn. Colleen hates being in the home, and Franny has been feeling guilty that she hasn't suggested Colleen come live with her now that Harley seems to be gone for good. Franny doesn't know why she is lying so blithely. Lying has always been her default setting. Maybe she's doing it to make the doctor feel good. Make him believe in himself. Doctors don't want patients they can't help. It makes them feel … inadequate.

Dr. Gold says, "So, have you been feeling more blue than usual, Franny? Is the Zoloft working at all?"

"No. Yes, I guess it's working. Some days are downers, though. Depends on the pain. Good days, bad days as I said."

He has Franny lie back on the table. He palpates her neck, her armpits, her groin, the areas around her breasts where tumors might be lurking. His man hands are warm, strong, satisfying. She recalls Dr. Zimmer, how arousing his hands were when she was a nineteen-year-old flirt. A man's hands should always feel like Dr. Zimmer's hands. Gentle but firm, yes. She closes her eyes. Falls under Dr. Gold's spell. He probes her stomach. Probes her bowels.

"Is this tender?"

"No, doctor."

"This?"

"No, doctor."

"Everything seems to be in order."

His touch works magic. Absolutely nothing hurts for the moment. She wishes he wouldn't stop. But finally he does. He sits her up. Listens to her lungs and tells her she is in pretty good shape for someone with so many problems. As for the sciatic nerve—"Just stay off that leg as much as you can when it hurts. You might try sitting on a heat pad while you watch TV or while you're reading. Sometimes ice is better. Everyone is different. You never know what will work. Take baths in Epsom salts."

"I do," she says.

"We could up the Celebrex. Take one more a day."

"It's killing my stomach. I knew it would."

"We'll change to Bextra."

"It's off the market."

"That's right, it is." Dr. Gold sighs. "They keep reducing our arsenal. You can bet none of them have rheumatoid arthritis."

Them?

The warmth of his touch, the well-being, healing-feeling vanishes. For the first time today, Franny feels totally hopeless. She wishes she hadn't come. But she smiles bravely, he smiling back at her, patting her hand. Good man, but she wouldn't want to make love to him. Dr. Zimmer was different. So handsome and young, so confident, so able. If he had wanted to, she most definitely would have.

"Just give me a second," Dr. Gold says, sitting on the stool, writing a prescription for prednisone.

Her mind rushes back to her father and the feather tickling her nose, the sneeze building. And the sun shining through the kitchen window. And her mother's worried look. And her sisters squealing when the bean shot out like a bullet ping! Franny wants to go back there. Even though people say you can't go home again, Franny wants to go anyway. Why not try it? What's stopping her?

Get real, Franny. Some other family lives there now. Your pa is long dead. Mama lives in the home. She watches TV, plays bingo, and growls, and orders the nurses around. That's how she was when you were little. She was the queen. She ruled the roost, always told you what to do. Wouldn't it be a relief if there was someone running your life and making it so you didn't have to think for yourself?

Harley. Harley used to.

For a time Harley was your crutch, but it's your own gimpy feet now, girl. Up to you, baby, no one to lean on. She sniffs. Rubs her eyes. Clears her throat for the umpteenth time.

Franny, don't you dare start crying.

10 - Mothers & Lovers

Comes Friday and Didi's time to meet her mother for dinner at Mimi's Cafe in Mira Mesa. On the way to Mimi's, she listens to a $29.95 CD, a lecture called The Art of Happiness. The speaker is His Holiness the Dali Lama. The CD contains meditations telling her how to ease angst, master insecurity, control anger and fear and hate. How not to give into life's letdowns-frustrations-defeats. His Holiness telling her to ride through life's obstacles on a deep source of inner peace. Empty your mind. Quit cataloging nonsense. Don't listen to drivel.

Pulling into the lot, she hears an alarm. Coincidence, of course. People annoyed because of the noise. A man saying, "Those things are fucking useless." A chirp follows. Alarm silenced. Cars creeping by, owners searching for parking spots. Wind shivering leaves loose from winter-gnawed twigs. The leaves twirling like Frisbees. The chilly air tightening her face. Breathing deeply: lungs feeling larger, she tells herself it is good to feel good. Good to feel calm. Thank you, Your Holiness. She fluffs her pale hair, checks for dark roots in the rearview mirror. Very faint, but maybe it's time for a touch up. She runs her palms down her slim neck to her ample breasts, her alluring waist and hips. How sweet to feel succulent.

●

Didi has been throwing up a lot. Purging. Also, she has a nervous tummy. Anxiety: about her ex-husband and their two kids, whom she hardly ever sees these days. But they're on her mind, perhaps more than is healthy, especially her son and daughter, although they're both in college, sufficiently adult and independent and don't really need her. She knew within six months she had made a mistake marrying their father, but she hung in there, stayed to raise them. Isn't that enough? For twenty years she let her husband drive her crazy. But now she has her own life to live. She has a soul mate. Well, maybe not a soul mate. Poor Harley is looking so old these days.

He can't help it. It's a heart condition. Stubborn man won't have the operation that would probably fix it. Didi doesn't know if she can stand it much longer. Love affairs can kill you. Yes, especially if your man isn't much of a man anymore and your mother vehemently disapproves of his and your behavior.

Didi, how could you?

Love is its own excuse, Mom.

She has already been dropped off by the courtesy bus and is sitting on a bench near the entrance waving, calling out "Didi, Didi! Yoo-hoo!"

"Mommy!"

"Baby!"

They hug kiss look eye-to-eye searching for disguises. "You're too thin," Helen says. "This much thin is not good. You need reserves to fall back on. You should get a reduction. You know breasts like yours will eventually make you round-shouldered."

"So you've told me, Mommy. I exercise like mad and keep my back strong, my spine is straight as an arrow."

"Wait till you're older, you'll see."

Didi rolls her eyes, shrugs and doesn't say how fat her mother looks. Beefy shoulders, matronly breasts. Her coat can't conceal how bloated the old girl's hips are. Glittering hair clapped on her head like a bronze tiara. Makeup doesn't obscure the sagging grooves beneath her eyes. A faint mustache, a pair of chin hairs stiffly white. Baggy jowls. A wattle.

Will I look like her when I'm seventy?

Jesus, Didi, don't think about it. You're only forty-seven .

Leaves scuttle behind them as they enter the café. The place is very cozy. The design and decor make Didi think of a Hobbit's hovel. They are seated at one of the window tables looking out on neatly trimmed bushes, a grass lawn, the sidewalk, the street, the stop and go traffic. Everywhere neon lights are beckoning.

Didi thinks of how Christmas had long ago lost its appeal. And what a relief it is now not having to deal with family gatherings, noisy relatives, rambunctious children, the preparation of all that damn food. And the cleaning up after. No more, no more. For the last three years she and Harley have celebrated the day by eating out. Home in bed snuggling by ten.

•

Behind thick lenses Helen's eyes are busy. The glasses sliding down her nose. She pushing them up and saying, "Too crowded. Look at them. Like ants crawling all over the mall. Look at the cars. Where they going, I wonder?" Her voice has changed with age. "Baritone gargle," Harley had called it. It's annoying how she keeps clearing her throat—it's an old age thing. When she talks her bottom teeth protrude. Seeming almost to float. Upper teeth hidden behind a pendulous lip.

"Well, how have you been, Didi? I've been missing my baby. You hardly ever call and all I get when I call you is that stupid machine. Whoever invented those things should be shot. I see you once a month. I don't see why we can't all meet here every Friday. I'm not going to be around forever, you know."

"Everyone is incredibly busy, Mom. Can't believe how busy we are. I hit the ground running every morning and don't stop until it's time for bed. Worn to a frazzle."

"You do look tired. Tired and skinny."

"I'm not skinny. Men still whistle at me."

"You're losing too much weight. What's wrong with you?"

"Nothing. Just tired."

Helen squints as if threading a needle. "I bet you don't weigh more than a hundred pounds," she says.

"A hundred and thirty, Mom."

"I don't remember your forehead full of worry wrinkles. How old are you now? Looking upwards she says, "Yeah, you're forty. Or is it forty-one? My baby has passed the mid-point according to the Bible. How did that happen? Where'd the time go?"

"Forty-seven, Mom."

"Baby Didi forty-seven." Wistfully, Helen shakes her head and wistfully says, "The fifties are tough. But not as tough as sixty, mind you. By seventy even the government admits you're too old for anything useful. Wants you to go live in old people's prisons, gated communities. Play golf. Take dance lessons. Do pool aerobics. Keep a lap dog for company. Watch TV and sleep. I do that a lot, my eyes close and an hour vanishes. Wait until you're my age, you'll see." When she laughs her teeth look volatile.

Didi cringes.

"Seventy the new sixty," she tells her mother.

Helen makes a sour face. "Don't you believe it, baby. People want to believe that shit, but it's twaddle. If I had better eyes I'd see the Grim Reaper beckoning. I see him in my dreams. I dream a lot about snakes, too. Wonder what snakes mean in dreams. Phallic symbol, you think?"

•

The waitress, a heavyset woman with flaccid cheeks and a drooping brownish-gray bun on the back of her head says, "Can I get you something to drink, ladies?" She hands out menus. They order drinks, a vodka martini for Didi, hot tea with lemon for Helen. As the waitress walks away, Didi notes she is wearing sandals with socks. Her ankles thick as her calves. Waterlogged.

Count your blessings, my girl, that could be you.

"It's not can, it's may," says Helen.

"What?"

"It's may I get you something to drink, ladies? Nobody knows grammar anymore. Nobody knows nothin but nothin when it comes to proper English."

Mother and daughter survey the menus. The silence is heavy.

"Harley has severe heart problems," Didi blurts.

Subdued shaking of her head, "I'm sorry," Helen says.

"He's losing weight and he's going bald. He said he won't have surgery. Rather die, he says. And he says, 'Let nature have its way.' They're giving him digitalis and nitro.

Imagine that, Harley with heart failure and he's only sixty."

"Such a big problem for one so young. Sixty you say?"

"Sixty-one in four months, actually."

"You reap what you sow."

"Harley is a good man. Don't dis him, Mom. He told me all about your visit to his classroom." Didi raises her palm, showing it like a wall to her mother. "Don't talk about it. I know all I want to know."

Helen smiles and says, "I've always been healthy as a horse. Clean living, you know? I don't even catch colds. Well, hardly ever. Daddy never caught colds. First time he gets sick and what does he get?" She pauses to take a bite out of the air. "Prostate cancer is flourishing. Yeah, flourishing same as breast cancer. Your grandmother never knew how lucky she was dying in her sleep that way. Not a second of torment. I mean she died too young, but at least she didn't have to deal with months of torture and chemo. That stuff is literally poison. Ugh, how terrible. Uncivilized. Vicious. Finally Daddy said no more. Turn on the Padres and give me morphine to ease the pain. That's what he told the doctor. No more operations, no more chemo. He was ready to go. Your daddy died with dignity. A brave man. You know what he told me before he went to sleep? He said, 'Helen, it's all been gravy.' His exact words. And then he napped. And then he died." She snaps her fingers and adds, "Just like that."

The two women have had this same conversation at least a dozen times already. Didi recalls rushing from San Diego to Poway to say goodbye to her father. The wasted body. The hollow eyes. But no fear in those eyes. Not a bit. He even laughed at not being able to stand up by himself. When he let her help him, all she felt were loose skin and tiny bones. Like lifting a sack of sticks—balsawood.

"Well, after all," says Helen, "here's a man who had been through two tours in Vietnam, right in the thick of things. Here's a man who faced death day after day and never flinched. And he came back without a scratch. He told me he fully expected to die over there. Out of his company, only eight men survived. He never understood why he was spared. The rest has all been gravy he kept saying. That was Daddy for you. A man's man to the end."

"Yes, I always admired Daddy as a man, Didi tells her.

Also remembering: what black hours, what head-trip horrors when someone you know dies and your own mortality opens its eyes. Strong, silent type, my father. Doubt I'll be that stoic when my turn comes. His dead face will haunt me forever. That inanimate skull, its waxy skin saying this is you one day, daughter.

"Even though he didn't much like me I liked him, Mom," she says. Also thinking: Waiting for him to die. Not wanting it. Wanting it.

"Well, it was all the trouble you caused. It made Daddy mad. He didn't understand why you couldn't behave. He never got over your leaving the faith and marrying Danny. He never understood it. Daddy knew Danny wasn't the right man for you."

"Because he wasn't Catholic."

"You married a Jehovah Witness, Didi."

"I don't want to go there again," Didi says. And then she goes there: "I shouldn't have married him, I know that now. I was young and had shit for brains. Two-thirds idiot, one-third moron. We couldn't have been more wrong for each other. However nice he is now, however pitiful he is, he was rotten and unfaithful to me for at least half the twenty years we lived under the same roof. God, I'm glad I got out."

•

The waitress hobbles back with their drinks and takes their orders: tomato bisque soup with sourdough roll for Helen; Cobb salad with garlic bread for Didi.

Background music is benignly neutral. Possibly Bach. She listens while sipping her martini, its fumes fumigating Dr. Danny Walker, dissolving him. She watches Helen stirring her tea, adding sugar and lemon, bottom lip hanging, wattle wobbling, chin receding.

How young and fresh she used to be.

Also thinking: I have that same oval face, long thin nose (though not as prominent as hers—age does that), almond eyes. The curly hair she keeps short used to hang on her shoulders like mine. Now she's no fuss. When you get old the last thing you want is fuss, she told me. At my age she was curvy as a stripper. She had better breasts than mine, but now look at how they sag, ugh, and that bulging waist and those short, fat legs. She could be mistaken for a five foot five fireplug.

•

When Didi was seventeen she had watched her mother strolling along the beach at Wind and Sea in her one-piece bathing suit, male gazes turning her way, and Didi thought how lucky Daddy was to have such a beautiful wife. And for well over forty years the two of them aging together, visibly declining but still in love. Cold father, but a good husband. As far as such lives go, Didi's parents had lucked out, until that last sad year. Didi had wondered what her mother would do with the leftovers. No one to look after her but her daughter. When the time comes to ease Mama out of this world, Didi doesn't know if she's up to it.

Does Helen dread the approach of death? Creeping toward her the way it crept in and stole her husband from her. Yes, of course she dreads it. Joining him in the graveyard. But before that she may have some hell of her own to endure: the frail phase—ripe for osteoarthritis and cancer and God knows what else. Thinning skin transparent as tracing paper. Brittle hair falling out from too many chemical dyes. Bones preparing more and more to announce their presence. Should Didi ask her what she thinks about it? About growing old and dying and what's happening to what used to be her beach-worthy body? You'll find out soon enough, Helen would tell her. And she would put that barrier of teeth between them. It's only since she's gotten older that she grins so much. A smile or a scowl? Hard to tell.

•

The dinners come. Helen sips soup noisily. She tears a roll in half and lathers it in butter. Looking at her daughter as if saying: why not, what the hell do I care about my cholesterol?

When they finish eating, Didi orders another martini. Helen frowns. Drinks more tea. Glaring over the rim of her cup. Showing Didi the familiar compressed brows that mean she's about to get ugly.

"What?" asks Didi.

"Also thinking."

"What?"

"Why do you drink that stuff? Bad conscience?"

"Excuse me?"

"Bad conscience, homewrecker?"

"What the hell?"

"Well, truth's a dog."

"Knock it off. I'm not here for a lecture."

"You never drank those things until you met him, that what's-his-name."

"Not true. I drank them all the time when I was with Danny. It's just around you and Daddy we didn't drink. You're so judgmental."

"Pulling wool over our eyes. Sneaking around."

"Can we change the subject?" Didi is feeling mildly high. She doesn't give two cents about anything her mother says right now.

"Hard liquor kills you early, Didi. You hate yourself enough for that? Quit being so unnatural and go back to your husband, take care of him and quit destroying your organs. God will reward you."

"So *not* gonna happen, Mom. And Danny's not my husband."

"Your Church says he's still your husband. You are living in sin with that … that creature. If you had stayed in the faith, you could go to Confession and be absolved."

Didi downs the second martini and signals the waitress.

•

Warmly inebriated, she can barely trust her tongue. Also thinking she doesn't hate her mother or anyone, not even Danny or Harley's wife Franny.

Helen says, "Break it off, baby. Get out while you still can, while you're still young enough to find someone to grow old with."

"I love him with all my heart. If you only knew him, how kind and generous he is."

"Love? Don't give me love." Again her brow washboards, her bottom teeth thrust. "The word is lust. Let me sum it up. He's bright. A man of the mind. Physically not so appealing anymore, but you're not put off by that, nor that he's decades older than you."

"Hardly more than a decade, Mom. Thirteen years."

Helen ignores her and continues, "Intellectually stimulating, sure. That's a perk, baby. Nice to get perks, but where it happens is between the sheets. Having the hots is not love. Don't give me love. What you've got is too destructive for love."

"What is love for, Mom, if not the perks?"

"Sometimes perks are not enough." She snorts. Adds: "Perks wreck you."

The downside of booze is the crying jag. Didi's eyes filling with tears. "I know you're right, Mom. I know in my heart what I'm doing is stupid and maybe even evil, but I can't imagine living without him. I don't think he can imagine living without me. I've never been so wrapped up in anyone, ever. He . . . he's enlarged my mind."

"Piffle. An obsession is what you got. Obsessions don't allow you to think straight. I know about obsessions."

"He's a good man. But I think this is killing him. He wants to get married. But he can't bring himself to divorce Franny. We're both torn I tell you. It's awful. I actually feel sorry for her. Sorry for Danny too, of course. Last time I saw him, he was miserable. He was confessing all kinds of things. I felt like a priest."

"Wipe your eyes, baby." Helen rattles her cup against the saucer, the noise snapping Didi out of her moment. Light glances off Helen's glasses like mute detonations. Phlegmy voice saying: "I'll tell you something, baby. The reason I never wanted to let you out of the house until you went to college was because I didn't trust you as far as I could throw you. You were willful. You were going to have your way come hell or high water. You did everything you could to manipulate me and your father. It worked when you were younger, but after puberty I had to put my foot down. You're the kind that would have gone out and got herself knocked up. That's why I was so strict with you. Why couldn't you have been more like me and my sister? God rest her soul. Never one day of grief and worry from us as my mother always said. Not when it comes to men, anyway. You, however, you had that look. I'll tell you the truth: IF I could I'd lock you up right now. Look what you're doing with your life. Look what a fool you are. You need to get right with God. Come back to the faith. Cleanse your soul before it's too late. Why can't you be more like me? Where did I go wrong with you?"

•

Swallowing hard, Didi tries to say something withering—fuck the faith, fuck those cocksucking pedophile priests, their stupid useless cannibal communions. Where were the priests when Jews and Gypsies and innocent children were being marched into gas chambers? If the priests stand for anything, it's hate it's suffering it's death. Christ said we should take care of one another, love one another, don't do unto others what you wouldn't have them do to you. That's all you need. Everything else is sanctimonious horseshit.

Naturally she doesn't say any of that. Keeps her mouth shut. Gazes out the window at two burnoose-draped women walking by, taking mincing steps as if their ankles are shackled, their eyes fixed on the concrete waiting to trip them. Didi thinks instantly of terrorism and feels a loathing she doesn't want to feel. Maybe those two women are suicide bombers wrapped in explosives. Could be. Anything's possible. A touch of a button and whoosh, crimson blossoms, bone shrapnel.

How mysterious Muslims are! How incomprehensible. *The Art of Happiness* told her to open her heart. Say yes to everything. Whenever you see people, remember you are seeing another *human* being. Leave your differences aside. Those differences are superficial compared to how alike we really are. Could she ever-ever do what the Dali Lama wants? If she had the power to make all Muslims vanish she would do it in a wink. So barbaric. So scary. She can see it now: a few more years and fury blowing itself to smithereens—nothing left but the husks to bury. The righteous in heaven with Jesus. Every priest and imam in the last ring of hell with Satan.

Helen is staring intensely at her hands, in the dim light her fingers looking crooked, knuckles swollen, digits curving. Old crone hands. Talons.

"What're you thinking, Mom?"

"Hmm? Oh." She winks. A teasing smile creasing her lips. "Well, strange to say I was just remembering that young man who lived next door. He just popped into my mind somehow. A ridiculous memory older than old."

"Alan Peters."

"Yes, Alan. Whatever happened to Alan?"

"Alan moved to L. A. Actually, I heard from him when Daddy died. Out of the blue he phoned me. He wanted to tell me how sorry he was about Daddy. He talked about how much he liked Daddy. How they both loved baseball. How they would go to games and yell at the umpires."

"Daddy's surrogate son."

"He said he was coming down for the funeral."

"He didn't show. Or maybe he was there and I didn't recognize him."

"So many years."

"Is he married?"

"He told me he was in a committed relationship."

"He lives with her?"

"With him, Mom."

Helen's eyelids flutter. "Oh go on, he's about as gay as your father was. I know a man when I see one." She pours more tea. Adds lemon and sugar. "Alan was a fine young man. I didn't mind him coming around. Bit of a flirt, you know. What does he do now?"

"He's a photographer. He owns his own studio. He takes pictures of celebs."

"Well, how about that. Good for him."

"I didn't recognize his voice at all. He must be about fifty-something now."

"People come, people go, people get timeworn."

"What is this leading to?"

"Nothing. It was just a thought." She pauses, stirring her tea. "Did he, by chance, mention me when you talked to him?"

"Mention you?"

"No reason why he should, of course."

"Actually, he did ask how you were doing. He said to say hello. I forgot to tell you."

"Still remembers me. That's nice. He was such a tease."

"What was it he called you? Calendar girl?"

"Pinup girl. He said I was his favorite pinup girl. Can you imagine? What a cheeky kid. Did I ever tell you about the time he took all those pictures? Me in shorts and a halter?"

"Wasn't it something about a magazine contest? He was going to send your picture in."

"That's what he said. I don't know if he ever did. Did he?"

"Beats me," says Didi. "That all happened before I was born."

"That's right. You were a year away."

"Alan said he was eighteen when I was born."

Didi recalls that every picture accentuated her mother's legs and breasts. And Alan wouldn't let her smile. He kept telling her to pout.

"He got you from every angle," Didi tells her. "Those were good pictures for an amateur. I wonder what happened to them. Do you know?"

Helen shakes her head.

"Alan said you were a fine fox. Those legs, he said."

"He said that?" Helen chuckles, shakes her head. Says, "Gosh yes, those were the days. Shapely me. Now look what's happened. Legs are stumps now. Geez, I wouldn't wish it on my worst enemy."

•

As they talk, Didi's mind flashes back to something that occurred when she was about ten years old. A morning when she walked to school as usual, but then realized she didn't feel well and went back home. When she opened the front door, her mother yelled up from the basement, "Who's that?"

"Just me," she answered. "I don't feel so good."

In a hoarse voice her mother said she would be up in a minute. Didi went to her room and flopped on the bed. Heard movement below, a faint pounding as if the washer was out of balance. A few minutes later she heard her mother climbing the stairs, her footsteps faint, tiptoeing. When the front door whispered opened and whispered closed, Didi went to the window. And saw Alan hurrying to his car.

She went into the kitchen. Her mother appeared wearing her robe. She blushed. "I didn't hear you," she said. "You say you feel sick?" She felt Didi's forehead and said, "You're burning with fever. Go straight to bed this instant, young lady."

The robe had sagged open. Didi saw breasts, nipples and all—all of it looking chafed.

•

The ugly knit in Helen's brow is gone. Her eyes have softened. "So tell me, baby. What's the future?"

"The future?"

"Are you still doing real estate? The bottom seems to have fallen out."

"I'm a senior partner now. We're doing fine."

Helen hesitates. She taps her forehead and says, "You know what you should do? You should write about your father. Write about his experiences in war and publish it."

"No one wants to hear about Vietnam, Mom."

"They don't? Why not? It's a timely topic these days. All these horrible wars going on."

"We lost in Vietnam. Who wants to hear about that?"

"Why on earth not? There are lessons to be learned even in defeat. Nothing's been the same for America since that war, you know. It was the turning point in our lives, the life of our nation. This country has been a mess ever since. Politicians! We need to keep a close eye on politicians. They're keeping secrets, you know. They want us to forget the past, so we won't question what they're doing and how they're repeating history and wrecking our country. How can we know where we're going if we don't remember where we've been?"

"We don't want to know," Didi says. "Ignorance is bliss."

"Lazy minds. Lazy souls. Gawkers letting TV run their pointless lives. Football and all that gibberish as if it's life and death. Bah! Maybe you shouldn't write about Daddy after all. They don't deserve him."

With a jerk of her head, she settles it, she settles them, whoever they are. The puddin-headed masses that don't want to know about her dead husband's sacrifices. Contempt for them long ago nested in her heart.

Didi feels immensely glum. Everything going to hell. She scrutinizes her mother. Her face a portrait of disgust. In the background a waltz is playing. There is a framed mist-hanging-over-mountain-lake on the wall above Helen's head.

Peaceful. So promising.

"He loved sports," Didi offers.

"What? Daddy?" Helen shakes her head. "Had nothing to give him but disillusionment. Those damn San Diego Padres. Those losers."

"I bet we all die disillusioned, Mom."

"Take a look around, baby. Everything is spoiled. We're killing our country as fast as we can. This President is a sociopath."

The low murmur in the restaurant is shattered by some woman's shrill laughter.

Helen frowns. "Another ignoramus," she says.

"Do you believe in an afterlife, Mom?"

"An afterlife? You know I do. Otherwise, what's the point?"

"Is it a Catholic afterlife? Or an afterlife for all faiths?"

"Sure it is. A place for Good people." Stroking her chin, eyes gazing upward, "Hmm," she hums, "hmm, well, sort of. I've been reading … books. Reading how it's all connected. One vast spiritual universe that can be seen if we only train that side of our soul. The third eye self, you see? The self that sees the other dimension. Daddy's there. Mother, my sister, my Auntie Aud, Grandpa, Grandma. With training we can see them. Meditation." She places her finger between her eyes. And says, "Right here, this is the place."

"What?"

"The home of the third eye."

Helen the mystic? "You really—"

Before Didi can say, You really believe there's a third eye, her words are smothered by Helen glancing at her watch and blurting. "Got to go. The courtesy bus will be outside."

She stands up. Buttoning her coat. Pausing. Saying, "What town did you say Alan lives in?"

"Los Angeles. I can give you his number."

"Los Angeles," Helen repeats.

"Do you want his number?"

"No, no, that's too far. I was just … Well, sure, why not. I'll give him a call. It would be fun to chat after all these years. Yeah, give me his number. Gosh, we probably wouldn't recognize each other. We've both aged so much. He would be fifty-seven now, I think. Yes, I was twenty-five and he was eighteen when you were born."

"You were twenty-three."

"Was I? Could be, could be. Yes, my mind is not as sharp anymore."

Didi searches her purse for her address book. She pulls it out along with a pen. On a napkin she writes Alan's phone number.

Her mother takes the napkin, looks at the number and says, "Men ruin women, you know. Men are destructive, baby."

Tears well again in Didi's eyes. She sees the destruction in front of her. Waiting for Danny and Harley and so many others. She feels lightheaded enough to faint. "You're right. I know you're right," she says, her voice quavering.

"You come live with me, baby," Helen says. "Move back to Poway. Will you think about it? My apartment is big enough for two. The rent includes breakfast and lunch. We have dancing and aerobics and swimming, all sorts of activities."

Hell no! Didi almost shouts. But also thinking: *maybe I should.*

"Maybe I should, Mom."

"A clean break with the past."

"Maybe I should."

Helen points an accusing finger. "Look, baby, I don't need to tell you you're living in sin. You might have quit the Church, but the Church never quits you. The Almighty sees what you're doing. He sees you're an adulterer. If you don't stop seeing this man of yours, you'll pay. You'll pay big. You're being tested, Didi. Don't fail."

Didi's face flushes. Her ears burn. She knows God has always had His snoopy eyes on her. She can sense His disapproval. "I know you're right. I know you're right. I'll pray on it. I'll pray for strength."

Helen nods. She looks out the window, squints. "It's dark and I hate the night, I tell you. My night vision is terrible."

"Harley has that problem, too. The night."

"It's old age, baby. That man is way too old for you. Wake up. Dry your eyes. Hey, things could be worse. You could have heart problems, too."

They hug. They kiss. Didi watches her leave. Sitting down, she orders another martini. The waitress gives her a scornful look.

Screw you, sister! Screw the world!

Sitting there brooding about her mother, God and adultery, Didi thinks: I wish there wasn't any god. I wish the Ten Commandments didn't exist. Wish I'd never met Harley. Wish she hadn't brought it up and ruined my day. I'll look like her, I suppose, when I get that age. She could use a neck lift. Some sculpting around the eyes. Contact lenses, instead of those coke bottles. But otherwise, hey, she still has her own teeth. I wonder if she and Alan …

•

Didi drives home in a vodka haze.

She finds him asleep on the couch. TV on the history channel—a World War II documentary. Always war, always people dying for this or that stupid cause. She puts the quilt over him. Watches him sleep. Notices how the crown of his head is balding, his scalp showing through scraps of hair when the light hits him at an oblique angle. He used to have such thick, coarse hair. His whole body is shrinking. Cadaverous is the word. Age giving no quarter. Smothering him. Hollow eyes saying I'm dying sooner rather than later. She smells it on his breath, the rancid odor of heart decay.

She enters the bedroom, sits at the computer, opens her journal file and types:

What if he doesn't die sooner rather than later? Men can live normal life spans with heart trouble. Next year I will be forty-eight. Nothing more pitiful to have clinging to you than a strong man brought to his knees. Nothing left to salvage. When it's time to move on it's time to move on. Is it my fault? Have I been a curse on his life? Would he have been better off if we hadn't met? No crystal ball. No Tarot Cards. No intuition. What have I accomplished this night? I've failed to do the Dali Lama's bidding of emptying my mind, failed to chill the agitations, failed to make a decision about leaving Harley, failed to believe I can hide out with my mother, start over, stop being a fool. I'll never be able to apply the Dali Lama's advice, the art of happiness: cool-calm-indifference. Inner peace? Forget it.

Also thinking: Not as long as Harlan J. Olsen darkens my life.

Save As Documents: The World According to Deidre Annaba Godunov.

11 - Ties That Bind

Franny's life changed evermore the night when her inebriated sister-in-law called with the news that Harley was cheating. "He's been fucking her for years. Did you know that, Franny?"

"Fucking who? What you talkin bout, Shanna?"

"I'm sayin your husband has a lover. He's an asshole I'm sayin."

Franny's heart was racing. She could barely breathe. "Harley?"

"Harley."

"Not Harley."

"*Harley.*"

"But ... but how do you know? Who told you?"

"He told me. I saw them having lunch at Pisano's. They were holding hands."

"Pisano's. Holding hands."

"You gunna repeat everything I say?"

"I don't need to know this shit. What am I supposed to do about it? Why you telling me?"

"Because I'm shitfaced and it's time you knew, you ignorant sap. I went over to their table and he introduced us. He said she was his friend. Hah, my brother's a fucker."

"Is she pretty? Is she young?"

"Both. She's pretty, she's young, maybe forty, I don't know, and a whore, of course. She sells real estate. Probably sold him his condo. He didn't say. But he did ask me not to tell you. I told him his life is his and my life is mine. That's what I said to his face. You know, goddammit, I kept my mouth shut till now. I figured it would burn itself out. Muck like that usually does. But I called him earlier today and asked point blank if he was still seeing her. He fessed up. And I said, what about your wife? He said you still didn't know. He also said he loved the slut and couldn't stand to lose her. But he loved you, too, he said. Now, how can that be, huh? Christ, Franny, you know what he told me? He told me he's been seeing her for six fuckin years and they're living together. Sonofabitch bastard."

"Six years."

"Six years. All that time you've been blind to it."

"This is not the way. A phone call from you. There are better ways."

"Like what?"

"I don't know. I don't want to know. But I do know you betrayed his trust, Shanna. Your own brother." Franny was stunned, shocked.

"Fuck him," said Shanna. "He never calls. He never comes see me. Out of sight out of mind. He wishes I didn't exist. I've loved him all these years and what do I get? Out of sight out of mind." Shanna was crying. Sniffling. Hiccupping. "Mother … fucker," she added, her voice choking.

Franny didn't know what to do. Confront him? Get a gun and shoot him? "I don't want to hear anymore, Shanna. I'm still a sick woman and I don't want to lose him forever. He still sees me on weekends. It's better than nothing."

"What?"

"Go to hell."

"This is the thanks I— "

Franny hung up. She held her cheeks in her palms and paced the floor.

What to do, what to do. Oh dear, oh dear. Her gut instinct was to ignore it. Let it run its course. Maybe he'd come back when it was over. She'd take him in. She'd be his emotional crutch when he needed one.

Unfortunately, even though she wanted to close her eyes, she found she couldn't. No, an hour later she called him and said, "Your sister told me you're living with a woman."

There was a long pause. A deep sigh. Before he admitted he'd been having an affair with a woman who came to one of his readings. Her name was Deidre Godunov. AKA Didi. "You know her," he said. "She used to date Norman Ten Boom."

Franny isn't stupid. In the jealous pit of her heart she knew something was going on, but she hoped she could keep it at bay. Let it blow over. But with Shanna's drunken call and Harley's confession, she felt she had no choice but to cut him loose, kick him to the curb. In fact, she surprised herself by telling him to go to hell: "You can both be damned to hell!" was how she put it. He didn't argue. Didn't beg forgiveness. He cried copiously. She cried, too. And that was the end of it. After twenty-nine years of a dreary, uninspired marriage she decided to get legally separated. She thought about divorcing him, but didn't have the heart. Also, she needed his health insurance. Goodbye. Drop dead, you prick.

The next morning one of the first things she did was call Mr. Lafayette at the Eighth Street Used Bookstore and invite him over to help himself to whatever he wanted. Mr. Lafayette bought all but a few books, the few which she gave to the library sale. Looking at the empty shelves she felt oddly satisfied. Those books were the beginning of all their problems together. To hell with them. To hell with him. To hell with men.

It took several weeks for Franny to process the feeling of finality, but slowly, doggedly she did. The shock wore off. She adjusted. Still missed her husband, but less and less as weeks became months. A woman can handle anything, including being alone in a cavernous house at night with only TV as a distraction.

Harley kept calling to see how she was doing. Usually he sounded depressed, subdued, sad. She was pretty sure he was drinking a lot. She didn't ask him anything more about that whore named Deidre. Didi. What a stupid name for a woman. Made her sound like a ditz, a dumb valley bitch. She wondered if he was being unfaithful to her, too. Had he seduced other women? Or maybe it's the other way around. Maybe some have seduced him. How many? HIV or not, one-night stands are very popular. What do they call it now? They call it hooking up. Would he go for it? A brief interlude. Sure he would.

Whenever they talked on the phone, their conversations were civil. He told her how hard he was working. He has to get up at four in the morning to get his daily stint of writing done. He sold another story. Well, actually he gave it away for a payment of two copies of the magazine in which the story will appear. Their exchanges often relied on the weather: it's cold it's hot it's dry it's humid it's crazy windy. Franny was always able to tell Harley about her continuing health problems. She knows how sensitive he is. She knows he frets about her, feels guilty. She knows that her ever-present ailments stopped him from leaving her long ago and will keep him calling her.

She knows where there is communication there is hope.

12 - Infidelity Times Two?

How it happened: She doesn't know. She didn't mean for it to happen. Maybe Harley needed to quit drinking so he could get it up and give her some loving, give her some release from the anxiety stressing her out day after day. She's too young and lusty to go so long without sex. And then what do you know, there's former fuckbuddy Carlson throwing himself at her. Pretending he wants to buy a house she's representing. What did he think? Did he think she was stupid? Did he think she didn't know what he was up to?

Somehow he knew she was ready. Maybe he could smell it on her? Hormones pulsing, nether-land drooling.

Small talk first: the fitness center is doing well, holding its own. Good idea to keep it small and not branching out too soon, not selling franchises after she sold him the property. He would have gone under for sure. But he was doing fine these days, and he was in the market for a house and since they were longtime friends he thought he'd give her the business, help her out. Truth is he said he *owed* her.

•

This is how things get started, how they spin out of control. For Didi it seemed the most natural thing in the world to go through the motions of showing him the home, leading him through the living room, kitchen, dining room, up the carpeted stairway, knowing he was looking up the skirt she had worn deliberately to show him she might be forty-eight, but she still had what it takes.

The master bedroom had a huge closet. Flicking on the light, she showed him the inside.

"Large enough to be an extra room, a nursery if someday you had children," she said. She saw him eyeing her, giving her that look. Standing before him wavering, she wished he would make a move, make her do it, force her, make it his fault, not hers. But he didn't do anything.

Those hot eyes scalding her.

Finally, she turned away, kept chatting about how versatile the closet was. So big it was like having another room. The owner could turn it into an exercise room, or a play room, or a nursery if . . .

"I've missed you," he whispered. "If you turn around I'll believe you missed me, too."

Now what were you supposed to do with something like that? Turn around.

Would you? Yeah, me too. She was in his arms before her qualms could ruin the moment. And when her mind finally spoke, all it said was, Too late, Didi. Nothing I can say will save you. Carlson kissed her, while reaching a hand under her skirt. Wrapping her legs round him, clinging to his neck, she kissed him as if he was the breath of life and she was dying.

•

At home later that night, she turns the computer on to make an entry in her journal. As the programs are loading, a porn site comes up: X-Videos-Threesomes. She knows Harley has been on her computer looking at porn. He's hinted at setting up a threesome. Something new, something to excite him. He needs stimulation. To hook up all she has to do is click on FIND INTERESTED PARTIES NEAR YOU.

•

But she doesn't. She's done that before, long ago when she was nineteen and fell in with some wannabes who were making a porn film. They wanted her to play Juliet and her boyfriend to play Romeo. He wouldn't, but she would, she did. Had to get drunk before she could let the other actor and the director have their way with her. Weeks later, she caught a bus for San Francisco. Ran with the Hippies. Did drugs. Had sex with strangers, both men and women. Until finally she was so exhausted she went home to her parents. Who said she could stay only if she went to college. She agreed to start with a community college, dropped out when she met and married Danny. Two kids later, she felt restless, but stayed and did her duty, until finally she went back to school and studied real estate. The rest is history.

She closes the porn site, but the offer stays in the back of your mind. Monogamy is tiresome. It's uninspiring.

•

What is happening to you, Didi?

What the hell? Happened what happened: Carlson made love to me every way imaginable, until finally I told him I had to stop. He said I was still the best ever. He should never have let me go, never married Sharon. He was preparing to leave, preparing to divorce her. He wanted to buy the house, he said, and not live in an apartment.

Nothing I can say, nothing I can do about it now. Except stay away from him. Except that would be very hard because he made an offer. Nearly full price: $435,000. I could have handled the rest by email and phone, or let a colleague take over, but I have a feeling he wouldn't let me do that. But on the other hand, looked at a different way: what we did is typical, is normal. It's what Harley and I did to his wife. Yeah, it bothered him. But not enough to leave me. Not enough to go back to her pick up where he left off.

As if he could. They haven't seen each other in over a year, maybe two years. I don't know. He phones her now and then. A call to soothe his conscience.

Let sleeping dogs lie. Right? If Harley could sneak around all those years and get away with it, until his sister finally found it fit to tell Franny, well ... Go on, get from Carlson what Harley doesn't give me enough of. The physical side is important. He knew that. It's what he told me himself. Years ago. Years ago he said the physical side of love is the most important element. We both agreed: it's not just a meeting of the minds. Sure the mind has its needs, but the body is neediest of all. And must be satisfied as long as it is able.

Was it because he got old and has heart problems that he lost his appetite for some Didi love? Or maybe he needed a change up? The threesome thing? Or was it me myself? Have I changed, gotten too relaxed, too blasé, too much taking the man for granted? Is it that? Maybe. But I have excuses. Not the least of which is – I'm emotionally frazzled. At night in bed, all I wants is oblivion, sleep.

Hey, he could be more romantic. Court me. Bring me flowers and take me to dinner. Seduce me. Why doesn't he want to seduce me anymore? That man used to be all over me night after night.

One day he said something that still puzzles me. I was trying to get him to talk. I was trying to get him to unburden his heart. Tell me why he was drinking so hard. All his energy going into booze and watching internet porn, playing video games and reading bios about artists, writers who had a moment in the sun, before they burned out and died angst-ridden and empty. "Reading your future?" I had asked him.

And he said: "You know, Didi, none of these authors was bad people. They might have done terrible things to their wives or husbands or lovers or children, but basically they were good, their hearts were good, their souls were good. That's the sad thing about them: the good doesn't matter; it's the bad that brings them out of obscurity and causes others to whittle them down to size, put a stain on their lives. Biographers are vicious. I hate them."

Okay, so here comes Carlson manly-man-macho. What was I supposed to do with him? Is it any wonder that I fucked him? At least for an hour today something was finally happening to make me feel like I was fully DIDI again. God, it had felt good. If it happens more, it happens. So what? Deal with it, girl. You're not hurting anyone. You're only being a healthy, active woman. Men get away with this shit all the time. Remember that when you have your doubts. Yeah, I have needs. My body is greedy. What am I supposed to do? Masturbate? Masturbating alone is lonely, it's pathetic. I want a man in me, not my fingers or a goddamn sex toy.

Hit delete hit delete: Oh, Didi don't relive it. Hit delete, erase this passage before it becomes a permanent part of your story.

Also thinking: what if Harley finds out?

Fuck him.

Save As Document: *The World According to Deidre Annaba Godunov.*

13 - Franny Adjusts

More months pass and Franny gets fanatical about getting her health back. Through an even stricter diet and more exercise, she goes from size sixteen to size twelve. Her sciatic nerve miraculously heals. The anemia and rheumatoid arthritis improve. Her use of pain medication falls to two pills a day, instead of four. She dyes her hair daffodil. Buys silver-rimmed glasses that make her look more intellectual. A dermatologist uses a laser and an abrasive acid on her face to slough off old skin, bringing forth an apple-cheek glow. She gets a boob job. Then a neck-lift. Franny is pushing fifty-four, but believes she looks thirty-five. Forty at most. Though still pudgy, it seems to her that in the right clothes, especially tush-lifting Levis and no-collar shirts that flatter her slimmed down neck, she is alluring in the way a woman of the world is, or at least should be.

Franny is wise to the ways of men. She knows she can get a man now, but she's gotten used to being independent, making her own decisions, not having to explain herself to an overbearing male. Who needs a man? Not Francis Austen-Olsen. Not Franny.

Her most pressing problem is money. Plastic surgery has drained the saving's account. Without Harley's income, the salary she makes is barely enough to make ends meet. Her greatest asset is her home and she thinks perhaps she should sell it. Move into an apartment close to work. But she loves the house and doesn't really want it on the market.

Judy tells her she can make extra money working part-time for Cecil at their restaurant, but Franny's arthritic feet won't allow it. And, truth be told, she feels serving as a waitress is beneath her. Also, Cecil gives her the creeps these days, his eyes always traveling to her cleavage, her newly uplifted breasts. What had she seen in him, anyway? It disgusts her to think of the times she had given him hand jobs and oral sex and came within a groan of actually fucking him.

Who was that stupid girl back then?

She doesn't know.

She doesn't want to know.

Ruthie calls to tell her, "Put that house to use. Rent out those extra rooms. They're just gathering dust." The idea of renting the extra bedrooms appeals to Franny. There would be life in the house again. Noise. Chatter. Someone to watch TV with. There are nights when Franny craves contact. Times at midnight when she is lonely and terribly depressed. Times when she weeps with self-pity and whispers, "Why hast thou forsaken me?" Times when she misses her husband and wants him back, no matter what he's done. But the mood passes. She tells herself she is doing fine and is better off without him. That cheater. That sneak. Two-timing liar. She hates him and hopes the whore is making his life miserable. The rotten bitch, spawn of Satan. How many years had it been going on? He told her six years, but she has a hunch it's more. Franny, you've been bamboozled. Harley said it happened when he got drunk and Didi drove him home. And stayed over. The rest is history. Franny doesn't know what to believe. Maybe it was many more years. Maybe it was seven or eight. Maybe he had been cheating throughout their marriage. Some men do. Right from the start they cheat.

In The San Diego Union she runs an advertisement:

Christian woman has rooms to rent in large, four-bedroom home in quiet Kensington. Must be Born Again, clean and sober female. No smokers. Call Franny Olsen at 619 543-2121 x 3 or 619 282-4412.

A week passes. No one calls. She runs the ad again. No one calls. She tells herself to be patient. In time it will work out. Blessed is she who puts her trust in the Lord.

Blessed is she who remains patient.

Late afternoon, home from work, the phone rings and the first thing she thinks is Harley. But no, it's her sister Judy calling to talk about health issues. Judy says her diabetes is giving her fits. She had a dizzy spell and found her blood sugar was 370. She could have gone into a diabetic coma. Her sugar is back under control now, but she still feels achy, feels poorly. She thinks she might be getting Franny's rheumatoid disease, or maybe anemia. Or possibly the flu. Pains in hips and shoulders especially bad. The sores on the soles of her feet refuse to heal. They don't hurt at all, but she knows they're there. She knows the nerve ends are atrophying.

"Oh dear, oh dear," says Franny.

"I don't want to end up like Mom," Judy says.

"Her mind is going," says Franny. "Every time I talk to her she says she's dying."

"I know, I know," says Judy. "There's this pain in my shoulder. Maybe it's a ligament or a tendon. Mr. Castor had a pain like mine and it turned out he had lung cancer. God forbid."

The litany of ailments continues back and forth, until Franny is worn out and tells Judy she will call back tomorrow. As soon as she puts the phone down, it rings, and again she thinks Harley. But no, it's Ruthie wanting to know how things are. Franny runs through her list of problems. But before she can finish, Ruthie jumps in with a catalog of her own. She coughs a lot. Her nausea is as bad as ever. For sure she has another ulcer. She asks about Harley. Does that self-centered sonofabitch ever call or no? What kind of a man leaves a wife trying to cope with so many ailments? That no good, rotten— Didn't he marry for better or worse?

"What could I do?" says Franny. "I couldn't hogtie him. I couldn't make him stay."

"He's so mean. He's running away from his responsibilities. I despise him."

Franny is feeling sorrier and sorrier for herself. She knows Ruthie is right. Harley has run away from his obligation to a sick wife. Most of their married life she's been ill. His compassion quota is tapped out. He doesn't want to deal with her anymore. Again she says, "I couldn't make him stay." She weeps, sniffling, clearing her throat. Coughing.

"My cough is worse than yours," Ruthie tells her. "Sometimes I think I'm going to choke to death. It's like I can't catch my breath."

"Crying makes me cough," Franny replies. "It's phlegm. Post-nasal drip."

"I worry about you being alone," says Ruthie, "and something happening and no one there to call an ambulance or take you to the hospital. Judy and I talk about that. We worry, sweetie."

"Don't worry, I'll be fine, honey."

The tears keep flowing. She grabs tissues and dabs her eyes. Wipes her nose. *Poor Franny*, a voice inside her keeps saying.

"Just the same, I'm going to keep calling you every day."

"Thank you, Ruthie. You're a good sis."

The topic switches to Mama. What are they going to do with her? No one has the health to take care of her. Or the patience. There is nothing to do but leave her where she is. It's a good nursing home. The caregivers are as good as they'll find anywhere, even if they are mostly Filipino. As long as the sisters are splitting the cost three ways they'll be able to afford it.

Franny has had this same discussion so often she's immune to it.

•

For dinner she juices carrot, cucumber, watercress, parsley, mango, an apple and blueberries. She also stuffs celery with low fat peanut butter and relishes it. She rides the stationary bike for twenty minutes working up a sweat, while watching TV, watching Dr. Phil analyze people living despicable lives.

Later, her feet aching terribly, she takes a hot bath with Epsom salts. Lying in the steaming water she recalls times in her youth when she and Harley bathed and showered together and fooled around. Just a pair of horndogs when they were first married and full of juice. And she got pregnant three times and had three miscarriages. It broke her heart, but Harley said it was better not to bring kids into this rotten world. And he said some vessels were not meant to bring forth life. "With seven billion people and counting, it's too bad there aren't more barren wombs out there. Who needs more martyrs to this mess we've created?" He told her there was obviously a good reason why she couldn't make babies. Nature, he said, was telling her something.

"What would I have done without God?" she murmurs as she heaves out of the tub and dries herself. Slips into her robe. Gets her Bible. Sits on the bed.

Reads—

A glad heart makes a cheerful countenance,
But by sorrow of heart the spirit is broken.

"But what if I had had those three babies?" she asks. "They might not have inherited my bad health. They might be running around like Comanches and taking my mind off things. I'd be too busy to be sick. I'd have a cheerful countenance. I might not be afflicted with sorrow of heart. My spirit wouldn't be broken. I'd have to keep it together for my children. Oh, Harley, what do you know? For all your reading, what do you really know? You know book stuff. You don't know anything about the human heart, that's why the things you write won't ever be on any bestseller lists. There's no heart in them. All flash, no content. You go off and leave your wife when she's deathly ill. No man with a heart could do that. I should have married Chata Johnson, you bastard."

Franny goes to the chest of drawers. Pulls a locked jewelry box from underneath her lingerie. Opens it with her secret key. Inside are two pictures of Chata when they were in love. In one he leans smiling on the fender of his white Camaro. In the other he is standing in the sun at the beach, the shimmering sea behind him. What a body. Lean, muscular, black as coffee. The swimming briefs bulging. He was big. Bigger than Harley. She turns her pillow sideways and uses it to support both pictures on the bed. She gets the vibrator, lies with her face inches away from Chata's image. She massages the pain in her fingers, her shoulders her hips her knees over and over. Is this another lump in her breast, or a cyst? And what is this new pain in her bladder? She massages it while it warms away. A sort of stitch, a sort of pinch. She keeps massaging lower and lower until she finds the right spot. All the while staring lustfully at Chata, remembering things he did with those succulent lips.

Which picture does she like best? She likes them equally. Where is he now? Is he still married? What if she Googled him, or looked him up in the phone book and gave him a call? Has he missed her as much as she's missed him?

Content now, she rests until her breath comes back. Looking down at herself, she thinks how pitiful she must look with a dildo crammed in her twat. It's all Harley's fault. She wonders if he'll even notice that she's lost weight. Still fleshy but heading towards shapely. Call her a full-figure gal. Call her well-rounded. Staring at the empty bookshelves lining the wall, she tells herself nothing looks the same as it did when he left how many years ago? She sold his precious books. She bought a hot pink nightgown and a yellow teddy with the book money. Rising, she washes the vibrator, dries it, puts it away. Locks the pictures back in the jewelry box. Slips it behind her underwear and closes the drawer. And says, "Now what?"

She wants a hot dog, a fat one with mustard, onion and relish.

Franny, Franny … *knock it off.*

At least another day is done. Her laboring over.

Going to the fridge, she pulls a pack of weenies from the meat drawer. She fries one and puts it in a bun with mustard and relish and a sprinkling of chopped onion. She pours a vodka rocks and goes into the living room. She will eat her hot dog and watch TV. Then go to bed early and start again tomorrow. She has some new pain pills (Percocet), and the Prednisone seems to be working. Each day she seems to feel less pain. Her fingers bend more easily. Blood circulation is obviously better. She looks forward to a good night's rest. And then tomorrow back to Harvest Home and more line-editing. So boring.

Folly is a joy to him who has no sense,
But a man of understanding walks aright.

She changes the line to a woman of understanding. It's what keeps her going through thick and thin. Franny believes she is a born psychologist. She gives good counsel.

Without counsel plans go wrong.

"And that's why they need me," she says. "And as long as I'm needed I can go on. Harley or no Harley, I've got God, my job, my sisters, my mom."

Settling back on the sofa, sitting on her heat pad, she eats and drinks and watches television. The phone rings. She lets the machine answer and hears Harley telling her he's wondering how she's doing. He hopes she's all right. He will call back later. "I suppose you're with your sisters," he says.

She plays the message over and detects notes of worry in his voice. "Let him worry," she grumbles. "Self-centered Narcissus."

Surfing the channels she finds a movie she has seen before. It is about a wicked man who gets cancer. After much suffering he finds Jesus and becomes a preacher racing against time, desperately saving souls for the Lord. When the cancer metastasizes and he is dying, Franny knows the best part is coming. She turns the sound higher. Listens to him whispering The Lord's Prayer. Asking God not to abandon him in his time of need. When he finally dies (bathed in choir music and holy light) Franny feels beatific. And she thinks: What a perfect death. The music, the light. The wicked man no longer wicked. The prodigal son returning to the fold. The arms of the Lord waiting.

Franny sighs. An epiphany of tears trickle down her cheeks and she sees that such a death is the greatest blessing God can give us. Death so perfect as to be—transcendent. No better word exists to explain it.

The phone is ringing again. It's him: Harley reaching out, making contact. Would he call if he didn't still love her? The ringing sounds very worried.

This time she'll answer it.

14 - Jealousy

It was another one of those devil days wherein Harley doubted everyone, even those closest to him. All liars and betrayers. All of them living sordid lives. Not just them, but all humanity. The whole world. Dishonest. Disgusting. He hated them and he hated that he hated them and hated that he had such hateful thoughts about them. His mother had always told him not to hate others because hatred destroys the hater. But he couldn't help it. He trusted no one and believed in nothing. Especially not himself.

Seven years now since he met Didi and lost his mind.

Five years since he left his wife.

Five years of pessimism.

Five years of self-loathing.

"God, I'm in a mood," he said. "And it's all her fault, the little bitch. Look at the time. Where is she? Why doesn't she call? Should I go looking for her? I could go to Carlson's house and see if she's there."

No, no you don't. That would be demeaning. It would be desperate. It would be pitiful.

"If she's there, I'll kill her."

Often it comforted him to remember that we all die tomorrow and all desire and pain dies with us. All striving caring loving hoping will end one day in the minuscule evaporation of a minuscule thought. Poof. That 5,000-year-old frozen corpse found in the Italian Alps had once been a living, breathing man. Just as greedy for pleasure as anyone alive today. But what did it matter? Embedded in a granite niche as the centuries ticked away and no one noticing. Maybe he had a family. No doubt they had wondered what happened to him. They cared for a while—where is Ugha? He went up the mountain and didn't come back. They searched for him. They called Uuughaaa! Uuughaaa! But all that returned were echoes. The moon changed shapes, rose and fell and life was for the living. Must go hunt and gather. Got to stay alive somehow. Ugha's disappearance remained a mystery to his friends and relatives. The memory of his voice faded as the months went by. The years became many. Eventually they forgot what he looked like. And his wife and children went on, until one by one they wore out and died. As did his grandchildren and his great-grandchildren, generation after generation, so on and so forth. All Ugha's descendants departing. And what was the point? Bodies in ice clutches. Flesh and blood morphing into tusks.

"Life is short," Harley growled, clenching his teeth, wishing he could bite someone. Bite Didi especially. "Better to acknowledge the brevity and the insentient state to which we sink, all of us large or small, great or guileless. Better not be fooled by an afterlife no one's seen. From whose bourn no traveler returns. Shrug it off. Be philosophical. It's coming. Who cares? It may not be today or tomorrow. But it will come. The readiness is all. Said Hamlet. Or was that Lear? No, Lear says ripeness is all. Actually no, it is Edgar saying it to Gloucester. And Gloucester says that's true too. Because everything is true. And then he died. Hamlet died. Gloucester died. Lear died. Uhga in the Alps died. My wife Franny will die. I'll die soon, also. Need to take death with a grain of salt. The only way to handle such an outrage. The trick is to know when to go. Give me the hemlock; it's time. Give me the morphine. Gimme the pistol."

•

Harley waited a moment to see if being philosophical made him feel better.
It didn't.
Where was she? Why wasn't she answering the phone? Something told him it was for sinister reasons. She was with someone. Maybe at Carlson's house right now, she and he thrashing on that Persian rug. Or was it Turkish? Yes, Turkish she had said. "I wish I had Carlson's Turkish rug. It's gorgeous. I wonder if he would sell it?" How come she knows that? She sold him the house. He moved in. Was there some paperwork follow up? Or?
Hell, who cares? She was probably out shopping. She was always wanting to buy things. "I want, I want," she was always saying.
Harley saw her lying naked on the rug, her head thrown back, her mouth open, her hands gripping her lover's arms. What did he look like? Harley could see him. Bulky and dark. Smelling musky like the dark ones do. He had seen how she looked at men. Always younger men. Older women were hot for young studs. An article in the paper this morning told of an older woman arrested for sexually abusing two teenage boys, fifteen and sixteen. The charges included oral sex and sodomy. She got two years. What perversion of the mind made those boys tell? Harley knew if such a thing had happened to him at that age, he never would have told. He would have made a sacrifice to Aphrodite. Given her a golden apple offering.

•

He went to the kitchen, grabbed the vodka, splashed some in a tumbler and added three ice cubes. Swirled. Waited for the drink to cool. Squabbled with himself: Why shouldn't she go for some younger guy? No reason not to, not when you're impotent half the time, old fart. Not when your face looks like a cluster of grapes hanging over her in bed. She never wants to make love with the light on anymore. Your body no longer turns her on. Wrinkly neck. A wattle beneath your chin. Rusty skin on the V of your chest where the sun used to burn you. Age spots surfacing like seaweed on your forehead. That tiny lesion on your nose is probably a basal cell. Not your fault. You tried to warn her. You told her she was too young for you, but would she listen? She said your age meant nothing. That you didn't look thirteen years her senior. Maybe ten years at most. That's when you were working out, lifting weights, jogging a mile every morning. And you had more hair. You had looked good for a man in his mid-fifties. Don't look in the mirror now, Harley.

He took a sip. Swished it like mouthwash over his teeth. Held still a moment breathing through his nose, feeling the vodka bite. After he swallowed, his tongue felt antiseptic. She claimed he hardly ever had bad breath. He told her it was because alcohol, plus Listerine kept his palate squeaky-clean. And that was why he never got sore throats or rarely caught colds. Germs can't multiply in an environment pickled in alcohol. She laughed at that. She joined him in a drink, laughing. She loved to drink one or two and laugh at his jokes and have fun. God, he *loved* her.

He loved that she had such control. Not him, not Harley. Once he started he couldn't stop. How many drinks had there been over the years, especially after Franny found out about Didi? Gallons of vodka, whiskey, wine to alter his moods. To tuck away truth. Seek oblivion. They had walled their love in a bubble for a few days every week, before he had to go home to his wife. He can't believe he did that for three years. Such a shitty way to live. Harley the adulterer full of anxiety.

Didi's willful behavior, the need to have her way at all costs, had taken a large toll on him. Knowing that if she would get rid of her husband and go after a married man and persuade him to betray his wife—she was capable of anything. She would betray him, finally. And why not? He was a burned out old bag. Heartburn, indigestion and bowel troubles. Arthritis in his knees. Constant guilt about Franny. More guilt about no longer measuring up to Didi. He told her he would edit her stories and poems. "I'll help you write them. Create a legacy. Harley is here. Harley will never leave you." He hasn't touched any of her manuscripts. Just thinking about them makes him suicidal.

Like Uhga, 5,000 years will mean nothing to Harley, eventually. For the past year he's been an impossible pain in the ass. A drunk haunted by dreams. Bad dreams. Dreams about Franny. The recurring dream about hearing her final breath exhaling: the sound of overwhelming fatigue. And how does one go on living when living means continual rewind and playback? No wonder Didi had that look on her face when she looked at him. The look that said what *am* I doing with this loser?

•

She used to say, "Sex is how I express my love for you. Sex is the closest we can physically be. You inside me is spiritual. I never knew I could love this way."

Stuff like that. Stuff she didn't say anymore. Like: You are my soul-mate, Harley. She hasn't said that in ages.

Soul-mate.

Cynic that he was, he used to sneer at such drivel. Before he made love to Didi, that is. As the weeks became months became years, he began to wonder if a mate for the soul might be true. Now he knew he was right in the first place. He was a sentimental dupe. He was a grieving ex-romantic, he was an double douche bag.

"That's me," he said. And then he said, "When I die there will be no one to give the folded flag to. Didi will bug out, I know she will. If a man does not keep pace with his companions—"

She was all that was left in his life, no one else to turn to. Children: no, he was still thankful he didn't have any.

•

He paced the floor. Went into the study. Frowned at the bookshelves, the rows of British literature. Shakespeare and his ilk and all things Donne—the Metaphysicals. All the lovely words he used to quote to his students. His mind overflowing endlessly able.

Things are not truly, but in equivocal shapes.

"Thomas Browne," said Harley, satisfied that he still had a memory.

And next to Browne on the shelf, incongruously (or maybe congruously?) was *Alice in Wonderland*. Down the rabbit hole. That's where he was. Has been. Will be ever.

Harley put forth a trembling finger, touched Alice and said—

Speak roughly to your little boy
And beat him when he sneezes!

A coughing laughter following. He blew his nose. Wiped his eyes. Laughed heh, heh: a mad scientist.

"*Thou shouldst not have been old til thou hadst been wise.* So where is she? Whose arms, whose hands, whose—Jesus, the thought is unbearable. I'll kill her. I'll kill myself." Eyes closed he whispered, "*Let me not go mad. Oh, Fool, I shall go mad.*"

He pictured the gun in the nightstand. Inevitably we die anyway, so why not get it over? Turn time to zero. You will not wake wondering. You will not feel guilt, you the man who broke your wife's heart. You the man wishing for her to die. Let her die.

Yeah, but you knew it would end this way. Alone. Stranded. Franny nipped and tucked and sexy again. She was doing fine. Harley an afterthought. Didi's passion for him has withered. You knew her passion would fade as you aged and the ills of aging started plaguing you, just as her mother had warned you that day in your office:

"You're too old for her. Have you ever thought about how she'll cope when time has its way with you and you start looking the way you feel?"

That bitch was right. Time has stamped your stupid face and corroded your organs. Those gall stones that won't let you digest fats. That burping routine after every meal. Disgusting. Even more disgusting is the IBS that comes and goes. And also your swollen prostate, the itching, burning in there that makes you short-tempered. Doctors can't help you. Forget those bastards, those pompous frauds, those phony fakes. It's a benign hypertrophism. It will be with you always. Nothing to be done. Don't drink alcohol. Alcohol is hell on stomachs and prostates. And stay away from spicy foods. Some day we may have to operate if the gland turns cancerous. But surgery is the last resort. They shoved pills at him for his indigestion. Tylenol for his arthritis. What a joke that stuff was. Might as well drink snake oil. His aliments overwhelmed every elixir, his courage especially. But, oddly, not his love for *her*. Why did he love her? No reason. Something wrong with your brain, Harley. She's a mental disease.

He wondered why, with so many ailments, he continued to drink.

Not true. He didn't wonder.

No, he knew. Every night at least five or six vodkas. Or as many as it took to calm him. Make him not care about anything. Stop caring. When you care that's when it hurts: that was what Buddha had said. In his cups, Harley tells himself that he most certainly has a death wish now. Several times he has taken the gun out and put the barrel in his mouth and pressed the trigger and thought—All I'd have to do is flick the safety off and this world will know me no more. Would you like that, Franny? Would that avenge you? And then Didi coming in and finding him with the back of his head blown off. She would freak. He can hear her screaming. He sees that funny eye of hers—that cast—if it wasn't a bad omen, Harley's not an adulterous fornicator.

But would she really care? She wouldn't care a fig. She had told him recently that his black depression was destroying her. She had given an ultimatum: See a psychiatrist and get some help or it's over. You're drowning and I'm drowning with you. You've got me halfway down the road to crazy, Harley.

He should walk away now. Give up Didi. Go live in a monastery and pray daily for Franny's forgiveness. But he has no will to give Didi up. She is his addiction. His obsession. A reason for living.

Let it be, let it be.

Basically it is for Didi that he hasn't killed himself. Maybe he should kill her first. And then: COUPLE DIE IN SUICIDE PACT.

·

Returning to the kitchen, he lifted the bottle. Two more and it would be empty. Should he go to the store now? Or should he finish the bottle first?

Finish the bottle. Then kill yourself, Harley.

What would she do if he were dead? What did Ugha's wife do when she realized he was never coming back? Harley can see Didi crying. He hears her asking why. She knows why, but pretends not to. He sees her running to her children and mother for comfort. Her friends would be there for her. She has lots of friends. Friendly, popular, always hanging on the phone. A social butterfly. He hates it every time the phone rings. Sometimes it's for him. But mostly it's some friend of hers, or her ex-husband. But would she miss you, Harley? Sure she would miss you. Then she would move on. She loves life. She loves her pleasures. She would find someone else. Someone closer to her own age. People have got to get on after a loved one dies. And besides, women have a life force that men don't have. Men die easily. Most women go kicking and screaming. But they die anyway, and 5,000 years later everything and nothing has changed.

•

Looking out the window, he watched wind tickling the trees. Ah yes, *Nature*. He used to care about the environment. Leaving it livable for the next generation and the animals. But that was no concern of his now. Who gives a damn? Not Harley Olsen.

Go now or wait for her? Where is she? She didn't used to be so evasive. Always kept her cell phone on. Always prompt. Phone calls always on time. If she said she would call at five, she always did. The past year or so she had spent lots of extra time at work, the housing slump. She's an optimist. She thinks soon she'll be raking in the dough again. She had asked him several times to invest, take a chance. But he had taken early retirement and lived on a fixed income. He has some savings for a rainy day, but that's it. Nothing left to gamble with. No risk left in a man sixty-two. And besides, he didn't really want anything more than what he had. The condo was comfortable. He owned all his furniture and his car. He didn't need more clothes. Except some new skivvies. The waistbands in the old ones were wavy.

•

Maybe she started pulling back after he retired and she realized he would never amount to anything more than what he was—a lazy-semi-functional-alcoholic-wannabe-writer who could no longer sell his work.

He could have taught longer. He could have hung in there and piled up five or six more years on his 401K and the bonds and Social Security and his State Retirement fund. He had thought retirement was what he needed. Give him time at last to work on his books. Write every day. Zone-in. Focus. Create something brilliant—a brilliant work of art that would outlive him. Time to read all those novels he had piled on the nightstand over the years. He hadn't realized that when you're no longer in the thick of things, the writing and reading don't mean very much. There is only you and the words. You and someone else's words. Only you and gestures unshared. On the page where no one cared to see it. She was far too busy to read his scribblings and encourage him. He belonged to no writing clubs. He didn't do readings in bookstores anymore. Because they filled him with even more anxiety.

No one buys literature, anyway. People wanted thrillers, mysteries, *crime*. Scandals that exposed the seamy sides of celebrated lives. Biographies that cut their subjects down to size. Literary novels? Forget it. And he was guilty, too. He hadn't made a dent in the stack he had been saving. He lacked the energy to read or write or eat out or go to movies or— How in the world had he become so boring? A man like him who used to strip nude and dance like a pagan for her. Stevie Ray Vaughan, John Lee Hooker blasting away. Those were the early days of their affair, days when he had had energy to burn.

No more. The backs of his hands, his corky arms tell him he is too old to be living. He should have died at forty, like Jack London. Or like Byron at thirty-six. Instead of this living on and on to no purpose. And becoming what he used to dread.

•

He finished the first drink and poured another, whirling the vodka, the ice cubes clicking. He went into the bedroom, opened the drawer. Took out the gun. Put the barrel in his mouth. Slipping the tip of his tongue round the rim of the muzzle, he tasted tangy metal. He backed up to the wall. She would find his brains and hair on the wall. He wanted that. He wanted an image that would haunt her forever. *You did this.*

He watched the secondhand sweeping a circle round the face of the clock on the dresser. Another minute gone forever. Just *do* it, he told himself. Flick the safety off and end time. You're going to die before long anyway. Get it over with, you fucking coward.

Taking the gun out of his mouth he snarled, "Where is she, goddamn her."

He put the gun in his waistband and phoned again. Nothing happened. No ringing. No voicemail saying, Please leave a message after the beep. He slammed the receiver down and swore. He said, "Fuck shit motherfucker whore." He poured the last of the bottle and said, "Harley, we got to make a booze run, my boy." He bolted the drink and felt dimly genial. He felt borderline fine.

"Harley's cool," he said. "Everything's cool."

He reminded himself to be philosophical. Let her fuck them all, he didn't care. What he really needed was another Stoli. What he needed was the indifference it brought.

•

After a stop at the liquor store, he found himself on the freeway. The university where he used to work was in the distance, its gold dome glimmering. He spent twenty-five years pretending before he managed to work up the nerve to retire. Telling himself, Now I'll really write. No more excuses, Harley. He threw himself into it, turning out two worthless novels that no one wanted. Numerous short stories: all rejected. He wasn't a writer after all. A sham of a writer making motions. And finally after two years of failure he stopped. He sent nothing out. He wrote a short story or a poem occasionally and put it with the others in the drawer beneath the drawer holding the gun.

Harley had no ideas. Everything he wrote seemed stupid. He drank as much as he could hold every night and tightened his grip on his anger. Dreamed of going postal. Striding down the hall at school and capping the director and the dean and maybe a vice-president or two. Then killing himself. Or maybe battling it out with the police. Take as many of them as he could. Before committing suicide-by-cop. He saw the headlines:

RETIRED UNIVERSITY PROFESSOR KILLS COLLEAGUES IS GUNNED DOWN.

Something like that. He fingered the gun snug behind his belt. Cars whipping by him on both sides. Six-thirty and the freeways still crowded. All these people, where were they going? These SUVs sucking up more than their fair share of gas. Polluting the air. It would be an easy thing to shoot out a tire, set the motherfucker rolling. Beside him he pulled the Stoli from the sack and opened it. Drank a lascivious mouthful. He felt buzzed. *Very.*

•

Carlson's house was dark, only the porch light on. The garage door was closed, so Harley didn't know if her car was in there or not. He parked halfway down the street and watched for signs of life. Instinct told him she was in there all right. Oral sex. Sodomy. She liked all of it. Older woman losing every inhibition with a younger man. Or maybe younger men plural. Two teenagers. What had possessed that bitch? Two years in prison for two blowjobs and her butt reamed. Was it worth it?

At the curb in front was a phallic Miata. Red: the color of passion. How typical. How cliché. Of course she would take up with someone like that. Her old fuckbuddy with his sports car. Her old fuckbuddy spreading AIDs. Fuck you, fuckbuddy.

The minutes ticked by. Half an hour vanished. The sky was still bright, but the sun had set. Harley got restless.

I don't really want to know, do I?

•

On the way back he pulled up behind three other cars at a stoplight. Standing on the center divider was a skinny, long-haired man with a stick in his hand. A homeless panhandler? The man walked over to the first car in line and opened the door and yelled, "Out! Get the fuck out or I'll brain you, you stupid bitch!" He brandished the stick. A woman jumped out of the car clutching her purse. The man ripped the purse from her and got behind the wheel and sped away. Crossing cars screeching to a halt. Ending sideways. Someone yelling, "What the fuck!"

The woman stood in the empty space gawking. People getting out of their cars. One woman screaming into her cell phone—"Carjacking, I said!" Others surrounded the victim and were talking to her all at once and waving their hands. Everyone was fuming. If they could just get their hands on that asshole. More cars pulled up behind the others in line. The light turned green. Horns honking. The air filling with bluster and *Carjacking! Carjacking!*

Harley sat benumbed and silent. He was drained. It had happened so fast. And he had not even tried to do anything. He could have jumped out of his car and shot that bastard. He could have run to the rescue. Saved the day. Freeze, motherfucker, I'll blow your fucking head off! That's what he could have said. Why hadn't he moved?

He didn't used to be so indecisive. He didn't used to be so scared.

Of everything.

Once long ago when he was thirty-five, he had stepped between a man and a woman who were yelling at each other in a bar. The man was threatening her, his hands reaching. Courageous Harley jumped off his stool and told the man to back off. The man had sized him up. Calculations spinning in his eyes—can I take this guy? Harley had been in his prime, all muscle from pumping iron. Behind him the bartender held a baseball bat. Everyone waited to see what would happen. The man pointed his finger at the woman and said, I'll take care of you later. And she said, Go to hell, asshole! And that was it. The fight was over. Harley sat down and finished his beer. The woman didn't even thank him. But the bartender did. Thanked him and gave him a free pitcher of Coors. Yes, Harley Olsen had been like a warrior that day—heroic.

"And here again I could have been the hero," he mumbled. And then reminded himself—"I'm too fucking old to be a hero." He burped. He rubbed his stomach round and round. He felt nauseated. He needed Maalox. Some Imodium too. He slid the gun and the Stoli under the seat. "Useless fuck," he said and burped again. Palm stroking his burning abdomen.

"Oh Harley, Harley," he whispered, almost sobbing. "Oh Harley, why do you do the things you do? Why have you done what you've done? What's wrong with you?"

The police arrived. They had witnesses pull their cars to the curb. Harley told a cop that he hadn't seen anything. He had gotten there too late.

•

Back home, he put the gun away and drank Maalox straight from the bottle. Sat on the pot and let the poisons flow. Then he washed his face and neck in cold water. Went to the kitchen and poured another drink. This will stop it, he told himself. This will deaden it.

He turned on the lights in the living room and sat on the couch staring at his reflection in the silent TV screen. His heart was still pounding fast. He wondered if every old man was a coward. Old and brittle and impotent and a coward. He wondered if a shot of testosterone would make him snap out of it. He wondered if he would do anything different if he could live the carjacking over again. He imagined himself in the thick of it. Ordering the motherfucker to freeze. But he doesn't freeze. And Harley shoots him. Harley shoots him and shoots him. There! That's for Franny! That's for me! That's for my mother! That's for—

What kind of car was it, anyway? What had the woman looked like? He couldn't remember anything about her except her astonished mouth. There had been an overturned sandal on the street. He could have gone over and picked it up and handed it to her. An act of kindness. A show of compassion. Poor thing.

But nothing. He had done nothing. Moment of truth. This is who you are now, Harley.

He set his drink on the coffee table and leaned forward, elbows on knees, head in his hands. Readiness is all. Ripeness I've got, but readiness, no. No readiness in you, you old, worthless fuck. He choked on the words ice-picking his brain. He tried to repeat them, to yell them at himself, but a sob gushed out instead. He wept into his hands. Big baby. Big stupid baby.

"What's wrong?" she cried. "What happened?"

He looked up. He wiped his eyes. Pulled out his handkerchief and blew his nose. She was saying over and over, "Honey, what's wrong, what's wrong, are you sick? Honey, what's wrong?"

He felt his lips moving. He listened hard, but he wasn't saying anything. The afternoon and evening passed through his mind, her dead message machine, the vodka rocks, the liquor store, the gold-domed university mocking him, the crowded freeway smothering him, the darkness of her fuckbuddy's house teasing him. The carjacker. That goddamn carjacker. He should have shot him.

"I … I thought you had left me. I couldn't find you. I called and called. I couldn't find you."

"My cell phone died, honey. I accidentally dropped it in the toilet. It's right there on the counter." She pointed to it.

There it was. Why hadn't he seen it? "I didn't see it," he said.

"Honey, you never see anything."

"It's been there all this time."

"I went to buy another after I left work." She fished in her purse. Showed him the new cell phone. "It cost me an arm and a leg," she said. "And they took forever. I hate that place. They knew I couldn't wait for a special. They knew they had me. They really stuck it to me this time. I paid a fortune for this phone. And I phoned you as soon as I could, but all I got was the answering machine. The freeway was a mess. I could have walked home faster."

He glanced at the answering machine and saw the red light blinking.

"I went out for more vodka," he said. Adding, "I thought you had finally had enough of me. I wouldn't blame you. I'm old and sick and ugly and all I do is whine. I'm like my wife; I'm like Franny. Physically a disaster. Actually, I'm worse. At least she didn't wallow in self-pity. She's moving on. She's taken charge of her life. I'm disgusting. I hate myself. I'm a failure as a man. What good am I to you? Good for nothing."

"Harley, why do you do this to yourself? Why?" She shook her head. Her eyes looked painfully sad. "Listen to me, you're not old, you're not at all ugly. I love you as much as I ever have. I would never leave you. I would never hurt you. I adore you. Only death can part us and that's the truth. You know in your heart I'm one hundred percent yours, Harley. Tell me you know it. Tell me."

"I'm so depressed," he told her, feeling the tears welling again. "I can't get over how I've failed. I shouldn't have retired."

"I wish you would get some help, honey. See a psychiatrist, please. Tell me you will. Promise me you will. A psychiatrist will give you anti-depressants, honey. You don't need to be so miserable. It's all chemistry. It's a chemical imbalance."

"Drugs will distort my mind. Turn me into a zombie. It will be someone else in here" (he tapped his head) "not me. A better me. A milder get-along Harley. The demon driven dead. Or at least anesthetized. Harley Olsen Prozac Person. That's what you really want. My moodiness made Franny crackers; it makes you crackers too. I'm driving you down the road to crazy you said."

"Harley, you hang on to your suffering like a masochist. You're after absolution. If you suffer enough you think you'll ..." She shook her head. Her eyes stayed infinitely sad. "I wish you'd stop. I wish you'd believe in life. I wish you'd believe in yourself again. Oh, Harley I wish, I wish you—"

"You wish I'd be the man you met seven years ago. I used to be what you might call a real man. Practically fearless. But conscience makes cowards of us all. You're lucky, Didi. You don't let shit like Franny or your ex or your children fuck with you. You blow off everything. Mom blew everything off, too, her dead husbands. Wish I was like her, instead of like my dad. That poor fucker never got over anything. Heartbreaker. My options have run out just like his did. Over the rail and bye-bye, baby.

Suicide runs in the family."

"Harley, oh Harley." She hung her head, her bright hair falling forward hiding her eyes.

He waited for her to tell him that he wasn't finished yet, he had a lot left to give and all he needed was to keep working and everything would be all right. Tell him he was going to start sending stories out again. Tell him he was going to get back to his desk and write. Tell him he was going to work on his novels. Rewrite them until they were perfect. Polish them until they were irresistible.

He desperately needed to hear her say all that. He needed her magic now. Eagerly, like a child, he watched her mouth. And he thought of Thomas Browne again, the end of that quote about equivocal shapes: . . . real substance beneath that invisible fabric. It was in him somewhere. Wasn't it?

She knew what he needed. She sat beside him holding his hand. Stroking his arm. Her voice was soothing. So soothing it calmed him down. And his tears dried and his heart slowed as she assured him again and again that his luck would turn. Everything would change. Maybe starting tomorrow. Maybe that soon.

"Whatever happens we've got each other," she said. "Don't ever forget we are soul-mates, Harley, and we love each other and ultimately that's what really counts. I'd die for you, honey I really would." And he was thinking, *Maybe tomorrow. Maybe that soon.*

15 - Cougar Lust

Franny sees a dark young man changing a tire at a curb near the mailbox. She parks her car, gets out and drops mail in the slot. That's when she hears the dark young man saying, "Piece of shit, son of a bitch!"

Oh dear, oh dear, his tone frightens her.

She looks away, sees people hurrying past storefronts, people who are scowling versions of the dark young man perpetually angry. She knows she lives in a world filled with hate, envy, seven deadly sins ubiquitous. A world that needs Jesus more than ever, but refuses to listen when he says, Come unto me, ye who are weary and I will give you rest. No, the ones who need Jesus open their hearts to the devil instead.

Probably this includes the dark young man barking at his car, a tire iron dangling from his hand, anger pumping blackness through his veins, his eyes two spheres of fierceness. Swarthy complexion. Possibly Mexican. Or Sicilian. Best keep away from him, so savagely handsome, his face intensely alive, honey-glazed skin radiantly sensual, the way Harley Olsen's skin had been when she married him. Harley Olsen gone. Harley Olsen, why did you leave your loving Franny? That slut Didi, what does she have that Franny doesn't have?

She gets back in her car, drives forward, the dark young man's eyes devouring her car sliding by. She has room to maneuver, but his stare so flusters her that she doesn't steer wide enough, her front bumper rubbing the side of his car.

He roars at her, "What you doing, lady! What the fuck!"

A low-slung Mustang abruptly stops. The guy sitting shotgun yells: "Hey, watch your mouth! Don't be yelling at ladies! Show some respect, shitbird!"

The dark young man hooks the tire iron over his shoulder and says to the guy, a college boy (no doubt about it), football player probably, big shoulders, thick neck, "What's your problem, man?"

"You the problem. Show some respect. You probably cussing someone's mother. How you like someone cussing your mother?"

"Fuck ladies and fuck mothers and fuck you too, dude."

The champion of mothers opens the door as if he is going to get out and teach the dark young man a lesson. The dark young man grins, says, "Come on, *dude*."

Meanwhile, Franny has parked in front of Pisano's. She struggles to open the Buick's heavy door. She sees the dark young man's attention riveted on the hesitating hero, who has one foot on the pavement, the other glued to the floorboard, a contemptuous sneer on his face—as if a dirty look, if dirty enough, will frighten the dark young man. Franny knows that the dark young man has the hero's number. Bad hombres don't stop long enough to sneer. Harley taught her that long ago, when he was bad like the dark young man. Bad hombres just come on as fast as they can. The dark young man keeps his fist wrapped around the tire iron. He seems to be waiting for the guy's other foot to hit the deck. There is a moment of suspension when everything happening gathers into a ball that will either explode or fizzle.

Franny hesitates, half wanting to see the boys fight because of her. But finally she manages to get out of the car, the door chunking hard behind her. "I've got insurance, boys," she says. "It was my fault, boys."

The champion of mothers says, "Well, okay. But somebody needs to teach these punks some manners."

"Punk?" says the dark young man. "Who you calling punk, punk?"

"It's okay," Franny says. "All my fault."

The hero withdraws his foot, closes the door. Franny sees that the dark young man is wired tight in his skin, needing action, a quick burst to get the fury out. He can't let the moment pass, so he steps closer and says, "I said, who you calling punk, punk?"

"You don't shut up I'll—" says the hero, eyes flaring impotently.

The dark young man strolls to the back of the car and pops a taillight with the tire iron. The driver hits the gas, the car bucks forward, roars away, tires tortured.

"You didn't need to do that," says Franny. "I've got insurance. I—"

"Nothing to do with you," says the dark young man jerking his chin at the fleeing Mustang.

"You were fighting over me," she says. She holds her hand in front of her mouth. Tries not to smile. Tries not to be thrilled. The dark young man looks skeptical. She has been to the hairdresser, where she had pink highlights sprinkled here and there in her hair. Her hair was teased. Poofed so it looks thicker than it really is. Fake lashes pasted to her lids. Parenthetical lines bordering her mouth buried in makeup. Pink lipstick above and below her lip-line—mouth appearing larger than it actually is. She knows she is wearing too much perfume, an invisible cloud of Femme Fatale enveloping her. It's as if she had been expecting to meet a dark young man and flirt with him. She takes off her glasses.

"Teach me a lesson," grumbles the dark young man. "Smart-ass college dude ain't teachin nuthin."

Franny coughs into her fist, trying not to be noisy about it. Tugging at the cross dangling between her breasts, she tells the dark young man: "You need college these days to get anywhere. That's what you boys need. Education."

"Who needs that shit? Shit, you couldn't pay me to go to no college." He pauses, his eyes boring into her. "Well, maybe if you paid me," he adds.

Is that an offer? Franny realizes she isn't afraid anymore. There isn't anything evil about him, not really. The steel in him shows he's full of vitality. Eyes throwing sunbeams. Teeth a miracle. She forces herself to breathe evenly. Her hand fluttering around her hair, pushing away some loose strands tickling her cheek. On her fingers are various rings glittering gold, turquoise, silver. The one on her third finger left hand is her wedding diamond. The one on her forefinger is a large, square emerald. She sees how he fixates on the rings, calculating their worth. She knows he wants them, but he wants the emerald most. It is the last anniversary gift Harley ever gave her. Most of the rings on her fingers, except the diamond, are gifts he doubtless bought during that period of his sneaky affair before he moved out.

•

Franny glances at Pisano's and says, "We need to exchange information, so I can notify my insurance and they can fix your car. But first I need to sit down. I have these feet." She points at her feet and adds, "They don't like standing." Raising her eyebrows gamely she grins. She is wearing pink tennis shoes, pink Levi denims and a pink sleeveless shell. A vision in innocent pink she called herself when she walked out the door earlier. "Could we go in there and I could write down my name and insurance and you could give me yours? That's the law. Uh, would you like to split a pizza? I'll pay."

"Bet your ass you will," he grumbles.

She cocks her ear. "Excuse me?"

He throws the tire iron back in the trunk and slams the lid.

•

A sour-mouthed waitress seats them at a table. Flips menus at them like she's dealing cards. Franny offers her hand to the dark young man as she says, "I'm Franny Olsen, what's your name?"

He shakes her hand limply and says, "Hector." He's wearing a broad leather band around his wrist. Is the band there for its tough look? Or maybe it's a gang sign? Or maybe to brace an affliction? She can see her emerald flickering in the mirror of his eyes.

"Hector? I love that name. Hector Trojan. Achilles killed him. Do you know that story?"

Hector looks suspicious of her.

"Well," she says, "what kind of pizza you like? The Works looks good."

"Yeah, I don't care. Except no onions."

Her coquettish heart tells her: He doesn't want his breath to offend me. She surveys the room. Five diners, two men, two women conversing at a table in the far corner. A man eating a torpedo and drinking a beer at another table. He looks familiar, but she only sees his profile and can't quite place him. Franny smells spaghetti sauce, baked bread, melting mozzarella, the underlying aroma of a musty pizzeria: ambrosia of her youth.

She orders a large Works with no onions. Saying to the waitress, "Well, there goes my diet."

The waitress gives her a forced smile and says, "To drink?"

"A pitcher of Bud," says Hector.

Franny indulges him. Says, "Well, if I'm going to be bad, I might as well go all the way."

The waitress asks Hector for his I.D. He shows her a driver's license that says John V. Harp. Harp's age is twenty-six. Franny can see that Hector's picture on the license looks pasted on. Pasted and laminated.

"John V. Harp," says the waitress, eyeing him. "You're not that old." She has a broad forehead, an upturned nose. His stare says she needs to mind her own business. She is looking at Hector as if she knows all about him. He snatches the fake I.D. Tells her to bring him a Coke.

"Do you still want a pitcher?" she asks Franny.

"And a large Works, no onions."

As he watches the waitress walk away, Hector's eyes narrow, his upper lip snarls. Franny knows he might do something to teach the waitress a lesson. He has such a cruel face now. Cruel but mesmerizing. She imagines him waiting for the waitress outside, and when she goes off-shift, there he is and he pounces. He grabs her by the arm, swings her into the wall. Does things with his hands that shock her. Oh dear, oh dear. Masochistic Franny sees it all. Sees his hands wounding tender flesh. Invisible wounds. Burning skin. Franny understands he is good at that, good at hurting. Good at humiliating. She sees him smacking the waitress, telling her that the next time she disses him he will totally put something painful up her ass. Franny closes her eyes and thinks: Thy rod and thy staff.

She bats her lashes for him. "So Hector, where you from? Around here?"

Again he gives her a withering look. She wouldn't be surprised to hear him say he is going to eat her. "Yeah, round here. Where you from, Pinky?"

"Pinky?" She looks down at her pinkness. "Oh, Pinky me." She titters. She covers her mouth. How old does he think I am? she wonders as she tells him, "I'm from the Kensington quarter." Her voice has an alliterating warble. She keeps giggling. Feels sixteen and harebrained.

"I know Kensington," replies glowering Hector.

"I've got a big house. Too big for little ole me. I've been advertising rooms for rent."

She reaches in her purse. Takes out silver-rimmed glasses. Puts them on. "Are you really twenty-six?" she says.

"Maybe."

"Older?"

"Neh."

"Nineteen?"

"I'm old enough," he says.

She puts her glasses away. "Old enough to know better, but too young to resist," she says. "That's such an old joke, isn't it? Does your generation still say stuff like that?"

"Nope. We grunt."

Franny giggles again. Feels bubblegum pinkish, moronically reckless.

When the drinks arrive, Hector opens his throat and pours the Coke down non-stop. He brings forth an air-rattling burp. Then eats the ice cubes, Franny wincing at the sound of his teeth grinding. She thinks of a wolf cracking a bone, getting to the marrow. When the ice cubes are gone, he helps himself to the beer. Franny is following his movements as if he is doing sleight-of-hand. She can feel a shadowy smile raising the corners of her mouth. She wonders how her mouth will look when she's older and her teeth fall out, sunken lips and jutting chin the same as her mother's. Who will want to kiss her? Will she look comical? Or tragic? An advertisement for mercy killing?

She notices Hector glancing at her purse on the table. He could grab it and walk out and she wouldn't be able to stop him. Oh, to be young and able. Able to—him and her. When she was in her prime he wouldn't have stood a chance. She would have gobbled him.

"I once knew a boy young as you." There is a pleasant ache in her heart. "Younger than you."

"So?"

She caresses the cross hanging below her neck as she clears her throat, words rushing out—"I had a summer job buffing eggs on a farm near Flynn Springs and this boy came to work there. His family was migrants. He was an Adonis already. And a hard worker. How good he looked going around with no shirt on. Tall and graceful, he had that beauty you only get in the bloom of youth, that fresh, polished beauty that goes away by the time you're twenty-five and been banged by life. He went shirtless all summer getting himself dark as an Indian. He looked like . . . like a pagan god, no kidding."

She closes her eyes, stretches her mouth, licks her lips to make sure her mouth shines. Does she still have kissable lips? She sees an image of herself as having a face hardly touched by age. Since Hector won't be honest about his age, she decides he is more than a generation younger. It would be robbing the cradle. People would call her a cougar. She tips the glass of beer and swallows without stopping, effervescence burning her esophagus. Hector pours her another. Franny can already feel it. Warm and fuzzy. She is fearless.

"Truth to tell," she continues, "I fell madly in love. But it was impossible. I was seventeen and he was fourteen." She winks at Hector. "Believe it or not, I had a come-hither figure in those days."

"You got one now," says Hector.

"Bless you," she says, feeling a little itch from the top of her head all the way to her toot-toot where things are liquescent. "My body made boys whistle. One old guy said my smile made him soppy. Whatever that means. He said he would give me his whole paycheck if I'd go to bed with him. But of course I did no such thing. He must have been fifty if he was a day." Franny bolts another schooner of beer and it occurs to her that the pains in her feet have vanished. Alcohol: blessed alleviator. She wants a vodka martini.

"I had saved my money," she says. "Five hundred dollars. My Adonis didn't have anything but his sexy self. I bought him presents whenever I went to town. Once bought him a red shirt, black pants, loafers. Dressed up, he looked like Bernardo in West Side Story. Did you ever see that picture? It's old, but it's really good. A musical. An opera.

Hector shakes his head. "I don't watch operas."

She says, "Whatever happened to George Chakiris, I wonder? He was one of the stars. Whatever happened to—"

•

Abruptly Franny feels close to tears. Eyes rolling upward searching for something, egg farm, lost youth, shirtless Bernardo. The time goes and we get old. We die and soon no one wonders where we went. She opens her mouth, laughs loud to keep from crying. The two couples in the far corner stare. To hell with them. The man with the torpedo sandwich stares as well. His eyes bulge. He has a round face, white hair and a double chin.

You know him.

"Franny, what's getting into you?" she murmurs.

Then: "He was a pagan like you. Something about pagans, I don't know."

"What?"

"People want forbidden fruit."

"Says who?"

"Says God." She snickers and thinks about telling him she lives alone and the nights are lonely. Blah, blah, blah. Are you drunk, Franny? Her fingers make adjustments to her rubbery lips.

She pours more beer, foam flowing over the edges of both their schooners. "Those were the best days of my life. But I didn't know it. You can't know your best days until you get my age. And that boy . . . that boy coming out of nowhere . . . well, he was a gift. Would you buy that?"

"Whatever, Madre."

"I never dreamed he would be so—"

The pizza shows up. The waitress eyes the beer in Hector's glass, but doesn't say anything. He grabs a slice of the Works, blows on it, crams half of it into his mouth and mumbles, "She won'd ged annuder pitcha."

"What?"

He swallows. "She won't give you another pitcher. She thinks you're contributing to the delinquency of a minor."

"Yes, let's hope so."

She knows by his eyes how sly he is. He wants to get her drunk and take advantage. It's okay with her, though. She will play along and when they get to her pad on Apple Ave, she will let him strip her of everything. For one warm night of him, she's willing to give him whatever he wants. Just for a touch, anything for a touch.

Franny is almost sick with desire, so horny she's antsy.

"So what happened with you and the kid?" he asks.

"What kid?"

"On the farm."

"Where is he now?"

"I don't know."

She taps her forehead. "Right here. This is the organ you want to take care of, Hector. In here is all you are, all you ever will be."

"You got that right," he tells her.

"Each of us a world."

"That's a way to put it."

"You have nice eyes, Hector. Your eyes look a little sad right now."

"Me? I ain't sad."

"He had eyes like yours. Sad and hungry at the same time."

"I ain't sad. And I ain't hungry no more neither."

She nibbles pizza, dabs her mouth with a napkin. It feels like her lipstick is traveling. She wipes her chin carefully, wondering if it is shiny with grease like Hector's is. He has finished two slices and is half done with a third. "I love to see a healthy boy eat," she says. "It cheers me to see you eat like there's no tomorrow."

"You never know."

"That's very true. But at your age you shouldn't be thinking such things. But still, it's very true. I wake up each morning wondering if it will be my last day on earth. I go to bed every night wondering if I'll die in my sleep. It would be a good way to go, don't you think?"

"Who gives a fuck?" A short burst, a deep breath. And then calmly adding, "But yeah, I think about it. Every New Year's Eve at midnight I wonder if I'll be around for another."

"Every New Year's Eve, yep," she agrees.

"Yeah. I know something's coming and it ain't good. Any second one of us might—"

"Me, most likely."

"So give it to me straight, you and West Side Story get it on?"

Her heart feels full again. "We kissed. It was . . . passionate. So young. So virile. Fourteen, but he was a man if you know what I mean. We kissed and kissed. I love kissing. One night he said, 'Franny, I'm seeing what you looked like as a little girl. The seventeen-year-old Franny is just a shadow hanging outside the real you. This little girl in my arms will always be the real Franny.' Isn't that romantic? What a sweet kid he was." Franny strokes her arms aching to hold someone. She touches her mouth, searching for vanished kisses. "Isn't that a strange thing? I mean, I was only seventeen. But to him I was already grownup. I don't care, he made me melt. I was ready to give him the world."

"Maybe that's what he wanted. Maybe he set you up."

She looks at her glass. Bubbles rising like seconds of her life ticking by. When will he make his move, when will he take what he wants and go? Maybe she should be upfront about it: How much you want to lay an old lady, Hector? How about this emerald?

"So one morning I woke up and their trailer was gone and so was my money. I waited and waited, but he never came back. I knew in my heart he wouldn't. But still I watched and prayed for the longest time."

"Yeah, he was using you. Fuck him."

"No, Hector, I was using him. The money, the broken heart was the price I had to pay for all those kisses. I would have gone all the way if he had pressed me." She gestures towards her face, her jeweled hands fluttering. "At least he'll always have that vision of me. That night when shadows were perfect. That moment forever young."

"I bet you was real fine," says Hector. "You still look good. How old are you, anyway?"

She pours another beer. "How old do I look?"

Hector shrugs. "I ain't good at ages. Maybe fifty?"

Instantly, she feels stupid. She switches the subject, asks him if he has a girlfriend.

"Sometimes."

"I bet you get around."

"So this guy, he steals your money and boogies?"

"At the end of summer."

"So you knew him what? Like three months, maybe?"

"I knew him ten weeks."

"Ten weeks and you're still stuck on him. That's lame."

"No, it's kind of beautiful, Hector." A warm sensation is flowing through her blood. "You know, I haven't been this close to a young man in years. Sharing pizza and beer. This is nice."

"Like this is a date, huh?" he says, grinning. She wishes she could lick his teeth.

"Well, no, it's not a real date. What were we— Oh yes, I meant to give you my—" Reaching in her purse she takes out a pen. On a napkin, she writes her phone number, address, email, plus her insurance carrier. "I'll let them know you'll be getting in touch. Your turn." She pushes the pen towards him. He ignores it.

She feels fifty-four again. And more. The pains in her feet have returned. He looks at what she's written, folds the napkin, puts it in his shirt pocket. The emerald sparkles as she holds it to the light.

"Isn't this the prettiest color?" she says.

He smiles thinly.

Franny pays the bill. She knows she can't handle him. Whatever made her think she could? That boy, that recycling of . . . of heart. But she has given Hector her address. She has made it easy for him. She watches him rise and wait by the door. She joins him. When she looks out the window she sees a cop car and the Mustang. The hero of mothers and his nervous partner are on the sidewalk talking to a policeman. Another cop is examining the inside of Hector's car. Franny says, "Oh dear, oh dear, the fuzz."

Hector says, "Fuzz?"

"Don't worry, I'll tell them it's my fault."

"No prob. I'm going out the back."

"But what about your car?"

"What car? That ain't my car."

There is a flickering feeling inside her head, brain cells firing. "I see," she says.

"I would have made two large chopping that car if you hadn't hit me."

"Two large?"

"Two thousand."

"Oh."

"You owe me."

Her face flushes, her scalp itching again. There is an arthritic hitch in her hip. "I don't have that kind of money on me."

"I'll be in touch," he tells her.

He starts to leave, but she grabs his arm. "Wait a minute." She twists the emerald off her finger, hands it to him. "Will this do?"

"Naw, get out."

"Will it pay my debt?"

"Let's call it collateral," he says.

"It makes me feel good to know you have it."

"You must be crazy, lady."

She is quiet a second, thinking maybe I am. Her fingers tighten on his arm. Her lungs feel smothery, like a hand is squeezing them. "I'm too old for trouble," she says.

"What trouble?"

"You didn't give me your information. I need your address."

"Get real, Franny." Hector puts the ring on his pinky, plays it in the sunlight coming through the window, dots of green strobing the ceiling.

"You won't—"

He turns away.

"Will you?"

"I don't know."

"I know how to keep my mouth shut," she says.

"So do I."

From the corner of her eye, she sees the familiar figure rising. He blocks the way to the back door. When Hector tries to go around him, the man steps the same way and holds up his hand. "Give it back to her, son," he says. And that's when she recognizes him.

"Norman," she says, "is that you?"

"This kid giving you trouble, Franny?"

"No trouble at all."

"What's it to you?" says Hector.

Norman's eyes glitter, his shoulders roll. He is, if anything, even more bearish than when she had known him years ago, when he was dating that damn Didi, who ended up breaking his heart because she wouldn't leave her husband and marry him. She had said his three former marriages made him a bad risk. At that time he had moved from Minnesota and was a professor at CSU. That's how Harley met him.

"I don't get into people's business," says Norman. "But I've known this lady a long time, and you're not ripping her off. No way."

She hears the sound of a police dispatcher speaking code. Hector glances at the front door. He looks Franny up and down. Shrugs his shoulders. Pulls the emerald off his pinky and hands it to her.

"I couldn't get shit for this shit."

She and Norman watch him leaving. She follows and hears Norman saying, "Where you going? That kid's trouble."

She tails Hector, with Norman trailing and saying, "Franny, I'm telling you." They walk to the next street over. Hector is scamming cars. A plastic bag flies in front of him exposing the shape of the wind as he swipes at it. The wind pecking his hair and hers, billowing her sleeveless shell, the wind peering inside at her renovated breasts. Hector stops, takes out the napkin with her name, address and phone number on it. The wind grabs it; he chases it. She hears him cussing.

"Shouldn't have given him that," says Norman.

"Always the idiot," she says. Turning away, she coughs hard. "Can't get rid of this sinus cough," she says.

The two of them return to her car. Police are gone. A tow truck is towing the stolen car away. She looks at her bumper, the scrape in the gold plastic. She will take the car to the car wash. Get it waxed. Buff away the evidence.

"So how you been, Franny?"

"No use complaining."

"You look good. Last time I saw you, you could hardly walk. I barely recognized you now."

"Dieting like mad."

"It shows." He pauses, looking away, rubbing his double chins thoughtfully. "I wish I could lose weight," he says. "The older you get, harder it is."

"Thanks for getting my ring back," she says.

"We should talk," he says.

"Do you think he memorized my address?"

"We should talk," repeats Norman. He looks at his watch. "I'll give you a call. You still working for that publisher?"

"Harvest Home, yes."

"Is Anita still there?"

"No. Anita left years ago."

Norman's eyes slide away. "She sure fooled me, Franny. I thought she loved me, you know . . . but she didn't. She used me just like that whore Didi did. One year together and Didi tosses me like an old toothpick. I couldn't believe it, how cold she was. All these years later, I still can't believe it. Cold broads, both."

"I remember Didi had a bad marriage and was saddled with kids."

"I know," says Norman. "So did I, but I was willing to try again. All for love, you know. She said she would never marry again. What about you? I see you're still married." Norman nods towards her wedding ring.

"Sort of, I guess. But not really. Harley and I are legally separated. Believe it or not, he's dating Didi. Last I heard they were living together. Isn't that weird?"

Norman looks stunned. "Mother*fucker*," he says.

"He still calls. We keep in touch."

Norman shakes his head. "The way of the world," he says.

"He broke my heart, but I got over it. Well, mostly."

"Good for you, Franny. Hey, good seeing you again."

"You too, Norman. Gosh, been a long time, huh?"

"Eight years, maybe?"

"Did you ever marry again?"

"Marriage and Norman Ten Boom don't get along. But yeah, I got a wife."

Franny nods. She gets back in her car, watches him wave as he walks away. "I won't hear from him again," she says. "But maybe Hector. Oh dear, oh dear." His brutal eyes searching her face, her body, making her shiver all over. Ah, she would give anything.

Anything? *Yes,* anything.

16 – Pleasure in Present Tense

Thursday morning she is at her desk trying to decide which manuscript to read first. The molester one sounds interesting. So is the one about incest. People do what they do and her job is to edit their writing and pray for them.

When the phone rings, she answers it and says, "Harvest Home, Franny Olsen. How may I help you?"

Gruffly a voice tells her, "You got my money, lady?"

"What did you say?"

"You got my money?"

Franny gasps and says, "Hector?"

She hears a throaty giggle and then, "Just kidding, just kidding. This is Norman Ten Boom. Look, Franny, I'll be in your neighborhood today. How about I take you to lunch?"

"Lunch?"

"We should talk about what to do to keep that thug from ambushing you."

"Hector? Do you really think? It's been awhile. I've heard nothing."

"It's a sick world, Franny. He's got his eye on you. I guarantee it. He'll show up when you least expect him."

"It's not the same world I grew up in, that's for sure, Norman. We used to say life was cheap in China. We used to pity people there. Now we pity them here." She moves her palm back and forth across her spastic colon. She can hear the Dutchman breathing the breath of waiting. "Where?" she asks.

"How about Balboa Park? The Prado. You're not far from there."

"That's thoughtful," she tells him.

"Ask anyone who knows me and they'll tell you it's one of my biggest assets, Franny. I've suffered a lot in this life. It's made me thoughtful of others." She hears him sighing. And then he says sprightly, "Twelve o'clock?"

"Twelve is fine."

"See you then."

After she hangs up, Franny murmurs, "What have I done?"

•

At noon she parks in the lot closest to the Prado Restaurant. She walks past the Museum of Art and the Sculpture Garden. Hundred-foot eucalyptus and pine scrubbing the air above the Colonial Revival buildings nearby. Not far away sits the San

Diego Zoo. She can hear birds calling. Ahead of her is "suicide bridge" and Sixth Avenue. She turns at the Museum of Man. Climbs the stairs. Sits on a bench in front of the Old Globe Theater not far from the Bell Tower. It's a beautiful day, what the locals on TV call "another patented San Diego day"—75 degrees in mid-May, sky cloudless. Air so bright it hurts her eyes. The park's stucco buildings, Old Spanish flare, make her feel as if she has stepped into another era, the nineteenth century possibly. The grass is lush, flowers blooming with extravagant health. Swallows fly by swift as thoughts. Sparrows squabbling. Heart thumping, nerves on edge, she stands up and paces until her arthritic feet start jabbing her again. "Where is that man? Is he coming?"

And you, Franny. what are you doing here waiting for that nut? Your husband may have left you, but you're still a married woman. God is watching YOU . . .

"That's right. What if Harley found out?" she whispers.

When the thirty-five minute mark passes she calls it an omen, a portent. She doesn't have time for this nonsense. She has Dear Bobbi letters to read, stressed-out psyches desperate for help. That Bobbi person is a fount of hope and faith for the forlorn, the lost, those despairing, yes and Franny, too. She's been working on numerous drafts of a letter she wants to send evangelist Bobbi and get her advice.

Dear Bobbi,

After many years of numerous ailments (chronic anemia, arthritis, gastro-enteritis and other disgusting problems), my husband's compassion quotient wore out and he left me and I can't get over the shock. So much for "in sickness and in health"— just words anyway. Everything comes down to actions that too often give the lie to what we say, don't you think, Bobbi? I believe in the Lord and tell myself that what is happening is His plan for me, my destiny, and I mustn't complain, just put one foot in front of the other and keep going. But life without my man is unbearably hard, Bobbi. I love him. We've been married thirty-plus years and I miss him awfully. Nights are numbingly lonely. My heart aches and I often find myself crying. What can I do? How can I cope? I'm constantly re-reading your book called Calvary Witness News. I've found it full of what I call hard-headed, no nonsense wisdom. So I'm hoping you can tell me how to get over him and move on with my life. Should I divorce him? But what will I do without his health insurance covering me? I'm on a diet. I exercise like crazy. I'm trying to get well, but it's an uphill battle. I hope you'll answer me. I am—a fifty-plus, full-figure woman suffering in San Diego.

Franny hasn't sent her own complaining letter to Bobby yet. She's not satisfied with it. She knows there is more to say, but for the past few days words have failed her. And now look what she's doing: waiting for Norman Ten Boom, a published poet whom she barely knows. If he shows up, what in the world will she do with him? She has no business acting like this . . . like a desperate woman, an eager ass waiting for her date. Is it just that she wants to get laid?

"Oh, Franny Olsen, you moron."

•

She makes her way back to the parking lot. A fifty-four-year-old fool, that's what she is. By the time she reaches her car, her sciatica has returned. She is limping. She might cry if she doesn't get a grip. When she takes her keys out, she hears a door closing behind her, a man's voice saying, "Hey, lady." Hector's primitive face flashes through her mind, his murderous eyes. You owe me is what she expects to hear.

Warily she turns and sees double-chinned Norman waving. Warmth flushes through her veins like an anesthetic. The pain in her lower back vanishes. She takes off her glasses and smiles, showing him her newly whitened teeth. "I thought you weren't coming," she says. "I thought you stood me up."

He grips his head between his palms. "No, no. The traffic. Huge mess on163."

"It's terrible how traffic is now. Everything terrible," she says. "It's a wicked world. It's murder." Her heart trips gaily. A teenage heart full of optimism.

"You look different," he says.

"Do I?"

"Off the pink?"

She blushes, remembering the pink ingénue getup she was wearing when they chanced on each other in Pisano's. "Pink isn't really my thing." She titters and he titters, too. Hopeful energy is rushing through her. This man is flirting with her.

Looking Franny up and down, eyes judging her hips first, then her boob job cleavage, a wink tells her he likes what he sees. What big round eyes he has! His irises make her think of brown sugar. The intensity of his stare increases, until she feels she is being X-rayed.

She has dyed her hair auburn. She wears a forest green rayon skirt and blouse and black pumps. The petite cross glitters against the green of her blouse, the three rings on her fingers twinkle, the big emerald reminding her of Hector and somewhere over the rainbow. She notices Norman's powerful wrists and forearms. Hands that know their business, hands that would have taken that punk apart if he hadn't given back her ring. Norman to the rescue. Norman the scourge of muggers. Is he still at the university, still teaching poetry?

"Are you still at Cal-State?"

"Nah, I retired. Not that I wanted to. I was forced out. I'll tell you about it sometime." And then he tells her about it: "I lost my cool with those bitches running things. It's the bear inside me what takes over and trips that anger switch. You know, Franny, a Dutchman is a calm, thoughtful human being, generally speaking. But the Dutchman in me has to stand back when the bear inside opens his eyes. During emotional moments the bear rules. I went ballistic, Franny. Lost perspective. The perspective that says time passes no matter what you do and people forget what seemed so important. They hung me out to dry, Franny. Threw me under the bus. That's the thanks I get. Hung me out to twist in the wind. Abandoned Norman Ten Boom. Told him to forget a full professorship. Told him to go fuck himself. I should never have left U of Minnesota. They appreciated me there. I should've stayed. It's the damn winter weather's fault." Norman's voice has risen. Passersby are glancing at him and walking faster. His face is flushed. His forehead and cheeks look sunburned. His finger is shaking at her. "Motherfuckers!" he bellows.

Abruptly he takes a deep breath. Sighs and says, "Sorry, Franny. Excuse my French. I know women hate cussing. I apologize. I respect you, Franny, but sometimes I lose my wits over how I've been so screwed by my enemies. What a chump they made of me." He shakes his head, shows her his sagging profile as he says mournfully, "I've won awards for my poetry, you know. Why don't they remember that? Who else on that faculty has been on NPR? Nobody. Just me, Norman Ten Boom."

Franny sees a tear trickling down his cheek. Or is it a drop of sweat? "I should have been treated better," he continues. "People should want a genius teaching their children. I was bringing big names in to do readings and lectures. For Christ's sake I got Ishmael Reed to come! It was standing room only. The newspapers were writing articles about what I was doing for the college. Did anyone appreciate it? Fuck no. They don't appreciate anything. They want you to be a cog in their wheel. I'm no cog in nobody's wheel." He wipes his eyes with the back of his hand. Takes out a hanky and blows his nose. "You know what?"

"What, Norman?"

"They took the heart out of me, Franny . . . tore it right out. I doubt it will ever heal."

Her sympathy goes out to him. She tells herself she can save him. Nurture his poetic genius. God would bless her for it. Behind her she hears classical music (Mozart?) drifting from the restaurant and she asks, "Are you hungry, Norman?"

"I'm famished," he says, giving her a big grin, showing her the Dutchman again. Furious bear retreating behind the huge orbs of his eyes. "Yeah," he says, "I might have lost the battle, but I'm gonna win the war, you'll see. Fuck em, let's eat."

•

After a small salad for her; spaghetti and meatballs for him, plus extra bread (of which he ate only the doughy centers and left the crusts), they stroll toward the botanical gardens. They stop on the footbridge, lean on the rail watching overfed koi slipping like gliding souls through fields of lilies. Franny chatters on and on about her strict diet, the exercise routine she adheres to. She hasn't felt this good in years. Where does all this vitality come from at her age?

"How old are you?" he says.

Without hesitation she lies to him: "Forty-nine. How old are you?"

"Sixty-nine."

"You don't look sixty-nine."

He nods agreement. "No, I don't. People tell me I look ten years younger. I swear to God, Franny, I feel like I'm no more than eighteen. Nineteen at most. Nineteen in my heart. Nineteen in my soul. Nineteen in my dreams. I still have big dreams, Franny. I'm still going to the top. You watch you'll see. How do you like my hair? I dyed it, can you tell? Does it look natural?"

His hair is sandy brown. "I liked the white mane you had, Norman. You looked very distinguished with white hair. It made you look like a noble lion."

"I'm not a lion now? I don't look distinguished?"

"Yes, but not quite in the same way."

"People tell me I have a youthful glow. I tell you I'm only nineteen." He taps his chest. "In here." Closing his eyes a moment, he smiles as if imagining himself at nineteen. Then he pulls a pack of smokes from his pocket and offers her one. She hesitates. Then takes it. Lights up. Doesn't inhale.

"My only vice," he says. "Mainly when I get nervous. You make me nervous, but it's a good nervous. I'm glad to feel nervous. It makes me feel more alive. Thanks for coming, Franny. You don't know how much this means to me. My wife and I don't get along. We're sleeping in separate rooms now. I get so lonely. I've got my son, but I hardly ever see him. He lives with his mother in New York. You don't have kids, do you, Franny?"

She likes how he talks rapidly, like a ventriloquist scarcely moving his lips. His face is old and tough. Picked on by the system. Who isn't? And picked on by Didi, too, who was only using Norman to get her poetry published. Oh dear, oh dear. Poor man. Franny wants to help him. Franny is here. Everything will be all right, dear. Trust in Franny and the Lord, the light of the world. He that followeth me shall not walk in darkness, but shall have the light of life. Franny hugs herself, covers her agitation with another pull on her cigarette, another expulsion of smoke into the crystalline air. She has forgotten how good cigarettes can smell. And pipes too. Harley had smoked a pipe when he was in college, until someone told him he looked like a cliché.

Touching Norman's hand briefly she says, "No, I don't have kids. Wish I did. But Harley and I quit trying. He said he didn't want to bring kids into such a godforsaken world."

"He's right," agrees Norman. "Ain't doing em no fuckin favor. Just look around. This planet is full of monsters. You got a gun, Franny? You got double-lock deadbolts on your doors? You got a security system?"

Franny wags her head.

"That thug out there preying on helpless ladies. He almost got you. If I hadn't been there I hate to think what would'a happened. For sure he would have kept your emerald. Maybe taken all them." Norman points to the jewelry adorning her fingers.

"Maybe take you in the alley and do some things. Fucking animal."

"Hector Trojan," she says in a timid voice, Hector's dark eyes menacing her again, his handsome face filling her with shameful hunger to be a wild thing once again in her life. "I didn't tell you I dented his car. I thought I was doing the right thing giving him the ring. I had no idea the car was stolen. The emerald was a down payment. He seemed like a nice boy, Norman." She pauses a second. Then adds: "No he didn't. He wasn't nice at all. He was scary. Killer written all over him."

"Killer written all over him is right, Franny. I was in the right place at the right time. It happens to me a lot. It's the instinct in me. I wasn't going to get a torpedo that day, but the bear wanted one. I had no choice but to go in Pisano's and order the bear a torpedo and get me a beer. It's mystical how things happen to me. I'm mystical. I'm a mystery to myself. But I know this: that thug would have ripped you off if I hadn't been where the bear wanted to be that day. Listen, we need to get you prepared. We'll get you a handgun. I hate guns, but the way things work in this forsaken country you're a damn ostrich if you don't have firepower. The biggest, meanest man in the world is no match for a gun." He pauses, narrows his eyes and continues. "What you really need is a man like me to protect you. You get me angry I can be your worst nightmare." Norman's fists swipe the air. "I was a hell of a street-fighter," he says, "back in Philly when I was a kid."

•

Franny is wondering how she looks in such direct light. Are her crow's feet showing through the heavy makeup? She turns toward the gardens, the huge lath structure full of tropical plants and trees and shade. He follows her while they slip inside, into cool green paradise. Stroll along narrow pathways lined with leaves so large she knows they could swallow her. She wonders if he will kiss her. The thought makes her panic and she starts chatting about how beautiful the gardens are, how they make her feel as if she has somehow been transported to South America, the equator, the Congo. She bends over and smells a white orchid, its musk saturating her sinuses, making her wish for proms, chiffon, tuxedos, romantic music, flickering stars, a full moon, the back seat of a Chevy. She wonders if he is staring at the slimmed down roll of her rump. She glances back and sees him sitting on a bench toeing the stub of his cigarette.

"I guess I better get back to work," she says.

"Do me a favor," he says.

"A favor?"

"Just stand in that sunbeam a minute. Let me see what happens." From his shirt pocket he takes out pad and pen and starts writing.

In a minute, he looks up and says, "Light beaming through lath squares brightens her breasts. Elephant leaves dip their eager ears towards her mellifluous voice. The veins in the leaves are heartstrings hoping to enfold her. My words beckon. Look at her, light of my life listening."

Franny blinks rapidly. Her breath quickens. "You just sat there and wrote that?"

"For you. When I looked up and saw you," his arms making an inclusive gesture, taking in the botanical scene, "the words flew into my Ursa Major mind. Inspiration. I haven't been inspired in a long time. Thank you, Franny. Thanks much, light of my life."

"I feel dizzy," she says. "No one ever wrote me a poem before."

"Harley never wrote you poetry? He's a writer."

"A wannabe."

"Ah yes, too many of those around cluttering up the slush piles. They get in the way of the good stuff."

"He did get four books published, but then he lost his creativity. Nothing he wrote seemed good enough."

"A common affliction," says Norman.

She sits on the bench next to him and fans her face with her hand while saying. "Harley never even bought me a Valentine. He's about as unromantic as they come. At least with me he was. Maybe with his latest lover he's different. She might insist that theirs is a great romance, don't you think?"

"Didi is an egocentric idealist," says Norman. "She's a selfish romantic like all romantics are. They're the kind who steal husbands. But I have to admit it, I'm a little bit like that too, Franny. A romantic. An idealist." His knee is pressing her knee as he adds, "Look here, let's don't be senile. We're too old to waste time. I feel you feel what I feel. Am I right, my darling? Have we found each other again after all these years? What we'll do about it is the question. You want to go to a motel, or shall we go to your house and find out how serious this is?"

The bluntness of his approach makes her unable to catch a breath. Her mind whirls. She's incoherent. She wants him. She wants him to go away. They're both married. Oh dear, oh dear. Adultery. "Your wife," she says.

"She's got her life, I've got mine."

Franny looks at the pathway between the botanical splendors and says, "You know, I still live in the same house I shared with Harley. It's too big for me, Norman. I've decided to rent the extra bedrooms. I have rooms to rent, Norman. Would you like to take a look and consider renting one from me? They're very comfortable. I had an ad in the paper, but no one answered."

"Right now?" he says.

She looks at her watch. "I'm a little late already, but okay."

"Let's go in my car. We'll come back for yours later."

She calls her boss and tells him she is sick and on her way to the doctor's. It must be something she ate for lunch. If she can't come back, she promises to work overtime tomorrow and not charge Harvest Home for it.

"What are you working on?" asks her boss.

She looks at Norman Ten Boom and says, "I picked it out of the slush pile. Mainly because of the title. It's a study, interviews about older women seducing younger men. It's called *Cougar Lust*."

"How younger?"

"Some are much younger. Like thirty years."

"The women aren't school teachers are they? That shit has worn out its welcome."

"No, they're from all walks of life. A lot of them are married."

"Sounds good. Pass it on if it holds up."

In her mind she starts composing the manuscript. Giving an imagined chapter a weave so no one can connect it with her life. She remembers a letter she read in Bobbi's book:

Dear Bobbi:

I am fifty years old and I have fallen in love with a younger man. Actually, he's hardly more than a boy. He's only nineteen, Bobbi. I'm ashamed, but I can't help myself. He's so—

As they drive in Norman's car to Franny's house, she tries to make sense of what she's doing. But she can't. This vigorous old man whose voice belongs on a stage has moved her in ways no one has moved her before—not even her husband. She tugs at her skirt, but it refuses to be ruled. Full of fire, the fabric clings, outlining her thighs and the hollow between them, where she hasn't been touched since long before Harley left her.

•

Dear Can't Help Herself: God sees your dilemma. What you are doing is damned by a social order that continually wars with itself over the meaning of Scripture. But be that as it may, the Holy Bible still contains the answers you need. Your personal relationship with God is paramount. Your understanding of His Word is more important than any interpretations held by theologians. Forget them. Flip to any page and you will find in code the path of truth and light and bountiful love. Get on that path and follow wherever it leads you. If it leads to the arms of this boy, then so be it. God has sent him unto thee for a purpose. Maybe you are meant to save him or he is there to save you. Listen to the urgings of your immortal soul. As long as God is in your heart, you won't do anything wrong, anything sinful or reeking of brimstone. Memorize the following lines from Holy Scripture and when you have doubts soothe yourself by saying over and over: "I came that you may have and enjoy life, and have it in abundance, until it overflows. *There is no fear in love; for perfect love casts out fear.*"

Faithfully yours, Franny Olsen

Glancing at Norman, she sees him staring straight ahead, his gaze so visionary it's as if he knows tomorrow. It occurs to her that God is satisfyingly mysterious in the way his wonders unfold. Just when you think your life is over, he sends you something new and exciting. He sends you a Bear Dutchman named Norman Ten Boom. He sends you a new pair of eyes and a poem. A security system. Maybe a gun. He sends you a warning that you need double-lock deadbolts for your doors.

17 - Going Down

Nothing to inspire Harley the way Franny had apparently inspired Norman whose tenth collection, *Shaman Bear Knows* had already earned The Walt Whitman Award and was nominated for a Pulitzer—*Finalist* was the word. The Dutchman was a big deal now, his poems praised for their insights into the death of "true" patriotism and the political madness of the "skulking President" who had gone into a self-imposed exile and was fretting about a special prosecutor ordering him to testify before a grand jury. Norman's poems were fearless in their righteous indignation, their ethical venom.

Harley wished that he and Norman could have stayed friends, but it was impossible after he found out about Didi. They had talked about what had happened after Didi left and Norman went crazy. And then went even crazier when he learned that Didi and Harley were having an affair. Norman had caught him at home one day and said, "You'll be sorry for this, you son of a bitch. I ought to kill you. Someone ought to kill you, you fucking traitor, you backstabber. You betray your wife, you betray your friend. How could you do it?"

Harley had tried to explain that he didn't know how such a thing could be. He hadn't meant for it to happen. It just did. She had shown up at one of his readings and later they had had drinks at a bar and the next thing Harley knew she was in his bed. He had been sure it was just a fling and she would pick up where she left off, not with Norman, perhaps, but with that guy who bought the gym. Carlson. She had confessed to Harley that she and Carlson had been fuckbuddies way back when. She had said that Harley wasn't merely a fuckbuddy. Sex with Harley was sacred, it was commitment. Carlson was out of her life forever, she said.

"If you believe that, you're dumber than I am," Norman had told him. "If she would cheat on me, she will cheat on you. She cheated on her husband with me and that's why they broke up."

Harley knew that wasn't her story, but he hadn't tried to contradict Norman whose huge hands looked lethal. "All I can say is I'm truly sorry."

Norman had answered, "You'll be even sorrier, just wait and see. That woman will destroy you. She nearly destroyed me, but I made a comeback. You, on the other hand, you'll go down in flames. Believe me, I know these things. You're a puny man, Harley. No strength to fall back on. I pity you, you stupid bastard. You should have stuck with Franny. You should have stayed home with your wife and done your work. What have you written since you left her?"

The answer was *nothing*.

•

Yes, Harley should have stayed with Franny and kept fiddling with the words. He would probably be writing, instead of wasting hours sitting at his desk harvesting failure.

But the thing was: living with Franny had made him miserable.

But then again the same thing had started happening with Didi. Harley was beginning to believe that he didn't really like women. A thought which made him remember his mother, how ambivalent his feelings had been about her. Feelings all over the spectrum.

He hears her voice the last time he saw her: "Harley, you look like death warmed over. How'd you get so old? Gray temples? Bags under your eyes? You're getting old. An old lug. How old are you anyway?" His fifties had seemed old when they happened, but now he was sixty-three. Definitely old age.

Leaning back in his chair, closing his eyes, he saw his mother alive chugging along beside him when he left Gateway. Did he ever love her? If you can't love your mother, you can't love anyone.

•

Harley rose and stood gazing at the spot where a huge hill used to be before it was dynamited and replaced by more condos. Nothing safe these days, not even huge hills. Or a mother's love. Is there such a thing as love? Beyond the word itself is there anything other than wishes? L-O-V-E. A word used to describe something incoherent, something illogical, something that comes in a rush of inarticulate feeling. Something that can be lost as fast as it's found. Or is it just me? Do other people know love the same way they know God? They don't need logic. They don't need to be rational. They don't need to think deeply about it. I know God exists because I know God exists. I feel God in my soul. I feel God in my heart. I feel God in every organ of my body. I know because I simply know. "Why hasn't that way ever worked for me? For how many millennia has the world run on such logic? Who is Harley Olsen to say none of it makes sense, none of it is reasonable? Who is Harley Olsen to say show me the data?"

But then again if there is God, there may also be Heaven, a place of many mansions where his mother floats in Eternal Bliss. Her essence knows nothing of pain or fear. It knows nothing of senility, loss of dignity. It knows nothing of children turning away with tears in their eyes and saying, "That's not my mother. That's just a shell we called Eve."

You'll carry that with you the rest of your days, Harley. And if you live long enough, it will be you they're talking about. Let him go. Let him die. He's making us sad beyond words. No one is allowed to do that.

"I wonder if I'll know if I'm going senile. I wonder if I'll have it in me to take my own life, rather than subject myself to the dying of brain cells and what my changing personality is doing to others. Is there some point at which you flip and no longer see that it's time?"

Harley watched an old couple walking by on the sidewalk. They were stooped and gray and holding hands and soon out of sight.

"Dying is an art, like everything else. What nonsense. There was no art to sticking your head in an oven. No art in blowing your brains out with a shotgun. Opening a vein, cutting your throat. Pills. Hanging. Leap into space. The water of San Francisco Bay beckoning my father as he waved goodbye. He must have been thinking of suicide for a long time without anyone knowing. The impulse to jump became overwhelming. How else could he have done it? In one of her honest moods my mother told me she would have committed suicide long ago if she had had the guts. 'I don't have the guts,' she had said."

It occurred to him that he was musing on an abstraction. It was easy to talk about dying, an event for the future. Maybe twenty or thirty years. Tonight he would settle into his easy chair with the TV on, the terrible news, the wars, the killings, 70 dead in a suicide bombing, innocence exterminated, fanaticism triumphant. He would watch it in security, knowing he would never be a part of anything like that. Yes, but Didi would be home soon. He might look at her and remember Norman's warning: "That woman will destroy you . . . you'll go down in flames."

18 - So Into You

The day after Harley's sixty-fourth birthday, Didi left him and moved in with Carlson. Days later, Carlson's wife called Didi and said he had bragged about fucking her when she showed him the house he bought.

"Fucking another woman's husband. Rotten-to-the-core—"

"He said you're separated."

"Separated. Not divorced."

"What's your name?"

"Maria."

"He bragged about making love to me, Maria?"

"He says whatever woman he wants he gets her. If I've heard it once, I've heard it a thousand times."

"He didn't get me. It was mutual."

"You think he loves you?"

"I don't know."

"He doesn't. Carlson loves Carlson. You know what he does? He calls all his ex-wives to make them jealous. Do you know he has kids scattered about? Yes, several. I don't even know how many. Listen, when you become an ex, he'll be calling you too, calling and bragging about what he did to whoever she is. He'll get you worked up. He'll try to have phone sex with you. He'll want to hear the sounds you make masturbating."

"Maria—"

"When he's finished with you, you'll be like I am."

"Who are you?"

"Number four whore. I'm warning you for your own good, don't trust him. He's cheated on all of us. He takes testosterone and gets B-12 shots and uses Viagra. He's obsessed with sex and will break your heart when you're no longer his fantasy. He says every man needs fantasy to energize him. I was his fantasy for a year before he tired of me and found you. If you think he'll divorce me, think again. I'm his shield now. I'm his excuse to end it when he tires of you."

Didi's spine stiffened. "Maybe he won't tire of me, Maria."

Maria hooted and hung up. And then sure enough, Didi couldn't reach him on the phone. She called numerous times that day, but he didn't answer. Where was he? What was he doing?

•

Word made flesh: It wasn't until after she started bedding him on a regular basis that she got back into poetry. She wanted to make flesh into words, wanted to pull from her soul lines like these: Your arms are outdone/only by the tenderness of your lips, Carlson.

Cornball kitschy shit like that. But she got off on it: I want to write you a love poem/ I want to write your eyes, Carlson.

No one had told her anything like that in her life, certainly not her ex. The beauty of her words went to her head. And the more poetry she wrote, the greater she lusted.

One night she quoted lyrics while kissing his feet. Sucking his toes. A breathtaking experience, which had never happened before.

Your toes tremble,
When I lick them,
Your feet shiver—
Your penis becomes jealous.
My poems
slip between
lines,
languid
touching you
in all those places
no tongue
has ever known before.

She watched him smiling down at her. She looking up at him, her eyes telling him: *See how I worship you?*

Harley huh? Danny who? What's a Norman Ten Boom?

●

He made her realize that the years of her marriage and the years with melancholy Harley were starving years. Under Carlson's spell she became drunk on sex in all its forms. Threesomes, foursomes. Nothing off limits. He got off seeing her making love to another man or a woman, or both at the same time. He told her he adored *watching*.

The next morning, she always felt ashamed. But each time he brought someone home for them to ravish, or be ravished by, Didi did it again. She had become addicted. Sex was heroin. She wallowed in it. Indulging herself, immersing herself in pleasure. The more whorish her behavior the more he loved her. Or so he said.

But did she love him?

She wanted to. He made her feel adventurous and special, HUGELY SO.

Price beyond rubies, he kept telling her.

The only things pestering her were (first of all) the tiny fact that he was another married man she had stolen. Also nagging was the fact that she had seduced Harley, taken him from his wife, and then abandoned him when he could no longer fill her needs. One other thing troubling Didi was the fact that her mother might find out. The old lady would never forgive her.

Every bad thing you do comes back to bite you. Yes it does, Didi. You're in trouble.

•

Erotic rewind: Now and then when he or someone else was in her, Didi conjured her husband's youthful engorgement. Long ago when they were new to each other, he had been a marvel—gorgeous blue eyes, slim, muscular body, perverse as porn, stamina of a race horse.

The first time he kissed her she nearly swooned. She saw him now in memory: saw him bending mouth to mouth, an intoxicating image. Didi thinking: I'm kissing the sexiest man alive. Wavy hair tickling her brow, silver highlights sprinkling through it like specks of tinsel. Were the specks natural? Or did he use A Touch of Sun? Prematurely going gray, Danny?

She had loved singing duets with him, her breathy alto blending with his tenor: I'm so into you . . . Feeling the heat of him. Licking the salty sweat of his skin. Zucchini is what they named his penis. Mouths magnetized and swiveling. What to do with lips so syrupy? Lick them like licorice.

Sweetest kisses, long, lingering. Tongue timid at times. Shy at first feeling her breasts as if they were part of a formula—obligatory. Though Didi didn't care if he did that or not. Fingers: find Netherland. Dreamily out of control was Didi in those heady days as in these days, seeing herself as a metaphor for luscious.

Also thinking: Didi is too far gone to ever love anyone else.

•

If anyone knew her past or could read her mind they'd call her the whore of San Marcos. No more morals than a chimpanzee. Maybe she's part Bonobo. One of her favorite daydreams centered around the first time she had sex with Danny, his whole mouth cupping her.

She saying, "What're you doing? I'm not wet?"

"Getting you wetter. Wetter the better."

Recalling that moment always makes her horny, always makes her giggle.

One night he drove her to a restaurant to meet Gloria, his mother. She was with her boyfriend, a dour, aging man with a receding hairline leading to a bald spot on the back of his head. His name was Rit. He didn't offer his hand, just nodded when Gloria introduced him. Eyes traveling up and down her were bloodshot, his nose was rosy, the nostrils patterned with broken capillaries, a mouth sour as the bite of a lemon.

Gloria was a portrait in platinum. Pale. Thin. Ghostly. Her eyes behind thick lenses had pink irises. Albino? When Didi saw the two of them together she almost laughed. In fact she tittered a little, an idiot utterance, which she offset by enthusing about how glad she was to meet them. Then adding, "Gosh, I don't know why I'm so darned nervous."

"Sid down, honey, sid down," said Gloria. "You're tractin tention."

Throughout the meal, Didi couldn't help noticing how people were staring at them. Rit smoked all through dinner and tossed off shot after shot of something amber. Whatever it was, it seemed to have no more affect than tap water.

She was so self-conscious she almost couldn't eat. Found herself wishing she could get up and leave. Danny's freckles, the blond and silver flecks in his hair, no longer charmed her. In fact sitting between him and his mother, she saw the resemblance and decided he looked ludicrous.

Rit never said a word. Now and then he grunted. Sometimes sighed. Occasionally he coughed wetly into his fist.

Gloria probed her about ambitions. What was she majoring in? Business? A minor in writing. What kind of writing? Poetry? Business is sensible. But a minor in poetry? Why waste your time on that?

Didi had chortled, simultaneously slamming her hand over her mouth. She told Gloria she wasn't sure what she would do with her minor. Perhaps work on a newspaper or magazine or teach? Maybe become a writer? All Didi knew for sure was that she loved reading, loved studying literature and poetry. Loved all types of art. Art made life interesting. And she said, "Someday when I have my own home I'm going to cram it with works of art. Art makes everything about life worthwhile."

Gloria raised a skeptical eyebrow. Glanced at Rit and then at her twenty-year-old son raking his knife over a bloody filet mignon. "Danny's working as a janitor while he finishes college," she said.

"A janitor, really?" Didi said. "You never told me."

"Yes, he's working to put himself through school. Next year he'll have his premeds done. Scrub those floors, kid. No handouts."

Didi said, "I thought you were on a full-ride scholarship?"

Danny shrugged, pointed his fork at his mother. "My nemesis," he said. "What she'll tell you is she's waiting for me to fall in line and show some respect for her who has worked hard all her life. But you know what? I don't want to be her clone. I want my independence."

"But you're going to be a doctor, right?"

"Whim of the day . . . who knows?"

"He's just saying that to irritate me," said Gloria.

"You said your father got rich trading stocks, and you didn't need to work."

"Do you know what his father did?" asked Danny's mother.

Didi shook her head.

"He mathematized widgets and whatnots."

Didi burst into shrill laughter. Rit looked at her with startled eyes. The mother was sneering. Danny winking, hunching his shoulders and continuing to work on brutalizing his steak. Didi noticed that he had rims of dirt under his fingernails.

When dinner was over and he was walking her back to campus, he said: "Now, when do I meet *your* parents? She told him that some weekend soon they would drive to San Marcos and meet her parents and brother and sister.

She imagined their faces. A janitor? You a girl at UCLA and you're dating a janitor with a ponytail? And he's iffy on becoming a doctor? What's wrong with this picture? Listen, you're only eighteen. Look at him, he's already going gray. Appears old enough to be your father.

Not only her mother would be appalled, but all Didi's relatives would have been offended. "He's beneath you in every way. I bet he's not even Orthodox," her mother would say.

Didi's father: "Whose damn daughter is she?"

Didi's sister and brother: "What a dumbbell."

So she started avoiding Danny. Stopped answering her phone. Pretended not to be in her room when he knocked on the door. She should never have let the affair happen. All that sex. She moved through life making one mistake after another. Doesn't everyone?

•

"Men want only one thing," her mother had always told her. "To them you're just a morsel named Deidre Annaba-Godunov."

Years later, she heard that Danny had his degree and was doing his internship, and she wondered if she should have stuck with him. Maybe he was one of the lucky ones. Maybe life on a golden platter that she stupidly threw away. She believed she had seen him for the last time. It had been lust, not love.

Not a bad experience, though. Certainly better than the experience she had had at nineteen with Jasper, the boy who worked as a dishwasher in Kensington. Wild, wild times with him and his friends making a porn film. Somehow dragging her into it. Playing her part had given her a taste for taboo. She knew she was far better than she was behaving. But at least the role she was playing was Juliet to Jasper's Romeo, a pornographer's take on those famous young lovers.

By the time it was done, Jasper had dropped out and the director had taken over his role. She had a copy of the uncut version and occasionally played it, marveling at how gorgeous she was, her hair its natural brunette, her body a vine of dazzling curves.

The later months in San Francisco flashed through her mind. Drugs and sex. The failed attempts to play the artist. The humiliating retreat to San Diego when she caught an STD. Trichomonas. Better known as Trich.

•

Didi had written a poem when she was thirteen:
Where are those dreams of yesteryear?
Those dreams are gone where dreams must go,
Where memories linger still.
Where our minds can capture them,
And bring them back at will.

Deathless stuff. It would be discovered one day. Probably when she had passed on to her eternal reward. Poetry lovers building a shrine to her. A secret admirer depositing a red rose on her grave every evening at sunset, where that certain slant of light was also a symbol of truth:

The eternal truth Deidre Annaba-Godunov gave us in her verse (some critic would write); our country has lost an American treasure. But at least we have her immortal words. Her voice will go on as long as we can hear, as long as eyes can see. As long as we are literate enough to read.

Such were the fantasies she clung to, even as an adult.

•

Home again, she went to see a doctor she had picked out of the phone book. He gave her antibiotics, which cured her Trich problem, but not the gloomy brainwaves living in her head. Days passing, Didi staying in bed brooding, unwilling to function. Getting up only when her mother came upstairs and said, "Get your butt out of that bed. I won't have you lazing about."

"What's wrong with you?" she kept asking.

"I don't feel good. I feel ishy. Flu maybe."

"That's it, Didi. No more of this shit. Go take a shower, and for God's sake wash your hair. It smells to high heaven. It smells like wet feathers."

She told Didi of a job opening at Stein News. A secretary. "Get down there and put your application in. See Matthew Stein. He knows you're coming. I've already talked to him. Smart as Einstein is Mr. Stein. His readers adore him."

•

A few weeks after working for Mr. Stein, he called her into his office and thanked her for straightening out the files. They had been a mess for months. The girl he had fired was lazy. Because of her there had been missed deadlines.

"At last things are the way they should be," he told Didi. Matthew had furry eyebrows, thin lips, narrow jaw, dimpled chin. He was tall. His movements fluid. At night in bed touching herself she thought of him, instead of Danny.

At quitting time one day he said, "How about dinner, Didi."

Dinner?

His treat.

After eating at The Golden Dragon they lingered, drank white wine while he told her about himself, how he was raised in Superior, Wisconsin, how cold and unemotional his parents were, just like the land itself. He got away from it all by joining the Marines and later went to journalism school on the GI Bill. His smile was self-deprecating. But his eyes were proud. (And proud he should be, Didi was thinking.) By the time dinner was over she was ready to do anything for him. Could anyone fall in love that quickly?

They had sex in his office, several times in his car, often in his apartment. Anywhere they could find to do it they did it. Two months later she was pregnant.

She kept it secret. Imagined their future together. True romance. Two kids and a house in an upscale neighborhood in San Diego or Los Angeles. The American dream come true. Didi and Matt holding hands as they walked into the future.

But then reality intruded. Matt didn't want to be married. Nor did he want a child. He told her he would pay for an abortion. Didi lost control. She slapped him and told him to go to hell. When she got home, she told her mother she quit her job because Matthew Stein kept patting her ass, making suggestive remarks, sexual overtures.

"See?" her mother said, "men only want one thing."

•

When Didi was in bed, she would run her hand over her abdomen to see how big it felt. She wondered how long it would take before she was showing. It was mad to dream that Matthew would marry her. Totally absurd. A girl who flunked out of college. A girl who had made a porn movie, caught an STD and had minimal social skills. A girl currently clinging to Mommy's apron strings. A girl who typed and filed for a living. She had nothing to offer but her body. Another silly girl knocked up out of wedlock.

Didi: a big zero. She was the same as all those other morons out there trying to hide babies under loose clothes.

She started daydreaming about Danny again, imagining the two of them eloping. The wedding in Vegas, the honeymoon after and soon she could tell him: Honey, guess what.

Who was she kidding? Danny would know she had bamboozled him.

She was in deep depression, so deep she couldn't get out of bed and look for a job no matter how much her mother scolded and threatened.

Didi knew the only way out was suicide. She asked her mother to ask Dr. Stevens, (the family's doctor for twenty years) to give her a prescription for sleeping pills.

"If I could get some sleep, I'm sure I would get better," she said.

Instead of giving Didi a prescription, the doctor made a house call.

He sat beside her on the bed, took her hand and said, "Now what's all this about, sweetie?"

"I don't know, Dr. Stevens," she said.

His eyes searching hers, she told herself his eyes were the exact image of Danny's eyes. Oh, if only—

"You look sad, Didi. Has something happened? Hmm? Tell me."

"If I could get some sleep," she said

"You're very depressed."

"I'm an idiot."

"I think I should exam you, sweetie."

Without waiting for her to say yes or no, he opened his bag, took out a stethoscope, pulled the sheet off and started listening to her heart. Listened to her carotid arteries. Listened to her stomach. Her bowels. Turned her on her side listening to her lungs. "Take deep breaths," he said.

He put the stethoscope away and probed her neck with his fingers. Slender, flawless hands is what she felt. He probed under her armpits. All this probing of this poor dumbbell Didi made her edgy. He lifted her nightgown and palpitated her tummy again and asked if anything hurt. His warm palm lay a long time on her belly. His gaze fixed on her abdomen. Could he feel the baby in there?

"I don't want it," she told him.

"Why not?"

"What would I do with it? How would I care for it, I can barely take care of myself. I'm . . . I'm hopeless, Doctor Stevens. Such a mess."

His little finger moved back and forth like a windshield wiper, the tip of it touching the edge of her pubic hair as he said, "It's been my experience that sometimes a little loving is what we need to change our chemistry and give us some relief from what ails us. His pinky slid over the edge and nested. "I should exam your pelvis," he said. "Just to make sure everything's in order."

Her breathing grew labored.

He pushed Didi's legs apart, lifted her knees, examined her and said, "Yes, I see.

Yes, I know what to do for you."

"I want you!" she told him. She grabbed his head. Kissed him fiercely.

She did everything to him. He did everything to her.

Then he made her an appointment to come to his office, where he would perform an abortion.

•

Afterwards, Didi had stared at the ceiling night after night praying for a sign of pardon. The opposite sign came one day when she walked to the store and bought caramel candy. Stuffing her mouth full of it. Caramel threatening to suck out her fillings, but she didn't care. The sticky stuff reminded her of Danny, the undercurrent breathing from him whenever they made love. She chewed caramel as if she were chewing his lips. And told herself: Damn you, Didi, you're still horny for that guy.

Passing a mini mall she saw a clinic. Saw a flyer on the window saying: ABORTION ALTERNATIVES. Underneath the heading was: ADOPTION AGENCY. And then: Pregnant? You have options. Our Services Are Confidential.

In the middle of the poster: a picture of a baby in a womb looking tragically vulnerable. Didi spit the caramel out and broke down sobbing.

•

Sum it up: Sex with five men and I was still only twenty. Am I a nympho? Are there many women like me who don't know how to say no? Never be that foolish again, Didi.

Who you talking to?

You talking to Me?

That sound you're hearing is laughter.

Save As Documents: The World According to Deidre Annaba-Godunov.

19 - A Terrible Beauty

Harley had never imagined that Franny and Norman would find each other, but not long ago he had seen them hand-in-hand crossing the Riverside campus, on their way to Norman's reading in the college theater. Harley had bought a ticket to the event. He had followed Franny and Norman inside, where he watched Norman's charismatic performance. White mane flowing over his shoulders, eyes burning, his booming baritone holding the audience spellbound:

Just yesterday, the bomb fell
Into the middle of the zoo
The cockatoos
Screeched, macaws went
Wild in their cages, screen
Wire shivering into
Countless fragments
Of death, piercing
The air,
Sending the raccoon
Into panic as shrapnel
Bit off his leg; the monkey's
Arm went limp,
Crushed by the blow
Of a shattered tree, hundreds of
Birds pulverized to atoms, all
Of their death cries crying out
Prophetically—cries
Merging with the wailing of
Women, the terrified
Sob-slobbering children.
O' innocence!
Innocence, welcome to the war
Welcome to the zoo.

•

Harley remembered how moved he had been. And how *jealous*.
Norman was in the sphere of the iconic and Franny was with him. Fortunate Nor-

man. Favorite of muses. Images blossoming like metaphorical spears thrown at those responsible for an immoral war. Storms of rupture, a terrible beauty formed from the mind of Norman Ten Boom.

I hate him! Life sucks!

Sour grapes, Harley.

Love dies daily. Gets waylaid, siphoned off, distracted.

•

Months later, he got an invitation to read at a community college in Escondido. His first inclination was to decline. He turned on the TV and tried to distract himself with the nightly news. Horrible horrors plaguing the world. He knew he was lucky to be ill and not far from dying. The Reaper would claim him and his own troubles and the troubles of the world would vanish in an instant. He was glad *not to be in his twenties* and trying to establish himself. No, he had had his life. Sixty-four years. Long enough for anyone. Those who live into their eighties look in the mirror and hate what they see. Such a thing won't happen to an eighty-year-old Harlan J. Olsen.

He went to the bathroom, peed, washed his hands. Looked in the mirror and told himself, "Not so bad. Thinning hair but not that many wrinkles. Lean, long, lanky. Girls always liked you, Harley. You could have had a dozen coeds, but you had ethics and refused to give in to something so tawdry. Look what happened the one time you did give in. *Didi*. Christ almighty, when did you get so stupid?"

He went to the kitchen and poured himself three fingers of vodka over ice. He turned the TV off and sat reading the invitation again.

Dear Harley Olsen:

I've been using your novel *So Much Heroism* in my creative writing classroom and I can't tell you how much my students have enjoyed it. I found out how close you live to our college and with urging from my students, I decided to take a chance and write you and ask you to please contact me if you have any interest in coming to my class and talk to them and read from your brilliant book?

If the idea appeals to you, please let me know and we can work out the details.

Sincerely yours,

Mona Washburn, Associate Professor

Palomar Community College

1140 West Mission Road, San Marcos, CA 92069-1487

Telephone: 1 760 744-1150 ©

monawanna@gmail.com

PS - We'd be so thrilled if you come!

•

Just like that, out of the blue. So you're not totally forgotten, Harley. *So Much Heroism* has been your most popular book. It hasn't fallen into the abyss with the others. Not yet. But doesn't Mona Washburn know how over the hill you are? Obviously not. Could you pull yourself together and give it one more shot?

Harley thought about calling Didi and telling her about the invitation. In an instant, he changed his mind: "Hell with Didi, that slut. Her and what's-his-name? Carlson."

Young, virile, handsome. Harley hates him. This is what jealousy feels like. He was jealous when Franny kissed that guy under the mistletoe. She caused a fistfight that night, the last one Harley ever had. *Stupid.* Her faithlessness showed its ugly head again and again. Young and horny and needed to go exploring. God knows how often she cheated on him. He cheated on her once. Only with Didi. Falling so hard he thought she was the love of his life. She told him she was, told him they were soulmates.

But then a man gets a heart condition and can't keep up. Can't get an erection either. Oh, it doesn't mean anything, she said. But Harley knew better. Slick Didi, lustful, perverted, Lesbian inclined—no way could she live without her pleasures. Saying to him, "I didn't sign on for this. I can't handle illness. It wears me out. It's too depressing. So sorry, honey."

"Fuck, go on," he had told her. I don't need you anymore than I needed Franny."

It's all fine. She's gone and Harley can live without her or Franny or anyone. He has a dog for company, a cocker spaniel. A female. Harley had found her on the street eating out of a pizza box. He had stopped next to the dog, opened the passenger door and said, "Come on, puppy." The dog had wagged her stub of a tail and hopped onto the seat as if she and Harley were longtime pals. When they got home, he had given her a bath in the sink. Dried her with a towel and the blow dryer, combed her hair out.

Because Christmas was close, he named the dog Holly. He lavished affection on her, took her everywhere, his companion, the one who owned the seat where Didi used to sit. He even allowed Holly to sleep in his bed, something he would never have considered when he was the old Harley, the walled off, distrustful pessimist who had said children and animals were irritations he could live without. Females in general had been added to the list of pests he kept on his shit list. Holly being the only exception.

•

At the moment she was lying on the rug staring at him curiously, as if she were asking why he was holding that letter and reading it again and again.

"What do you think, Holly?" he said. "This teacher wants me to come talk to her class about writing. She wants me to read. I don't know. Do I want to? Shouldn't I just leave well enough alone?"

Holly sniffed the letter, head cocking back and forth, obviously thinking over what he had told her. She licked the letter and his hand. Sitting on her haunches before him, she smiled and nodded.

"You're saying I should?"

All of her gestures seemed to be saying, Do it, Daddy.

"Okay, I will if she'll let me bring you."

•

And that was how he came to be where he was on a certain Thursday evening, Holly on the floor beside him as Harley, half-hunched, his butt resting on Mona's desk, reading to her class a scene he hoped would titillate them, shock them, perhaps. Although he understood that (unlike his generation) their generation was practically shock proof.

Almost bought the farm again. Lots happening. The gods of war have suddenly noticed me and they say Hey, we need to fuck wit him. We ain't fucked wit him enough. Yup yup, I got wound number two, a graze along the right side of my head that opened a seam. I felt it sizzling through my hair, but I didn't equate it with a bullet at first. It felt like white heat, like a swipe of lightning. It took forty stitches to close. It give me a monster headache like I never had in my life and I was temporarily blind in my right eye. The whole side of my face ballooned. I still have a black eye. Not swollen anymore. It looks like it was splashed with tar. So I have two Purple Hearts now. I do not want a third. Third time is the charm, they say.

He put the book down, his lips smiling tightly. Most of the students were staring at him with riveted eyes, but one young man in the back was yawning. Harley knew they were waiting for him to entertain them. He had his writer's mask on, the one he put on for thirty years when he was teaching and doing tours, his mouth opening, words pouring out. Hoping he wasn't making a fool of himself.

"Any questions?"

A loaded pause. Then Mona Washburn raised her hand.

"Yes."

"Mr. Olsen, in what category would you place your story? Fiction? Creative non-fiction? Or simply non-fiction?"

"Maybe historical fiction. Much of *So Much Heroism* comes from letters my father wrote to my mother when he was in the war. I worked around those letters to create the story of a soldier who earned three Purple Hearts and lived to tell about it. He also won a Silver Star."

"Your father won all those medals?"

Harley nodded. "He was extraordinarily brave."

"His suicide a few years after the war, is that true, too?"

"Yes, I saw him dive."

"You end with the last line saying, 'If you're falling, dive.' The hero in your book, based on your father, as you say, seems metaphorically to be falling from the time he's discharged to the moment when he dies."

"The war . . . broke . . . something . . . in him," said Harley, his voice stumbling.

A hand shot up. A chubby girl wearing gold-framed glasses, thick lenses. "I think he had PTSD. They didn't have the name for it back then."

"You're probably right," Harley agreed. "I think they called it shell-shocked in those days, but my father was never given that label. As far as anyone knew, he was well-adjusted."

Another hand, another female voice, "I read an interview that you did for South Carolina Review. At one point you sort of admitted that you mined your own life for your books. So, is *Bodies in Motion* biographical too? I read it on my own, after reading *So Much Heroism*."

"Only to the extent that I once saw a dancer in a bar take a man's hand and lead him out the back door. Everything else in that novel is pure imagination."

A young lady, brunette ponytail, studious face, raised her hand and asked, "Did you write *Bodies in Motion* to show us how one moment of impulse could ruin a man's life? Harry seems most likeable and kind, until halfway through the story when he becomes a recluse. He quits bodybuilding and takes to drinking and in general falls apart. Did you know that was going to happen?"

"Yes. I needed to find out who he was, which took me an entire four hundred page draft, but when Harry finally opened his mind to me, I realized he was the sort of man who allowed an errant impulse to rule him. Over time, that one out-of-control moment turned into an obsession. As a child and as a teen, he was impulsive, but then he went to college, studied philosophy and literature, took up weightlifting, did everything in his power to be good and kind and generous to his family. He tried to live a healthy life. When Harry is in that bar enjoying a pitcher of beer with his buddies, suddenly this thing happens. Blame it on alcohol and how it destroys your inhibitions. Or blame it on Harry's genes, the ones that made him so impetuous all those years ago. Whatever the reason, Harry is toast when Karen takes his hand and they end up having sex. It should have ended there, but she was relentless, kept after him, until, under the onslaught, he gives in, gets married, has a son. He didn't know that there was a time bomb ticking away inside him. Did I answer your question? Sorry, I often get spacy when I'm in front of people."

"Are you part Harry?" she asked.

Harley laughed softly and said, "No, I'm just a boring old writer who dotes on his dog and hopes to write books that will entertain you. And perhaps make you think."

A bald fellow with a silver ring in one nostril, a tattoo of a tear beneath his left eye said, "We all read the same interview. In it you also said you hated book tours and readings and wish they weren't so necessary. Why do you hate them, and why are they necessary?"

Harley cleared his throat, coughed lightly, all the while wondering how to answer the question.

"These book tours/readings/signings are necessary if you want to please your publisher, who wants you to become famous and sell lots of books, so that he or she can justify making you an offer you couldn't refuse. Let me be clear on this point: I don't do these gigs to win fame or fortune. A modest fortune would be welcome enough; it would allow me some independence, allow me to indulge my love of reading and writing and communing with whatever story might be living inside my head at the moment, over which I have little control. Unlike those sloppy stories everywhere else (war, pestilence, accidents, death, death, death) that makes me wonder how we can possibly make it through another day without an implosion. The advantage of which would be how . . . how inwardly coiled we would be sealed inside our own madness. We wouldn't have to deal with anyone else's neurosis. Every morning I open my eyes and the first thing I think is: How are we are able to go on? What perversity makes us able to go outside and participate in the futility of being human?"

"Do you have an answer?"

"We have to find something to do."

"Like what?"

"I don't know. I write, I read, I nap, I walk my dog, fix dinner for both of us, have a few drinks while I watch TV. Go to bed at ten. Get up at six and repeat, repeat, repeat. Beckett famously said, 'I can't go on. I'll go on.' "

"Do you get angry when reviewers criticize your work?"

"No. Sometimes yes. In interviews I have argued with the critical assessments of my books, explaining how I am trying to write a small slice of life as seen through the light of my own distorted lens. A prism that can't quite catch the entire spectrum. A light that ebbs and flows according to some inner chemistry, whose formula I do not know. I insist that my work isn't plotless. It isn't edgy or literary. Those critics who have tagged me with being literary have done me no favor. Think about it. As necessary as reviewers are, they need to remember that the word literary turns readers off." Harley shook his head and surprised himself by chuckling.

"Are you being ironic," said teardrop.

"No, no," said Harley. "It's true. The tag of *literary* dooms you."

Laughter rose and fell in the room.

Teardrop added, "I would think it would be an honor to be called literary. Isn't literary the sort of pinnacle you're trying to reach?"

Harley shrugged. "Maybe. But then again the word means work for the reader, no coasting. The word means elitist. This bastard thinks he knows something." Harley paused, smiled playfully and said: "I will be the first to tell you that I don't know anything—except that I don't know anything. I write mainly to keep myself sane and out of some psychiatrist's office, away from anti-depressant pills, Prozac, Zoloft, you know the drill. In care of a psychiatrist is where some people, including my mother (may she rest in peace), have claimed I should be. At least once a week on a couch: Doc, save me, I'm losing my mind." He cleared his throat and finished: "Leave the mind of the writer, the poet, the painter to find its own blithering way. No brain pickers. No experts."

Another hand climbed upward. A young lady very much pregnant. "You give your mother any credit for becoming a writer? My mother says writing is a fool's game."

Harley nodded. "It certainly can be. Maybe mostly it is. But you have to ask yourself if there is anything else you'd rather do. If there is, then go do it. Last thing this world needs are more writers clogging the system. As to the first part of your comment. Yes, I do give my mother credit. My mother told me, when I was growing up as a whirlwind of energy making her climb the walls, she would say, 'I can't figure out what I've given birth to, a genius or a moron.' Harley hesitated, wondering if he should continue.

Go ahead, Harley—shock them. All those rapt eyes, spellbound faces.

"Both the genius and the moron weren't sorry when Dad died jumping off the Golden Gate Bridge. His last words were, 'I can't stand this kid's incessant chatter! I can't stand his maniacal hopping up and down anymore!'" A mirthless chuckle broke from Harley's mouth. A number of students chuckled with him.

"I think it must have been more than that. I mean for the last two or three years of their married life, he and my mother were always at each other's throats. Sometimes it was over me, but most the time it was over her. She had such a mouth. Before she died she lived in an assisted care facility, and she still threw her mouth around like a drill sergeant berating recruits. No malingering Get off your asses, girls, and lets march! Hup two! Hup two! And geez, believe it or not, they would do what she said. Well, some of them. She had the equivalent of a squad marching to meals and daily water aerobics and Bingo and Saturday night dances. Move it or lose it. Mom was an inmate. She was put away for wearing stripes with polka dots and wandering off in the evenings. It's called sundowner syndrome. Early stages of senility. Or Alzheimer's. She had her good days and her bad days. On good days, she got her squad shipshape. On bad days, she stayed locked in fetus genre. There was no talking to her. Forget about coaxing her with her favorite chocolates. You offer her a Pepsi and she wouldn't even look at you. The only thing that might make her stir was her little dog Pepe. If I brought him over on Mom's bad days, she might actually open her eyes, she might sit up. For the sake of the mutt. She might hold him on her lap and call him, 'My kid.' Hey, whatever works. For a few weeks I paid an extra fee so Pepe could be with Mom all the time, but that didn't work so well. I would visit and the dog would be hiding under the bed. His fur would be matted. He would need a bath and a haircut. I would pick him up and he'd be trembling. The final straw was when Mom started putting dog poop in plastic bags inside the refrigerator. I took Pepe home for good after that. Kept him well-fed and groomed. He died of heart failure a month before Mom died." Harley looked at Holly and said, "How did I get off on this tangent?"

"Your mother, your father," said someone.

"Ah, yes. Well, here's the thing: all I'm telling you is grist for the mill. Never trust a writer to keep your secrets. Writers have no conscience about stealing your stories or their mother's stories, their father's, their own. Much of my work comes out of my own life. In a hundred years we'll all be dead and if anything remains of us, it will be the work we have accomplished. Otherwise it's all *poof.*" He gestured as if throwing confetti. The dog sat up, raised her head, her eyes questioning. "It's okay, Holly," he soothed. "I'm just trying to make a point. Now, where else was I going? Oh, I was going to tell you how Dad would plug his ears when Mom would get going. Can you imagine her on one side of him, me on the other? So maybe it's true that my hyperactivity and ventilation in the back seat of the car (my uncontainable noise) was the last straw for him. But the groundwork had been laid long ago when he was a soldier killing to keep from being killed. My story depicts a desperate father trying to cope with nightmares, war memories, the bombardment of his ears by his son and his wife. People tell me they liked the book up to where the father took the long dive. A witness said he was smiling. Another witness said he waved bye, bye and shouted Wee! Can you imagine how it felt? The air tearing at your hair. The seagulls thinking you were one of them and had spotted a school of fish down there. The sparkling water so bright it was like diving into the sun. A moment of clarity: maybe I shouldn't have done this. And then—"

The students seemed fascinated, or maybe stunned is the word. Harley recalled Norman saying after a reading from *Love Poems for Lovers*: "I had them in the palm of my hand."

Bending down and running his palm along Holly's head, Harley said, "I love this dog, Yeah, found her wandering and took her home. She's smarter than anyone I know. Yes you are, Holly."

"She's a pretty dog," said Mona. "Is she pure bred?"

"Cocker is all I know."

Mona was smiling sweetly at him. He smiled back and said, "Thank you so much for saving *So Much Heroism* from the abyss. Got to love you for that."

"Our pleasure, "she said.

She started clapping. They all clapped.

•

Afterwards, he signed books and chatted with students who wanted to talk about getting an agent, getting published, independent publishers (are they the death knell for a writer?), are contests you pay to enter worth it? (generally no, but no harm in trying), how do you support yourself until you've made a break-through? (Get a job or marry someone with lots of money.) And so it went until finally they ran out of questions.

Mona hung back until he was ready to go. She asked him if she could buy him a drink. "Hell yes, I needs one," he told her.

"There's a nice bar a block away. They have an outdoor area. They let you bring your dog if you sit out there."

"Come on, Holly. You hear that? Dogs are welcome."

They took a table under a large umbrella. The night was warm. No breeze.

Inside, a band played shrilly.

Harley was glad for the open air. He knew Holly was glad, too.

Mona complimented his reading and the way he held the students' attention. She called him a natural. As was Harley's way, he switched the conversation to her, Mona's past. She told him she was once an aerobics instructor who owned her own fitness center. Sold it to a bodybuilder whose name she can no longer remember, but he was movie star stuff, quite a hunk. She had her M.F.A. and had been teaching for eleven years. She had a calling, she said, a true passion for literature and poetry and teaching. She liked being an aerobics instructor because it taught her how to focus and go with the flow. Which spilled over into how she approached her writing and teaching—"Keeps me in the zone."

"I used to work out," said Harley, a vision of his youthful body nipping at his mind.

"You still look good," she said.

"It's an illusion," he said. "Or you need new glasses."

She smiled sympathetically. He smiled back. *Oh, if only.*

Even being outside, there was too much shrieking music. Harley wondered whatever happened to quiet lounges and murmured conversations over a cocktail table, drink in hand—the atmosphere a whisper.

Mona and he sat at their tiny table, hardly more than a toadstool. She bought him a martini and ordered a glass of white wine for herself. She spoke about her writing, reminding him of Didi, how insistent she could be that he look at her latest poem and analyze its do's and don'ts. Mona's eyes were fixed on him as if he might bolt or utter an oracle. She wanted his secret to publishing. There had to be a formula. He went over what he'd said to others. "Read great literature. Write every day. As novelist Thomas E. Kennedy says. 'Be the water that wears away the stone.' There really isn't any other way to do this thing. It helps to be lucky. Luck is ninety percent of any writer's success."

"Oh, I'm never lucky," she said. "Whatever I get I have to work hard for. But I'm not lazy. I'm liberal, but I don't think the world owes me a living." She kept chatting, mouth working.

The third martini made him mildly high. He felt himself smiling stupidly. She was very appealing. And she really did have beautiful eyes. He found it hard to keep up with what she was saying. Something about who? Margaret Atwood? She had a passion for Atwood.

"What do you think of her, Mr. Olsen?"

"Call me Harley. What do I think of Atwood? I find her tedious and boring and lacking invention. I find her derivative and repetitive. She's at best a B-writer. She'll be forgotten as soon as she dies."

Mona's loose mouth became looser. "Really," she said. "Oh my god, I'm kinda shocked."

"Don't let it shock you. It's one man's opinion. A writer who himself will be forgotten as soon as he dies."

"That's so sad," she said.

"Not a bit."

She became quiet. Leaned back. Looked away.

"Have you been imitating Atwood?"

"Yes, I have."

"The music's too loud."

She nodded in agreement.

"You want to go back, Mona?"

She gestured to the waitress to bring the check.

As they walked towards campus and the parking lot, he tried to make amends. "Look, Atwood has a million fans. What do I know?"

"Did you ever like her at all?"

"Maybe a little bit. Until I met her."

"You met Margaret Atwood?"

"At a writers' conference, I saw a fan go up to her and say, 'MS Atwood, I love your work. I teach your books to my students.' The fan held out her hand, but Atwood didn't take it. What she did is frown and stick three fingers down her throat and pretend to vomit. That's the arrogance of too much adulation, if you know what I mean. Sorry, but I haven't liked her since, and, honestly, I've never thought much of her work, anyway. She's overestimated."

"You sound misogynistic."

Harley took a few more steps, stopped, looked down at Holly and said, "Holly, am I a misogynist?"

Holly shook her ears, making clapping sounds.

"She says no, Mona. Really, some of my favorite humans are women." He laughed.

She frowned. "I'm sorry," she said. "You've burst my bubble."

"Ack, don't listen to me. I'm juss an old curmudgeon. I don't like much in this world, but I like you and I like your students. And I like reading and writing. Just about everything else can go to hell."

"No women writers you admire?"

"Sure there are. Of contemporary writers: Andrea Barrett. Hmm, Alice Munro. Others, but vodka is blocking my memory cells just now."

She stopped. Her face came close. Her breath caressed his cheek, reminding him of the first time Didi kissed him and how she smelled of wine. He wondered if Mona needed kissing. Impulsively he took her arms and drew her to him. Liplocked her. Her lips responded, and when the kiss was over she said, "Oh, my god."

"Thank you," he said. "I've been needing a kiss for such a lonely time."

"I'm so sorry, Mr. Olsen, but I've got to go."

Harley's ardor fizzled. "Goodbye, Mona. Nice meeting you."

"Yes."

"Thanks for the martinis."

"Thanks for listening. And the reading, of course"

"It was great. Good luck, Mona. I hope you write a masterpiece."

She headed for the parking lot, her waiting car. Dew encircled the lights and also the moon in her path. The cool dampness of the air cleared his head. Did he really kiss her? Tasted wine. Perked up below. Could have. Probably. But didn't. Good for you. A woman like that, she's been riding that hedonic treadmill and God knows who you would be sleeping with. No point in taking chances, not at your age. Sixty-four. You should have learned something about the futility of it. It's never really worth it. Think of Franny. Better yet, think of Didi.

20 - Shaman Bear Knows

Life is good. Franny gets over her doubts about being a married woman involved with a married man. Tough, practical, pragmatic: that's our Franny these days. You don't think you can survive, but you do. In fact, as the saying goes, you not only survive—you thrive.

Norman is warm. Norman is wunnerful. Norman is a major poet, a famous man, a famous major Verseland star. And he loves this rejected, washed up woman named Francis Olsen. He loves her to the bottom of his soul. "I love you, my darling, to the bottom of my soul," he tells her. She can't get enough of it. Can't get enough of his poems, of going to readings and listening to his voice mesmerizing her and every woman in the audience. The advertisements for his readings call him

PULITZER FINALIST.

ANNOUNCING WALT WHITMAN AWARD-WINNING NORMAN TEN BOOM READING FROM *SHAMAN BEAR KNOWS*.

Everyone in the world of poetry knows who Franny is these days. It doesn't matter to anyone that Norman is married. She is his Intended. Just a matter of time before his wife trickles by. What Franny needs to do is file for divorce. Get rid of that two-timing Harley. Move on with her life.

When some biographer eventually writes Norman's story, she will be part of it, the woman who came late in his life and brought out the best in him. In every way: creatively, spiritually, psychologically, physically. She's the best lover he's ever had he's told her. She believes him. She's told him he's a million times better in bed than Harley ever was. She doesn't mention Chata Johnson who could definitely hold his own in comparison to Norman. But what does that matter? (Secrets of the heart she will take to her grave.) Nothing matters but here, the moment, the two of them.

Only a year ago she would never have believed life could be so inspiring. Some days she feels that if she really wanted to, she could write poetry, too. Maybe even write stories. A novel. Why not? Nothing stopping her. Norman would help her. He'd make sure she didn't make a fool of herself. Maybe she could tell her story, the story of her childhood and growing up and finding Harley and marrying him and all those years of humdrum leading to where she is.

People like stories about winners. Make a million bucks with a memoir like that. Get you on TV. Make you famous. A huge book tour, a tour Harley could only dream about. Wouldn't that flatten his ego, eh? Turn him into particleboard. Hey, it could happen. You're in the zone.

Did you like the Fallujah poem?" Norman asks.

"The Fallujah one? It's very good, Norman."

He quotes it for her again:

Tonight, in Fallujah
We wait
For the known
For the follow-up
To the fighter planes
To the rockets
To the long days of shelling
To the depleted uranium killing us slowly
We wait
To see their tanks
Their tanks will come first …

"Gives me the chills," she says.

"It came out of nowhere, my darling. It was a voice in my head. Let me tell you something. Years ago, back in the sixties when I was teaching at U of M, I went to the Notre Dame Book Festival. I was writing every day, every morning, poems flying from my fingers. The festival put me in a room with Tennessee Williams, Ken Kesey and William Burroughs—three of the craziest bastards alive in those days—and I asked them if they believed there was a muse. They all agreed there was a muse. None of those guys were morons, Franny. If they could believe in a numinous world, so could I. Last night the muse inspired the Fallujah poem and it felt the same as when I was writing at Notre Dame. It was another Revelation."

"I believe Revelation is the breath of God," says Franny.

"I believe in the Shaman Bear who lives in me," says Norman combing her hair with his fingers. "The Shaman Bear is my muse. He lives in my mind and gives me the brilliant talent I have. I'm truly blessed with a stable genius. The bear gives me my prodigious strength and energy, too. Brings out the primitive side as well, my bear."

(Listen to him, Franny, so mystical, so otherworldly.)

Norman continues, "You know what John Milton said? He said, 'Great poets drink their water from a plain wooden cup.' That's the way it is. Nothing fancy. You got to have talent and passion to say things meaningful like that. To speak for humanity. At times, poets like me are able to see beyond the beyond, like some fortuneteller or medicine man. I've had this happen to me many times. Years ago in a trance I wrote a first draft of Shaman Bear. In it I saw myself walking through a snowy field in Minnesota. I was wearing a white coat and my hair was white, as it is now, and I looked like a polar bear. I described the field, the fences, the snow, myself like a bear (because I am part bear, you know) and I was filled with this magical feeling and I knew that my first draft was an omen.

"A year later, I bought a little farm in Minnesota, and the snow came and turned everything white. And my hair turned white in the two years I lived there. Everything: the farm house, the fields, the trees, the fences, all that stuff was already in my poems. I knew then I was a shaman. 'There are more things in heaven and earth than are dreamt of in your philosophy.' Better believe it, Franny."

"I do, Norman. If you say it, I believe it."

"I love being an artist. Being an artist is the highest calling. When you're an artist you do what artists always do if they're for real. Artists take chances. Artists can't be too concerned with what's called common morals, the hoi polloi ethics of the hoi polloi. Artists have their own compass, their own code, a code that says if you live with the herd, the muse will abandon you. Nietzsche said, 'Go the way your art demands. Or go to hell, you washout.' That's Harley, you know? He abandoned the muse and now she's abandoned him. I don't feel sorry for that bastard. Maybe he had potential, but along came Didi and she finished him. I'll tell you what I said to him, I said, 'That woman will destroy you.' I told him right to his face. And I could see he believed me. Believed, but didn't have the courage or the sense to get away from her. You see what I'm saying? I know these things. I know and when I tell you I can see the future, you need to believe me. I'm always right. I've never been wrong when the shaman bear talks through me."

As he spins the world, Franny absently strokes her breast, her finger circling the left nipple. She is wearing a black rayon blouse, the material helping the finger move smoothly. There is a moment when she touches something familiar. A lump. She feels it and yes, a pea. A familiar pea. "Not again," she says. "Jesus no, not again." She unbuttons her blouse, lifts the offending breast out of its cup, sucks her finger slick and runs it round and round the growth. It's in a different place this time, a few inches away from the one she had removed years ago. "No fair." She interrupts Norman. "Cancer is back," she says.

"You think so? You think it's come back?" His tone is fearful.

Ice is racing through Franny's veins. Anxiety filling her. Mouth dry. Bowels watery. Hands and feet cold and sweaty. "Maybe," she says. "I don't know, but it feels the same as before. This is creepy, Norman. This is creepy déjà vu all over again that's what it is." She pauses a moment. Then adds in a breaking voice, "Cancer … is never … cured, you know. It always … comes back, eventually."

The look on Norman's face mirrors the horror she is feeling. "We've got to get you to a doctor," he says.

She is panting. "Scared shitless, Norman. I've been through this and I know what I'm in for."

"Maybe this one is encapsulated, too. I bet it is, my darling." He reaches out to take her hand, but she jerks away.

"No, don't touch me. I don't want to be touched right now. I have to get calm. I have to calm myself. You're right . . . this one might be encapsulated and no big deal.

Think positive. Trust in Jesus. He wouldn't take it all away. Not when I've just found reasons to live. I don't want this. I don't want to be frightened. I want to be what we were one minute ago. God, I wish I hadn't, Norman. I wish I hadn't found it."

"Sorry, Franny."

"Breathe, breathe," she commands herself. "Breathe and pray. I believe in God the Father Almighty. I shall not want. He maketh me to lie down in green pastures. Surely goodness and mercy. Goodness and mercy." A voice inside her says: *Goodness and mercy, your ass. Coming for the adulteress, coming for you, Franny. You've been asking for it.*

"I've been asking for it, that's the thing. Having an affair." She glares at Norman. "You men." She grabs the shawl draping the back of the couch . Pulls it over her head. Scoots downward, the shawl tenting her body, like a woman wearing a burka. "That kid, that Hector, I wanted him. God read my mind. Everything unraveling. That boy on the egg farm I dry-fucked him when I was only seventeen and got him off. God never forgets those things. No screwing out of wedlock! Harley and me fucked a lot out of wedlock. After we were married I fucked Chata Johnson plenty. And almost my sister's husband Cecil. I sucked his cock. My boss, Mr. Pulliam. Jesus, what a . . . what's the word for me?"

"But you said—"

"Hector reminded me of that boy and my thoughts went to the devil. And then comes Norman Ten Boom to the rescue. Ahg!"

"You were seventeen when you first had sex?"

"Seventeen! No, no. I said 'dry-fucked,' not wet-fucked. I was nineteen when I lost my cherry. This guy got me drunk on Sake and I let him have me. I was so sloshed I hardly felt anything. After I got married, Cecil, my brother-in-law, and I did all kinds of shit. Harley was living in a cocoon. Hardly touched me. That's my excuse. But what about later . . . what about now?"

"So you lied to me about not cheating on Harley?"

"I know better. I've always known better. God oh God, I lost all that weight, did all those exercises, bought clothes to look sexy. I wore pink! God was watching me. He was inside my mind knowing all my thoughts when I bought Hector that pizza. You were there you saw it yourself. You saw me at my worst. That boy made me lusty. I hate him. If you hadn't been there, I'd have taken him home. God knows I would. God knows and now I've got cancer again."

"You can't believe in that kind of God," says Norman. "C'mon, God isn't going to hold that against you. It's just being human."

"You don't know Him like I do. I've gone through hell because I strayed. God save me."

"Gosh, I didn't know you were this . . . this . . . this is a whole new personality. I don't know you. Take the shawl off. Come out of there."

She lets him pull the shawl away and wrap her in his arms. "You poor thing," he says. His palms on her back are clammy. "You've suffered enough. Who knows why these things happen to good people. But I'm here, my darling. I'm here to see you through it. I want you to be brave. Be strong. I'll stand by you. I'm very strong. It's probably nothing, my darling. It's probably just like before. They'll cut it out and you'll be fine. Hey, I know these things. I've got a poet's soul. Poets have a sixth sense. The shaman bear knows."

"I'm such a liar," she whispers. "Such a fake. All my life I've been a huge liar, a pervert."

"Oh, who cares about that? Big deal, c'mon. Your past is your past, just like my past is my past. What matters is—"

"Forgive me, forgive me." Franny is weeping on his shoulder, feeling his damp hands running over her blouse. "What a baby," she blubbers.

"No, no. It's understandable. All you've been through."

"I want it over. I want to have my health and a life with you."

"I'm here, my darling. Don't worry. It's gonna be fine, darling. You'll see. I know these things."

Of course, she wants to believe him, just like she wanted to believe Harley's assurances when the first lump was found all those wasted years ago. She also wants to believe that God would never be so cruel as to put her through such torture again. Even if she hasn't behaved well lately. Even if she hasn't been a good girl. What's wrong with trying to find a little happiness? What is wrong with having sex when you're fifty-seven, desperate, forsaken and lonesome?

21 - Bubbling Love

Spoon-love over one evening, she turns onto her back, breathing the breath of satisfaction, while he cuddles her.

"So you love me," he says in a voice that seems the essence of what honey would sound like if honey could talk.

"With all my heart," she tells him.

"More than you loved him?"

"I loved him a lot."

"How many lovers have you had, Didi?"

"You and Harley."

"Two?" His tone is doubtful.

"Well, first there was Danny. Then Harley. Now there's you."

"Is that true? You were a virgin when you married, and you never strayed till me? And then Harley? Tell me the truth."

"Why would I lie? There were flirtations, of course. Fantasies. But I was always true to my husband." She's sure Carlson is pleased. She knows him well enough to know what he really wants to hear.

He says. "A couple of my wives cheated on me. It's hard to trust a woman after that. At least we do everything together. It's not adultery if we both consent, right?"

"What's the feminine equivalent of cuckold? Cuntkold?"

Carlson snorts.

"I've given myself to you, body and soul. You never have to worry about me. Your Didi knows what she's got. She knows when things are good."

"Dear Didi, my heart, I love you so."

"I love you so, too."

"You don't miss Harley a little?"

Didi looks away. She doesn't want him to see deceit in her eyes. There is a vicious sensation in her fingers. Her nails wanting to slash him—she doesn't know why. But she knows no matter how long she lives, some part of her will never forgive Harley for getting sick. Her thoughts bring forth tainted words: "I wish to God Harley had been killed in an accident or something. I could have handled his death much better than I've handled this endless illness of his. Death is final and you have to deal with it, no matter what. But because he's alive I will always have this ache inside me. This grief and sorrow, this anger. It's funny, but there are days I believe I don't care at all. And then it'll hit me what happened and I want to throw up. I left Danny and my kids for him."

"A selfish guy," says Carlson. "He seduced you."

"Even after I knew what was going on, I thought his being ill wouldn't break me. And it wouldn't have if he hadn't drank so much and called me stupid cunt and threatened to beat me."

"I'll kick his ass if he ever fucks with you again, Didi."

She thinks about how long it had gone on: Harley going back and forth from her to his wife. Every weekend, back again to Franny's arms. Again and again, Didi hears how anguished he was, especially when his heart started failing. She will never forget what he told her after the diagnosis. "Relieved," he said. "Like a death row prisoner tired of it all and hearing there are no more reprieves. A few months, maybe. A few weeks. I could use the rest, Didi."

All she felt that day was repugnance, she tells Carlson. "I can't stand a self-pitying man. When he refused to have a bypass, I knew it was just a matter of time before I left him. Shame on him, self-absorbed sonofabitch." She coughs to the side. Pulls the sheet up and wipes her eyes.

"I'd never do that. I'm here for the long haul," he says, kissing her shoulder. Sliding down a bit, elbow cocked, head resting on his palm. He stares at her, his eyes incandescent. How does he make them shine so bright?

"You've been a tonic," she tells him. "I thought my life was over and then came you sweeping me off my feet. It's miraculous. Let me tell you—I never dreamed I'd have sex like we've had these past months. But look at us naked in bed and banging away like honeymooners." She breaks into joyous laughter. So glad to be alive and in love and living with a man who is even more brilliant than Harley. Lots more brilliant. And definitely a better lover, a studly male nympho.

"All I ever wanted," she says, "was the love of the man I loved. I dreamed of being happy with one special person for the rest of my life. A love that lasted forever. I thought I had found it with Harley, but that was delusion. The dream shattered. The last time I tried to have sex with him, he said he was having a nervous breakdown. He was crying. You should have heard how he sobbed. It was the sobbing of a wretched man. What kept me from going to pieces? I don't know. I masturbated a lot. You need to get off sometimes, you know what I mean?"

"Course I do. Five times a week."

"At least." She pauses. Giggles. She's glad she has someone she can talk to about anything. "And then came you out of the blue."

"You say his sob was the sobbing of a wretched man," says Carlson. "That's poetic, Didi."

"I'm going to write that into a poem," she says. "You're so thoughtful. When we were fuckbuddies before, I didn't see that in you, your sensitive side. Back then, you were simply a hunk. It was simply sex. Lots of plain old lovely sex. What a tonic. Danny was never as fun as that. Well, in the beginning he was. But those honeymoon months vanished when I got pregnant. From then on, it was Mister Serious. Mr. Morose. Always fretting about this or that. Usually the kids. God, I got sick of it."

"Did he ever fuck you the same day after me?"

"No, never. I wouldn't let him touch me."

They linger a moment, looking at each other, both of them partially grinning.

"Well," says she, "maybe two or three times."

"It's okay, it's okay," he says. "Wish I could've seen it."

"You'd like to see Danny do me?"

"Yeah, it'd be a turn on. Harley too."

"An awkward threesome."

"I love threesomes. Hell, foursomes. You know that."

She thinks about it. His smile is erotic. She feels her organs stirring.

"Amazingly, impossibly, I've found the male side of me," she says. "I used to think you were crazy, a wild nutcase, but you're not. You're sweet and considerate. And you make me feel like the most desirable woman on earth. With you, I feel like nothing bad can happen to me. I've never been so content. I never thought I'd be contented again, but I am."

"I'm a perverted bastard. I was born with three balls, you know. Freaky, huh?"

"I'm a perverted bitch," she says.

"The bitch. The bastard."

They both laugh.

"Bastard and bitch deserve each other," she says.

•

She feels prophetic. She understands how the pieces fit, and how, in the end, her life will prove to have been a journey full of significance.

Because? Because she and he fit so well together. Like-minded. Compatible. Harley is a loser, a cast away. Why didn't she see that sooner? Bad things happening to him. As sure as the sun rises and sets Harley is fatal.

So hey, Harley, was it worth it? Harley, you're such a damn fool.

She bends to Carlson hard as rebar. She twists her head and, as if his penis is a microphone she's holding, she says to it, "I believe there is a world we can sometimes tap into. Some people say that's nonsense, but I believe it's true. You know what I mean? I feel it deep inside me. Right here." She touches her breast. "Here in my heart."

He kisses the top of her bobbing head. Ten minutes later, she feels something else rising. How can a man? So many times!

Three balls, indeed. What if he had four?

•

After a night of love, he sleeps like the dead, but I can't. Harley is in my head. I can't get over how much he changed from when I first met him. Tough, courageous, reliable, a man from top to toe. Fabulous lover. As smart as Norman, but not at all so damn conceited. Harley has hardly any ego at all. Self-deprecating so much it irritated me. I blame his mother and father. Always saying hey stupid to him. Kids are basically prone to dumb behavior. They're kids, what else would one expect? My kids were borderline, until they graduated from high school and went off to college, where they learned how wide the world is, how complicated and multifarious human beings are. Whenever Harley said anything foolish in his mother's presence, she would always say, "A fool is known when he opens his mouth." Which is why he doesn't talk very much. That's my theory.

I wonder how he's doing these days. Last time I talked to him, he said his ears were making whooshing sounds, the whooshing timed to the beating of his heart. He thinks it might mean he has an aneurism. I told him to see a doctor and find out. Aneurisms can be fixed. He said the same thing he always says: "Let nature take its course." See, that's stupid. So maybe his parents had a point? What's so bad about life that he won't do anything to prolong his? "We all have to die," he tells me. Yeah, so why let it happen sooner than you have to? I'm never going to be ready. I want to eat the rind of life till there's nothing left. Life to its fullest, is what I'm saying. Food and drink and as many wild experiences that I'm capable of enjoying. Especially sex, of course. Carlson has been a revelation. I never knew I'd do the things I've done with him. I think back to the porno I did at nineteen and can see the connection with the way I'm behaving now.

Maybe it's genetics? My mother was a fox on fire when she was younger. Men hitting on her. I'm absolutely certain she banged Alan. Did it for years. How many? I don't know, but I'm certain they made love every chance they had. And then how funny he turns out to be gay. How weird is that? Or probably he's bi. Goes both ways, depending on what's happening. I guess I have to admit that I'm bi-sexual a tad. I enjoy girls, but mainly I'm hetero. Is it something everyone has inside them and all it takes is a certain unguarded moment and out pops the Other? What an assortment we are, so speckled. Fuck it, I wouldn't have us any other way. Anything cut and dried would be an unbearable bore.

Save As Documents: The World According to Deidre Annaba Godunov.

22 - Cancer Déjà vu

So the cancer has returned and Franny didn't have a clue. Except for her chronic cough, she had felt incredibly well. But then again cancer might explain why losing weight had been so easy. The tests show the malignancy has metastasized to the left lung and the liver. Stage four. Inoperable. When Franny asks about chemo, the oncologist, a balding man with white tufts in his ears, says bluntly, "Why put yourself through it, Mrs. Olsen? It will make your life hell and the end result will be the same."

On screen, he reviews the C.T. scan with her. She's sees the shadow of the breast and lung tumors and the tumor deep inside her liver. He says she also has "a small thrombus in the inferior vena cava, plus lymphadenopathy."

It's all a blur to Franny.

He taps the scan with his pen and says if she had only the breast tumor, it could easily be removed. But the metastasis, especially the deep liver location, well, all this is more than problematic. He compares the liver to a peach and says the tumor is the pit at the core of the meat. Again he repeats the word inoperable. He also explains that chemotherapy and/or radiation are not viable options for something so invasive. He keeps tapping the spot on her liver.

"Perhaps even in the bones," he grumbles, his tone dispiriting. Shaking his head, clearing his throat he adds, "Systemic. It's—I'm sorry, really, really sorry, but it's—" He looks away. She watches him chewing his lip. Watches him close his heavy-lidded eyes as if he can't stand the sight of her.

Breathlessly, Franny says, "I'm fifty-seven years young. You've got to give me a chance."

"Mrs. Olsen—"

"I need some hope."

He explains that if the liver tumor had been more on the surface, then he would have recommended surgery; but because of the core location, an operation would destroy the organ, and even if it didn't, well, lymph nodes, breast, maybe both breasts. Multiple locations, multiple operations, followed by aggressive chemo and radiation. "You see what I'm saying: the body's ability to heal and recuperate would be so compromised that in the end you couldn't survive. There is no effective treatment for you. I don't know how to say this without sounding callus, but I've always found it best to be straightforward." He clears his throat again. Eyes and voice authoritative. "You need to go home and prepare yourself. In my experience, cases such as yours are always terminal. You have six months. Perhaps less. It's that deep liver location, I'm saying."

She hears the word terminal and finds it impossible to process. Little Francis terminal? After all the illness and suffering for so many years, how could she be terminal now?

"Chemo," she croaks. "Radiation." The magic word *abracadabra* flashes through her mind.

His mouth is fretful, but his tone remains firm. "We can keep you comfortable and mostly pain free. You'll be able to travel. You'll be able to visit your relatives, spend time with your children. You can do almost anything for a while. Eventually, of course, you won't have the energy, your strength will drain away, but while you are able, I hope you'll take advantage of the remaining days."

"I don't have any children. Three miscarriages. One was two months from being full term." Franny thinks about it. If she had had children, they would be there for her now. They would take care of their mommy.

"You have a husband, yes? Relatives?"

"I've got a mother in a nursing home. Two sisters with health issues of their own. A husband, but we're legally separated. He left me for a woman who left him when he was diagnosed with congestive heart failure and started becoming a burden. Thank God I still have his health insurance as well as mine. I've got a boyfriend who may be too high-strung to handle this sort of thing. He's a famous poet. He's very preoccupied. Very egoistic."

"Famous? What's his name?"

"Norman Ten-Boom."

"That name's familiar. Has he been on TV?"

"PBS and he's won major prizes. He's always in demand for readings and speaking engagements. Somehow I don't see him willing to nurse me through this." She smiles grimly.

"Your sisters?"

Her voice quavers again as she tells him, "Well, like I say, they've got health issues of their own. But maybe I'll have to ask them to lend a hand." Her saliva tastes vile, it tastes cancerous. "Look, I'm sure you're right about the surgeries. But I believe in miracles. I believe God loves me and wants me to live. I believe my illness is part of God's cosmic plan. There's a reason for what's happening. God doesn't play dice Einstein said. So I'm asking you to at least give chemo or something a chance. I don't want to give up. I want to fight. Won't you help me fight? Won't you? For God's sake, say you will, doctor. Tell me you will." Franny buries her face in her hands.

To her own ears she sounds disgusting.

So, even though it is hopeless and is going to look bad with the HMO statisticians who calculate year-end bonuses, the oncologist eventually gives in to Franny's pleading. He looks at the experimental cancer treatments available and manages to get Franny's name added to a new clinical trial.

•

Franny goes to the clinic every other week, checking in for three hours, lying in a recliner while a needle is inserted into a port in her chest. A cocktail of cancer killers are given to her and through the first two treatments she feels fairly well. Maybe she is going to be one of the lucky ones? She concentrates on thinking positively, imagining the tumors surrounded and putting up a fight but slowly shrinking under the onslaught of medical miracles.

The third treatment leaves her weak and weepy. She goes home, goes to bed. Wakes later with shortness of breath, a severe pain in her chest. Norman takes her to urgent-care, where the doctor on duty says it sounds like a collapsed lung. The doctor orders chest X-Rays, which confirm that Franny's left lung has collapsed. There is also fluid surrounding it. Franny is admitted and spends two days in the hospital. When asked if she wants to continue with chemo she says, "Of course. Why wouldn't I?" The doctor sends her home with a portable oxygen tank.

As the adverse effects increase, she begins vomiting for three to four days after each treatment. She can't keep anything down, so what comes up is whatever she has eaten, along with a foul-smelling mucus that reminds her of her garbage disposer when she forgets to clean it with soap suds and lemon peel. Sometimes her lips are coated with a sour pink froth. She has dry heaves as well. The heaving makes her belly so sore it feels as though someone has taken a club to her ribs.

If Norman is home when she's vomiting, he comes into the bathroom and holds her head, rubs her back and says, "Let it all out, my darling. Good girl." After she's done, he washes her face with a cold cloth and picks her up in his arms as if she's a child (she is down to size zero) and carries her to bed. He holds her and says that he can be brave as long as she can be brave. He sticks it out with Franny, driving her to the clinic now that she's so weak. He listens to her agonized heaving, he watches her hair fall out, watches more weight peel off, watches her eyes grow dark-ringed hollow.

Words in the Bible usually calm her, so every night before going to bed he reads to her. Best of all she likes the passage at the end of Job: "And the Lord restored the fortunes of Job . . . and the Lord gave Job twice as much as he had before . . . and Job died, an old man, and full of days."

She sometimes says, "Jesus is testing me again. He won't abandon me." Childlike she chants, "Jesus loves me, this I know."

Nights when he is home, Norman sits her in front of the TV and slips comedies into the DVD. She likes the old ones with Walter Matthau and Jack Lemmon playing grumpy old men. She is amazed at how much she can still laugh at such silly stuff. And also amazed to think that Matthau and Lemon are dead.

Two or three times a week her sisters call. On weekends they come over and sit with her and chat about things that don't really interest Franny anymore. They tell her sternly not to give in. Miracles occurring every day. Trust in the Lord. Hey, who says she can't get well? What do doctors know? The sisters usually leave as soon as it is polite to do so. She sees them sitting in the car, their hands gesturing as they babble. Franny knows they are frightened at how awful she looks. Franny knows she is becoming a burden. Dying people are very problematic.

•

After twelve treatments the first round is over and she is given a break to see if her body will regain strength enough to allow another series. A second C.T. scan shows that the tumors have stopped growing. The oncologist scratches his chin, looks perplexed as he says, "Non progressive . . . for the moment."

Gradually she recovers some strength. Within a few days she is able to bathe and dress without help, walk the path to the sidewalk and back, getting only a teeny bit winded. She starts forcing herself to make dinner. She and Norman sit at the table like regular people. He drinks a little wine each night because it is good for his heart. She drinks green tea because it is full of anti-oxidants. She has read about alternative cures for cancer and kept to her diet of vegetables and fruits. She takes free-radical cancer-curing herbal pills as well. She eats a bowl of blueberries every morning.

After she reads an article in which a woman says that victims of cancer have to take control, she tells Norman that she has decided to take control of the cancer, rather than be controlled by it. With permission from her boss at Harvest Home, she goes off disability and back on the payroll. She starts working from her living room, on the couch with her laptop, mailing in her edits. She buys evangelist Bobbi Poe's newly released book: *Advice to Suffering Sinners* and takes solace in the knowledge that she's not the only person whose life is cruel.

One of the first Bobbi letters she reads concerns a subject dear to her heart. The letter is from a woman terrified of aging.

Dear Bobbie,

I'm divorced and alone and turning 40 next month. I can't believe I'm getting so old! I feel that if the next 40 goes as fast as these first 40 years, my life will be hardly more than an insignificant blip. It's a dead end, isn't it, Bobbi. No man wants a woman over 40. Even now I notice the difference when I go to the Mall of America and very few male heads ever turn my way, even though I am dressed for war. I see old people shuffling along with their bowed backs and feeble legs, their stiff necks, the look of fear ringing their eyes. Everything about them says they won't last much longer. And they won't, of course. They'll end up dropping dead or getting some awful illness that puts them in a hospital, all of them becoming bleached out bundles of skin and bones wondering why they still wake in the morning. Young, healthy relatives will want the sick ones to die. That's human nature, don't you think? I'm thinking it's better to die in middle-age, instead of bumbling along year after year turning into a pitiful old crone that people can't stand to look at. I wish I was dead.

Demoralized Janice

Dear Demoralized Janice,

Your problem is Pride. So you're turning forty and losing your looks. So what? Nature isn't picking on you, so knock off the pity party and take a look around and see all the good there is to be found in God's astonishing world. Hear the giggle of the baby, the song of the bird, the wind whispering through the trees. Watch the clouds floating like silver boats through the bottomless sky. Watch them cover the sun and darken the earth for a moment before the sun emerges beaming a smile of welcome. Feel its warmth on your face. Remember that feeling! It is one you won't have in the grave. The wind, the rain, the sun will be nothing to your earth-bound remains. A kiss from your mother or your lover or your child will be unobtainable. All the good things you have felt while alive, the food you've eaten, the hugs, laughs, the sheer joy of living on God's good earth will be wasted on you if you continue with your boohoo attitude. Count your blessings like I do. Celebrate with friends and family the gift of being alive and turning forty. You really need to get your priorities straight. The rest of your life will be a journey through misery if you don't.

I will give thanks to the Lord with my whole heart.

I will tell of all Thy wonderful deeds.

I will be glad and exult in Thee.

I will sing praise to Thy name, O Most High!

Pray the above prayer three times a day every day for the rest of your life and you'll get out of your own moping head and find meaning in every breath. And you'll find God and light at the end of your voyage from here to Eternity.

Faithfully yours,
Bobbi Poe

After finishing the letter to demoralized Janice, Franny feels better. She believes God has used her as a vessel to show His power to cure incurable cancer.

Incurable cancer?

Maybe the cancer is her own fault and God has used it to open her eyes. She knows she will conquer, she knows she will win. She knows the cancer is cowering before God's omnipotence. She has never felt so enlightened. "Praise God from whom all blessings flow," she sings.

Despite a chronic, blood-thin feeling of fatigue and twinges of pain in this-or-this area, this little spot, this tender zone, she senses that her body is nearly normal. She sticks to her schedule, which includes line-editing in the morning, followed by a nap, followed by reading new manuscripts from aspirants, followed by mild exercise (usually walking half a block and back). Along with the new cancer-controlling diet, she listens to relaxation tapes, sets time aside for reading the Bible, chats with her sisters on the phone.

Franny stays optimistic. Cautiously so.

Most of the things she used to think were so important, like her philandering husband, she currently sees as absurd, meaningless, a sideshow. One of the inspirational books on tape that she especially likes is *Head First: The Biology of Hope,* by Norman Cousins telling her that laughter is the best medicine. She increases the hours she spends watching comedies. She laughs as much as she can. Jovially she chants—"a merry heart doeth good like a medicine." She doesn't feel cured, but she feels definitely better. Tired, but eventually not so tired, not so stressed, not so terrified of dying, not so full of defeatism and wonder at the ways of an angry God picking on her for not obeying one of his major commandments. Yes, Franny knows the main reason why the Lord has chastised her. It comes down to Adultery with a capital A—living in sin with Norman Ten Boom, both of them married to others, both of them breaking their holy vows. What on earth had made her think she could get away with such heinous depravity? You're a fool, Franny—*a fool!*

23 - The Seventh Commandment

She remembers a poem she had learned years ago when her first cancer occurred, the one that was "cured":

Come to the edge He said.
They said We are afraid.
Come to the edge
He said.
They came
He pushed them and
They flew—

The poem comforts her. Death is a metaphor for flying. You leap over the edge into the arms of Love. What could be better than that?

She knows what she has to do. She has to get the source of sin out of her life. She has to break off with Norman. Send him back to his wife, his much abused Maria. Franny already knows she has worn him out, anyway, gotten to him, so to speak. There is no mistaking the message written all over his face. Yes, and only a few nights ago, she caught him crying and whispering into his hands, "Dear Lord, how will I ever stand this?"

After she had recovered enough to start working again, he started going out to more readings and speaking engagements and spending time with his friends. She knows he needs to get away from her.

Who wouldn't?

When he had become her lover he hadn't dreamed he was signing on for a terminal ride. Caretaker, nursemaid, last witness to a dying flame. A woman with her eyes fixed on a future labeled *forever.* Poor Norman, how good and courageous he is. Who would have thought so? Not any of his lovers, not any of his four wives. No one. She feels she loves and admires him more than ever, and because she loves and admires him, she is going to make it easy for him to get on with his fabulous life.

She asks Judy and Ruthie about it. Both agree that living in sin is undermining her spirit, which in turn is undermining her body's ability to heal itself. "Get rid of him," they counsel.

She waits for a sign from God. The sign comes in the form of the oncologist saying that non-progressive has become progressive, "No more chemo, he says. "A new trial: immunotherapy. It's T-cells, it's your T-cells not doing their job."

Her T-cells are harvested. Billions of them are grown in the laboratory. Then infused into her bloodstream.

She needs fully-loaded spiritual powers to make the most of God's obvious intervention. Without question, she needs Him engaged in healing His adoring Franny. No more wagging the censorious finger.

She also needs her sisters.

"Don't worry, I'll be over every day to check on you," says diabetic, overweight Judy who no longer does water aerobics.

"Me too," gasps COPD afflicted Ruthie.

This is how it should be, they all agree. The family pulling together the way things were before everyone got so me-*ish*, when everyone knew the rules, especially the rule that says we don't depend on others, we take care of one another because blood is thicker than water, blood is blood, your blood is my blood. When none of us is prepared for the slings and arrows of outrageous fortune, what else have we got but family? The family bonds. That's the way we were raised—sisters. Sisters stick together. Especially in times of crisis.

The sisters embrace. They cry their hearts out. They feel lucky. They feel grateful. God is smiling down on them, perhaps crying too, crying to see them behaving like Catholics and Evangelicals should. With their love coupled with His love anything is possible. *Wonders: commonplace.* Cure for cancers created with the flick of an omnipotent finger. Hold off tragedy. Hold it at bay until you're Mama's age. When you're her age it's sad, it breaks your heart, makes you melancholy for days and days. But it's no longer tragedy. At Franny's age it's a different story. Fifty-seven aligns with death, which is a disaster. It makes you look like a woman born to failure. Lost your health. Lost your husband. Lost your purpose for living. The meaning is no meaning. Whatever you've been taught about behaving and striving and following the rules becomes a joke on you. A joke on you is calamity. Death at fifty-seven? No way. An army of T-cells is on the attack.

And then:

Evening. Dinnertime.

"Norman," she says. "Honey, we have to talk."

They have finished eating. He has a little wine in his glass and is swirling it. "Yes, my darling," he says. "Talk about what?"

When she tells him what and why, Norman Ten Boom, panda bear of a man, puts his face in his hands and weeps as if he's the one who has cancer. Franny cries too. For a while they cry together. The sobs constricting her throat won't let her talk. She has done a thing she thought impossible. She has given a man, her lover, the boot. She feels indescribably sad about it. But also vaguely relieved. She tells herself that she has nothing to weep about, but the tears continue flowing. Why? For love that almost was but now is lost? Lost illusions? Hopes of a future with Norman on top of the world, a future moving beyond her husband, a future wherein he could never hurt her again?

She hates him, she hates Harley.

No, she doesn't.

But then again, it is probably the stress over his sordid behavior that has given her cancer again. An acute sense of loss assails her.

Norman.

Harley.

Her own bewildering life. No wonder she's crying. The terrible contrast between what had been and what is now makes her heart ache and deepens her pessimism. The mixture confuses her. She doesn't know exactly what she feels. An hour ago she was weightless and walking on air. And now? What is she going to do without Norman? Maybe she should take back what she said. Maybe she should tell him she didn't mean it, she was only trying to give him a way out.

"Norman—"

"Franny, you're right, of course. This is a time for you and your family. I'm just a stranger in the way. Even if my heart is in the right place, I can't give you what your sisters can. And if I'm making things worse by making you doubt your connection to God, I mustn't do that. In times like these, what is more important than your immortal soul?"

"Are we living in sin?"

"I don't happen to think so, but if you think we are, then we are. That's what matters. If it's eating at you the way you say it is, I'm only making things worse. It's like sugar feeding the cancer. This is no time to weaken you further. I'll pack up and go. Maybe Maria and I will try again, I don't know. But I'll keep in touch, and if there is anything you need, just let me know."

He bolts his wine. He stands. She stands. They embrace. A sense of panic seizes her. She has all she can do not to cry out, "Don't go, Norman. I've made a mistake."

She goes into the bathroom, locks the door, hears him packing. He is hurrying. Can't get away fast enough. She hears his car starting and she remembers when Harley left her and she had wanted to chase after him and say "Harley, don't go." She leaves the bathroom. She runs to the kitchen window, sees Norman pulling out and yells, "Norman, don't go!"

He goes.

"Dear God, what have I done?" she says. "What'll I do now? Who will help me?" She walks back to the table, her fingers fingering the vacancy where Norman finished his dinner.

•

The sixth month passes. She is fifty-eight and still alive. She should be dead, but truth be told, she's more vibrant than ever. The tumor inside her liver had been steadily shrinking and finally it vanished. The spot on her lung is gone. The pea-sized lump in her left breast has gone away, too. She has gained eight pounds and her hair has grown back, although not quite as thick as it was before chemo and radiation made it fall out. She doesn't dye it anymore. Her hair is brown. Natural. Peppered with gray, she styles it so it swirls out and over her ears, curling in on the sides of her neck. She still wears wavy bangs to hide the lines on her forehead.

It's the day of her two year assessment. The oncologist says her cancer is in remission. He shakes his head, swears that in all his years in medicine he's never seen anything quite like it. It must have been the immunotherapy trial. He's baffled. He's amazed. But she isn't.

No longer living in sin with Norman was the beginning of the end for the death sentence she was facing. Though they generally have lunch at the Prado every other week, she's been untainted since he left her. When they meet they kiss hello and good-bye and go home. Maria has taken him back. They've renewed their vows.

And Franny has returned to the Church. She attends mass Sunday mornings. She goes to Confession every Friday. She whispers prayers and eats Jesus at Communion. She knows God has forgiven her. She wants to believe her cancer is gone forever, one more miracle the loving Lord granted her. But she knows not to be foolish. Eventually cancers such as hers always revive.

"But anything life throws at me, I can take it," she says.

Tough woman our Franny.

•

She proves how tough she really is one night when she's sleeping in the midst of a dream, a haze of imagery, naked bodies his and hers. Has Harley returned? Harley on top of her? Harley making love to her? She spreads wide to help him. Her mouth finds his mouth, her tongue his tongue. Which is when it hits her that something is wrong. This is not Harley's mouth, these are not Harley's lips. This vigor inside her is definitely not Harley. The musk she's breathing is unfamiliar.

"You're good, you're good," whispers a voice in her ear. "I knew you would be. Oh Jesus, oh Jesus." His body shudders. His hips keep pumping awhile. When he stops, he pushes upward with his arms and looks into her eyes. "Madre," he says. "Madre, you still owe me. I'll drop a C note from your bill if you let me rest a minute and we do this again."

"Hector?"

"Hector," he says.

"After all this time?"

"I never forget nothin, Franny. I've been watching you for a little while. I saw you leaving church today. I followed you home."

He rolls off her. When she tries to rise, he grabs her arm and pulls her down.

"Where you goin?" he says.

"The bathroom."

"We're not done."

She lies still, her mind awash with wonder and fear. Is Hector there not only to rape her, but rob her, too? Kill her as well?

"What do you want, Hector? What you gonna do?"

"No worries," he says. "Ain't gonna hurt you, Madre. Gonna get what you owe me and go." He chuckles and adds, "But when I saw you laid out like this and moaning like you wrapping cock, I says what the hell, Hector, do the whore a favor. You're lookin good, Franny. You lost weight."

"I have cancer, Hector. I lost weight because I have cancer."

"No shit? Really?" He rises to his knees and looks her over and says, "Cancer suits you. Look at this body it give you." He pauses. In the grayness of night his eyes are bright. Surrounding him are shadowy halos. Hair black, a swath of it straying over one eye. A minute passes while Franny's heart hammers.

"Don't hurt me, Hector. Don't hurt me."

He says. "Round two?"

Franny starts crying. "Please, please," she says.

Hector slaps her so hard she nearly passes out. "Stop that shit," he says.

For perhaps an hour he uses her. At first she feels it. Then a switch turns off and delirium takes over. This is a dream.

Dreams end.

"Move your ass, Madre," he says. "Wiggle. Do something. You like a dead woman. You wanna be a dead woman? I can make it happen."

His hands encircle her throat. He chokes her.

Franny welcomes it.

When she wakes later, the overhead light is on and Hector is squatting at the foot of the bed, his face, his body leaning forward. To her he looks like a gargoyle. Her hands are tied to the headboard with silver duct tape, her feet tied wide to the footboard. Her throat throbs. She's not sure she can talk. Her voice raspy, almost inaudible as she says, "Why?"

"Are we having fun yet?" he replies.

She knew he was bad, but she hadn't known he was evil. This is the boy she had fantasized, the boy she had almost propositioned, the boy she had imagined asking how much he wanted to lay an old lady.

"You on display," he says. "Bush and all. You stink, Madre. You need a bath. And . . . and you need give me my money. I need my money, Franny. Times is bad. There's a warrant on my ass. You give me my money, I go far away. You see me no more. You don't give me my money, you stay tied to this bed. Maybe a week, hmm? How long it take a body to starve? How long before it dies of thirst?"

"Don't know," she rasps. To her ears she sounds like an ailing crow.

Hector stands, his hands touching the ceiling for balance as he toes her vagina and says, "Feels good?" His eyes take in the room. "What you got here? Anything worth having?"

Bouncing off the bed, he starts rummaging through her jewel box sitting on the vanity table. He makes a pile of rings and bracelets, chains, lockets and pendants. His calves are skinny, but his shoulders and arms are roped with muscle. As he goes through her drawers, tossing clothes to the floor, he mutters, he cusses. In the second drawer down he finds her precious box, the lid locked. "What here?" He shakes the box. It rattles lightly. Bending to his pants beside the bed, he reaches into a pocket and pulls out a switchblade. Flicking it open, cramming the tip of the blade into the lock, it's no more than five seconds before he's got it open. The pictures of Chata fall out. "That's it?" He looks at Franny, his expression puzzled. "A dark lover, Madre?"

"Long ago," she whispers.

"Was you married when you hooked up?"

She nods.

"You a funny lady. You carry the torch for that boy you knew back at the ranch. Egg ranch, right? And here you are getting your rocks off with two pictures of a cock-hound name of . . . what's his name?"

"Chata."

"Chata. I can see you and Chata sneaking round on . . . what your husband's name?"

"Harley."

"Sneaking round on Harley doing the deed with Chata in the back of his car like a teeny bopper. Fuckin in closets and bathrooms and motel rooms and shit. I bet he was married, too. You probably was the best friend and you fuckin her man. You women, you got no morals. What the pussy want the pussy get. See what I'm sayin? You deserve what I'm doin."

She agrees with him. "Most my life I've been bad, you're right."

"Pay back, Madre. You got baggies?"

"What?"

He goes to the kitchen and starts opening cupboards. In a moment he's back with a zip lock bag into which he drops her jewelry.

"Every little bit helps," he says.

He goes through her wallet and finds forty dollars. He pulls out her ATM. "Four hundred dollars," he says. "Every day until your account's empty. What's the pin? How much you got in there?"

She gives him her numbers and says the last bank statement said she was down to eight hundred seventy six dollars and change.

"That's all? What the fuck you do with your money?"

"Pay bills, buy groceries, get gas."

"Yeah, always something, huh? You don't get paid until the first? It goes directly to the bank?"

She nods.

"Two days," he says. "Fuck."

He opens the bedside drawers. Finds the vibrator. Laughs. Says, "Oh, no, oh pervert." He slides between her legs. The dildo vibrates. He plays it over her legs, rubs it up and down the labia, slithers it inside back and forth, lays it on her clit. She doesn't feel anything but a distant numbness.

"Wiggle. Wiggle, Franny. Move."

"Untie my legs, "she says.

"Ah, yes." He cuts the tape clutching her ankles. Pushes her legs up, leans back a bit. "Get your rocks off. How cool would that be?"

"Don't hurt me, Hector. Don't kill me."

"You some slut," he says.

"Please."

"I like that. It's what you are. You were Orgy in another life. Look how you drooling."

He kisses her, his tongue slipping inside. Franny gurgles. She gasps, coughs. She says, "Oh no, oh no."

When he's finished he says, "I'm hungry. What you got to eat?"

Climbing off her, he goes back to the kitchen and clatters around. She hears the cast iron skillet getting slammed on a burner. Soon she smells toast. She hears eggs being cracked and scrambled. The aroma of coffee noses into the room. He eats he drinks he burps. Says, "Hmm, not bad."

Next thing she knows he's staring down at her. His mouth is crooked. A plate of food gripped in his hand: eggs, toast. He's sitting on the bed shoving a fork full of yellow at her. She turns her head away and says, "I eat anything I'll throw up. I need to go. I need to go bad. You don't get me into the toilet I'm gonna make a mess here, Hector. I feel like I've had an enema."

She can see he's pondering. Finally, he unties her wrists and marches her to the toilet. Plops her down, steps back and sits on the edge of the tub waiting. She pees a quart. Then her bowels move and diarrhea lets loose. When that happens he stands up and flicks on the overhead exhaust.

"I need to take a bath," she says, wiping herself several times before flushing. "You could use a bath, too. You're ripe, Hector."

He laughs.

And then his eyes morph into knife-edges regarding her as if she has a trick up her sleeve, as if she might be trying to lure him into some plan in her head. But there is no plan. She wants to bathe. Wash him off her. Douche him out. "Please," she says.

"Please, Hector. I've suffered so much. I was inches away from dying. Hector listen: We're just humans alike. Let me take a bath."

He stands back while she pours the tub full of water as hot as she can stand it. She lowers herself, sits staring at the reddish tape burns on her wrists and ankles. Her throat is sore. He has gone out and brought back a cigarette. His clothes are on now. She wonders if that means he's done with her. He smokes. Watches her, his eyes alien.

A minute passes before he says, "Don't get stupid, Madre." From his pocket he pulls out the knife, pushes the button, waves the blade at her. "Jugular. Hot water speeds blud. Turn you into a hydrant."

"I'm not stupid," she says. "I'm trying to figure out how to get the rest of your money. So you can go. So you can run from whatever's after you. The law. What did you do? Why they after you?"

He touches the blade to her lips and says, "Shh."

She soaps up. She scrubs her body with a washcloth. She washes between her legs. She lathers again and again, uses the washcloth like a Brillo pad, rubbing, scrubbing as if she might rub layers away.

"That's enough," he says. "Get out."

She opens the drain, takes a towel from the rack.

He lets her wear her terrycloth robe. He lets her sit in the kitchen and sip vodka. He sips vodka, too. What to do, she asks herself. Oh dear, oh dear.

"Take my car, Hector. Go empty my bank account. Almost nine hundred dollars. Take it. I won't say a word."

"Neh," he says. "Neh, you'll give me up five seconds after I'm out the door."

"I swear to God. I swear on the Bible."

"Neh."

"So what you want me to do? I give you all I got."

"Two days to payday."

She thinks about two days of this. "You staying till payday?"

"That's a plan. I'll feed you. Fuck you some, too. You liked the dildo. You were into it."

She sighs, lowers her gaze, shakes her head. Sniffs. She tries not to cry, but she cries.

"I told you stop that shit," he says. "What the fuck. You ain't got it so bad. I'm not torturing you. I'm not pulling your toenails out or breaking your fingers. I could do that, you know."

She forces herself to stop crying. She tries to smile as she says, "It won't work, honey. Two days? No way."

"Why not?"

"My sisters call all the time. My mother. My boss at work."

"You just say you sick. You say you got flu, they better stay away or they'll catch it. You tell em that. And right here I'm listening. You make it sound real, or I will be bad to you. I promise I will fuck you up worse. I don't want to, but don't push me, I'm a desperate man." He pauses, his eyes looking upward, his lids blinking. "Two days is good," he says. "Gives time to cool them cops. Lay low and they think I'm gone. Another country. Maybe Mexico. Or Canada, the Yukon. Crims disappear up there all the time. It's known fact. Everyone knows it. Big-wild up there. But no going half-cocked, Hector. You will plan this thing. You will know what to do when the time comes. Maybe you take her along. Keep an eye on her." He laughs. "Yeah, disappear her in the desert maybe, if she don't behave. What would your mother say about that? Your sisters?" He beckons to her. "C'mon, let's watch TV. Find some news, so we know what's happenin. Maybe you learn somethin. C'mon."

•

They watch the noon news, but Hector is never mentioned. Afterwards, he leads her back to bed, ties her hands behind her back. Ties her right leg to his left leg. "Don't you move," he says. "I need sleep."

Around quitting time her boss calls, leaves a message. "You okay? You at the doctor's? Gimme a call, Franny."

Judy calls and says she's sick again. An hour later it's Ruthie complaining.

Hector finally has Franny call everyone back and talk flu. Her voice is still hoarse, so the ruse works. "The flu, yeah. A little fever. You don't want to catch it. Stay away, okay?"

When the last call is done, Hector pats her butt and says, "See how easy?"

No more calls come.

Her mind keeps reminding her of how bad she is, how bad she's been all of her life.

I deserve it. Slut I've played since I was played with by that boy at the matinee. It started there. That boy fingering me and I am not ten years old and he is a stranger, but I am so frozen I can't move, can't stop, can't cry out for my sisters sitting a row away. It started then, and running out screaming didn't change my fascination with it.

She sees him again. The boy with tousled hair and half-closed eyes. She smells his smoky breath, feels his hand parting her legs and feeling around down there for ages, until something hurt and she sprang up and ran out of the theater shrieking, while both her sisters yelled behind her, "Franny, it's just a movie, it's not real!"

But this is real. No denying it. "I'll never be able to tell anyone," she whispers.

"That's the way, Madre. You tell em about this and they know you a whore. You know what I'm saying?"

She nods. "I'm way tired," she says.

"Yeah, me too," he says.

He ties her to him. Plays with her a while before passing out. She passes out, too.

•

Morning light. Franny opens her eyes and he's gone. Her hands are tied to the headboard, one ankle tied to the footboard. A strip of tape dangles from her other ankle.

After taking a shower, she changes the sheets and sleeps all day. Rising at 7:00, she eats a light dinner of yogurt and strawberries with Melba toast. She drinks a martini. She drinks two. She drinks three. She watches the shopping channel till midnight.

24 - So Into Didi

Taking the 8 west from Kensington, she finds the freeway claustrophobic as usual. She thinks about turning around, going home, calling him and saying she tried to visit but couldn't get through the traffic. He would understand. He would tell her it's okay. He would say he was doing fine, no need to burn that four dollar gas, no need to play dodge-car today. He knows how much she hates driving in traffic, how unnerving it is.

For several minutes she sits unmoving, surrounded by trucks and cars. Letting her mind wander, she tells herself, I shouldn't have let my ass rule, that's the thing. If I had tried harder, we would have stayed together. Only myself to blame. Oh, shut up, Didi. Get off your case. What's done is done. You can't hit rewind. And you know what? He's a masochist, a self-flagellator in more ways than one. He pushed his heart over the edge and refused to be repaired. How dumb is that? Yeah, but I'm another thing he didn't need in his life. Didi the perpetrator.

The traffic crawls. Stop and go, riding the brakes. There doesn't seem to be any reason for gridlock, no accidents, no suicide leap off the overpass, no stupid dog meandering. Just vehicles, vehicles, too many cars, too many semis, too many people, all of them jerking forward trying this or that lane, a bizarre dance filled with clusters of sound, engines pounding like one irresistible will that insists on moving.

After she takes the on-ramp to the 15, the crawl turns into a trot. Mission Valley falling behind. The freeway leading her north. She can keep going if she wants to—drive all the way to Oregon or Washington, or Canada or turn round and head south into Baja, lose herself in one of those charming little Mexican towns along the coast. No one would find her. She could do it. She could take all the money out of savings and live like a robber baron exchanging dollars for pesos. When she turns sixty-two she could claim half of Danny's retirement. In Baja her income would be fine. A little house near the beach. Fresh fish for dinner. An adoring senor to cook for her and warm her bed. Someone to cuddle her. She would go barefoot on the sands. She would listen to waves rolling onshore and breathe pure air again, the way it used to be before the country was overrun by greenhouse gasses—all these goddamn vehicles!

She tries to drive in the slow lane but keeps coming up behind monster trucks going slower than she is. In the fast lanes, cars are doing eighty and ninety. "Burn that gas as fast as you can," she grumbles. She stays at sixty because her reflexes are slow and sixty is safer and everything scares her. Giant SUVs and pickups ride her bumper. She keeps pulling over, but then another asshole fills the rearview mirror. Another and another.

"I need a drink!"

•

The last time they talked he told her, "The bridge abutments beckon, Didi." He said he had been plagued by thoughts of suicide after she walked out. Why didn't he do it? Why don't we all? Why do we rush from desire to fulfillment to desire? Satisfaction/ dissatisfaction—endless cycles. What are we looking for? Thirty-three years he has been married to Franny. Thirty-three years and never content, losing himself in books, teaching and writing. He needed to keep himself calm and producing, instead of chasing another woman, always wanting more out of life than life gives anyone.

"Oh, Harley, what are you doing? What have you done?"

He told her it was the newness, the intensity she brought into his life that made her captivating.

"I get it," she says. "But now I'm living larger than he is. And I'm not going to stop. When it comes time to check out, I want to have experienced everything possible. I want adventures. Escapades. Dalliances. Affairs. I want romances. You get none of that when you're dead."

•

The car drifts and a horn honks. She swerves barely missing a collision with a pickup. She retreats to the slow lane again. Her mind wanders back to him. "He should have settled," she says. "Should have stayed home and written novels and sent out stories. Why didn't he do that? Why didn't he apply himself more? God knows he has talent. Four novels and two dozen stories published, productive until he ran off with me and started drinking. And now Franny tells me he's all but disabled. Here's the thing: he wasn't happy with her. 'I'll never be happy with Franny,' he told me. Yeah, and he also told me I was the sword of Damocles hanging over his head."

Hoping a profound thought will make sense of it all, she pauses. A minute passes with nothing but fragments entering her head: "If Franny were a real woman, I wouldn't be driving to the rescue. This will probably kill me. I bet it does. I can feel the blood in my temples. There's a raw pain in my throat. Am I coming down with something? It's common knowledge that the caretaker often dies first. That man will kill me. 'The coward does it with a kiss, the brave man with a sword' Quoting what who? Am I desperate enough to kill him? Would be merciful. Do it for dogs and cats. No more fear of dying after you're dead."

A jacked up four-wheeler roars by, cleated tires howling. On the tailgate is a magnetic ribbon telling Didi to SUPPORT OUR TROOPS. Next to it is a flag decal: UNITED WE STAND. Didi (glaring at the truck weaving in and out of traffic) mutters, "Patriotism, my ass. 'A thing is not necessarily true because a man dies for it,' Harley told me time after time."

With seething resentment in her heart, she continues dawdling towards Temecula, towards ailing Harley waiting like a spider to wrap her in his web.

•

Rain is starting to fall. It makes her anxious. She turns the intermittent wipers on. Every ten seconds: swish. Past the Retirement Village she cruises, where the old ones putter their final days away in woolgathering comfort. She can see the building where his mother lived. He had pointed it out once when they were driving to have dinner somewhere.

She wonders if she will end up in the same place. If not there, another box equally repulsive.

This aging thing: God's comedy.

Turning onto Rancho California, she goes to the lounge at The Country Inn. Something to take the edge off. Something to mitigate the glooms. Salvation sans lucidity. She hurries out of the rain, enters the bar and finds she is the only customer there. She sits on a stool and orders a vodka martini straight up, no vermouth, no olive. The bartender is a willowy woman with streaky blond hair pulled back in a ponytail. The dim light is flattering to her, but when she leans over to place the martini in front of Didi, she sees wrinkles on the woman's forehead. In her mid-forties, Didi decides. Bottles of liquor create an arch over the cash register. The lights embedded in the counter and on top of the mirror create charming rainbows.

Bolting the first martini she asks for another. The bartender adds extra, a smidgen. She knows Didi needs it. The rattle of the shaker makes music. When she serves Didi again she smiles curiously and says, "Are you all right?"

What does the bartender see? Does she see how fretful Didi is, how angst-ridden, worried and angry? The woman's slim hands are on the bar. She is leaning forward, showing what Didi would call first-class cleavage, head cocked, eyes coaxing. A scrap of song flashes through Didi's mind: *it's a quarter to three . . . there's no one in the place except you and me.*

"I've got one hell of an evening ahead," she tells the bartender. "Waiting for me is someone I definitely do not want to see. But I have to."

The bartender nods, her eyes coaxing Didi to continue. Light too dim to tell what color her eyes are. "I could tell something was wrong," she says. "When a good-looking woman comes in late-afternoon and guzzles a martini, that's definitely a sign something's amiss."

"I'm Didi."

"I'm May."

"Yeah, you look like May ... May flowers."

"Really? I wish I felt like May flowers."

May's smile is sensual. Is she Lesbian? They're out of the closet, they're everywhere now. Gay women all the rage.

The vodka is already persuading her to talk. "I imagine you get all kinds of stories. You're the neighborhood listening post, the advice giver. I need your advice, May."

"I'm listening, Didi."

"One more." She twirls her finger over the glass.

Sipping the third martini, she thinks she ought to down it quickly and take a walk. A woman should never let anyone know her secrets, not even a stranger she will probably never see again. Play your cards close to your vest.

"May," she says, "I have so fucked up my life it's a wonder I'm able to function at all. I've made so many mistakes I doubt I'll ever recover."

"We've all been there, honey. I'm no angel."

"You look like an angel. You're a nice change of pace on a gloomy day. I expected some gruff old fart bent with age working the early shift, not you looking like some surfer girl. Do you surf, May?"

"Used to when I was younger. But I'm forty and don't have the time or the skills anymore. I have to work whatever shift they give me. If it wasn't for the tips, I couldn't make it. But we're talking about you, honey. You fucked up your life and can barely function. What's fucked up? I bet it's a man."

"You see before you a woman trying to rub her belly while patting her head and doing an Irish jig at the same time."

May laughs, and Didi feels a burst of giddiness. She wants to take May's hand and run away with her. Life can still be good. Sure it can.

"Actually, it's three men," she says. "I've got a lover and an ex-husband who pesters, and an ex-lover who I'm seeing today. Can you believe me when I say I love them all? I do in different ways. My ex is more like brother love. My lover is more like lust love. My ex-lover, the sick one, is giving me a guilt trip because he left his wife for me. Then after seven years, I left him to take up with my current lust. It kills me to hurt any of them, but I couldn't stand married life, so I left him. To add insult to injury, my ex-lover has a dangerous heart condition. He needs a bypass but refuses to have surgery. I don't know what to do about it. I feel responsible. I feel like I've got to take care of him. How long he'll live is anyone's guess. The doctor said maybe a year. That was nearly two years ago. I'm thinking I can get a caretaker to come over. Someone from hospice, maybe. But I'm burned out already. Can't handle it. What it's doing to him, you know? His wife, her name is Franny, called me, wanting me to step up to the plate. I know I should, but I don't know if I have it in me. I want to be brave and strong about this, but inside I'm quaking. I can't do it. But if I don't do it, how do I live with myself? Wish I could just walk away, say to hell with him."

"Jesus, you've got your plate full," says May. "Have one on the house."

Didi is willing. If three martinis make her feel able, four might sedate her. She can handle her liquor. She's so used to it she could drink a pint or more and still drive like a coded robot.

May puts the drink on a fresh napkin and says, "How old are you, honey?"

She adds another lie to the lies she's already told. "I'm forty." That puts them even, a pair of forties at the peak of their sexuality, according to whoever. There is some flirt in May that has captured Didi's interest. Ever since she and Carlson did their first three-some, she's been thinking more and more about women and how much she enjoyed their softness, their soft, wet kisses, their hairless lip. What would she do if May—

Booze talking.

"God, I hate aging," May says. There is a grave turn in her eyes. Aging is serious business. "Can I tell you something? Time and tide wait for no woman. You're forty. Won't be long and sixty will come, sixty-five, seventy."

"If I live that long."

"Yes, lots can happen between now and then, but my point is time is closing in."

"Like a vise."

"I feel it too. I used to be fourteen and suddenly I'm forty. If the jump to eighty is as fast as forty it's the blink of an eye. How did I get here? I can't be forty. Yes I am. And so are you. And you still got some looks. I mean you look really healthy. Listen, one thing I've learned from the breakup of two marriages and trying to make nice, it's mainly a waste of time. People get along fine without you. You only think you're needed because you're the one who needs, not them. I know this sounds selfish, but it's the way of the world: you don't take care of yourself, people will eat you alive. Those are my philosophics."

Didi agrees: "I've always said that once you're dead it doesn't take long for people to forget you. Ten, twenty years tops before you're pulp in their heads. In a hundred years you're not even that, unless you're Elvis Presley or Marilyn Monroe. And even they're ephemeral ultimately."

"You're proving my point, honey."

Didi watches her turn, grab a bottle of Cutty Sark. Pour herself a shot. She salutes Didi who salutes back. Warm desire uncurls in her. They could lock the doors. Use a booth. Just let yourself go like Carlson does, his three women in one night, satisfying all of them, including herself. His many affairs, the down and dirty details he tells her. Hearing them making her lusty.

You only live.

Once.

And you want to try some of that, don't you? You've come a long way since you abandoned Harley. Wild sex with Carlson. Wild sex with Harley when he was up for it. And now on your way to him. Because Franny called and said he's dying and wants to see you once more. Even when you were lovers, you were no more faithful to him than you were to your husband. How come men are such suckers? What kind of low-life skank have you become? Come on, you've always been this way. This is the real you. You're no longer undercover. Sure, you kept yourself in check till the children were grown, but meeting Norman and then Harley unleashed the Other in you.

●

Didi, you know it's the Devil talking don't you? She looks at her left shoulder and sees him there. His forked tongue sticking out as if he's going to lick her ear.

The door opens. In come three men in suits, one of them saying, "May, what's up?"

"Nothing much," she says, smiling. "You want another, honey?" she asks.

Didi puts her hand over the glass. "I gotta be able to talk civil. One more and I'll be calling him names." She puts down two twenties and tells May to keep the change.

The men take a booth and call for a pitcher of brew. Didi rises.

"What names would those be?" May asks her.

"Heartbreaker," tumbles out of Didi's mouth. "Sad prick. Leach. Parasite. Vampire." She stops. Then says, "No, I'd never say any of those. He's really a good man, mostly. A fine person. A gentle human. He doesn't deserve what's happening to him."

"Hmm, don't believe you," says May. "Come back. Let me know what happens."

"It's a date," she tells her.

In the car, she sits awhile gathering her courage. Taking out her phone, she sends her computer an email:

I stopped at the lounge inside The Country Inn. I had four martinis, but I'm not drunk. At least I don't think I am. But I probably couldn't pass a Breathalyzer. Inside the lounge I met a bartender named May. She's forty. I lied and said I was forty as well. I want to come back here and feel her out about joining me and Carlson for dinner and fun together. So this is my life lately. I look for sexy women in order to find those that have the same predilections that I've developed over the course of a year. Somewhere in my head is a premonition that eventually I'll negate men altogether and become one of those out of the closet Lizzies I've read so much about. Men are too much trouble and you can't trust them. Case in point is Harley. He dropped a twenty-three year marriage to shack up with me for seven years. And then what does he do? Contracts heart disease and won't do anything to cure himself.

I'm on my way to visit him. Lord knows what I'll find, but this is something I do not want to do. So why do it? Why not turn around before it's too late, go home, maybe take May with me? The answer is: I don't have an answer. People do what they do and life fucks them for it.

Also thinking: I'm curious to see what he looks like after an entire year of not seeing him. Call me Ghoulish.

Save As Documents: The World According to Deidre Annaba Godunov.

25 - Conciliation

Harley isn't muscular anymore. Shoulder blades suggesting coat hangers. Arms and legs unable to hide a sickly thinness beneath pajamas and robe. The face: *skeletal.* Eyes cradled in scoops of darkness that look like bruises. Irises glittering with what seems to be wonder or fear. Wrinkles like the specter of cobwebs. This is Harley J. Olsen. This is what life has done to him. This is what he has done to himself. Once upon a time a man with the body of a weightlifter, the one she had a crush on because he was so smart, a professor, a published writer—ages ago and who could know the heartache they would cause each other? Best not to know. Knowledge: *dangerous.* Knowledge: *paralyzing.* What woman can walk out the door in the morning without the veil of illusions propping her up? What if it was all stripped away and she saw tomorrow—and tomorrow looked like Harley?

•

When he opened the door, she had winced to see how changed he was. He hid his face in his hands, spidery veins interlacing beneath paper-thin skin. It had been unnerving. Balding Harley, whose hair had once been something out of a shampoo commercial.

She didn't run, but that's what she wanted to do. Leave it all at his doorstep. Write him off. Behind the shield of his hands she heard him say, "Oh my God, Didi, oh my God." Then he was on her, saying her name over and over, "Didi, Didi, oh Didi." His scrawny arms hugging her. And she was hugging him, too. Her fingers repelled by the knuckles of his spine. The smell of him: fecal breath and body rot. Finally she had let go, took a step away and slapped him (her slap: the brush of a butterfly) and said: "Goddamn you, Harley Olsen, you're breaking my heart!" Bowing to her, he took her hand. Kissed it. "So sorry, sweetheart. Couldn't be sorrier."

"Have that goddamn operation. What the hell is wrong with you?"

He smiled but didn't answer. Turning, he left the hall, shuffling like an old man needing a cane.

•

The walls of the living room are pale yellow. Beyond the windows the world is gray, the sky thick with clouds heavy with rain. There is a blond-brown dog that has come out and is sniffing Didi's ankles.

"This is Holly," Harley says. "My best pal. Holly, say hello to Didi."

The dog pants. As he strokes her head, she whines and licks him.

He turns to Didi and asks if she knows that Franny has cancer again.

"Yeah, we've talked. She said she's beating it. She said, unlike you, she refuses to die. Harley nods. "I thought maybe my betrayal did it. Gave me my heart condition and gave her cancer. Do you know how many millions in this country alone have cancer? Twelve million. Twelve million people. Wrap your mind around that. I heard cancer kills more people than heart failure now."

He gives her a ghastly grin as he sits on the sofa, one hand resting in the pocket of his robe, the other patting the dog, while she leans her muzzle against his leg.

Harley's skin is as yellow as the walls. The whites of his eyes yellow as well. Probably cirrhosis, she thinks. Even with the heater blasting, Harley is shivering. "My heart flutters almost continuously now. A few more days it's over. I'm finished."

"C'mon," she says.

"Yes, yes," he says.

"I don't understand you, Harley. They want to operate, but you won't let them. For God's sake why?"

He shrugs. "Free will. Chemistry. Death wish. I don't know. We all have to die, sweetheart. If not today, tomorrow. If not tomorrow, someday. No getting out of it."

"I don't believe you. Listen, Harley don't give up so easily. Hang in there. People have been worse than you and came back to live plenty of years. What about my uncle? Remember what I told you about him? Eight years he lived after having that nasty bladder cancer. Eight years and he died of a stroke. Think of that."

"Sit down, Didi. No, not by me. I know how bad I smell. I have a touch of cirrhosis as well. Cirrhosis smells. Did you know that? Sit in the recliner." He pulls up his pajama legs and says, "See how swollen my ankles are? It's water. Liver and kidneys not doing their jobs." He pushes his thumb on one of the swellings and leaves a dent in the skin.

She sits in the recliner and wonders what to say to him. Rain patters steadily on the roof, runs over the eaves, rivulets distorting the world beyond the window. She dreads the long drive back. California drivers are always idiots when it rains. Maybe she'll stop by the bar and see May again. Have more martinis.

Leaning forward, elbows on knees, he asks about Carlson. "Is he good to you? You gonna get married?"

Didi shrugs. "Same as always. Some days we're in love. Some days we're not. I think he's cheating on me."

"Who doesn't cheat?" he says. "Franny, as good as she is, cheated on me when we were first married. Twice that I know of. She excused it by saying it's *only* sex. As if having sex is just a sort of more intimate hugging." He smiles, laughs breathlessly.

"It was more than that with us," she says. "Way more. I loved you. Part of me still does. Even though you're willfully dying, a thought that nearly drives me out of my mind."

"Some of us are just doing it faster. All babies are born to die, you know."

She shakes her head. Says, "If people knew what suffering they were creating with the birth of a baby, maybe they wouldn't do it."

"They'd still do it."

"My two are all grown up and won't talk to me."

"So sorry," he tells her. "Be a comfort to you if they would, I'm sure."

Instantly, she feels combative. "Are you sure you're sure? What do you know about it? You never wanted kids. You hate kids."

"I grieve."

"Liar, you couldn't tell the truth if your life depended on it. Even when the truth wouldn't be a problem, you won't tell it. The first thing out of your mouth is always a lie. Just like your mother. You told me she was a compulsive liar. So are you. And you said Franny was worse than both of you put together."

"Franny is a compulsive liar, yes, and you're a liar, too, Didi."

"I don't lie, Harley."

"Just to me, huh?"

"To protect you. I tried to protect you is all. I couldn't tell the truth because I knew how it would hurt you. All your health issues—telling you would have been callous, you see? I mean it would be . . . rotten, a rotten thing to do. So I chose to torture myself by lying. I lied and lied and lying ate me up. But I did it for you. You made me a liar."

"And you made me a liar as well."

"Ack, no talkin to you."

•

This isn't the way it's supposed to be. She is there to show her concern and to help him if she can. And maybe absolve him. Yes, forgive him for giving up on life. Forgive him for letting her go. He doesn't want to hear about how bad he is. He knows he has no excuses. He is not the person he intended to be. And neither is she.

She feels woozy, a little disoriented. She shouldn't have drunk those martinis.

"I've always been a coward," he says.

"No, you're no coward. If that were true, you wouldn't have done what you did. It took courage to walk out on a sick woman. You must have been really desperate. Did living with her make you desperate?"

"I don't know."

"Because she was always sick?"

"Maybe." He shrugs. "Being around illness wears you down."

"And now you're old and falling apart. Franny's vamoosed. She wanted me to come see you and call her back, but she won't get off her ass and help."

"What would you expect her to do?"

"Who knows? She waves her hand as if shooing away hopeless notions. "I figure when you didn't want sex with her anymore, that's when you started searching for a way out."

He shakes his head. "Not true. Sex was never the thing. But when I couldn't respond, I admit I started wanting her out of my life. It happened between you and me, too. In spite of how much you tried to keep things spicy, I just couldn't keep up. When you brought that guy home, that's when I knew we were done."

"I brought him for you. You're like Carlson, both of you hardcore voyeurs."

"A younger, healthy Harley might have been able to get into it. Or maybe not. I don't know. As I've aged I've become more aware that sex with strangers can be demoralizing. And deadly. Let's not forget deadly."

"What do you care? You don't care if you die."

"Not like that. Not that way."

"You've still lots to live for. Look, you have your books. You have your writing. You have your work."

"I have nothing."

"God, you're so fucking exasperating."

"You cheated on me, Didi."

"What? Is that bothering you still? Really? Big deal. I'm a flirt, a stupid, flirty girl. And besides, you started it. You showed me the way to behave."

"Sure. Blame me. Must be nice."

"And besides, I knew I wasn't doing it for you anymore. I wanted to make you happy. It was the only way I could think to keep us together. Lots of sex."

"Didn't work."

"Nope."

"I'm over it now, Didi."

"You don't get over anything. Here you are within days of meeting your maker, and you're still holding those mistakes over my head. I enjoyed it. Did I ever. That's what really got you."

"Yeah."

"Why?"

"Sometimes fantasies shouldn't be brought to life."

A crushing sadness grips her. In a thin whisper she says: "What does any of it matter now? Shouldn't we be talking about what we can do for you?"

"We?"

"I want to help. What can I do? Tell me how to help."

"Naw, I'm beyond help." Copious tears start falling. Nose running, he keeps wiping it with tissues. There is a pile of tissues on the coffee table that look like chrysan-themums.   The dog is nudging Harley's hand and whining again. His whole body continues shivering. And still the heater is blasting.

Didi glances longingly at the door. *Open it. Go on leave. No one can stop you.*

"I'm frightened, Harley."

"What?"

"I'm scared. This is awful."

Now she is weeping as well. He passes the Kleenex. "If only I could do some-thing," she says, blotting tears. "I'd give anything to save you, honey. I really would. I'd cut my arm off if it would save you. I've prayed and prayed and nothing happens," she says. "Tell me it's a dream, Harley."

He nods. "We are such stuff as dreams are made on. Our little life is rounded with a sleep."

"Who said that?"

"Guess."

"Shakespeare."

"*The Tempest*, yes. His farewell to the stage."

The rain sounds like fingers tapping on the panes, trying to get Didi's attention.

Harley continues, "Doesn't it comfort you that when you die you'll stop suffering? You won't know anything."

"Hell no."

"You won't be far behind me."

"Shut up," she says, and blows her nose, wipes her eyes, stares at him.

"I . . . I'm only trying—"

"Give it up," she tells him.

"Don't be mean, Didi. Don't be mad. I've had a hard life, you know."

"Oh boo-hoo, it's all about you," she says. "It's always about you. Poor Harley. Your whacky family, the death of your father, who hated you because you wouldn't shut up and sit still. That and . . . and your mother's promiscuity after she was free of that asshole."

"You, you're promiscuous, too."

"I am not, Harley. Not like that I'm not. How many husbands did she have? Four was it? Was it six?"

Harley defends his dead mother. He tells Didi that everyone has a reason for be-having the way they do. Everyone driven by forces beyond their control. Life is full of misery and it makes you do things you don't really want to do. The only way to handle life is distract yourself. That was what his mother did after his father died, distracted herself by creating a beautiful facade, a magnet to men. She put on a persona everyone loved. In his mind she was irresistible to both men and women.

"Your mother was a monster. You used to say it yourself, but now you're saying she had reasons for what she did and you forgive the pain she caused. Harley, c'mon."

"She was not a bad person. She could be stupid at times, but who doesn't do stupid? You?"

Didi shakes her head. "You," she says.

"No. You, it's all your fault. If I hadn't met you I would never … Well, I should have met someone normal. A boring woman, but trustworthy. A boring woman, but dependable. Instead, I got you. Got carried away by your looks and talent. Wanted to support you and help you and be an important part of your life. Maybe not the center of your life, but close enough. I was never the center. I was never anything but a person who could get you published. I didn't mind you using me. I never complained. I should have complained. I should have left you and met someone who wouldn't betray me and abandon me and—you gave me heart failure, Didi."

She knows that the old Harley wouldn't have been so blunt. The old Harley would have felt compassion for her. She knows he's dying, but she doesn't have time for coddling. She tells herself what she told herself all through the years of her marriage to Danny—he's not the man she used to know.

When the phone rings, she leaps to answer it.

"So you're there," says Franny.

"Yes . . . yes, we've been talking."

"Now you know what I was saying. You see how he is?"

Her eyes are on Harley dabbing tears. That cadaverous face. Those fingers: twisted twigs on a dying tree. The dog is still making sympathetic noises.

"Yes, I see how he is," Didi tells Franny.

"So what you gonna do?"

"I don't know."

"You don't know?"

"Yeah, I think I do." Didi slams the phone down. Goes out to the porch. Calls Carlson on his cell.

He answers on the first ring and says, "What's going on?"

"He's really sick. Really, really."

"What does 'really' mean?"

"It means heart failure. And he also has cirrhosis of the liver. He looks like the wrath of God."

"Shit."

"Shit is right."

"What are you doing?"

"Listening to him cry. He has a dog here. It's crying, too. Jesus."

"Fuck that, Didi. You don't owe him nothing."

Mournfully she watches the rain slanting, hears it drumming on the porch roof. She is trembling, not from cold but from fear. "What can I do but help him through this? He's at death's door. He smells like he's decomposing. It's the strangest smell, I can't explain it. Like meat going bad."

"He probably needs a hot bath. Who takes care of him?"

"Nobody."

She hears Carlson clearing his throat. Then: "How did it come to this?"

Feeling trite she tells him, "God's will. All I can do is help ease him over the threshold."

"Then you're gonna stay?"

"Yes," leaps out and surprises her. "I'll keep in touch. We'll talk."

"You got guts, lady."

"Guts?"

"I thought I knew you. But nope, I don't know you. Not really."

"Truth is I haven't a clue either."

"Are you getting a cold? You sound congested."

"No, I'm fine."

"You been crying?"

"What do you think?"

"So sorry."

"Yeah." As she hangs up, a voice in her head says, What did you ever see in him? He's conceited. He's narcissistic. He's way more perverted than you.

•

When she goes back inside, she finds Harley leaning forward groaning. The dog is on the sofa pawing him. Harley glances up at Didi. "Nitro," he whispers. "Over there." He points at several bottles on the kitchen counter.

She hurries through them, reading the labels: Prilosec, Xanax, six other bottles, one of them labeled Digoxin another one says it's a Vasodilator for Chronic Angina. "How many?"

"One."

She opens the bottle.

"Give me two."

She shakes two tiny pills out. Brings them to him.

Seconds after slipping the pills under his tongue, he gives her a sleepy smile and curls on the couch, the afghan over him, the dog as his pillow.

She watches his face relax, the cords in his neck softening. She sees his eyes shifting beneath their lids, lips making puff noises. He used to make that noise when they were sleeping together. She hated it. She finds herself wondering if May snores. She thinks of calling the lounge.

But doesn't.

26 - Near End Stop

Harley sleeps a full hour, occasionally moaning, sometimes smacking his lips as if they're dry. Does he need water? She doesn't know what he needs. She wonders if she should fix him something to eat.

In the kitchen she finds cans of consommé and chicken broth. She heats the consommé. Butters some saltines. Makes a cup of tea. Puts it all on a tray and carries it to the coffee table. Harley is murmuring, "Nuh-uh, nuh-uh . . ." as if denying something someone said. Maybe the man with the scythe?

When she holds the bowl of broth to his nose, his eyes open. Holly sits up. She sniffs the air. Her tongue pants. Her eyes are riveted on the bowl of broth.

"You need to eat something," Didi tells him.

Making an effort, he puts the broth and buttered crackers on the floor and tells Holly to eat them, which she does immediately. After sipping the tea he says, "I might throw up. Get me a pan."

Watery vomit spews over the afghan.

After he calms down, he whispers, "What a stinky mess. Why don't you just shoot me?"

"How about I give you a bath first?"

At the kitchen sink she rinses the afghan. Wipes the coffee table and the rug with paper towels. Throws all the crushed tissues away. She pours him a bath and half-carries him to it, the panting dog trailing behind them. She takes off his robe, pajamas and slippers. Eases him into the water. After he's up to his chin he says, "Oh, this feels good." She soaps her hands and washes what is left of his hair. She washes his face, the canals of his ears, his neck, his chest and belly and between his legs, his shrunken penis. She washes his feet, noticing the length of his toenails, the one next to his big toe has a nail so long it curves all the way under. The water is filthy gray. Didi pulls Harley out. Dries him as he stands there trembling and saying, "Did you know that the penis shrinks as you get older? It's true, another indignity of aging."

She is looking at his penis and yes no doubt about what he says is true.

After escorting him to bed, she massages lotion into his skin. He seems content now. Grateful. His wisps of hair are shiny and slick with lotion. She puts fresh pajamas on him. He wants his sweatband around his head and over his ears.

When he lies back, she clips his toenails. After her pedicure is finished, she looks up and sees he is sleeping again. Holly lying beside him. It is dark outside. Didi leaves the bedside lamp on.

•

For the next two hours she does the washing and drying. Vacuums the rug. Dusts the furniture. Folds the laundry. Puts it away. When she checks on him she finds he is on his side angelically cuddling the dog. She remembers the man he was when she met him, the muscular shoulders and arms, the deep chest, the narrow waist, the strong legs—all of it dissolved now behind veils of illness. She feels like crying but refuses to. Bending over, she kisses his cold cheek, and his eyes open. "You're still here," he says.

"I'm still here."

"I won't blame you if you go."

"I'm not going anywhere. I'm not worth much, but I'm here, Harley."

"Harley Olsen—bedlam." He chuckles.

"Me too," says Didi. "Inside my head is total chaos."

As they stare at each other the years fly by:

So this is you now.

And this is you.

This is what we've come to.

"Listen to the rain. So soothing," she says. "Think of it. Think of flowers."

"It's a blessing, Didi."

"You make me feel brave," she says. "Promise you'll stay."

"I'll never leave you," he says, hand over heart. "Never, never."

"Never say never," she tells him.

"Vodka," he says. "I need it to sleep through the night."

"Whatever works," she says, rising from his side. "I'll have one, too."

"Or three or four," he says smiling.

•

In the morning, she rises, showers, dresses in the clothes she wore the day before. She lets the dog out. Then feeds Harley buttered toast and tea. She sponge bathes him. Dresses him in sweat pants, heavy socks, his robe. Coaxes him out to watch TV, while she cleans more of the house, mopping the kitchen floor with a germ-killing cleanser, changes the sheets on his bed, puts the dirty ones in the washer to have them ready for tonight.

•

Later, she drives home, packs a suitcase full of clothes. On the way back, she stops at Wal-Mart and buys purifiers/ionizers for every room. She means to run them twenty-four/ seven.

Day follows day while she watches him wasting away. Every evening the three of them watch TV, preferably something silly. Maybe a movie on the Turner channel, an old one that ends happy. At nine she gives herself and him a six ounce glass of vodka poured over ice. Then she tucks him into bed with Holly and kisses him goodnight. She's learned not to give him any vodka until bedtime. When she gives him vodka, he always dozes off quickly. He sometimes mutters, occasionally moans or whimpers. He looks like a little old man lying there imploding, holding the dog as if she's a symbol of life he's clinging to.

But Didi has faith she can save him. Love and caring and sanitary conditions will work miracles. She knows what she's doing. She knows why she's obsessed with cleanliness. She's cleaning illness out of the house. This is one more way she can help. This is one more way she can hold off what he calls his coming quietus.

Sterilize every inch of the place.

She works hard for the next two days, dusting, mopping, vacuuming, Windexing the windows, Cloroxing the tub, the toilet. By the time she's done, the living room, kitchen and bathroom sparkle. The air smells wholesome.

She inspects her handiwork and says, "Didi Godunov, you've earned your place in Paradise."

·

In the evening, she calls Franny and asks her to take over for a day or two. "I need a breather," Didi says.

"Harley might mind," says Franny.

"Not at all. Let bygones be bygones. He's a short-timer. Maybe a week. Maybe a month."

"That's all?"

"Definitely."

"I never meant anything bad to happen to him."

"Me neither."

"I tried to be a good wife. Failed miserably in the first decade of our marriage. Cheated, you know. "

"I failed my marriage, too. We all fail. Things never turn out the way you plan." Didi knows she and Franny are speaking platitudes, but she can't think of any other way to answer.

"So what time do you need me?"

"Noon would be fine."

"I'll be there. And listen, thanks for nursing him. I just didn't have the strength to face it."

"But you do now?"

"I think so. I mean if it's only a day or two."

"Two at the most, Franny."

"Sure, I can handle that."

"Of course you can, you're a trooper."

•

Again she uses her phone to post an entry on her computer:

I just checked on Harley. He is snoring. I shake my head in wonder. Harley Olsen, the single best lover I've ever had, and I've had plenty. When was the last time we made love? I mean real love. I don't know. I should remember, but I can't. Everyone has a last time. Here's the thing—you never know if this particular time is it. You've had sex with him and then it's over. Forever. No more Harley-generated orgasms. How sad is that?

At noon I'll be on my way to the lounge. I'm hoping to catch May starting her shift. I'll invite her out.

Let's be optimistic.

I need to call Carlson and tell him what's up.

Also thinking: Maybe I shouldn't. Maybe it will only be me and May. Why have a man hogging all the attention?

Save As Documents: The World According to Deidre Annaba-Godunov.

27 - End Stop

Franny lies on the sofa watching TV. At eleven o'clock she turns it off, turns out the light and stays awake sorting through her memories, the ones that bring back her childhood. In the glow of the streetlight filling the curtains, she often sees her grandmother. Images of the old lady comfort her. Gammy, the hostess, the welcoming one. Franny would like to see her father and grandfather, too, but they never come. Or haven't come yet. Franny has a notion that when they show up, her time on earth is over. She imagines herself looking down on her mother and two sisters. She imagines her mother finally beside her. Franny the guardian angel. She hopes when she dies, her sisters will sing "Beautiful Dreamer" at the funeral service. Pointing at her grandmother, she murmurs, "Gammy. My dear Gammy."

Peeling back layers, Franny giggles at what she comes across. She tells herself she'll write it down someday when things are better and she can concentrate. She'll write about the time when she was innocent and sweet and had a peaches and cream complexion. "I was so cute," she whispers. "Cute as a button. Boys touching me, wanting a kiss. I should have kissed all of them. Well, not the ugly ones, not them."

Sitting with Harley the next day, Franny tells him about her adventure in the theater when the boy molested her. "Oh, Harley" she says, "I was so clueless." She talks about the boy trying to get his finger in her, and how she ran away in terror and told her mother, and the cops came.

Harley wants to know what the cops said.

"I remember their guns. And I thought that nasty boy was in big trouble. He better run, he better hide." She laughs. Sees her mother yelling at the cops, demanding they go arrest that horrible pervert and teach him a lesson.

"My mother said, 'Charge him with child infestations!'"

Franny and Harley cackle. It is a good day for laughing. He laughs until coughing stops him.

A policeman asked questions that Franny did her best to answer:

"Who was the boy?"

"Big boy,"

"Name."

"Dunt know."

"Where touched you?"

Franny pointed to her forearm, her knee, up inside her thigh.

"Hurt you?"

"Nuh-uh."

"Scared you."

"Uh-huh."

"This is one of them things kids do, ma'am. They grope each other," said one of the cops.

"No harm done," said the other.

Franny winks at Harley and says, "My mother looked like she was going to explode. She was so mad her eyes were nearly out of their sockets. You remember how big her eyes were? Just imagine."

Harley nods his head and smiles. His smile is tender. "Poor molested Franny."

"Mom said it could mess up my psyche. She said it's one of the reasons so many women end up in therapy. Because men can't keep their damn hands to themselves. She wanted me to take the police to the theater and show them where the boy was sitting, but they convinced her that he was long gone. I couldn't give any description. He was just a blur. Except his smile. I told them I liked his smile. And Judy said I was stupid. Ruthie was shaking her head in disgust. Mama tried to defend me. Saying I was just a little girl. And they started arguing about that, about how she spoiled me. Those cops slunk away, got in their car and boogied. It was funny, Harley. Not at the time. But thinking back on it I gotta hoot at my sisters bickering, while I wander to the piano and start playing 'Heart and Soul' and singing it, singing heart and soul, I fell in love with you heart and soul. They stopped yelling at each other and yelled at me, Ruthie telling me to get my head out of my tokas. Oh Lord, oh Lord, I can see it like yesterday. Daughters. Daughters and mothers."

Even as ill as he is, Harley's face is full of good humor. She can see his gratitude that she is there with him.

"What do you think?" he says. "Did that nasty boy mess up your psyche?"

"Oh, who knows, honey? It's just part of growing up, isn't it? Every psyche gets dinged along the way." She imagines herself sitting at the computer writing it down, creating a book full of giggles.

"Yeah, we all get our dings," he agrees. "God knows you've had more than your share."

"What I know, honey, is that I can handle anything."

"Yes, you're strong. Lots stronger than me."

"You handle what you have to handle, honey. I know you'll handle it. You're a strong man. You're a rock." She taps his head, says, "In here, inside your head."

He doesn't agree. "Not me. I'm mush compared to you. I can't handle anything except feeding Holly and letting her out to go potty. I can barely handle getting up in the morning, but I do it for her, while thinking *nother fucking day to get through.* Life costs too much, you know."

"It's worth it," she says. "I'd pay the price over if I ever got the chance."

"The whole thing? Years of illness and me letting you down?"

"Absolutely. I'd live it all again with you if I could. The good and the bad. We've had our moments."

"I'm sorry I hurt you, Franny."

"Let it go. Let it be. Hey, no regrets. Today let's not be sorry for anything."

She is feeling sleepy again. She wants to think up more stories, dream up more amusing scenes for him. She looks toward the window and yep, her grandmother is there. No hurry. Take your time, Francis.

She yawns. She tells Harley, "I think I'll make a drink."

"Make mine a double," he says.

They lie on the bed, the dog between them getting strokes from both sides. They talk about her. What a good dog she is and how worried Harley is that she'll end up in the pound or worse. He extracts a promise from Franny that she will take the dog, give it a home.

A moment goes by. Then she says, "Thinking about Didi. How long were you seeing her before you left me?"

"Three years."

"Sneaking around three years. Must have been hard on you, I bet."

"I'm not built for it. It was awful. It ruined my insides. High blood pressure, IBS, ulcers, depression, insomnia. I drank constantly. Which fucked up my liver and my heart. And all I could think of as I was getting sicker and sicker was that I deserved it."

"That's right." Franny pauses. "No, not really. I'm doing fine now. At first I was a basket case, but after a few months things changed. I pulled myself together. It was either that or die."

"Yeah, and look at you now. You're a fine looking woman, Franny."

"Oh, for my age I'll do."

"I mean it. You haven't been this slim and youthful since you were twenty-five."

"Cancer mostly. I was already taking weight off by exercising, but when the cancer came along, it melted the fat right off my bloated ass."

He shakes his head and says, "What a way to lose weight, eh?"

"Stupid," she replies, her mouth a wicked grin.

"And you're in remission for sure?"

"It's what they tell me, but you know the Big C."

"Sometimes people beat it." He shakes a finger at her. "I mean they beat it for good. Remember that whenever you're down but not out."

"I guess so. Yeah, we'll see. Today I'm not scared. Tomorrow I might be terrified."

She muses the meaning of it all: His affair and her affairs, the quick years of what seems a very short life leading to this. His illness, her illness. Hector raping her. His disappearance after emptying her account. Norman Ten Boom in and out of her life. Grand love not so grand. "In the meantime," she says, "I'm going to enjoy everything as best I can."

"Make love. Raise hell," he tells her. "But don't drink, Franny. Don't be an idiot. Booze is insidious."

"So Didi chickee-poo? Isn't that what old men do, they find someone half their age, so they can feel virile again."

"Didi's fifty-two, only six years younger than you."

"Really? Your sister said she was half your age. Young, she said. Slim and a slut with tinted blond hair."

"Not as slim as she'd like to be. You met her when Norman was dating her. Did she seem like a slut?"

"She was cheating on her husband. But no, you're right. Not a slut. I have to give her credit for stepping up. She could have told me to go to hell when I called, but she didn't. The way I figure is she owed you, this woman who broke up your marriage, then abandoned you for someone else."

"He's a major stud. Big bodybuilder. Balls her brains out. She needs that. She's addicted to sex. I'd be addicted to sex if I were healthy enough. You too. You should get all the sex you can before it's too late."

"I've had my share," she replies. "Not much interested now." She wonders if she should tell him about Hector. Decides not.

"Didi's full of get-up-and-go. She's vivacious and you know what? She sings wonderfully. Oh, what a voice. Could have been professional in my opinion. Yeah, and she writes publishable poetry. I'll tell you, she sort of overwhelmed me with her talents and intellect and the way she made me feel I was the center of her world. There seemed to be nothing she wouldn't do for me. She said I was the love of her life. I think maybe it was true, true for a while, true until I got sick. When I got sick, we started having fights and I saw a side of her I didn't like. She can be ugly. But my illness scared her, you know? She begged me to stop drinking. It's ironic, the fact that alcohol was killing me, but without it I felt I couldn't keep living. Drink or face reality and die." He pauses before adding, "Faulkner drank himself to death. So did Hemingway and Fitzgerald and James Joyce and Steinbeck. Lots of people do. It's a slow suicide. If I were a real man, I'd take the gun and shoot myself."

"Don't be in a hurry. It comes soon enough for all of us."

"Didi and I had a fight the night she packed up and left. I told her if she didn't want to be with me get the hell out. Go, I said. And by god she did. But first she screamed at me to shut up. She got right in my face, nose to nose, and she shouted as loud as she could fuck you! fuck you! fuck you! There was pure hatred in her eyes, eyes so beautiful I never dreamed they could be hideous. The next thing I knew she was gone. I might have been in shock a little, I don't know. Pretty fucking amazing. I broke *your* heart for *her*. I snuck around like the lowest low-life for her. I lost contact with all my friends for her. I stayed away from my sister for her. Shanna's always been a blabber mouth and I knew if she knew I had a lover, she would eventually tell. She would get drunk one night and call and tell you. It was inevitable."

Franny nods and says, "You're prescient, honey. That's exactly how it happened."

"Predictable."

"And some people aren't. You aren't. You changed so much since we first met, it's like you're a totally different person. To this day I don't really know who you are."

He chuckles and tells her not to feel bad he doesn't know who he is either.

"I'll go to my grave not knowing," he says.

"Probably me, too." Franny says.

"I should tell you something about Didi."

"What?"

"Didi goes both ways. She sees nothing wrong with it. To her, sex in whatever form it takes is beautiful. Sex is the sea. Immerse yourself in it. Nothing compares with the feel of it when it's good."

"Are those her words or yours?"

"Hers."

Franny thinks of when she fantasized about making love to a woman. It was when she and Norman were watching a movie, two women, two men, the men kicking back watching, stroking themselves and watching. For a moment she, Franny, wanted to be one of the women. Would I ever? Why not? What's the harm?

To him she says, "I'd argue with her about it, I think. I mean the world sure has changed since I was a kid. Sex used to be this tremendous, life-altering experience. Now it's almost like . . . like French kissing."

"Well, maybe a little more than that, but I get your drift. I blame our current lack of morals on pornography."

"To some extent."

"Yes to some extent. But before the flood of porn, people were more cautious. It's monkey see monkey do now. No limits, let your imagination dictate."

"That's right, honey, you're right. Even HIV hasn't slowed us down. Powerful stuff. Even when I had cancer, I wanted sex. I made Norman move out because I thought God was punishing me for having sex with him. And maybe He was. It was after Norman left that I started getting better. Look at me now."

"I'd make love to you if I could."

"No, no, I didn't mean that, honey. I'm fine. I'm not at all horny these days." She leans over and kisses his cheek, crinkling her nose at the odor of decay as she says, "We've had some good times, honey. I'm thankful. Most lives come down to that, don't you think? I mean memories, the good ones."

"I got nothing else left," he says, taking her hand. His eyes filling with love for her. A look she thought she would never see again. It makes her heart swell. It makes her happy.

When he dies, I'll always have the memory of his look saying better than any words: Harley loves me. Harley still loves his Franny.

28 - Harley Gone Green

San Diego Union: Obituaries:

Harlan James Olsen dead at 65. Mr. Olsen was a retired English professor. He was also a published writer of novels and numerous short stories. According to his wife, Francis Olsen, her husband continued to write every day, until his final illness forced him to stop. He leaves behind his wife and two unpublished novels and dozens of stories, which Mrs. Olsen will edit before she looks for an agent to represent the deceased. Olsen passed away at his desk. Mrs. Olsen said it was a fitting death, the kind of death every writer should have. She said Mr. Olsen wanted to be buried in the recently certified Green Burial Section at Miramar National Cemetery, 5795 Nobel Dr., San Diego. Services: Friday, October 24, 11:30 A.M.

The cemetery is framed by rolling hills, enormous oaks, maples, evergreens. Ubiquitous tombstones. Brittle leaves spiraling, prisms made of leaves. No clouds in the sky. Cold sun approaching noon. No rain expected.

Mourners are gathered around a rectangular hole in the ground. The deceased lies on a pallet wrapped in a white shroud suspended on straps over the grave. No longer a warm, living man, Harley is an *it* now.

Didi is singing "Amazing Grace", the song a spontaneous reaction to the images surrounding her. She wasn't supposed to be part of the service, but her voice mesmerizes.

Sob suppressing Franny admires the ethereal beauty of Didi's voice. Harley was right, she could have (should have) been professional.

When the song ends, Franny thinks: *No Harley no me. He was the lucky one. Dear God, what do I do now?*

A chill wind toys with the mourners, their hair, skirts, suit pants. Ties tousling.

Bending over his shroud, she touches it. Recoils. It feels rubbery, inhuman.

She stands beside her mother slumped in a wheelchair. Judy puts an arm round Franny, bracing her. Franny is blotting her eyes with a hanky. Judy is whispering, "It's okay. It's okay." Round and round Ruthie rubs her back while murmuring, "Almost over, sweetie, almost over." Ruthie and her mother are scowling at the corpse.

Now that's she's started, Franny can't stop weeping. Other mourners are weeping with her, some holding back stiffly. When she first saw so many people gathered for Harley, she told herself: There must be sixty to seventy here. Harley more admired than he ever knew?

He once told her that no one would come to his funeral.

Wrong again, Mr. Olsen.

Famous poet Norman Ten Boom clears his throat to begin the eulogy.

He starts this way: "I've been asked by Francis Olsen to read the tribute she has written for her husband." He clears his throat and continues. "These are her words: Here lies my spiritual companion. Here lies Harlan James Olsen, one of the most talented men I've ever known. I was lucky enough to call him husband and friend. I already miss him so much I can scarcely bear it. Could I have done something more? Could I have somehow saved him? These are questions that will undoubtedly hound me. Questions that can never be answered, but I take solace in remembrance of all the years we had together. Thank you all for coming."

Norman holds the note in his hand while he extemporizes: "Let our prayers and good thoughts go out to Francis and her family in this time of trial. The great love of her life is gone. Her soul-mate no longer here in the flesh. But take comfort, dear ones. Harley's soul waits for his wife and all of us somewhere beyond this vale of tears. I know these things, so believe me when I say take comfort that Harley waits in a place where suffering ends. We haven't truly lost him. We have his published and un-published work, his writing. So only his body leaves us today. And the body is merely a shell for the immortal soul. Remember that these slumbering trees will reawaken when winter gives way to spring, and Harley Olsen will be part of that renewal. He is giving the last thing he can give to the earth. His body will nourish this oak behind me. Its roots will seek him out. It will take him molecule by molecule into its living system. He will feed the trunk, the bark, the branches, twigs and new leaves budding year after year. When you see this oak flourishing decades from now, you will know, in part, that it is reaping the harvest that used to be Harlan James Olsen. This is how he wanted it. This is the way he insisted it should be."

Norman's resonant voice quotes a poem he has written for the occasion:

Dying grass   scattered leaves.
The wind is cold   for those grieving.
Who are these grieving?
Not I, says the bird flying.
Not I, says the field mouse.
Not I, says the bee in its waxy hive.
Autumn has returned to the land,
Reminding us that winter always
Follows fall.
And life renews itself when winter
Winds its way to another Vernal Equinox.

Norman stops. Raises his confident eyes and stares at the crowd before continu-ing:

We survive our father's dying.
We survive our mother's dying.

We survive the deaths of our lovers.
We survive every loss that touches us,
Knowing ultimately our misery ends
When we join countless multitudes
Suspended in God's infinite bliss.

"In the days ahead when tears are falling, I hope you'll recall my words of comfort and be comforted. Let us leave the remains of Harlan James Olsen to the earth's embrace and carry his spirit away in our hearts. On behalf of Francis and her sisters and her mother, I, Walt Whitman Award-Winning Poet Norman Ten Boom, once shortlisted for the Pulitzer Prize, thank you for coming. Go in peace, dear mourners, go in peace. May God bless you."

On the boom box at his feet Norman presses a button and a bugle is heard playing Taps. The mournful sound has most of the grievers tearful again. Standing next to Harley's sister, Shanna, is Didi weeping. Freshly dyed hair pale, long and lush, shivering on her shoulders. She is wearing black jeans, a black leather jacket. Arms hugging herself. Her sturdy body looks slightly overweight, mostly round her hips and thighs. With sudden insight Franny thinks: *Gosh yes. No wonder Harley couldn't resist her.*

One by one and in groups the crowd departs. The mourners leave for their cars. Some pausing to embrace Franny and shake Norman's hand and tell him how lovely his words were, how in the midst of so much sorrow, his words were an inspiration.

"I've always been known as a speaker of uplifting and inspiring words," he says. "My words have a magic that touches hearts and gives hope in cases like this. It's the paranormal power in me. It's the Dutchman and the bear using me as their medium."

His fans, including bald Cecil and chthonic Mike, her sisters' husbands, surround Norman as they stroll over the grass, past headstones and plaques, Norman telling the people, "It's a gift God has given me. It marks me special, of course. But I'm not special. The Dutchman and the bear who speak through me are special. I'm only a humble vessel."

Hypnotically the followers nod their heads. Eyes glassy as if enchanted, as if they're in the presence of a palpable sacredness. They gaze at Norman. This is the poet shortlisted for the Pulitzer. This is the poet with ten books of collected verse published. This is the poet who has won a dozen awards and been on television talk shows. This is the poet that has stepped in and stolen the show at Harley Olsen's burial service. Oprah Winfrey interviewed him. Touch him he's famous. Apply his wisdom and your life will be better for it.

•

Franny trails to the side of him, listening and observing his admirer's faces. A light shimmering around him. Shafts of autumn falling through barren trees. His white mane glittering. This is the man she dumped because living with him was a sin and her heart really wanted Harley. This is the man who is past seventy now. A man who looks like a tubby white-haired bear rumbling through a litter of gravestones.

Harley *dead*. How *strange*.

No, not really, not strange at all.

Count your blessings, Franny. You have your sisters. You have the love of your mother. You don't have Harley, but soon enough you'll find someone else to share your life. A companion. Not Norman. Norman is yesterday. Tomorrow and tomorrow good things will happen again. Enjoy the breeze teasing your hair. Chin up. Shoulders back. Walk tall.

And keep repeating he's at peace, no longer guilt-ridden. No longer distressed for what he considered his moral failures. No more regrets No more moaning over moments of truth that broke him. No more remorse plaguing him for a weakness he couldn't help. A weakness *you* don't have any more. One more perk that comes with old age.

Glancing over her shoulder at the gravesite, she sees the rigid figure wrapped in white waiting for workers to remove the pallet and lower the remains, allowing Harley to begin the recycling process: "Gone green. Good for you, darling man."

Norman is still surrounded by worshipful fans, all nodding, smiling. Eyes filled with adoration. When he sees Franny and her family coming, he breaks away with a laugh and a wave goodbye. A colossal grin on his face, he hustles over to open the limo's doors, bowing and gesturing like a chauffeur. The husbands of her sisters hurry behind him.

Behind the wheel he starts the engine and says, "Well, I have to say I think that went well, don't you?"

"As well as it could," Franny replies.

Norman nods and says, "I had them in the palm of my hand."

29 ß- Requiem for a Superfluous Man

Every evening after the funeral, Franny holds the dog on her lap and gets drunk and feels ugly and fatter than ever. Heavy breasts. Heavy legs. Heavy, swollen feet. Heavy heart. Nothing will change, she reminds herself. *The tipping point was reached with the death of my Beloved and everything coming is downhill for the rest of my life. A holding action here and there, an excess survival to kill.*

It is curious how things work out: Harley hasn't been buried a week before Franny hears the doorbell ring and finds his former lover standing on the porch.

Her subdued voice says, "Franny, can we talk?"

She is stunned. Her mouth falls open. Her ears start ringing. She feels a horrible flushing in her neck and cheeks. "Why . . . why are you here?"

"I wanted to talk at the funeral, but I didn't think it would be right."

"Awkward," Franny manages to say.

"Yes," agrees Didi.

"You've got my number. You could have called."

"I wanted it face to face. May I come in?"

Franny hesitates. Then steps back and gestures toward the living room. Didi comes inside. The dog is standing in front of her wiggling welcome. "Holly! You remember me?" She pets the dog, kisses her nose and is kissed in return. "Oh, I'm so glad you took her," Didi says.

"Have a seat. Sit down," says Franny.

Didi gives the place a once over before sitting on the sofa. Holly hops up beside her and gives her more love. Franny sits in Harley's saggy recliner (over thirty years old) picturing her husband kicking back, feet up, watching TV, probably something on the history channel.

"I'm sure you hate me," says Didi, her voice restrained, her words scarcely more than a whisper.

"Not really. Oh, I hated you at first, but Harley is more to blame than anyone. If it hadn't been you, it would have been another, no doubt."

"Within a month of your phone call telling us to go to hell, he was falling apart. He had seemed so strong to me, but almost overnight he weakened. That's when he really started drinking. The drinking soothed his conscience and gave him courage, I think."

Franny feels a flush of triumph. "Weak? I never saw Harley weak, not even when he was dying. That's a side of him I didn't think existed."

"Alcohol calmed him. It helped him sleep."

"No more insomnia where he is now." A surprising laugh erupts from Franny's mouth. She waves her hand in front of her face. "Nerves," she says. "Nerves."

Didi's lips are trembling the way they had at the graveside. She tries to say something but can't speak.

Franny says, "If you need to cry, go ahead, but pardon me if I don't join you. I'm all cried out. I won't waste anymore tears on him. It's too hard, you know. It leaves you drained. Leaves you wanting to die. The thing to do is wait for time to heal. It always does, you know. Well, to some degree. If you can quit pitying yourself and blaming others. Easier said than done, of course."

"You're strong, Franny. He said you were strong, said you have a strong life force. He said eventually you'd be all right."

Is Franny strong?

She casts her thoughts backwards, rewinding the morning he left and how she wasn't sure it wouldn't kill her. Of course it didn't. She got out of bed, went to work, kept one foot moving in front of the other. She hadn't believed he would stay away forever, not even when she found out about Didi.

If he was so miserable why didn't he come back?

"Was he writing when you were living with him, Didi?"

"Off and on."

"Stories or . . . ?

"I'm not sure. He never shared anything. I'd show him poems and things and he'd comment and edit and give me advice. He always made them better, but he never showed me what he was doing. Before we started dating, I read most of his published work. I thought he was brilliant. A brilliant unknown keeping his day job, so he could write on the side like many do."

She's talking fast now, in a rush to say how she noticed things in him she hadn't seen before. He was more than merely special. He was gifted. A genius, perhaps? Perhaps an immortal who will be resurrected in some far off future. In her opinion, he should have been hugely famous.

"'Tomorrow is ours for the taking,' he said when we were first together. He was so optimistic then. It was that phone call of yours that plunged him into despair. Telling him you knew about us and we could go to hell. He tried so hard to make sure you'd never know. He wanted spare you."

"Poo, fuck that. Look, none of it matters now. It was an impulsive curse, but I can't regret it. One of my many faults, I'm sure."

"Harley said your only fault was an inability to control your appetite."

"Appetites plural. I'm full off appetites. I'm not talking about food."

"I'm full of appetites, too."

"Fifty-eight and full of appetites. I thought age was supposed to slow us down."

"He never wanted to hurt you, Franny."

"Well, too bad. Because I sure as hell wanted to hurt him."

"And you did."

"It's that fucking Shanna's fault. I didn't need that phone call, you know. Why couldn't she keep her damn mouth shut? I didn't need to know any of that shit. She wanted to get back at me because Harley loved me. She loved him, you know. Do you understand? She loved her brother in an incestuous way. It's true."

Didi nods. Her eyes are spheres of sadness. "Yes, he knew that about her. He said she probably thought the news about us would destroy our union and she would have him all to herself."

"Sounds like her."

"In the end, it worked, it did break us up. But he would never have gone to Shanna. He couldn't forgive the betrayal. That and the pain it caused you."

"The betrayer betrayed." Her smile is bitter.

"Gradually, he became more and more suicidal. When his heart trouble started, he wouldn't do anything for it except nitro and digitalis. It drove me crazy and finally I couldn't take it. I couldn't stay there and watch him inching toward extinction. I had to get out. I didn't want to abandon him, but he was driving me mad."

"The man was crazy-making. After you called me and I went to his place, I didn't recognize him. What a change."

"Forgive me, Franny."

"Is that why you came here? To be absolved?"

She shakes her head. "I don't know, I don't know." Tears falling, nose snuffling. The dog keeps licking her hand. "Dogs," she says. "They tune in to humans. Right, Holly? You know something's wrong. Where's Harley? Where's Harley, Holly?" The dog yips weakly, her head turning right and left as if searching for him.

"Harley did it to himself," Franny says.

"What?"

"Harley's conscience ruined him. Let's face it: he burned out long before he died. Sabotaged by his own body protesting against the way he was living his life. How frail he was. How tough I am by comparison. It's Darwinian. It's survival of the fittest. My future is long. I will live to be ninety. Maybe a hundred. Live long enough and everything is forgiven, unless you're Hitler or Stalin or that bozo Trump. That's what Harley should have known but didn't."

They settle in for hours. Franny makes martinis, which loosens their tongues even more. At one point in the conversation, she tells Didi about finding Harley dead with the gun in his hand. It hadn't surprised her. Something had prompted her to open the door to his study. When she saw he was dead, she told herself of course it was bound to happen like this. Deep down she always knew how he would end. She imagined him taking the gun (as he often did), putting the barrel to his head and playing with the safety. She remembered him showing her that no matter how hard he tried he couldn't pull the trigger with the safety on. He would get drunk and do it and she would yell at him to stop being stupid. The explosion never came.

Not even when he meant it to happen.

Also, imagining him on his death day, a heartsick Harley pulling the gun from the drawer. Voices prompting him to do it quickly. No thinking, no reflecting, no debating points of procedure. Take the gun into the room. Sit at the desk and think of Conrad dying in harness. Put the barrel to your heart. Pull the trigger. Since your heart is broken, it's appropriate you shatter it with a bullet. You feel it racing like you are near the end of a marathon closing in on the last yard. Sitting down. Leaning your elbows on the desk. Hand holding cool steel against your cheek, you abruptly feel a pain in your throat. Yes, it feels like the carotid artery is blocked and the blood can't keep up with the furious lub-a-dub inside you. In the blink of an eye your heart will stop beating, and you will feel nothing. Nothing ever again. Not here. Not anywhere. Your thumb flicks the safety off. The tiny red dot tells you: READY TO FIRE. All remorse will end. You will cease to be. You'll never have to face another second of your floundering self, nor despise your being.

The greatest sin of all is despising your being.

Time and memories of you passing. It's not even peace. It's nil. It's Hemingway's NADA. The pain in your throat runs a tentacle into your arm, into your hand. This is what stress can do. Stress can kill you.

"Could have killed me, too," continues Franny. "But I managed to get out, managed to save myself and get above it and win the war with cancer and win the war with those who tried to destroy me. I vanquished my enemies. Something Harley could never do. Hammers the heart hammering his throat, hammering his hand, hammering his chest. Let me in! If you're not going to pull the trigger, let me in and I'll do it. Would you really leave me like that, you bastard?"

If ever I would leave you . . .

"Sing me no songs, Harley."

When Franny finishes, Didi wants to know who won. "Was it suicide and you got them to report Harley's death as a heart attack?"

Franny shakes her head. "The way he handled his life was suicide. His heart burst, Didi. The coroner said he was dead before his head hit the desk. I took the gun out of his hand. I clicked the safety on. The gun is in the drawer beside my bed. It makes me feel safe. It's my protection against whatever comes my way, bad boys like Hector, who should be dead, but is probably still alive. Hector, Hector."

"Hector?"

"God knows there are thousands of Hectors stalking us. Lurking out there. I refuse to be helpless."

"Who is Hector?"

Franny blinks several times. "Hector?"

"You keep mentioning Hector."

"Another martini?"

"Why not?"

When she returns with fresh drinks, Franny sits on the sofa next to Didi and sips. She looks into Didi's delectable eyes. Pouty, kissable lips. Breasts to match the size of her hips. Franny sees dark roots beneath the bright blond hair

When she finally speaks, her tone is chilly. "Yes Hector. Didi, can you keep a secret? If I tell you something, can you promise not tell anyone? Not a soul."

"Ask anyone who knows me, Franny. I'm quiet as the grave. I don't tell nobody nuttin."

"Hector was a young man who broke in here one morning and raped me. Raped me several times and beat me. He was going to empty my bank account and dump me in the desert."

"Oh my god!"

"Nasty piece of work."

"But what happened? How did you get away?"

Franny puts her drink down, stands up and crooks her finger. She leads Didi into the kitchen and picks up the cast iron skillet sitting on the stove. "I bashed his head in with this," she says, brandishing the pan. "Like I was hammering a nail. Bash! Bash! Bash!" As she notes the astonishment on Didi's face, Franny feels the glory of murdering him and wishes she had actually done it. "Buried him in the desert."

"Are you kidding?"

"I did it."

"Holy fucking Christ what a woman!" In an instant Didi has her arms around Franny and is kissing her, Franny liking it. Mouth against mouth Didi murmurs, "You're my hero. By god, Harley said you was tough."

Franny steps back and says, "Survival of the fittest. It was him or me. He wanted me to make him dinner, you see? He sat right there at the table, right in that chair. He put a cigarette in his mouth and bent to his lighter and flicked it. That was my chance and I took it. Bash bash. His head caving like a melon. I did it for me, but I did it for all women who've ever been treated like shit."

Didi's eyes idolize. "I mean it, Franny. You're my hero. The woman who roars. The woman I've wanted to be." Nose to nose Didi shouts, "Fuck you! Fuck you! You're my hero." Her words hit Franny's ears like thunderdents.

She spins away, her feet carrying her and her frying pan back to the sofa. Franny Olsen a hero? "I'll drink to that," she says and empties her glass. "I think we're drunk," she adds.

"I'm sure we are," Didi agrees. "Tell me more. Give me details."

"Details. Yes, let me see. Hmm . . ."

Franny goes over the rape minutely, the two days of being at Hector's mercy.

Didi keeps saying, "And then what happened? What happened then?"

"Well, I'm in the kitchen and Hector is gobbling a chicken leg. Yeah, a chicken leg."

"And?"

And behind her the door opened and there he was. It was Norman using his key to get in. He stopped dead. His eyes stunned. And then he said, "Him?"

Hector threw the chicken bone at him, yeah, that's what happened. Norman putting his hands up, warding off the knife. Franny, as if pricked by a needle, flew to the stove, grabbed the skillet and ran behind Hector, laid a two-handed blow on the back of his head. Hector falling like a stone. Franny hitting him again and again, the sound of it like crushing a cantaloupe. Hector was at Norman's feet, Norman looking down at him, mouth agape, eyes bursting.

Finally, he said, No more, Franny. He's dead, you killed him. He's dead.

"Oh, the blood, Didi," she says. "Blood pumping out of Hector's head timed to the beating of his heart. Fountains of it"

"I see it," says Didi. "So Norman, he's your boyfriend now? Crazy Norman?"

"Just a friend. Sometimes we sleep together, but basically he's my friend."

"A fuck-buddy."

"Those are good to have."

"I've got one. I should call him, have him come over. I'm sure he'd like you."

"Ahh. . . "

"So okay, you lay the bastard low. Then what?"

"Let's see, let's see. What did I do? I dropped the pan, backed up, my legs finding a chair I could sit on and stare at my handiwork."

"What did Norman do?"

"No man? . . . I mean Norman?"

"Poor man probably shit his pants."

"He stood there saying, 'He was going to kill me. You saved me.' I saved him. I saved Numan. Shock turning his face to parchment. Then . . . then he was shouting, 'What's going on here? What's he doing here?'"

"I told him Hector broke in and raped me in my sleep, he tied me up, doing it since Sunday. Or Monday, maybe? Doing me two days of hell. Don't think I enjoyed it, Didi."

"I don't."

"Nope, not one second. I hated it. I never been so scared in my life. Even cancer didn't scare me like that kid did. He was waiting for payday and then he would take all my money and take me somewhere in the desert and dump my body for the coyotes."

"Did he say that?" asks Didi.

Franny replies, "It was in his eyes. I could read his thoughts. I not only saved me, but Numan as well. It gets better, it gets better."

"And?"

Franny sees the scene: the frying pan, the body. Stupefied Norman wobbling into the kitchen, sitting down, his head in his hands. "He said he thought I was shacked up. All that God stuff I pulled on him and then he's thinking I'm a cougar shacked up committing adultery with Hector."

The phlegm in her mouth burns. "Don't give me anymore God, that's what I told him. I prayed and prayed. For two days I begged. But all there was is a voice saying it's my own fault, sinner that I am. Whore. No wonder Harley left me. He doesn't believe in God, you know. He says God's world is a child world and we need to grow up. The species needs to mature and stop killing each other over something not even there. There's no proof of it. Not a speck. Mathematically, God is impossible. Occam's Razor, Harley says. Cut to the chase. Harley quoted some philosopher who said, 'Faith is believing what you know ain't so.' And you know what, Didi? You know what? He's right. Has God ever shown up when you need him?"

"I don't know," says Didi. "I don't know. I tend to think Harley is right."

"God . . . God." Franny hears contempt in her voice. "We're all babies, we're such fools."

Franny points to the bare wooden floor. "I rolled him in the rug. That's where the rug was, Didi. Ancient old thing."

Didi says, "It had to go."

"It had to go and him with it. Do unto him as he would have done unto me."

"Justice," says Didi firmly.

"Roll him up. Tie him in there and take him out the eight to the desert. Out there near the turn for Ocotillo Wells. Norman helped me. Don't ever say a word to him about it."

An invisible key in her hand locks Didi's lips.

"I promised him cross my heart and hope to die."

"Never, Franny, never," says Didi. "But hey, I would have helped you, too. I wouldn't bat an eye, I'd help you."

"Norman was jealous, you know. Jealous of Hector."

"Jealousy," says Didi, scoffing. "Jealousy ruins a man. Makes him stupid."

"We rolled the rug over him. Wrapped it in duct tape. And all the time Norman keeps repeating 'Franny, what the . . . Franny, who are you?'"

She and Didi throw their heads back howling with laughter.

"Who am I?" Franny pauses to consider. "A woman who woke up. A woman who took off blinders. If you're *not* gonna help me, get the hell out of here."

"I'll help."

"I mean Numan. Thas what I says to Numan."

Didi downs her drink and says, "I'll make anutter. A double."

"His shoulders sag. You notice that? How his shoulders have gotten saggy? His face droopy, his double chins drooping so far they obliterate his neck. Did I tell you how fat he is?"

"I saw him at the funeral," says Didi. "He's going to pot. What did I ever see in him? He fuckin drove me crazy."

"I'm wondering the same thing about me. What did I see in him? Poetry? A little fame rubbing off on me?"

Franny, hesitating, trying hard to construct what the next segment should be, finally says, "Hector choked me. He choked me till I passed out. I could hardly swallow, my throat was so sore. What did I ever do to him but buy him pizza and beer? What gets into guys? What makes em so fucking evil?"

"Between their legs, Franny. Men are slaves to that thing."

"We did it just as I said we should. Rolled Hector in the rug and duct taped him." Franny laughs shrilly. Didi lifts her glass and says, "I'll drink to that. What a woman, what a woman."

•

The day passes. Night arrives. Franny turns the lamp on, igniting the aura around Didi's hair. "You have great hair, Didi."

"I like your hair, too."

"Auburn fits my complexion best, I think."

"Yes, fits your face. I'm actually brunette, but blonds have more fun." She sniggers into her fingers.

"Are we the same size?"

"I'm a ten."

"I'm a ten, too. God, I used to be an eighteen. Men never hit on me back then. Lots hit on me now."

"Oh, me, too," says Didi. "They always have. I was so ignorant about men. One time, this was over thirty years ago, maybe thirty five, I made a movie with some guys. We did a satire on Romeo and Juliet. Some really wild stuff. That movie lost me my boyfriend." Her eyes roll. "Eh, it wasn't much of a loss. I have a copy if you ever want to see it."

"I'd love to see it. A movie, huh?"

"Naughty."

"I wonder if I could ever let go long enough to do one of those? Probably I could now because I'm really, really buzzed."

"I was drunk at the time. Most porn stars are on drugs, you know. The drugs let them do the things they do. Not all of them, but quite a few. Men, you know, they don't need the drugs the way women do. Except Viagra, maybe."

Franny pauses. Then says, "I'm pessimistic about men. I'm thinking women make better companions. Sweeter by far. More trustworthy."

"I'm generally an optimist," says Didi. "Man. Woman. Whatever. Everything is for the best if the time is right."

Franny is not negating anything, complications, intricacies, intrigues. "When I rise in the morning these days I'm generally optimistic," she says. "I breeze through the day believing death is way away. Time is on my side. But when night comes, it's different. Darkness tells me that I, too, must follow Harley. No getting away from the void. And the only thing between me and it is a god I no longer believe in. Gathering unto, you know? Rising out of the darkness into the brightest bright. Everything a dream and then you're dead. Nothing satisfies us for long. But let's be satisfied whenever we can. And stare it down: mistakes, betrayals, lousy luck, bonehead decisions. Don't let any of it crush us. To hell with your conscience."

The look in Didi's eyes says she agrees with Franny.

"It's bad we wasted so much time," Franny continues. "The clock ticking." She cackles. "We had to take long way round. We had things to learn. Time to evolve. I don't regret one second I spent with Harley. But what a relief he's gone. Ain't I awful? He was so testy before he finally took off with you, so unhappy and testy and touchy." She pauses, remembering Harley laughing that day before he died. "Well, not always. I mean, he was light-hearted the day before he died. When you were somewhere. Where were you? Did you have a date with that guy?"

"Carlson and I had a threesome that night with a looker named May, a bartender. Think of that: the night before Harley dies, I'm an orgy. I should have been with him. I owed him that much."

"Look at the positive side. He got what he wanted: oblivion. Free from all anxiety. You're *SERENE* now. Ain't you, Harley? Ain't you serene?"

Didi says that she loves life. Death wishes baffle her.

"Harley was sooo miserable," says Franny.

"Bad attitude," says Didi.

"And irritable."

"Foolish man. A fool."

"Couldn't win."

"No matter what."

"Determined to end a loser. But this Franny is not gonna let it stay that way. She'll write about him before she starts editing the manuscripts he never tried to publish. Leavings that tell the world we had a life together. I'll write a biography. Style it fragmented, like Harley's life. I'll tell everything I know. The world will see him for what he was, a man with talent but fatally flawed. The world will want to read his work because of me. I'll make it happen. He couldn't do it, but I can. He was always pathetic in that respect. He needed to toot his horn, but couldn't."

Didi says, "I can toot my horn. I'm not shy."

"Neither am I," says Franny. "We're a match, me and you. Once I was fragile like him, but after all I been through I'm stwong as a beer. We're survivors. We're shamans. I'm part beer, you know and we endure."

"I'll help you with Harley's junk. We can work on it togetter. I give it poet touch."

"Bingo! We conquer the world. I know these things, you see. When I get this feeling I know I'm right. The spirit invades and I know what tomorrow brings."

The sofa: comfortable. The room: warm. The dog: sleeping, light beams falling on Didi's radiant face. No bad memories plaguing Franny as she continues to calculate for the dead man, making plans for him, probing the future with a mind made prescient by ill-fortune and the audacity to admit no limits.

Thinking:

Dear Bobbie,

My beloved husband has died. His heart quit. Dying of a broken heart because he couldn't keep his vows and left his wife to cope on her own. I went on a diet, lost tons of weight, had a facelift, breast implants, teeth whitened, hair dyed auburn. Made myself so sexy that a young man less than half my age raped me and kept me captive for two days. He stole all my money and disappeared. I got a gun. It's loaded and in the drawer of my nightstand, ready action. He comes in my sleep. I fantasize killing him. I'm sure he's marked for the seventh ring of Hell. Harley is probably in the second ring. Isn't that where adulterers go?

He was a writer, Bobbie. He quit publishing two or three years ago. I have a stack of manuscripts that I want to edit and find an agent to market. I want to do that for him, give him the notice he should have, a wonderful artist too long ignored.

I believe that out of the deep, out of the bitter cry of the heart, out of loss, remorse, out of grief too deep for tears—art is born. 'Ashes and sparks: my words . . . if winter comes can spring be far behind,' said Shelley in some poem. Wave welcome to the quiet man. Wave to the Harlan James Olsen still living in me: a still point in a turning world, a new me in the moment, the now because I knows cancer is coming back. It always does.

It scares me.

Some days it doesn't.

Time.

Life.

Gotta go some day

Join Harley.

The dead in their tens of billions.

Till then, I and my friend Didi, Harley's former lover, have work to do. She's as dedicated to preserving his memory as I am.

At this moment, we both had too much to drink. It's making us feel grandiose and close as sisters (or lovers?), but I don't care because I think it's right we wallow in alcoholic inebriation :)

Yours in Sin-Filled San Diego.

Franny glances at the vodka bottle sitting on the counter, not empty yet. "Anutter?" she asks.

"Anutter," says Didi. "You got any cheese and crackers? Any bologna? How about sugar on bread and butter?"

Franny rises. Staggers. Cackles. Coughs.

The startled dog awakes, looks upward, eyes full of questions saying: What's goin on, lady? Why you walkin that way? Franny pats the dog's head, kisses her nose and says, "Ain't life freaking golly, Holly?"

The dog nods her head agreeably and says, "Yip. Yip."

Duff Brenna is the author of ten books, including *The Book of Mamie*, which won the AWP Award for Best Novel; *The Holy Book of the Beard*, named "an underground classic" by The New York Times; *Too Cool*, a New York Times Noteworthy Book; *The Altar of the Body*, given the Editors Prize Favorite Book of the Year Award (South Florida Sun-Sentinel), and also received a San Diego Writers Association Award for Best Novel 2002. He is the recipient of a National Endowment for the Arts award, Milwaukee Magazine's Best Short Story of the Year Award, and a Pushcart Prize Honorable Mention. His collection of short stories, *Minnesota Memoirs*, was awarded first prize at the 2013 Next Generation Indie Awards in New York City. His memoir, *Murdering the Mom*, was a Finalist for Best Non-Fiction at the same 2013 Independent Publishers Awards. He also received a second-place award under the Grand Prize category. Brenna's work has been translated into six languages.

www.ingramcontent.com/pod-product-compliance
Lightning Source LLC
Chambersburg PA
CBHW022042240626
47154CB00007B/2530